T0367816

Taking
Texas

by Niki Chesy

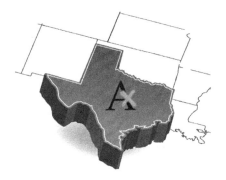

BOOK ONE OF A TWO-PART SERIES

authorHOUSE®

AuthorHouse™
1663 Liberty Drive
Bloomington, IN 47403
www.authorhouse.com
Phone: 1-800-839-8640

Published by AuthorHouse 04/08/2015

ISBN: 978-1-4969-3563-2 (sc)
ISBN: 978-1-4969-3564-9 (hc)
ISBN: 978-1-4969-3554-0 (e)

Library of Congress Control Number: 2014914921

Print information available on the last page.

This book is printed on acid-free paper.

Cover Concept - Tim Rod
Cover Photo - Allison Shacklett
Cover Model - Matt Lederle

For my little pieces of Heaven

MY EVERLASTING GRATITUDE.

Mrs. Jackie Tancredo - my junior high and high school Russian teacher and friend. You have been a great example to thousands of kids.

Matt Lederle - a friend that came to me through an unconventional path. Thank you for being the cover model and showing support for my book. You have been there every time I've asked and I appreciate you so much.

Tim Rod - a title doesn't fit him; my ex-husband, my best friend... he knows me better than anyone... he is, with my animals, my family. Thank you for giving me the time and support to write this book. You are a good man!

My Mom - for telling me I could do anything I put my mind to. As she put it, "so figure it out and get to it!"

Thank you to those of you who made me think and stretch my mind; my mentors and friends: GK, DR, DB, RS, ME and BV to name a few.

BOOK 1

TAKING TEXAS

PART 1
DOSSIERS & THE BEGINNING

OPERATIONS DIRECTORATE

TOP SECRET – EYES ONLY

27 FEBRUARY 2013

INTERNAL MEMORANDUM

TO: Director, Operations Directorate

FROM: Marc Wilson, Information and Privacy Coordinator

RE: Individuals Under Surveillance

- - - - -

Please find four (4) profiles attached for surveillance on the individuals we discussed. This information has been collected over the last 15 months, in reference to the alleged underground movement known only as AmendX. Background information is available for a period in excess of 15 years on each individual.

Please be advised that, although these individuals have been determined <u>NOT</u> to be a threat to national security, further surveillance is highly recommended.

Please contact me directly for additional comments or concerns.

Marc Wilson
Information and Privacy Coordinator
Operations Directorate

CENTRAL INTELLIGENCE AGENCY

INDIVIDUALS UNDER SURVEILLANCE (IUS) PROFILE
PROFILE ID: 3-EPWwWhac47ztcQ

Name: Michael Earnest Bishop

AKA: Mike, Bish

Age: 39
Date of Birth: April 11, 1973

Current Address:
100 Memorial Drive
Cambridge, MA 02142

Other Residences:
930 23rd Street
San Francisco, CA 94131

PHOTO CLASSIFIED

SEE ADDITIONAL FILE CONTENT FOR MORE INFORMATION

Brief Summary:

The subject, Michael Bishop, has come under surveillance per a multi-agency task force initiative. It has been determined that the subject, with the aid and assistance of multiple other individuals, may be involved in efforts that would lead to grave harm to the United States and its interests.

The subject has been under surveillance for a period of 14 months prior to this report, and has been observed by operators from CIA and DIA, with support from FBI. Continued efforts are ongoing under Counter Intelligence Program (COINTELPRO) program office.

The subject has been observed to be in primary contact with other IUS to include Nikoli Borodin and Samantha Sloan (see IUS Profiles 3-bdQh2CZxZywi4D and 3-fZtMPB9Ap9rric). Captured communications reference is NSA-1-f7p-QZFF-tcy7-DXNP-gg-PBvWD. Communications should continue to be monitored for these and other associations with known IUS.

No foreign contact noted

Completed by: Agent Steven Harrison
Date: 16AUG2012

Niki Chesy

PROFILE ID: 3-EPWwWhac47ztcQ

PHYSICAL DESCRIPTION

Height: 6'4"
Weight: 200-210lbs
Eye Color: Blue
Hair Color: Dark brown
Hair Style: Very short, sometimes buzzed
Distinguishing Marks: Mighty Mouse tattoo left shoulder/ upper arm
BACKGROUND INFORMATION
Father's Name: William Bishop
Father's Status: Living
Mother's Name: Olivia Thompson Bishop
Mother's Status: Living
Number of Siblings: 1
Ethnic Background: German and Russian/Irish American
Religion: Catholic
Degree of Religious Practice: Non-practicing
Place of Birth: Menlo Park, CA
Citizenship: United States
Brief Description of Home: White stone and red brick loft/condominium in Boston
Other Occupants of Home: None
Current Occupation: Researcher at MIT
Education: Harvard undergraduate, attended Stanford for under one year.
Marital Status: Never married
Spouse's Name: n/a
Name by Which Subject Addresses Spouse: n/a
Spouse's Occupation: n/a
Children's Names and Ages: n/a
General Health: Excellent
Chronic Health Conditions: None
Current Health Conditions: Excellent
Dress (describe dress): Upscale casual
Grooming: Meticulous
Speech - Pace: Average pace
Speech - Voice: Soft spoken, casual, confident
Speech - Favorite Words or Phrases: None
Speech - Usual Cuss Words (if any): None used with any regularity

MANNERISMS

General: Projects a calm image
Gestures: Doesn't gesture much
Favorite Gesture: n/a
Habits - Home: When in Boston, subject reads/studies
Where does subject live? Boston, MA but travels frequently
Décor of personal space controlled by subject: Modern, minimalist
Basic Overall Style/Impression: Modern

Habits - Pets
Number and Type of Pets: No pets
How well does subject treat the pets/animals? Very well

Habits - Waking up

5

Who else is sleeping in the same bed? Periodic girlfriends
What time does subject wake up? Between 5:30 and 6:30 am. Runs first thing.
Is subject cheerful in the morning? Seemingly so
Does subject eat breakfast? If so, what? Eggs, Protein shakes, yogurt and chicken breasts.

Habits - Dinner
Who prepares subject's meal? When eating in, self.
Who does subject eat with? 30% with friends and girlfriends, the rest of the time alone.
What does meal typically consist of? Wine and food is quite varied.
Does subject enjoy the meal? Why/why not? Seems to enjoy wine, eating slowly as to "experience" the meal.
Who cleans up? Subject

Habits - evening
What does subject do on a typical evening? Reads and watches sports
Is bedtime consistent? If so, what time? Varies
With whom? Mostly alone.

How does the subject get along with:
Spouse: n/a
Parents: Well
Siblings: Well
The Opposite Sex: Well
Children in General: Well
Neighbors: Well
Friends: Well
Anyone that challenges subject: Calmly
Anyone who angers subject: Logically and calmly
Anyone who helps subject: Well and gratefully
Anyone who asks for help from subject: Well and gracious

END OF REPORT

CENTRAL INTELLIGENCE AGENCY

INDIVIDUALS UNDER SURVEILLANCE (IUS) PROFILE
PROFILE ID: 3-bdQh2CZxZywi4D

Name: Nikoli Leonidovich Borodin

AKA: Niki

Age: 39
Date of Birth: October 30, 1973

Current Address:

Primary Residence
3 25th Avenue
San Francisco, CA 94121

Second Residence
1701 Sunset Drive
Pacific Grove, CA 93950

PHOTO CLASSIFIED

SEE ADDITIONAL FILE CONTENT FOR MORE INFORMATION

Brief Summary:

The subject, Nikoli Borodin, has come under surveillance per a multi-agency task force initiative. It has been determined that the subject, with the aid and assistance of multiple other individuals, may be involved in efforts that would lead to grave harm to the United States and its interests.

The subject has been under surveillance for a period of 10 months prior to this report, and has been observed by operators from CIA and DIA, with support from FBI. Continued efforts are ongoing under Counter Intelligence Program (COINTELPRO) program office.

The subject has been observed to be in primary contact with other IUS to include Michael Bishop and Samantha Sloan (see IUS Profiles 3-EPWwWhac47ztcQ and 3-fZtMPB9Ap9rric). No captured communications are available for this subject. Attempts at communications capture should continue subject. Note: Communications capture has been deemed by NSA to be obfuscated by technology in use by subject. Patterns are under investigation by COINTELPRO, as well as NSA branch office 8QR.

Subject is a founding partner of Sensedatum Technologies. This position provides for significant financial resources for subject (see related COINTELPRO financial files created by Office of Navel

7

Intelligence (ONI), related to main file number). Subjects status formulates a very public persona, and subject is often found in very crowded venues. Personal security appears to be minimal and discreet, and is provided by a private contractor (origin unknown at this time). Personal and business air travel within CONUS and OCONUS is done via private aircraft only. Subject's substantial resources allow for pre-arrangement of secure ground transportation when traveling outside continental United States (OCONUS).

Foreign contact noted. Subject continues to maintain communications with family members in Russia. Due to subject's occupation, foreign contacts are numerous and frequent.

Completed by: Agent Steven Harrison
Date: 6NOV2012

PROFILE ID: 3-bdQh2CZxZywi4D

PHYSICAL DESCRIPTION

Height: 6"1"
Weight: 180lbs
Eye Color: Hazel
Hair Color: Dark Brown
Hair Style: Short
Distinguishing Marks: 3/4 inch scar above right eyebrow

BACKGROUND INFORMATION

Father's Name: Leonid Borodin
Father's Status: Living
Mother's Name: Tatyana Mironov Borodin
Mother's Status: Living
Ethnic Background: Russian
Religion: Russian Orthodox
Degree of Religious Practice: Non-practicing
Place of Birth: Moscow, Russia
Citizenship: Green card 1984, Naturalized 1995
Brief Description of Home: Brick and glass condominium
Other Occupants of Home: Wife
Current Occupation: Entrepreneur
Education: Harvard undergraduate, attended Stanford 16 months, on leave from Ph.D. program.
Marital Status: 1st marriage - 6 years
Spouse's Name: Haley Reynolds
Name By Which Subject Addresses Spouse: Haley
Spouse's Occupation: Researcher, evolutionary development
Children's Names And Ages: Leo Nicholas Borodin, 3 years old
General Health: Good - above average, but not excellent
Chronic Health Conditions: None
Current Health Conditions: Good
Dress: Unkempt
Grooming: Average grooming and cleanliness for group
Speech - Pace: Talks fast, faint Russian accent
Speech - Voice: Average
Speech - Favorite Words Or Phrases: Amazing
Speech - Usual Cuss Words: None

MANNERISMS

General: Moods change, and body language with it a bit fidgety
Gestures (doesn't gesture much, gestures are deliberate and controlled, gestures mostly when excited/upset, gestures much of the time, gestures wildly, even weirdly): n/a
Favorite gesture:
When does subject use it?

Habits - Home
Where does subject live? San Francisco, California
Décor of personal space controlled by subject: Casual
Basic Overall Style/Impression: Contemporary, casual

Habits - Pets
Pets: One cat, one dog
How important are pets to subject? Moderate
How well does subject treat the pets? Well

Habits - Waking up
Who else is sleeping in the same bed? Wife
What time does subject wake up? Wide range: 4-6 am
Is subject cheerful in the morning? Does not seem so.
Does subject eat breakfast? If so, what? Wide range of breakfast foods

Habits - Dinner
Who prepares subject's meal? Live-in housekeeper prepares meals for family, subject eats with them when home from work
Who does subject eat with? Family or at work
What does meal typically consist of? Balanced diet at home, full range at work.
Does subject enjoy the meal? Why/why not? Moderately, seems to be in a hurry.
Who cleans up? Housekeeper or staff at work

Habits - evening:
What does subject do on a typical evening? Spends time with family or at work
Is bedtime consistent? If so, what time? Not consistent
With whom? Wife

How does the subject get along with:
Spouse: Hard to tell - from outside seems fine
Parents: Does not see them often but keeps in regular touch
Siblings: None
The opposite sex: Good
Children in general: Well
Neighbors: Well
Friends: Well
Anyone that challenges subject: Challenging
Anyone who angers subject: Ceases to engage
Anyone who helps subject: Well
Anyone who asks for help from subject: Generously

END OF REPORT

CENTRAL INTELLIGENCE AGENCY

INDIVIDUALS UNDER SURVEILLANCE (IUS) PROFILE
PROFILE ID: 3-fZtMPB9Ap9rric

Name: Samantha Chloe Sloan

AKA: Sam

Age: 38
Date of Birth: March 13, 1974

Current Address: Several (in order, most to least time spent)

Broadmoor Hotel Cottage 18
1 Lake Avenue
Colorado Springs, CO 80906

Rented from 2005-2006, purchased home 2006
1311 Hurst Creek Road
Austin, TX (Lake Travis)   78734

Parent's Residence
1117 Crest Lane
Menlo Park, CA 94025

40 Steamboat Wharf, Unit 1
Mystic, CT 06355

PHOTO CLASSIFIED

SEE ADDITIONAL FILE CONTENT FOR MORE INFORMATION

Brief Summary:

Subject has been selected for inclusion as IUS based on associations with
other known IUS. It has been determined that the subject, with the aid
and assistance of multiple other individuals, may be involved in efforts
that would lead to grave harm to the United States and its interests.

The subject has been under surveillance for a period of 11 months
prior to this report, and has been observed by operators from CIA
and DIA, with support from FBI. Continued efforts are ongoing under
Counter Intelligence Program (COINTELPRO) program office.

The subject has been observed to be in primary contact with other
IUS to include Michael Bishop and Nikoli Borodin (see IUS Profiles
3-EPWwWhac47ztcQ and 3-bdQh2CZxZywi4D). Captured communications reference
is NSA-1-Pau-g4ch-cKLn-EB9X-oK-uUiXP. Communications should continue to
be monitored for these and other associations with known IUS.

Subject travels frequently, and current location is unknown. Subject possesses exceptional capability to detect and deter surveillance efforts. All current residences are under observation. Ongoing efforts to overcome circumvention have been deemed appropriate, and electronic measures are being employed.

No foreign contact noted.

Completed by: Agent Mark Cole
Date: 14AUG2012

PROFILE ID: 3-fZtMPB9Ap9rric

PHYSICAL DESCRIPTION

Height: 5'3"
Weight: 95-100lbs
Eye Color: Blue
Hair Color: Blonde
Hair Style: Medium length to shoulders
Distinguishing Marks: None

BACKGROUND INFORMATION

Father's Name: James Grey Sloan
Father's Status: Living
Mother's Name: Chloe Barnes Sloan
Mother's Status: Living
Ethnic Background: German and Austrian American
Religion: Raised Catholic
Degree Of Religious Practice: Non-practicing
Place of Birth: Palo Alto, CA
Citizenship: US
Brief Description Of Home: Current living arrangements unknown. Owns house in Mystic, CT, and Austin, TX
Other Occupants Of Home: None
Current Occupation: Clinical Psychologist
Education: Ph.D. from Stanford
Marital Status: Never married
Spouse's Name: None
Name By Which Subject Addresses Spouse: n/a
Spouse's Occupation: n/a
Children's Names And Ages: n/a
General Health: Excellent
Chronic Health Conditions: None
Current Health Conditions: Excellent
Dress: Professional or business casual dress - in black only
Grooming: Meticulous
Speech - Pace: Fast
Speech - Voice: Shrill to average
Speech - Favorite Words Or Phrases: None
Speech - Usual Cuss Words (if any): Fuck has been heard on multiple occasions

MANNERISMS

General: Projects calm posture but can get fidgety
Posture: Stands straight but not stiffly
Gestures: Gestures much of the time
Favorite Gesture: Hand movement for descriptions
When does subject use it? When speaking with others

Habits - Home
Note: Have not observed individual at all residences
Where does subject live? Multiple locations
Décor Of Personal Space Controlled By Subject: Stylish, but sparse
Basic Overall Style/Impression: Minimalist

Habits - Pets
Pets: Many; dogs (Saint Bernards), cats; (multiple breeds)
How important are pets to subject? Immensely
How well does subject treat the pets? As if people

Habits - Waking up
Who else is sleeping in the same bed? None. If she has male companion, she visits their residence. Rare.
What time does subject wake up? Between 7 and 8 AM when able to observe.
Is subject cheerful in the morning? Seems quiet
Does subject eat breakfast? If so, what? Yes, breakfast sandwiches mostly, or smoothie shakes

Habits - Dinner
Note: Eats out often
Who prepares subject's meal? Self, when observed at home in Connecticut
Who does subject eat with? Friends or alone, rarely male companion.
What does meal typically consist of? Wide variety, but typical protein, vegetables, and starch.
Does subject enjoy the meal? Why/why not? Yes, but never eats all of it.
Who cleans up? If at home, self.

Habits - evening
General Note: Reads a lot, seems to have interest in research and watches television.
What does subject do on a typical evening? Reads or is on computer during dinner, plays with animals after dinner, watches television for an hour or so, then reads until retires.
Is bedtime consistent? If so, what time? Yes, between 11PM and 12 AM
With whom? Alone

How does the subject get along with:
Spouse: None
Parents: Well
Siblings: No relationship seems to exist
The opposite sex: Well
Children in general: Have not observed with children
Neighbors: Well
Friends: Well
Anyone that challenges subject: Can be quick tempered

Anyone who angers subject: Can be explosive
Anyone who helps subject: Very appreciative
Anyone who asks for help from subject: Very accommodating

END OF REPORT

CENTRAL INTELLIGENCE AGENCY

INDIVIDUALS UNDER SURVEILLANCE (IUS) PROFILE
PROFILE ID: 3-M7bj4xghCqvKAL

SPECIAL FILE STATUS: This file must be maintained as a special file, per CIA 32 CFR 1909, and as such, is NOT subject to the Freedom of Information Act, Privacy Act, or Executive Order 12958. Subject to redaction.

Name: Jackson John Cooper
AKA: Jack

Age: 53
Date of Birth: February 12, 1960

Current Address:

Governor's Mansion
1010 Colorado Street
Austin, TX 78701

Personal Residence
1770 Lakeshore Drive
Austin, TX 78734

PHOTO CLASSIFIED

SEE ADDITIONAL FILE CONTENT FOR MORE INFORMATION

Brief Summary:

Subject has been selected for inclusion as IUS based on circumstantial evidence of participation in extremist activities. It has been determined that the subject may have first-hand knowledge of individuals that may be involved in efforts that would lead to grave harm to the United States and its interests. Subject observation basis is intended to identify other individuals.

The subject has been under surveillance for a period of 25 months prior to this report. Subject maintains a Department of Defense (DoD) Top Secret - Secure Compartmented Information (TS-SCI) clearance based on Single Scope Background Investigation (SSBI) conducted in 2010. Subject currently occupies the Governorship of the State of Texas, and was confirmed as Governor without election, based on elevation from Lieutenant Governor. DoD clearance was deemed appropriate based on status as Commander-and-Chief, Texas National Guard. Subject has access to credible foreign intelligence data based on Department of Homeland Security (DHS) daily briefings. Note that file is granted special status based on subject's access to intelligence data. Subject was re-elected as Governor in subsequent election.

Communications capture for subject is maintained by National Security Agency (NSA), in accordance with standard practices in counter-terrorism.

The subject has not been observed to be in primary contact with other IUS, although based on circumstantial evidence,

Subject travels frequently, and current location is unknown. Subject possesses exceptional capability to detect and deter surveillance efforts. All current residences are under observation. Ongoing efforts to overcome circumvention have been deemed appropriate, and electronic measures are being employed.

No foreign contact noted.

Completed by: Agent Mark Cole
Date: 17JAN013

PROFILE ID: 3-M7bj4xghCqvKAL

PHYSICAL DESCRIPTION

Height: 6'2"
Weight: 210lbs
Eye Color: Brown
Hair Color: Brown
Hair Style: Short
Distinguishing Marks: None

BACKGROUND INFORMATION

Father's Name: John Cooper
Father's Status: Living
Mother's Name: Emily Shaw Cooper
Mother's Status: Living
Ethnic Background: English American
Religion: Christian
Degree Of Religious Practice: Practicing
Place of Birth: Midland, Texas
Citizenship: US
Brief Description Of Home: Governor's Mansion
Other Occupants Of Home: Family/Staff
Current Occupation: Governor, Texas
Education: Undergraduate of Texas A&M
Marital Status: 1st marriage - 27 years
Spouse's Name: Lily Clarke Cooper
Name By Which Subject Addresses Spouse: Lil, Lily
Spouse's Occupation: Medical Doctor
Children's Names And Ages: Two boys, 23 & 21
General Health: Good
Chronic Health Conditions: Mild asthma
Current Health Conditions: Good

Dress: Professional casual
Grooming: Above average grooming and cleanliness for group
Speech - Pace: Average pace, but slows to make point
Speech - Voice: Deep, authoritative
Speech - Favorite Words Or Phrases: Repeats sentences or words twice when making a point.
Speech - Usual Cuss Words: (if any) None

<u>**MANNERISMS**</u>

General: Project a calm & confident image
Gestures: Gestures are deliberate and controlled
Favorite Gesture: Right hand first finger to lips
When does subject use it? During speeches or talking to five or more people

Habits - Home:
Where does subject live? Austin Texas
Décor Of Personal Space Controlled By Subject: Traditional
Basic Overall Style/Impression: Traditional, comfortable

Habits - Pets
Pets: Two dogs
How important are pets to subject? Moderate
How well does subject treat the pets? Well

Habits - Waking up
Who else is sleeping in the same bed? Wife
What time does subject wake up? Early 6 am or before
Is subject cheerful in the morning? Quiet, takes a while to wake up.
Does subject eat breakfast? If so, what? Eggs, meat, toast every morning

Habits - Dinner
Who prepares subject's meal? Wife or housekeeper
Who does subject eat with? Family or business dinners
What does meal typically consist of? Meat, potatoes, with salads or vegetables with wine
Does subject enjoy the meal? Why/why not? Depending on who he is eating with, he can be quick or sit and relax and enjoy
Who cleans up? Staff or housekeeper

Habits - Evening:
What does subject do on a typical evening? Working or spending time with his family. Many political functions
Is bedtime consistent? If so, what time? Not consistent
With whom? Wife

How does the subject get along with:
Spouse: Well
Parents: Strained
Siblings: Not well
The opposite sex: Well
Children in general: Well
Neighbors: Well
Friends: Well
Anyone that challenges subject: Does not back down but is polite

Anyone who angers subject: Abrasive
Anyone who helps subject: Humble and respectful
Anyone who asks for help from subject: Gracious and giving

END OF REPORT

CHAPTER 1
HARVARD, WELLESLEY & RUSSIA (1993-1999)

Friday, February 26, 1993 – 1:00pm Eastern Standard Time (18:00 hours Zulu Time)

"Man, something's gotta change, or it's only going to get worse." Michael Bishop stood in the doorway, as if he were physically unable to move.

"What are you talking about? What's going on?" asked Nikoli Borodin.

"You can see on TV exactly what I am talking about," said Bishop, pointing at the television. "I'm talking about the fuckin' insanity happening at the World Trade Center. Someone set off a bomb in the parking garage of one of the towers." He threw his book bag on the couch with a little too much force.

"We know about the bombing, Mike. It's on every channel. What do you mean when you say that it's going to get worse? The ATF just said there were no more bombs in the building," said Samantha Sloan, not taking her eyes off the television. She had already been watching when Bishop had walked in.

Nikoli spoke, instead of Bishop, "He meant this country, not this bombing incident, right Mike?"

"Yeah," was all Mike could muster. He finally stepped out of the doorway and threw himself on the couch next to his bag.

To Bishop, it was appropriate that they were together on a day as momentous as this. These three had been friends for as long as he could remember. They were even referred to as "the three", by parents, professors, and other friends because they were inseparable. A year younger than the boys, Samantha Sloan had skipped sixth grade, so she had entered Junior High School with the boys. She was currently attending the all-girl college, Wellesley, but would graduate the same year the boys would graduate from Harvard, and then they were planning to head west to Stanford to pursue their graduate work together. This weekend, though, they were still on the east coast watching the horror. Samantha had hopped the senate bus, also known colloquially around campus as the "Fuck Truck," to

19

visit the boys at Harvard. She hated the nickname, and even more so, despised the girls that justified the name in the first place. It was simply a shuttle bus that ran from Wellesley, stopping once at Harvard University, then moving onto The Massachusetts Institute of Technology, and finally dropping students off on Beacon Street in Boston. The real name, senate bus, was given for the Wellesley College Government Senate, which worked hard to establish such a circuit. She didn't have classes on Fridays, so she had wanted to get a jump on the weekend and catch the early bus. Now they were all sitting in the living area of the boys' room at Kirkland House, watching something the country wouldn't understand until the days and weeks to come. No one fully grasped that this country had just experienced a terrorist attack on its own soil.

"Mike you don't know how bad things can get," Nikoli said softly. "After coming here from Russia, things look pretty good. I mean, I don't remember too much because I was nine, but I do remember it was a hell of a lot harder there than anything I've seen here. I mean, kids here have it *cushy*, and in ways they don't even think about, like supervision, and how their time is filled with activities instead of having to work to help the family out... those kinds of things. I also remember my parents, and the weight that had been lifted from them once we got here."

"Oh, I agree Niki, totally. I'm not saying this country isn't great... it is. I'm just seeing its greatness slip away a little at a time. It seems like the bar keeps getting a little bit lower while we get a little bit fatter, accepting less for a higher cost. Mediocrity over striving to do your best," Mike said almost sorrowfully. "No one loves this country more than me. Really. I guess I am sitting here wondering how the hell this happened? Who was looking the other way, while lives of good people were being compromised? Plus, it happened in New York. That is a little close to home, right? We are literally just up the road."

Most people that knew Michael Bishop while he was younger called him Mike. His newer friends and college girls called him Michael, and his closer friends called him Bish, but Samantha called him Mike. She hated the name 'Bish.' Mike had grown up inside the Great American Dream, in a normal house, almost too normal – a house with two point four kids, a family dog they called Darwin and a cat named Sigmund. Mom worked part-time in real estate while dad was the major breadwinner, working as an engineer for a private contracting firm that did most of their work for the US Navy. Their neighbor, and Michael's namesake, Michael Pearson, was a close friend of his father and a constant source of inspiration for those that knew him. Mr. Pearson and his father met on the job and he became known as 'Uncle Mike.' For only a junior officer in the Navy, Pearson had known where he wanted to end up; Mike really looked up to the male role models in his life and wanted to be just like them. So, he did well in school, joined the Cub Scouts, played sports, went to the prom and never had any of those teen-angst run-ins with his parents. At Harvard, he was the co-captain of the rugby team, varsity crew, and helped organize the activities at Kirkland House. He enjoyed playing sports but he wasn't that "jock" that Kirkland house has been known for, and that was one of the reasons he chose not to be a Master of the House when his peers asked him to be. For all intents and purposes, he was the perfect child.

Handsome – beautiful actually – but he either ignored it, or was unaware of his good looks. With flawless, sun-kissed bronze skin that glowed, he turned heads. His eyes were his best feature by far, almond shaped, and large, icy, sky blue. People would comment that he could look coldly right through you, but once you got to know him, his looks softened. Plus, he had a Mighty Mouse tattoo on his left shoulder, which sure made the girls giggle. He was rather tall, about six feet, four inches, and weighed about two hundred pounds. Everyone that met Mike liked him, especially the girls. Girls went crazy for him. He certainly had a great time with women, but he found himself enjoying his friends and sitting back and watching them enjoy themselves more often than dating. His soft-spoken nature was more that of an observer than in-the-middle-of-the-action kind of guy, unlike his pal, Nikoli. Mike certainly wasn't a player, but he didn't stay interested in the same girl for any real length of time. What seemed even more amazing, especially for teenagers, was that Mike somehow remained friends with the girls he had dated. His solace and guilty pleasure, though, was the golf course. He didn't really find his stride until his twenties but he always made time for the sport. He often tried to get Nikoli to play but was usually unsuccessful; Niki had no patience for the game.

Always curious about how things worked, Mike experimented with everything from reverse engineering video games to trying his hand at day trading. He was successful at both; the trading allowed him to make quite a large sum of money before he even had his undergraduate degree. During that time he also discovered that, although he didn't need them, he had an eye for the finer things in life. After a particularly good month in the market, he rewarded himself with some German engineering and bought a sleek, black BMW M5. His dad said it was pretentious... and then Mike let him drive it, and his dad realized the guilty pleasure as well.

They all sat looking at the television not saying much. It was reported that a truck bomb had exploded in the parking structure below the North Tower of the World Trade Center. Not much was known at the time; except that electricity had been cut off due to the blast and over one thousand were reported injured and six killed. Almost immediately following the explosion, an Al-Qaeda group of conspirators took responsibility for the attack, spouting that the goal had been to bring down the tower. In the days to follow, a videotape was released by one of the masterminds who had escaped to Pakistan just hours following the attack. The message was clear: This group and other splinter groups were out to kill Americans at any cost.

"The world is changing – I can't say exactly how and I'm sure our parents, and their parents, have said the same thing, but I can just feel something ugly creeping in," said Bishop.

Nikoli and Samantha both nodded in agreement.

Mike Bishop's best friend, Nikoli Borodin was also extremely bright; he naturally excelled at everything he tried, and did even better than Mike and Samantha scholastically. Having emigrated from Russia with his family when he was nine, it was very important to him to act like an American, sound like an American – be an American. Unlike Bishop, Nikoli was a risk-taker and had a wild side to him. He classically rebelled against his parents and was often smarter than his teachers and professors, which proved him to be too smart for his own good. While he earned a reputation as a 'problem' student, and taking Mike's lead, he frequently forgot about school and spent the day hashing it out in the market. To say that his wins and his losses were substantially bigger than Mike's was an understatement, but Nikoli must have been born under a good sign; he always managed to stay on top. A few inches shorter than Mike, and finding his hair thinning at an early age, he took it upon himself to take the proactive approach, and maintained a buzzed, almost bald look, which the girls seemed to like. With hazel eyes, leaning more to the green than the brown, he could produce a twinkle at will. His pale Russian skin made him look a bit frail, which he also used to lure the ladies, even though he was quite robust and healthy. Unlike Mike's ambivalence, Nikoli considered the ladies a much higher priority. He liked watching sports more than playing them, even though he was quite athletic, but never turned down an opportunity for a good time throwing around the football. Almost the polar opposite from his best friend, he liked and believed he needed nice things, and stopped at nothing to acquire them, but he always worked for and earned what he wanted. He was taught a good work ethic and as he grew older, it just became stronger. That was one of his favorite things about America: if you worked hard and did well, you were compensated for it. His father would tell him stories about how the system worked in Russia, being a very different tale. He felt blessed to be in the United States and he wasn't going to waste the opportunity.

When they were in high school, the three kids were always together, and a classic love triangle blossomed, although Mike was completely unaware of it. Samantha had been quietly in love with Mike since she was six, but through high school, observed Mike's inability or lack of desire to connect with girls and realized he was a much better friend than a lover and put any thoughts of dating Mike out of her head. Nikoli, however, was obsessed with Samantha; she represented to him all the great and beautiful things about America and it strained their relationship for a short time. Samantha gave in to Nikoli's charming and heartfelt courtship and they dated for a year. For Samantha's eighteenth birthday, Nikoli took her skydiving, while Mike watched from below. It had been a wonderful and difficult year for both of them. They had wild adventures, romantic moments, and they matured together. They knew they weren't "it" for each other, and, after a very awkward and rocky period, took a lesson from Mike and stayed great friends.

Nikoli would eventually continue his education at Stanford, and would stay very close to Samantha and Mike but would also meet someone that would become his business partner and together they would change the Internet forever. Langley Ford was a lot like Mike in that he was very levelheaded; Nikoli needed to be kept grounded, and Langley did that. Ford didn't pierce the bond the three had, but nonetheless became an integral figure in Nikoli's life. Also while at Stanford, Borodin met the woman who would become his wife. College provided good times, he met wonderful people, learned a great many things, some relating to education, some not, but most of all he became a good man.

Samantha walked over to the couch that Mike and Nikoli were sitting on in the Harvard dorm room. "Wouldn't it be great to have California secede from the Union?" she laughed. "Then we could just go home, start over and do things right."

"California is going to crack off into the ocean someday… that isn't the way to start off anything right. We don't want those problems, trust me." Borodin said smirking.

"You know, Sam, you've got something there." Mike said, his whole face changing and moving deep into thought.

"Let's go get something to eat," Niki said ignoring what Bishop had just said. "I'm starving."

"Me too," Samantha agreed.

Standing just under 5 feet 3 inches inches tall, and weighing maybe one hundred pounds, Samantha Sloan did not look intimidating. Her blonde hair and bluish eyes often went unnoticed at first, but once someone gave her a second look, they did not want to look away; she was very inquisitive, and had an intense stare. With an angular jaw, slightly turned up nose and porcelain skin, she could look grayish pale if she wasn't careful. She looked more like she should be hanging out in the fashion industry. But she wasn't a girly girl; she like to look good and appreciated nice things, but she gravitated toward stereotypically-male activities and that often alienated her from other girls. Throughout her life, she wanted to ride motorcycles, play poker, play football, and go shooting. Her parents both shot skeet and that was how the hobby started. After a close call in graduate school, when a cafe was held up where she was eating, she pursued obtaining a concealed weapons permit. Plus, her father always taught her the old adage of "walk softly and carry a big stick." Her big stick was a Smith and Wesson M&P 9mm compact. She was not a girl that would be a victim. She studied martial arts, she learned how to safely shoot and defend her firearm and she believed in the responsibility that carrying a gun required. She was not a fragile flower, even if the boys didn't let her play football with them anymore.

Another thing was that she wasn't necessarily good at being a girl. She acted like a boy more than a girl most of the time, and while she was dating Nikoli, she sometimes joked with him that she was the man in the relationship. Even though she went to an all-girl college, she had her fair share of trysts with boys, never getting attached to any of them. Growing into adulthood, the romances continued the same way they always had, but the one thing she did take seriously was school and her education.

Her relationship with her brother was strained and not as close as she'd always wanted. Her brother, Stuart, was quite lazy and content living off of the family money. He was kind of a jerk, and she felt like he never liked her. He was much older than Samantha and deep down always saw her as being the cause of messing up his perfect life. She tried repeatedly to have a relationship with him, but he never reciprocated. He went to college simply because his parents insisted, but as soon as he got his bachelors degree in business, he was done. She, on the other hand, loved school. She sailed through high school. Wellesley was hard, but she studied until she understood the subject matter. She would eventually graduate at the top of her class with a double degree in psychology and philosophy. Stanford would be the best time of her life; she got to be with her two best friends, get her masters in psychology in under two years, and would feel like she really found her stride. She would ultimately continue on at Stanford to receive her Ph.D. in clinical psychology. Her dad wanted her to go to Yale but she really didn't want to go back east again and Stanford had a great program, and then she would live happily ever after and all would be grand, or so she thought.

As the three were eating, Samantha thought to herself that she agreed completely with Mike and she knew to her core that something had to be done about what was happening in their world. She wanted to better understand the root of these problems, and she felt the psychological perspective would help her reach that goal. She wanted to have the background and knowledge of the human mind, and the corresponding behavior that humans carry out. At least having an understanding of those things, she would be able to appreciate and think through why certain things were happening and maybe, hopefully, be able to do something proactively to help.

Not very talkative, and a bit standoffish, she was always analyzing the best next move. Her instructors called her 'analytically literal' and it wasn't meant as a compliment. She felt as though she had to eat up and spit out every question that was asked. She often asked why certain wording was the way it was on a test, and it drove professors crazy. As an avid chess player, she understood the need for strategy; Sun Tzu's Art of War made her all too aware of how critical making the right move could be. Often she would miss social queues when having a conversation with someone, and just not respond to a query or help carry the conversation; she simply wasn't interested. The flip side to the silent treatment was the fact that she could cut someone off at the knees with a verbal beating that no one that it happened to could soon forget. She wasn't proud when she did it, and ended up disappointed in herself. She found it disparaging, and thought it was the main personality trait that she needed to work on.

The strangest, most quirky, idiosyncratic trait Samantha possessed was the fact that she only wore black. Everything from suits to jeans, all black all the time. It drove her mother crazy and she thought Samantha was a bit neurotic to not bend on the subject. Her mother often wondered, out loud, what would happen once the day came when Samantha was to get married. That was one of the times Samantha just went about her business as if nothing was said. When Samantha was a little girl, her grandmother bought her a black cotton jumpsuit with velvet accouterments. She wore it until it was literally falling off of her body. It didn't matter that she was growing out of it as well; she loved that outfit. From that day on, the only thing she would wear was black. In her 20's, she fell in love with pajamas from Lanvin Paris, but the only color they had for the particular style she wanted came in white, so she did acquiesce and get them. At $2,200 a pop, she wore them and loved them even though she thought she looked strange in them. The second trait that could be considered a bit odd was her fanaticism to be clean. Her personal hygiene, her home, her car, and her animals... the list was endless. She strongly believed that clean and organized surroundings leant to a clean and organized mind. The third thing that made her quirky to other people was the fact that she connected more easily to animals than humans. Close friends often teased her about it, prompting Samantha to demote those people from close friends to mere acquaintances. Anyone that didn't understand her enough to know how she felt about her animals, and even animals in general, were not worth her time. She had cats her whole life; at Wellesley she had a five-year-old half Ragdoll, mutt mix named Big Kidd. She and Big Kidd were soul mates; with his grey body, white paws, a little white mustache, white chest, and on his belly a white spot shaped like a heart. He was her special man! At the time of the bombing she was on the hunt to get him some companions, looking for a Ragdoll breeder to grow her family a bit more.

Sam was the most loyal friend anyone could have once you got to know her and once she trusted you. Her stress coping mechanism was music. She would put on her iPod, go for a run, a drive, anything that one could do with the help of music, and was miraculously healed. Some of her trust issues related directly to her family money. She was raised wealthy, her mother coming from old money and her father being an ex-professional football player and current sportscaster. Samantha didn't know if her friends liked her for her, or for her money. Her mother had also gone through the realities of hangers-on and tried to protect her children from the not-so-attractive side of life that having money could bring. The one thing that Samantha believed about having money was that it offered her time and peace of mind to figure out who and what she wanted to be, and then she could make her own money. Most early thinkers, albeit men, didn't have to sustain a living because of family money, giving them the opportunity to make great strides in our history. Descartes, Darwin, Newton; they all might have been very different people if they had to get up and go to work every day just to live. She was lucky that she did not have to struggle to make the house payment while discovering how she wanted to contribute. Other than that, she knew she would be successful in her own right.

Time passed and the three finished their undergraduate work, and moved on to Stanford. With Sam's family home in Menlo Park, it was an easy and convenient commute to Stanford, while the boys would live on campus. Living on campus was misleading for the boys. They were at Sam's parent's house more than they were in their rooms, which kept the house alive. Even though she was a west coast kid all the way, she missed the sense of history back east provided during her time at Wellesley. Following graduation, she and her parents had purchased a small but beautiful townhouse on the seaport in a little town in Connecticut called Mystic. She knew she would use that hideaway as a retreat to recharge whenever necessary.

It seemed like very happy times, and many of them were, but always in the back of Mike's head he was thinking of ways to change this downward spiral that the country was in, that the three could not help but see. Graduate school at Stanford seemed to be over in the blink of an eye. After the 1993 bombing, and through 1997, more of the same trend continued; there was nothing as horrifying as the bombing, but nevertheless, it was enough to keep it clear in Bishop's head that something would need to eventually change.

Bishop starting talking to his neighbor, 'Uncle Mike', Mike Pearson, about his thoughts, and Pearson started talking to others, and so on. They were gauging how the people they respected felt, and to their surprise, most felt the same way. A great country was slipping away, so what were they going to do about it?

And so it began, toward the beginning of 1999, as Mike started to work as a research architect at MIT by day instead of finishing his Ph.D. work in Mathematics at Stanford, and in all of his spare time he researched; he researched secession laws, what different resources each state had... he wanted to know if there were any states that had not come into the union as part of a territory, and on and on and on. He was relentless; for two full years that was all he did. Between the first bombing of the World Trade Center and then the Oklahoma City bombing in 1995, he just felt that the idea of what life was supposed to be was being forgotten to complacency and apathy. Nikoli and Samantha were as interested, each with their own part to do, and amazingly over the course of those two years, an underground movement started that brought in people from all backgrounds, jobs, and ages. Borodin, however, had another project he was working on, with his pal Langley Ford, that would catapult him into the limelight by inventing perhaps the greatest search engine technology of all time. Samantha continued her doctoral work while researching topics that Bishop had asked her to do. As another one of her "what ifs" she suggested this new group call themselves the AmendXers, and the name stuck! The name came from the 10th amendment to the U.S. Constitution, thus the X, representing the Roman numeral for 10. It stood for states having independent rights not delegated to the federal government. Essentially, it was under this amendment's framework that they could secede. AmendX became a covert organization that lived among the unsuspecting. Michael Pearson was now much higher in the military ranks of the Navy, and during his years of service had become disappointed with the lackadaisical attitude that the country had adopted. Once he joined the movement, it secretly but quickly spread like wildfire through major areas of the government. Each person that joined continued to work in their given professions, while as a hobby of sorts, researched and built plans on how to improve areas that they felt were in need in this country. Some member's projects stayed within their professional expertise, others had completely opposite interests, but they all had a passion for solving a problem. Samantha, for example, started by reviewing law enforcement and the historical problems associated with it. She was adamant that the mistakes with early police corruption, private security mishaps, police and military force not be repeated. She was hardly a bleeding heart; those jobs required force and brutality that not just anyone was cut out for. Nevertheless, over time, those jobs often made people corrupt, power hungry, bitter, racist, or numb and lifeless as a result. She was not going to let this happen and that was the primary reason she completed her Ph.D. work in clinical psychology. She would go on to develop programs to profile for personality type as it would relate to job fitness to be successful in the police and military roles, as well as keep them mentally healthy during their service. In fact, that was the topic of her dissertation. There were many avenues she wanted to pursue, post doctorate. For now though, she needed to partner with someone outside of government and military, but that knew the internal ropes as well as the privatization of business.

Mr. Pearson thought he knew the perfect person, and that meeting would come in time.

Michael Pearson introduced Samantha to Jackson Cooper and told her he thought Cooper would be the perfect partner to team up with, both for help with her Ph.D. work, as well as for the group. Cooper was disillusioned with politics and wanted to be the guy to make some changes from that domain. Working as the Agricultural Commissioner of Texas, Cooper's position offered Samantha very valuable experience within politics, something she had none of. She and Cooper became fast friends and he fit into the group as if he had been there all along.

PART 2
NUMBERS TALKING (2009)

CHAPTER 2
CONTACT FOR 44

Friday, January 9, 2009 – 3:00pm Eastern Standard Time (20:00 hours Zulu Time)

44's first contact came anonymously.

Before he was even sworn into office, his whole world turned upside down. Number 44; he was going to be the 44th President of the United States and it seemed like from the minute he would take office, everything would be turning to shit. Not in the sense that the economy was still down, unemployment still high, healthcare sucking epically, he knew these were issues that every president would go grey over. No, this was a whole different ball game. As far as he knew, he was the first president to receive these communications. It was delivered to the Hay-Adams hotel; he was staying there as many past incoming presidents had as well as dignitaries from other countries, it was a famous and respectable hotel. And as the President Elect, he had some meetings he had to attend, some final security briefings to go over and someone from the transition team would be there to go over what to expect on inauguration day. He had a stack of mail delivered to the hotel, and this envelope just blended in. At first he thought it was a joke or friendly jabbing from 43 because it was anonymous but it had only the number 44 and his code name on it and so few people knew it. He and 43 weren't close, being from different parties and having very different views, but they did have this post in common and only the people that served in this capacity could have any idea how the others felt, so there was a bond between the two men. When the secret service needs to communicate about a principal in their guard, they use code names; POTUS, which stands for President of the United States, and is globally recognized from the movies and television dramas so in addition to using POTUS they also use another, individualized code name. As soon as he read the letter, he knew it wasn't from 43...How the hell did they know his code name? He was just told what it was a week ago. It would surely be changed but that made him feel uneasy immediately. If it could be found out that easily and quickly, couldn't it be again? He gave the letter to the head of his security detail that had just been assigned to him and then didn't think of it again.

Wednesday, June 10, 2009 – 10:05am Eastern Daylight Time (14:05 hours Zulu Time)

The second envelope came to his home just outside of Philadelphia, a few months into his term. Another envelope that again said only his presidential number and that first code name; if they could find out that first one, they could surely find out the new one so why are they using the first one still? How did it make it through security he thought; once you become President, everything is scrutinized and evaluated including mail, even though it isn't the residence at the White House, it is still previewed before it just lands on the kitchen table. It was his wife, of all people, who brought it to him, so it had to have been screened before she got it. She had spent the week at home in Wyomissing, Pennsylvania preparing for the kids to move schools. A group that called themselves AmendX signed it. They promised more communication. Again, he turned it into the proper personnel and went about his business running the country.

Monday, July 6, 2009 – 9:47am Eastern Daylight Time (13:47 hours Zulu Time)

It was mid-morning when he had returned from a jog; feeling energized when he opened the door to the Oval Office and saw it lying in the middle of his pristine desktop. "Kate! Come here, please … when you get a moment … what is this?" as he lifted the package. "I don't know, Sir … it was brought up here by Mark Gonzales. He said it he found it on his desk, but your name, excuse me Sir, your first code name was on it." He moved closer but he already knew what it said; first the hotel, then my house, now the fucking Oval? Why didn't Kate open it? How does it just land on my desk unobstructed? An uneasy knot began to form in the pit of his stomach. What did this mean? He wasn't sure just how many of them there were, but he knew by the notes that the number had to be large. It took six months for the third envelope to come, maybe they would just stop coming. He glanced around the room and cleared his throat before he quietly asked, "Would you ask Mark to come to my office for a minute? Wait a minute, Kate – have you seen this envelope before today?" "No sir – I'll call Mr. Gonzales" was all Kate said with a flat expression on her face.

As soon as she closed the door, his personal cell phone rang, with a blocked number. He stared at the ringing display and the room began to hum … he braced himself as he slowly made the movement to sit on the couch, never taking his eyes from the phone. Small beads of sweat began to form on his upper lip, as it started to dawn on him that this could be a terrorist group…but then none of the notes indicated any terrorist demands, not any demands at all, really. Thank God, the phone stopped ringing and he set it down on the side table. The moment he removed his hand, it rang again… again, a blocked number. He didn't want to admit to himself he knew what was happening, so he hit the button and said nothing. "You don't have to answer, Triumph, but I know you are in possession of the envelope. You have five days to review its contents and one of us will be back in touch. And passing these communications onto your Secret Service detail will glean nothing, they will never trace it, plus it will not make a priority listing because as you can see there are no threats. Good day." Click. Shit! It is one of us! How the hell did he know to call me Triumph? Did he have an accent? Did he sound young? I am freaking out, he thought to himself … What the hell is going on?!

He still couldn't get over how they knew his first code name. Pre-inauguration, he had met with his security detail, he was returning late from a half marathon he had just run. The head of his detail, Mark Gonzales, noticed his running shoes and that became his code name; is that really how code names are created? He was wearing Saucony Triumph 8's.

Where did it all go so horribly wrong? He leaned back on the sofa and gazed absently around the room; his eyes landed on his favorite leather chair across the room and considered moving, but he was too tired. Just minutes before he was full of energy. He thought about the last time he sat there and wished he could transport back in time, before he'd even heard the name AmendX and what it meant. He closed his eyes, with a fatigue that he wasn't used to. He certainly wasn't to blame, but he was absolutely powerless to stop this awful machine that now seemed to operate on autopilot. He thought back to a time when he was naïve enough to think that by getting into politics, he could actually make a difference in the world. Hell, even by the time he was old enough to understand government, it was too late to stop this self-propelled monster that once was a great idea created by a group of extraordinary individuals.

There are those that would say it was FDR that was to blame; a bunch of ill-planned programs his administration laid out with little thought to how future generations would handle paying for it. Others would say those were great programs but since FDR's administration the programs have been run horribly; with spending out of control, programs extended without any thought as to the incremental cost. But then again, has any administration since Washington really cared about the national debt? The United States forged ahead with zero regard to the wise forewarning contained in the first President's farewell address, which he remembered very clearly, as it is read in Congress every year in observance of the President's birthday:

"... As a very important source of strength and security, cherish public credit. One method of preserving it is to use it as sparingly as possible, avoiding occasions of expense by cultivating peace, but remembering also that timely disbursements to prepare for danger frequently prevent much greater disbursements to repel it; avoiding likewise the accumulation of debt, not only by shunning occasions of expense, but by vigorous exertions in time of peace to discharge the debts which unavoidable wars may have occasioned, not ungenerously throwing upon posterity the burden which we ourselves ought to bear. The execution of these maxims belongs to your representatives, but it is necessary that public opinion should cooperate. To facilitate to them the performance of their duty, it is essential that you should practically bear in mind that towards the payment of debts there must be revenue; that to have revenue there must be taxes; that no taxes can be devised which are not more or less inconvenient and unpleasant; that the intrinsic embarrassment inseparable from the selection of the proper objects (which is always a choice of difficulties) ought to be a decisive motive for a candid construction of the conduct of the government in making it, and for a spirit of acquiescence in the measures for obtaining revenue which the public exigencies may at any time dictate."

None of that matters now, the problem at hand is so damn big…too big for him to try to keep it contained by himself or his administration. He had special interests who helped get him elected he had to answer to as well, and in his mind money was the only thing that could fix it, spending money. There was a time he believed that he could, with his office, really make a difference. But the "system" was so convoluted, it seemed like nothing could get accomplished. It chewed administrations up and spit them out, and the partisanship was worse than ever. The founding fathers never intended for this to happen. D.C. was now a self-serving machine that would eat you alive if anyone dared go up against it. And now, whom could he trust? Who would even have the power to help him mitigate the guaranteed shit storm that was ahead in the next days, weeks or possibly longer? He rubbed his temples as he squeezed his eyes shut as tightly as he could, hoping the pressure would bring an answer to mind. Nothing…absolutely nothing. Didn't he ask to see Gonzales? It seemed like days ago when he walked into this room.

CHAPTER 3
CONVERSATION WITH 43

The meeting with Mark Gonzales got him nowhere. Mark, the head of his security detail, seemed utterly baffled. For something to get to his desk, it had to be vetted at the highest levels, so he had thought it came from within so there was no reason for Kate to be alarmed by it either. He suggested that Kate open everything from now on or he would. 44 said he wanted Mark to open anything that looked out of the ordinary, even if it came from within. Mark thought it was a hoax, someone playing a huge joke on him. Maybe this is how the new president gets hazed he said. He tried to calm 44 by laughing a little and said to try to see the humor because the only way it could get through was if it was a joke. 44 wasn't laughing.

44 asked 43 for a private meeting, as private a meeting the President of the United States could have. He asked 43 to come to the oval under the guise of some presidential charity dinner that was coming up. He knew past presidents from 41 on, including himself would be in attendance, so 43 coming to talk about it wouldn't seem strange at all. He felt like a fool that he couldn't get to the bottom of these notes and with, as much access as they seemed to have, the only thing that made sense was to ask 43.

He found out this "note" thing had been going on for years. 43 said that this group, incidentally, has been unable to be identified. They had been trying for years. It started, to the best of their knowledge, during 42, but the letter-senders thought 42 was such a complete waste of skin, "I'm paraphrasing, but that was the gist," 43 explained, "they didn't feel the need to reach out until I took office. It took me completely by surprise and put me on edge at first, but they were never violent, nor insisting on anything. They gave ideas and possible solutions to an array of issues, much of what I was already trying to advance anyway. Then, I wasn't sure they would continue to make contact once I left office and that is why I didn't tell you. But if you don't listen to anything else I say, listen to this...they are within the ranks and they are smart. Smart in a way I can't even describe. They exist, and they don't exist, you know? It is almost like the Illuminati, Bilderberg or Bohemian Grove."

44 looked at him smugly, giving away nothing. "What do you mean?" he asked.

"You know exactly what I mean. I will say this once because I know how important it is that what really goes on at Bohemian Grove stay covert, but just like the Grove, these people could be from anywhere and everywhere. We all know about the Grove and how it makes or breaks presidents, but the public thinks it's a myth and that is how it will be kept. That is the biggest difference between the Grove and the AmendX group. The Xers are choosing not to directly call any shots, but they certainly aren't shy about dropping some hints, and I have to tell you, their recommendations are usually right on." 43 continued.

44 jumped out of his seat. "*What!* You have done what they have *said?*"

"Hold up, Sparky," 43 said in a condescending tone, "First of all, they have not dictated a move-by-move directive, they have issues with very specific problems and suggest possible solutions. Most of the time, the solution matches what many of our advisors come up with anyway. One of their major issues that we can't seem to do anything about is time. Even though I personally agree with the ludicrous amount of time things take, politically there was nothing I could do about it. The partisanship in this town is getting worse everyday and if everyone keeps thumbing their noses across the isle nothing will get done. I'm thrilled to be out of it frankly. It's your problem now, but heed my warning, they could be anyone and anywhere; Christ, your wife could be one of them."

"Yeah, sure. I think that is highly unlikely. Besides, she tells me when she disagrees with something I'm doing, and that is rare so it wouldn't make any sense anyway…I can't even believe you have me giving it any serious thought. But fuck, what are you thinking anyway? You can't acquiesce to some nut-ball group's demands." 44 was getting worked up shouted, "I don't care if they are right or not! The country doesn't run that way. Who the hell do they think they are that they can just send the President of the United States a note and something will get done? And you did it! Holy shit, what am I up against here?" 44 got up and started pacing.

"What are you up against?" 43, remaining perfectly calm, asked back to him. "Well, I'm only here as a courtesy to you. You can do anything you want. I'm done. I'm done with the media making fun of me, I'm done with image consultants giving politically correct advice…here stand on the left, you will appear stronger, make sure you sit down only after the other dignitary does, don't smile so much, you won't appear strong. FDR had polio for God's sake, you think he would be elected now when looks are more important that substance or brains? I'm sick of this, and I'm done. My family has been in public service forever and I'm done. My wife and I are going to just fall back, away from this scrutiny and ride off into the sunset. You think that I did something wrong for this country, and that's fine, though it couldn't be further from the truth. But you know what? I don't give a shit. I'm done. Once you start to see what they are talking about, I hope you realize they are right. I don't agree with how they are choosing to do it, the way they go about it, but I can understand why they are doing it this way. And hey, chief, soon you're gonna realize that they are all around you so blabbing to someone about it might get you in a mess! I could never figure out who was and who wasn't a part of the group. I had people followed for months that I was convinced played a part in the group and came up with zilch every time, so I stopped wasting time and money. So go, knock yourself out and waste your resources on doing the same damn thing I did. You will get the same result and only piss them off. And like I said, they are smart and they are savvy with, from what I've seen, incalculable resources. But do it your way. I'm done."

They stared at each other for a few minutes. 43 sat there as 44 let it sink in. After that the conversation went differently. 44 knew enough to know that without 43's help, or at least his take on the situation, things would be harder so he calmed down and apologized. He said he didn't mean to imply he did something wrong and asked him detailed questions about what the past messages said, how they came and everything else he could think of. He'd hoped the conversation lasted longer, but he believed 43 gave him everything he knew, so there was no use badgering him; he was utterly exhausted when they stood, shook hands and parted company.

PART 3
TEXAS, COLORADO & A PLAN (2011)

CHAPTER 4
THE LOCATION

So much time had passed since those early school days, yet it went by so quickly. In school, Sam had studied awareness, perception, and cognition among other things and through that learning, she had tried to live in the "now." It had been particularly helpful when, at times, she thought she might not have a 'later,' when things with the group got dangerous or they might get discovered. She tried to spend meaningful time with people when she was with them, to stay engaged, not working on other things, or being distracted by her phone. She tried to make the most out of moments that were good and even those harder times where she had to search out the bright spots were significant to her. And the bottom line was she had always secretly hoped it would not have to get this far. She had hoped the group would get powerful enough in the areas of concern that things could be fixed here, without having to do what they were planning, but she knew the problems were just too big now. A huge shift had to be made.

Friday, March 18, 2011 – 9:15am Mountain Daylight Time (15:15 hours Zulu Time)

The first official policy meeting of the AmendXers would be held in April of 2012 in Colorado. They had been meeting for years putting together reports from countless hours of research to make recommendations at these meetings. The conferences would involve lengthy discussions of very detailed issues to reach consensus within the group. The conferences would be split up by topic and stretch over an undetermined period of time. Now that the group was in full planning mode, there was a level of urgency, but it was more important that the issues get covered in their entirety and correctly, so there was no timeframe written in stone.

Colorado was a central location for many, while many others had homes in Aspen and could come down from the mountain quite easily. Bishop didn't want it to be smack in the middle of Denver; with so many famous people gathering, not to mention the strong military contingent that would be coming and going, he knew that would attract attention they didn't want or need. He asked Samantha to find a suitable meeting place, book it and provide false names where appropriate to mitigate any unnecessary identification. Samantha chose the Broadmoor resort in Colorado Springs. It was a large, five star campus, stretching over three thousand acres that would accommodate such guests without any suspicion. It had also proved an excellent location for the celebration when Jackson Cooper became Governor of Texas. The smaller teams had met there, as Samantha herself had stayed there several times over the years. This was a perfect location. The resort touted over seven hundred rooms and cottages, eighteen restaurants, seven tennis courts and three golf courses. The group could come and go with relative ease and never be suspected of all being there for the same purpose. Plus, they were pet friendly and she could bring her dog Oliver as well as her cats. She thought to herself and chuckled, the only problem with the Broadmoor's golf courses were the fact that they were world renowned, and Mike might lose focus on the task at hand and wish he was on the course, if even for a moment.

She decided to buy out all but one of the cottage complement, located at the southern tip of the property; this would allow for maximum privacy. One, the management said, had to be available for other guests and since the purchase had no end date, Samantha couldn't argue. There were five, eight bedroom buildings with dining tables and seating in each as well as a grand parlor in the center of each of the buildings. These areas would be perfect for breakout groups to come and discuss ideas and plans. She also booked the adjacent three-bedroom building with a one bedroom and a two-bedroom cottage. Mike and Nikoli would be very comfortable in the two-bedroom and she would take the one bedroom to be close in case anyone needed her for anything.

In scouting for a location Samantha had been to the Broadmoor several times during the previous year to plan and organize the final conferences. She had planned for this necessary time; she specifically had taken time off from her practice to dedicate herself full-time to this endeavor and it was worth it. It would change life, as she knew it, and it had to happen correctly. The end of March was quickly approaching as she was putting finishing touches in place for the conference. She decided on the Broadmoor South meeting space. The conference room was on the same side of the campus as the cottages, with the spa wedge in between, there might be time for a quick massage during her stay, she thought. The room held around sixty-five people depending on the configuration. Mike was adamant about a hollow square seating arrangement so there would be no possible misunderstanding that preferential seating was at hand. This was impossible, however, because with sixty people, possibly more, everyone would be shouting just to be heard from one side to the next. She settled on a banquet style with a twist; with the help of the wonderful staff, there would be six executive conference room type tables holding between 12 and 13 people at each. There would be so much commotion and exchange of ideas, she knew people would be getting up from their seats and moving around constantly so this worked well. The room was quite conducive to the type of work that was to be accomplished; big over-sized black leather tufted chairs, mammoth dark mahogany tables, state of the art audio visual and IT equipment, natural and ambient lighting. The room was tastefully done; it was lush and comforting while also ideally professional. This was the room history would be made in.

With rooms blocked for group members, she had begun the long task of confirming who was coming and when. A large subset of major players would all come in at once for the initial introductions; she had to moderate egos as well as practical items such as schedules. One military general would be on vacation at the same time a defense contractor met with a real estate investor about possible expansion to Colorado, while the CEO of a major tech company had meetings all in the same hotel. It was a maze of misdirection, but she believed she was ready. As far as the egos went, after ten plus years of working with some of these people, egos were the last thing any of them were going to allow to get in the way, but egos were egos and she had become an expert on when to use the kid gloves. She often stood back in awe at the uniting of such incredible minds that had decided to give up the tremendous accomplishments they had made here in the world to create a better one with a renewed focus on integrity, hard work, production, ability and most of all the balance of community responsibility and individual prerogative. She was getting more excited by the minute, she had not seen some of these people in person in at least a year, some more, and now everyone was finally coming together.

CHAPTER 5
THE COMPANY

Thursday, March 31, 2011 – 3:45pm Pacific Daylight Time (22:45 hours Zulu Time)

The distant sounds of Led Zeppelin seeped through the open door, from his son's room, into Quinn's home office. "…If the stores are all closed," the song continued. "…With a word, she can get what she came for… and she's buying a stairway to heaven."

Quinn loved this music, and was happy that his son, now 14 years old, could appreciate it as well. Some of what his son listened to seemed to literally grate against Quinn's soul, but for father and son to connect as they did, over something that reached its heyday even before his son was born, was satisfying.

As the song ended, and the next one began, Quinn continued his work on the project that he had stayed home to complete. He was working on dissecting the notes from a brainstorming session he had conducted the day before with his creative team. They were working on envisioning the next generation of his revolutionary technology. Even though he bought in to this "future world order" as he called it, he also loved his company, his processes and the idea-generating machine that had become his life. It wasn't enough to just phone it in where his company was concerned, he would continue to strive to bring new technologies to the market and make them as beautiful to the people buying them as they were to him during the creation process. He also knew that 13-C was the technology backbone to the group, and that came with tremendous responsibility.

He thought back to how it had begun back in 2008. He had always been fascinated with video, and ways to make it even more useful than it was today. While working with a small group of people studying subliminal messages in video, he had a thought that hit him like a bolt of lightning. Instead of looking for the few frames that existed within the video itself, instead of trying to influence the viewer without their knowledge, what if they were to add data to digital video in such as way as to make it interactive? In essence, could they design a viewing screen that allowed a viewer to interact

44

with what they were seeing, and extract unseen information? That's exactly what they ended up doing. This new encryption was borne from the Point-and-Click technology, KAI, which he had released to the public. KAI kept the money was really rolling in, making 13-C the most profitable company year after year, but it wasn't about the money to Quinn, he had long since had more than enough and really never cared about money anyway. He was about design and innovation. He loved making beautiful things that people could use to personalize their whole technological experience, and this bit of technology was only rivaled in popularity to the iPod so many years ago.

After its initial release, they were able to secure a 20-year patent on the KAI technology. The operating system, Sense, that they purpose-built for the special TVs, was rapidly transformed for use on phones, PDAs, and computers. It drove the mass adoption of touch-screen televisions, as well as remote controls that would act like a mouse. Point, click, and buy, simple, yet brilliant. In later years, the same concept would be applied to digital books, and would give the reader access to nearly endless content associated with what they were reading, and would be called an x-ray. Their idea was revolutionary, and was unmatched by any other technology.

He wasn't satisfied. Ever. He was relentless in his pursuit of improving the technology. That's why he had conducted a series of brainstorming sessions to try to create a future vision. As the music from his son's room continued to permeate his office, he strained to put these random thoughts together into something useful. He enjoyed the process, but it always left him completely drained. The result of today's session gleaned a new type of steganography that he would turn over to Derek Holden when the time came. This was not to be sold to the public, which was foreign to Quinn, but it may keep the group's digital traffic a secret beyond what Nikoli Borodin had spun up.

He thought back to another world-changer that he had personally been involved with. As the Internet had grown in prominence in the early 1990's, there was no ability to know what kind of computer people would be using to access the Internet, so a technology needed to be developed to allow any computer, regardless of operating system, to run a program. His friend, Tim Conrad, had been so instrumental building the necessary software to access the Internet, it made sense to work together on this new concept. Their creative talents fed off each other, and eventually produced the capability to virtualize software. In essence, they mastered the ability to operate a fully functional computer, but completely encapsulated in a simulated environment. Essentially, it was running a software-based computer inside another host computer, and independent of the type of computer the host happened to be. They created programs to run identically within IBM PCs and compatibles, Macs, and many other machines.

Eventually, their revolutionary techniques got the attention of Dean Kinsey. Kinsey had the necessary resources to develop this technology further, and through many iterations, this capability eventually became the basis for cloud computing. Now, as Quinn surveyed the landscape of huge companies like Amazon.com, and other giants, he knew their existence would not be possible without what he had done. He laughed, thinking that at one time, when Kinsey had just gotten involved, the initial code name of the project had been *Stealth*. Those were the days, he thought. They had all amassed fortunes and made the world better for the creations they had dreamt up. Things in the world weren't exactly how he imagined them. He was behind what this group was trying to accomplish, but the one thing that was true to being exactly like he had imagined was his company, and he wasn't going anywhere without it.

He gazed out the window for a moment, as the Southern California sun was shining down on his view of the ocean in the distance, and now his son was playing *Beautiful Day*, by U2. How fitting.

***

The meetings began with relative ease and quite naturally. Michael Pearson was the natural middleman between Bishop and Derek Holden. Then through Bishop Holden would meet Samantha Sloan, so planning could commence. Through Samantha, Holden would meet Jackson Cooper and be introduced to the political and physical planning. Holden was key in the construction and foundation of this undertaking; he had to be heavily involved with other members initially. This would slow down though, as he had to spearhead a part of things that were to be completely removed from any other members. But before Holden could be out of day-to-day introductions, Cooper introduced him to a wildly fascinating kid that was obsessed with all things energy, Sakti Sharma. Holden and Sharma didn't have much in common, but everyone, including Holden, was taken aback by Sharma's enthusiasm and drive for his projects. It was Sam, Cooper or Holden that facilitated major player meetings.

CHAPTER 6
THE INTRODUCTIONS

May 2011

She couldn't get over this remarkable group of people. She had no idea how much she missed the company of great people until she was standing in the middle of this room. Every day, outside of administering the charge for AmendX, she had to bear the mediocrity and the status quo, no one wanted anything better for themselves anymore, and if they did, they certainly didn't want to work for it, and it had gotten worse over the years. Now that the conferences were starting she could see a light at the end of the tunnel, things were going to change. She chuckled to herself, that this could also be the union of the bald heads convention! So many of the men in this room had a bald head from necessity or style, and it certainly was a style these days.

Everyone looked around the huge Colorado Hall. She had three rooms of the gigantic seven available, allowing for upwards of 700 people coming in and out. There weren't that many tonight, both from a security perspective as well as scheduling ability, and not everyone could be in one place on one night, but it was a sea of people. This would be the only time that this many leaders of the group were in one place, and each of them brought many of those that followed them into the group. Samantha loved and dreaded tonight. She was so worried about another leak, someone hearing something they shouldn't, or someone noticing this gathering. The most recognizable guests came in at all different times with groups of the unfamiliar, and defense contractor Derek Holden made sure to post covert security at each entrance and exit to make sure no one approached that shouldn't be there. The easiest way to signify those that should be there, Samantha decided after Nikoli's wedding, was that there should be a physical announcement of sorts; a rhodium X in the form of jewelry, or ID bracelet as a signifier that this person was a member of AmendX. Rhodium's high reflective property made it easily recognizable, when looking for it, in even small pieces of jewelry. It could also be mistaken for costume jewelry, which was fine because the lack of added attention was a good thing. Critical mass had been met for the group, so there was no way for everyone to know everyone else, and that was to be expected. It wouldn't be until post-Event that members would be able to walk freely among each other. But even over so many years, some of the major organizers hadn't met yet. They dealt with the people they had direct business with, and didn't worry too much about peripheral happenings, thus, this identifier would help immensely.

Many of the original members were top entrepreneurs or executives in their fields, but many were everyday people, and of course there were the famous celebrities among them. Those that couldn't keep their own private lives a secret, yet somehow managed to keep their involvement in the group on the Q.T. Samantha still believed the big leak had come from within that particular rank, those famous ones that couldn't keep their mouths shut. The problems that brought everyone here were essentially all the same, and it was the group of unknowns that would stand tall and united to be heard, and that hadn't happened in a very long time since the country was founded. The complete confidence they had in Bishop truly showed now, and the assurance that he knew who to recruit, assemble and have trust in was demonstrated so perfectly while everyone was sitting down. It became almost overwhelming; this was the true meeting of the minds...*The* think tank!

There was a small stage with a podium for one speaker, Michael Bishop. He would say a few words, but nothing about the plan. Tonight was about introductions. He walked over to the podium to speak and in his usual way, grabbed the microphone and sat on the edge of the stage. He constantly avoided being set above anyone else in the group, and even the literal pedestal wasn't going to work. He began, "My goal was always to find the pure and perfect balance between competition and cooperation. This country's founders were the best-of-the-best, and taking second was not one of their talents. Having said that though, they also knew how working together bettered them and to that point, I believe that is the area that has been forgotten. Also, let me point out the fact that I am aware that the statement is an easy one to make, and I know that everyone sitting at this table here today understands the concept. Bringing it to fruition via policies, and..." He paused for just a second, "ways of being, is not easy in any meaning of the word. That is why you are all here, and have been a part of this for years, trying to adjust and tweak things about where this country is, and how it can become the best once again. Many of you still do not know each other personally, but surely know each other by reputation and trade. Let's take the time to meet each other on a personal level tonight and resume our work tomorrow. It will become important to know each other on a deeper level one day, and I don't want to miss such a vital piece of the puzzle because we are all in hurry. You all know me, probably better than most of you ever wanted to, but I'm around if you need me." He paused again and while he walked out of the room he said, "Things are going to change, I can *feel* it," and without turning around, he heard Sharma yell out, "Beck!"

Samantha laughed, the song game had been going on for years, some comic relief inside of a pressure tank she thought. The song game was a twist on a game they used to play in the car when they were younger. The first one to guess the name of the artist that came on the radio, won. Mike's new method was to just say a line from a song and wait for someone to get it. She looked at Mike with complete reverence. She remembered him as a kid; he had always been able to get groups of people talking, he could bring out the best in everyone, and this was his swan song.

Many chuckled at his self-deprecation while others laughed at the song game. He had some work to do, and the members were there to get to know each other, so for the next few hours he parked himself in the adjacent office, hearing robust laughs and important whisperings that told him people were getting comfortable with each other, and that was a good thing.

Introductions ensued.

Vassily Novikov was a Russian citizen that Nikoli's family knew back in Russia. When Nikoli's family came to the US, the two men stayed in touch but were never close. It wasn't until Novikov made millions in the financial sector, and was running Russia's largest precious metals producing company, that he got back in touch with Nikoli and they rekindled their acquaintanceship. Novikov, like Borodin, had that American entrepreneurial spirit and drive. Actually, Novikov embodied a work ethic and drive that was unparalleled, and when Bishop had his first conversation with

Novikov, Bishop couldn't believe all he had accomplished and how he had done it. Bishop was often impressed and pleasantly surprised at many of those whom he talked with, but this was almost scary. Novikov was definitely one of a kind and not just because of his success. His unique looks also made him stand out. He stood 6 feet 8 inches tall by the time he was 23 years old and had extremely severe features, and as a young man he modeled. It was at that time he became acquainted with life outside of Russia. He was drawn to the party life and as he became more successful, his exploits became more famous. A complete health and sports freak, he bought an American sports team and met and brought along other owners into the group as well. They were an exclusive bunch unto themselves and many looked at them in awe. Novikov himself brought about $10 billion to the table.

In one corner of the room, Nadal Dani spoke with four other men, and one woman. Nadal had come to the group through Nikoli as well, and had been part of the effort almost since it began. All it had taken was an eye-opening conversation with Bishop. Nikoli had many friends, many through his amazingly wide social network, and if he saw them having the same difficulties and entrepreneurial spirit that sought out solutions, he introduced them to Bishop. Those that Nikoli invited in didn't need much further coaxing, but as everyone in this group had learned, a conversation with Michael Bishop could be life changing. Many that Bishop came across did not have the fight in them anymore, and although they were great people, they just did not fit the mold of an AmendXer. But many did fit that mold, and Nadal Dani was one of Nikoli's favorites. This man just didn't know the word "quit." The boys ran across him while at Stanford, but only Nikoli really kept in touch with him, and after Dani sold his email service company to a multinational computer company, he had a few hundred million dollars burning a hole in his pocket, and a mind burning through new venture ideas. After he talked with Bishop it was clear he was on board. He was currently working on a pet project that could poll extraordinary amounts of people, allowing them to vote and insert their opinions on different issues both confidentially as well as a completely anonymous feature. It also had a collaboration piece to it that interested the group very much.

Dani was listening intently to one of the men, who's contribution to the effort would involve the dissemination of information through the media. The man wasn't a media mogul, or even someone that the country would consider a well-known figure, but he understood media production inside-out, and would be instrumental in spreading information that suited the group's purposes. Since Dani's experience was all rooted in gathering information, the man's outlook on information dissemination was the exact opposite, and complementary, view. For one to gather information, it had to first be disseminated, yet to be disseminated, it had to be researched and well-understood. These two men would work well together.

The woman in the little group was dressed casually, in jeans and a light, lavender collared shirt. She was older, yet still very attractive. She had eye-catching red hair, and bright green eyes that made it impossible to hide her Irish heritage. She asked several pointed questions as the media producer was talking, and Dani had to smile in that the questions she was asking were the same as those circulating through his mind. It was clear that although many in the room, and even within this group of five people, disagreed with each other, the spirit of cooperation and the unified goal was apparent. Score another one for Bishop.

The conversation continued for the better part of 30 minutes, at which point the little group split up and sought out others to introduce themselves to. This small group of people together was able to contribute well over a half a billion dollars to the cause.

Nikoli stood with a few others near a table that was festooned with coffee, tea, soft drinks, and bottles of water. Nikoli was introduced to another powerhouse in technology and champion of the early web browser, Tim Conrad, while at a renewable energy conference with energy guru, Sakti Sharma, whom he met through Dean Kinsey. Both Nikoli and Conrad shared a passion for renewable and alternative energy, and the fact that technology was such a focal point in their lives a friendship was destined. After several years of friendship, and one very important conversation with Bishop, here they were. Nikoli and Conrad stood and drank coffee, getting to know a few others that would march with them along the path to what they hoped would be a new existence. They chatted briefly with a couple of computer guys, a gentleman that owned a car-wash franchise, and a woman that had worked in senior management in the Department of Labor for two presidencies. All had keen insights. Sharma, Conrad and Kinsey were good for a billion and a half.

Not totally bought in as a member, Collin Nelson sent many people to the group. At first, Bishop said you either had to be with the group or not. Then, in a much more complex conversation with Nelson, he realized collaboration with some people that might remain 'outside' might not be a bad thing. Plus, Nelson was completely a unique situation and man. Trailing the Montes family by too slim a margin to count, he came in as the second richest man in the world, with resources in the tens of billions. But, instead of using it for an extravagant lifestyle, he used it to help myriad industries, countries and individual people. He believed in a strong work ethic and had a heart the size of Texas, pun intended. He was a compassionate man interested in helping those that helped themselves. Plus, it didn't hurt that anything he touched turned to gold. Of all the wonderful people Bishop was able to have conversations with, it was Nelson that he enjoyed the most. He was part mentor, father, boss and friend. He brought in Robert Gilbert, the man who always ran neck-and-neck with Randall Quinn, who Nelson also brought to the group. Gilbert and Quinn were always on opposite sides philosophically regarding technology, but collaborated occasionally to write software for Quinn's company, 13-C. That type of collaboration wasn't something that Quinn enjoyed at all in his younger days, but grew more comfortable with in his maturity. Gilbert also chose to remain outside of the group but contributed significantly, giving about $10 billion to be used as Bishop saw fit, and offered counsel when needed. The politicians David Merchant and Marc Blair were in with both feet, as was media heiress Kylie Chamberland. It was rumored Quinn had a steamy affair with Chamberland's daughter prior to meeting his wife, but it was never confirmed. These three brought about $24 billion to the guild.

Another politician and first-string Xer, Jackson Cooper brought in Rex Morrison Jr., who had taken the reins of King Ranch from his father, Rex Morrison Sr., five years before. From a financial perspective, he could only contribute about $300 million, but one of the reasons he was so valuable was because his knowledge of real estate surpassed most, plus he was the CEO and controlling partner of the largest working ranch in Texas and second in the world, not to mention one of the U.S.'s most plentiful resources of oil. Cooper was also friends with Morrison Sr., but although Morrison shared his son's beliefs and enthusiasm for the group, he felt he was too old and too tired to be of any service. He stayed in the background and offered counsel to anyone who needed it. The resources that King Ranch provided were of limitless benefit to this group. Cooper, bringing with him $2.5 billion and more brilliance and innovation within his industry, also brought in Anderson Glennis, not in attendance. A stodgy older man that "didn't have time for bullshit" he would say. An aerospace engineer by trade, he worked tirelessly on private space travel, removing it from government purview saying it was the only way to actually get something done. He was a big believer in free trade and entrepreneurialism; for that, in his mind, was the only way to succeed. He didn't have the patience to sit at a multi-day conference that, for the most part, would have nothing to do with him, but he was happy to be a contributor; if the group needed anything from him, they had just better come prepared to ask the right questions and get out of his way when he was done answering them. One of his biggest concerns was how to inspire our children to do something great, not just worry about the next upgrade on their smartphone or video game, or that Johnny had to get in A in class but had no idea of the material being taught. He would point out that you didn't just get an A… to get an A, you studied hard and learned the material and even if sometimes you didn't get an A, learning was the payoff. Through Glennis, Cooper met and recruited Ryder Burns, a British industrialist and another non-citizen that was equally as interested in starting a new culture as any American in the group. He was in attendance and after some conversations with Bishop and Sloan; he wanted to be included on the team that was working toward a solution for a new educational system. As an early dropout from high school, he understood all too well the difficulties and struggles involved in trying to improve a system designed to educate its peoples even through such a wide spectrum of interests, skill and ability. His involvement also gave the group a global airplane fleet, among other things. To Quinn's dismay, Cooper also brought in a great old nemesis of Quinn's, Adam Edelstein. As the co-founder of one of the world's largest computer technology corporations with a net worth of approximately $30 billion, he was another ego that was guilty of magical thinking; it was his belief that it was his personal greatness as a leader and executive that made his endeavors successful. There might be many elements of truth to that, but his lack of any shred of humility also often caused large amounts of accomplished people to withdraw from him. He knew that he and Quinn would butt heads, but he sincerely believed in the cause and was there to assist whenever needed. He was interested in the future direction of education, energy and of course the Internet and technology.

From the Holden contingent came the famous pastor and televangelist from Houston, Paul Olson. He was not in attendance, and he was another member who would not be very involved, but he was sympathetic to the cause, would remain in Texas following the transition and was available to help when necessary. Mark Gonzales was there, the head of the Secret Service detail for the President, and a former Navy SEAL. That was where he and Holden met and had been friends ever since. He was tall with a shaved, bald head. His mother was African American and his father was half black half Latino. He was handsome with an angular jaw and giant black eyes. On this night he wore a black suit, white shirt and red tie. He believed in looking your best. Gonzales got many a panicked call from 44, wondering how messages from this group infiltrated their security. Gonzales didn't have to play stupid; it was arranged before hand that the messages would come in from other sources besides Gonzales so he had plausible deniability. He had worked under several presidents, but on this one he was the head of the detail so everything had to carried out perfectly. Whether he agreed with the politics or not, he was the president and with that came a level of respect for the office. Finally, long-time family friends of Holden's were the Needham brothers. Collectively bringing in excess of $18 billion, the many industries these brothers owned or were involved in had tentacles so far reaching, they would be a fantastic resource for the group. But their lives and extreme right wing beliefs kept them in controversy and in the media. The group would have to be careful whenever they were around because some drama was sure to follow. Kevin Needham was much more conservative than his younger sibling. He stood about five feet eight inches tall with salt and pepper hair. He was extremely active for a man of seventy-five years. His brother John, ten years younger and few inches taller, actually looked older than his brother with a full head of white, silvery hair. Both men wore dark blue suits, Kevin with a red and white striped tie and John without a tie, but a red handkerchief in his lapel pocket.

Samantha heard John Needham say to Reagan Mills, a woman he had just met, "We are so splintered, I'm amazed this hasn't happened yet to be honest. I mean we really are getting to a civil war, we can't come to any kind of compromise in Washington, so why not break off and see who has it right."

Samantha thought for a minute and quite agreed with the idea.

From Michael Pearson's group was Joseph Bailey, the Assistant to the President for Homeland Security and Counterterrorism, which was a civilian post, but knowledge and power came with it. Pearson also brought Harlan Mackay, who had risen to the rank of General in the Air Force. Mackay held positions as Director of the NSA as well as for the CIA. Being an avid football fan, he and Samantha Sloan got along famously, often going to games. Mackay loving the Pittsburgh Steelers and with Sloan behind the New England Patriots, they had many great debates during games. Harrison Corrigan, also a General, but in the Marine Corps, attended the US Naval Academy and went on to graduate school at George Washington University. He eventually ascended to the position of Chairman of the Joint Chiefs, and had since retired. He and Pearson held a special bond because Pearson held the post currently and both knew the level of pressure the job came with, as well as the discerning sensibilities the job required. Dylan Sterling came to them following the big leak that had almost brought the group down, bringing the only good thing to come out of such a sloppy error. He simply approached a staffer and made a cryptic remark, including wanting to talk with Pearson. It made many members doubt him at first, not knowing if he was infiltrating the group or really one of them, but after some time, it was obvious he was one of them. Having once worked under the presidency of Ronald Reagan in the Management and Budget Office, and with a Ph.D. in economics, Sterling agreed to oversee the group's budgetary concerns. Most of the major players had met these men before both in "real" life and during some interactions within the group. Pearson brought quite the powerhouse collective. Recently, Corrigan brought two more men to add to the arsenal; William Brahe, a former White House Chief of Staff, and best friend of Corrigan; Christian Adams, former head of the US Cyber Command and current Director of the NSA. He and Mackay often diverged widely on philosophy but once both discovered they were in the group, they realized that they had more similar ideologies than originally concluded.

Randall Hawking Quinn, brought in through Nelson, was a major contributor to the group. He was born March 13, 1955 so a bit older than the designers, but the same age as first devotees. His parents were brilliant students; his mother with a Ph.D. in Sociology and his father was an MD, his specialty neurology, finishing his formal education with a fellowship from Harvard Medical School. Despite all of the western training his dad had received, the family sought holistic approaches to life and to health, and Quinn took the hippie, holistic lifestyle to the extreme growing up. His parents were much older than the parents of his friends, deciding, he thought, to have children later in life. When he was 16 he found out that he had a sister whom his parents put up for adoption. They said they were just about to embark on school and they would never have been able to move through their respective college careers with a child. His sister was 15 years his senior, and would eventually find her birth parents and track him down in his early 40's. But as a teenager, he believed he was produced to be an only child, an heir apparent to something special.

His uniqueness and success was not inherited, however. His parents were perfectly contented doing mostly research in their given field, which did not glean a great deal monetarily. His father, fastidious to the core, taught his son detailed, careful examination, and discriminating quality. He developed his tenacity, arrogance, and narcissism all on his own.

As a teenager, he and a friend began tinkering with electronics in his dad's garage, mostly early computer game boards and radios. His friend, Paul Scagglietti, who they just called Scaggs, had a knack for programming these devices and before long, the two had amassed a huge following of other tech geeks from all over Northern California. He was certainly in the right place at the right time.

IBM, Atari and some fledgling computer companies were smack in the middle of a technological revolution that no one could have predicted. Quinn immediately knew what he wanted to do, and that was to start a company. He worked briefly at Atari. He struck up a strange friendship with the COO over a summer in his youth and the man gave him his first chance in tech. His partner-in-crime Scaggs, worked at IBM. At Atari, Quinn sat in a cubicle at the very edge of the development group's area, and the cubicle was, ironically, right next to the Chief Operating Officer's executive assistant. From this vantage point, he could still be involved in development, but was able to remain tapped into how the company was actually operating, and the other aspects of its business. The cubicle number, which became his inspiration and company's name, was 13-C. Quinn was not known for being sentimental but the time spent in that cube gave him the tools he needed to move forward without hesitation and do it his way.

Quinn believed both companies that he and Scaggs worked for were being run incorrectly, and Quinn's complete lack of experience, coupled with his narcissism, made him believe he could do better. And he did. With Scaggs' unwavering devotion, they built a computer company that would become one of the biggest in the world, 13-C Computers. 13-C had it all, beauty and brawn. In the early days, Quinn was the designer of both how the functionality should exist for the user, as well as the interface that the user saw. Scaggs was in charge of making that functionality happen.

It wasn't until he met his wife Christina that he showed any kind of personal connection with anyone. But even after they were married, he was still completely, over-the-top rude to anyone outside of her, except maybe Samantha. He could still give her a rip-roaring tirade, but he would know to stop when he saw something in her eyes that told him he was about to get just as good as he just gave. There was a thread of mutual respect that allowed these two to become friends. Even his kids sometimes received his wrath of outbursts and tongue-lashings that were famous at the office. Ten years into a profitable partnership, Scaggs couldn't take Quinn's brutality anymore, cashed out his stock and retired an extremely wealthy man. Quinn never went to Scaggs to say goodbye.

From Quinn's faction they met Elam Highfield, who definitely fit in this group, but he was more there due to loyalty to Quinn. At 13-C, he was Quinn's right-hand man and was here to be the same. Next, they met Reagan Mills, heiress to a mammoth investment firm and the $15 billion fortune that came with it. She was a former model, and left that life to pursue her education in anthropology and get more out of life than "glam surface values," as she put it, that left her empty and lonely. She certainly didn't start out caring to be the brightest bulb, but over the years she tuned into things that interested her and found that she had much to contribute. So much so that as Bishop and Sloan got to know her, she surprised them with insightful questions and ideas; as her education progressed she bloomed into an articulate, highly intelligent and confident young woman. Then came the Hungarian-American philanthropist and his daughter, George and Asher Rabin. Their net worth and bestowal to the group was about $14 billion, but George was a very controlling man and wanted a say in everything before he would commit any money, so much planning was done without the endowment of the Rabin money initially. George was also ill, and Asher was quite a bit more level headed than her father and was in this fight for the long haul. Asher also didn't want to be bothered with day-to-day details; she had several philanthropic interests that took most of her time. She was, however, very astute and picked up information quickly, so keeping her in the loop would be important. George died a month prior to the final conferences.

At different times during the night everyone milled around the table in the back of the room to catch a glimpse of the very quiet the man sitting in the corner alone, save for a single member of his security detail, taking it all in. So few had even been allowed to meet this man; Quinn was friends with him simply because he loved everything that 13-C produced, as he was a self-proclaimed tech junkie. Quinn knew having the world's richest man, or rather the son of the world's richest man, with a net worth in the multiple billions, on your side had to have its benefits. But now, he was allowing himself to be known. Antonio Montes wasn't just the son of the world's richest man; a brilliant businessman in his own right, through his intelligence and boldness, he had inherited the collection of companies and made them more profitable and efficient, and was truly a visionary for his home country, Mexico. Antonio's father instilled great values in him as well as his siblings and he wanted, as a gift for his father, to show him that he could change the world. Montes had big plans for Mexico that many in his country were against. The group saw him as a perfect ally and positioned perfectly geographically. If they were to take Texas, having the neighboring country with you made success more achievable. He saw the group as trying to accomplish the same thing so partnering could only benefit both causes, and he was ready to put his money where his mouth was. Montes was in cleanup mode in a big way. He was a sought-after person because of his businesses as well as his money, but now he was getting serious about clearing out the drugs from his country. He believed, like many in the room, that the huge amount of drug use in both countries, Mexico and the US, was causing staggering amounts of people to lose their lives, figuratively and literally. He believed that drugs infect a person from the inside out causing them to make decisions based on an internal need to feed the monster. He had seen first hand the horrors that drugs cause; rampant violence, the loss of any self-respect or value, mothers selling themselves and their young children for drugs. He was done; he was about to embark on the single largest destruction of drug makers, suppliers, sellers and all persons involved in any of part of it. He put his family, including his father, in protective custody, in the care of SOURCE personnel in undisclosed areas around Texas, and he himself would not be back to Mexico for quite sometime. His first attack would be on shutting down the Mexican Mafia, both in Mexico and its contingent in the US. His legacy would be one of transforming Mexico into a place where the culture and values expressed hard work and integrity, and sent a really strong message that the people were sick and tired of the drugs and "*degenerars*" that go with them. The good people of Mexico would stand behind him, and Texas was a means to that end. His fellow Xers would build Texas up in the same image that he envisioned for Mexico.

Each of these people had involvement and investments from people in every walk of life, plus some of the top in their field, the first woman billionaire, a screenwriter known for his super leftist tendencies even came with the thumbs up knowing that partisanship is one of the things killing this country, but it was the every day people willing to sacrifice and give up what they had and the life they knew to start fresh. Some were running, screaming from what they knew; bad streets, bad parents, no future, but willing to work and work hard for a new future, a new beginning. While others loved their lives, had material things and nice families, but wondered how much longer it would last on this current path. Both saw a shining light of opportunity that they, themselves, could be a part of building.

CHAPTER 7
THE PLAYERS

Introductions continued, from domestic divas to gritty trade union leaders to world famous media mogul billionaires to Nick and Suzanne Graham who lived down the street from Samantha's childhood friend in normal-town USA. Everyone had a personal investment in correcting the ship.

Dean Kinsey was another top mogul in his field, except he didn't have the motivation of Nikoli or the massive ego of Quinn. A business major, he met the three at Stanford. Actually, he met Bishop on a golf course just off campus. Both men were obsessed with golf and made it out for early rounds a couple times a week. After Stanford, a group approached him to help with a fledgling company that originated as the Stanford University Network. Having the head for business, he took the company global from a small town in Colorado and made his first billion at the relatively young age of 42. Self-deprecating with a fierce sense of humor, he joined the Xers under the condition that his wife and five kids be included as well. He and Bishop often had long, philosophical talks. Kinsey being very independent politically, he wanted his children to understand how important it was to look at things based on the issues, not the people, but even he had a hard time looking past Bishop the man. During their talks, he often went into the conversation disagreeing with some of the points Bishop raised, but when he explained his thinking, his logic or his methodology, Kinsey came around every time. Bishop agreed, though, that the issues should be looked at not the charisma of a person. He looked forward to a day when kids got to learn the issue at hand, not the hype, the skewed statistics and the out and out lies and bias around them. Bishop appreciated the relationship Kinsey and his wife had. With their financial security, this was not a women who needed to work outside of the home, but he would have put her in charge of any company. She ran the house very much like a company and provided her kids with a stable, loving home to feel safe in. Bishop believed that home-makers were severely undervalued as if the jobs they had to do were not worthy of "pay" but in reality those that did work in the home often did more than those who went to a job every day. The two made a great team, and Bishop was glad to have them a part of the Xers.

The partnership of Nikoli, Quinn and Kinsey was not as easy a task. In the "real world" these guys were going head to head on a daily basis, Quinn couldn't stand them for different reasons; for one, he thought Nikoli and his pal Langley Ford were thieves of almost everything they were working on. He had a minimal professional respect for Kinsey although his ego would never let him admit that. Bishop had to keep Nikoli under tight reins because he knew Quinn had the experience and tenacity to keep people on task whereas Nikoli was easily distracted on fantastically creative ventures, and thus his team would also become distracted. Quinn was laser focused and they both agreed to let their outside competition and quarrels drop at the door. That was easier said than done, and just their innate nature guaranteed head butting, but so far, so good.

The detailed information that came of the prior years of work for the upcoming conferences would be retrievable only by two members of AmendX, Jackson Cooper and Michael Bishop, using retina scans associated to individual passwords as well as twenty-five digit random number key-fobs. It was not a matter of trust, but one pointing to two things, security and collaboration. It was decided even before the first in-person meeting that information gathered or retrieved should be done in groups; in this case only two group members were needed to retrieve information from the archive, but the point was to always have fresh eyes, another perspective, even a devil's advocate. It wasn't that the AmendXers didn't believe in or have great respect for individual thought, ideas, creativity etc. Xers, of all people, were individuals to their core. Their belief was that individuality is what makes a society great, but it is the ability to meld these thoughts and ideas into the values and policies of a new nation that will make them triumphant.

13-C's longtime VP, Elam Highfield, was not so much a friend of Quinn's but a loyal slave. He was trustworthy, infinitely capable and probably as brilliant as Quinn, he just didn't have the panache Quinn had. Plus, he was intensely private; he had carried on a secret relationship with 13-C's chief designer for six years and no one knew about it, including Quinn. If Quinn said he would take care of something, ninety-nine percent of the time, it was Elam that did it. He wasn't the sort of man that ever wanted to shine in the spotlight like Quinn, but he did believe in the same things that Quinn did; he thought creativity and the arts were an integral part of our development and without it, we wouldn't excel in the hard sciences either, as they were each part of the fragile balance. Like others interested in education, Elam believed our schools were lowing the bar far too much for our kids and we would soon see the results of all program cuts. Focused heavily on creativity, and how children learn and think, he believed that if the arts are cut out of school curriculum due to budgetary constraints, and the aim is set at rote learning and standardized test preparations, then we, as a country, would produce people that cannot think for themselves, solve problems, or invent anything new. Each of those things being part of what made this country the greatest country on the planet.

Then there were the unrecognizable and non-famous people that were the meat of group, one being Sloan's long-time friend from college, Victoria, who had gone on to a very successful career as a physics professor at NYU. Victoria was one of the only people that could run circles around Samantha in intellect. They met as freshmen getting coffee one morning; Samantha was intrigued to meet a fellow double degree student, much less one who's second degree was the same as her own, philosophy. Sam's first degree field was psychology, Victoria's was physics. Samantha was just in awe of Victoria's mind and the speed at which she could process information. They didn't get to see each other as much as Sloan wanted, but Victoria was wholeheartedly part of the group. Victoria lived and breathed by the famous book by Ayn Rand, Atlas Shrugged, so it was no surprise that she advocated the value of one's mind and the ability to produce. She pursued physics and philosophy because of the book, and although her love was the hard science, she also appreciated the benefit in the quest for the primordial nature of our existence, our knowledge, and of our mind's ability to elevate both.

Even though Nikoli recruited many techie people, that did not necessarily mean their main interest to focus on was technical. Adam Edelstein and Randall Quinn, for example, were both intensely interested about how education was progressing in the country. They had very different ideas about how to fix what they felt was broken, but were willing to work together nonetheless. Uncommon groups often came together and worked on all different tasks. Nikoli brought in energy savant Sakti Sharma, and he worked well with Rex Morrison on land resource ideas.

Vassily Novikov wanted smaller government and less big brother controlling the people. He believed oversight naturally happened. The more regulations you put into place, people looked for more ways to get around them, but when someone takes advantage of him or his company by unethical or verboten ways, he would make it his priority to make sure that company fails, and he believed that other businessmen felt the same way as him. The sandbox he played in was policed enough without the purview of the government getting involved. They only made it worse.

Reagan Mills saw a growing entitlement attitude and wanted to go back to the days of her grandfather and the hard work he put in for his own benefit, because he wanted a better life for himself and his family. Now the kids are bored in the suburbs, so instead of working to accomplish something for themselves, they go try drugs and get addicted. A lady Mills used to model with, and whom she thought was a good mother, but just didn't instill any kind of work ethic, morality or self-respect, had just died of a heroin overdose. Mills believed that if any rules should be dictated, it should be directed at drugs. Antonio Montes shared this belief. Montes was much more brutish on the subject; if the people wanted the ability to waste themselves away, and give up the greatest gift of life that has been given, then he would be the one to hand them the fatal dose. Otherwise, he would work tirelessly to get drugs off the streets and give children opportunities to do well. He believed people had to be accountable to the consequences of their decisions. If, or rather *when*, the abusers sought out criminal acts to obtain more drugs, then they should be taken away from society. Not necessarily a prison, but a place dedicated to keeping them removed, the savages they will have become because of the use of such horrific substances. Let them sort it out among themselves. Mexico might be able to restrict access to groups of people based solely on the lifestyle they chose and then couldn't control, but this country, even breaking off and creating a new one, would be hard pressed to be able to justify it. She wasn't sure exactly how to manage it, but she did believe, maybe naively, that when something was illegal and the country truly did not want drugs within its borders, something could be done to stop the access to it. She was fully committed to being involved and helping the group in this endeavor, and she had many people in the group ready to work on the problem as well.

Sakti Sharma, being from India, had a much different take on the state of affairs. Much less aggressive than his cohorts, the same idea of the self was shared by all. Michael Bishop's view of the self was to do as much for yourself as possible; challenge yourself to attain perfection. So then, with a wink of his eye, he would say you get a whole bunch of selfish people doing very well. The byproduct of that, then, is a large group of successful people not needing anything from anyone. Sharma looked at it as by loving and honoring the self, all relationships flourish. In speaking with Sharma the night the introductions were made, a young lady likened his concept to what the flight attendants said when going through the safety checks before the plane took off. "If the oxygen masks drop, put yours on first and then assist others in getting theirs on." Many people hearing the conversation thought it was funny and chuckled, but they also thought it was dead on. You can't be of any service to others, when you are incapacitated, and the same goes for life, Sharma thought.

Derek Holden and Paul Olson being men of extreme faith, albeit different sects, believed many things, but the two items that were most discussed during the evening were the issues the country was struggling with currently, from honoring God to the tremendous overspending of the government, both effecting future generations. The second thing, and a major message of the ministry, was living in abundance was not a sin. Working hard, earning a good living was any human being's right, and there should be no guilt or shame associated with it. Some in the room asked if the ministry took criticism for that message, as many had always heard to give wealth away for those in need was the responsibility of the church. Olson's response was simple; there are always great causes in which those with the means can choose to involve themselves with. The operative word being 'choose'; never should there be a time when a directive of what one can do with their earned money should be handed down. When there is real need, there can be real help, but now there is the idea that one should be given the abundance with no work for it, and that just undermines, in his words, what God wants for us all.

Good, honest, hard work equals bounty in the form of self-respect, efficacy and good, spendable cash. When that is taken away, we are not doing God's work and we certainly aren't helping those become liberated and independent.

Jackson Cooper and most of the military pack, specifically Harlan Mackay and Harris Corrigan wanted to settle the issue of the security and the price of freedom. Cooper would get infuriated when he would hear someone misquote (or quote out of context) Benjamin Franklin's thoughts on liberty and security, "Those who sacrifice liberty for security deserve neither." First, he thought, having both was not an either-or consideration. Second, in Cooper's definition, it was not liberty or freedom that good ole' Ben had in his mind when discussing deliberate, illegal acts. In today's time, those who don't like the idea of drones surveying the homeland because they might catch a glimpse of the marijuana field growing behind their house are firmly missing the point. Our liberty was not fought for to use as an excuse to commit criminal acts. If you are not doing anything wrong, you shouldn't care about the homeland drones, being asked to search your car during roadside checkpoints for holiday DUI's or any other act that you consider an act of invading your privacy. There was much discussion, that given that kind of authority carte blanche can also be abused, and no one disagreed, but Cooper believed the baseline had to start with security within liberty, and move the line from there.

Dylan Sterling brought the views of the Needham brothers with him, and of non-members like Collin Nelson and Robert Gilbert, regarding money management and how to deal with the myriad issues surrounding the financial state of the country, and where the monies should be spent. Although conservative, he often shared more moderate views with his long-time personal friend Ben Stein. The Needhams, conversely, often pushed so far to the right that it alienated anyone that had any ability to compromise. Nelson and Gilbert did business with them because it was almost impossible not to with the conglomeration of businesses within a wide range of industries. Plus, in business they were both savvy, shrewd, and decisive. Traits that both men found necessary where business dealings were concerned.

CHAPTER 8
THE PLAN

The Conference would span an undetermined period of time, and include the members that had been working on primary areas of concern. Even though a time deadline was not set, the idea was to flesh out the issues in question in detail and precision, and not move on until each issue was firmly in hand and organized. Samantha knew she would be at each of the conferences as the consistent member that everyone knew and saw, so she made a deal with the hotel to accommodate an indefinite stay. As issues were fleshed out following the initial conferences at the hotel and then she would invite those participating to come back and work through the details in the relative comfort and privacy of Bohemian Grove, California. This would be the new location were the world could be changed. The items would be discovered and discussed in Colorado Springs, then finalized in Northern California. Having two locations was also smart because of how members had to move around the country; arriving at the same place repeatedly was not reasonable or recommended.

Some had joined the group for moral and financial support but were unable for one reason or another to participate in any more depth. Just over thirty people of incalculable wealth, power, fame, and importance started the movement's momentum, and after that the numbers took off. It was those original, founding members that would have to move discreetly around the country holding meetings, talking with each other in secrecy. Much of this might seem out of the ordinary of daily operating procedure to anyone who might be watching, so precautions needed to be made. They couldn't all go on vacation at the same time, schedules needed to be planned, coordinated, and diligently kept. The numbers of members actively involved on a daily basis would reach the hundreds and members in total would reach the thousands. Measures had to put in place and followed with absolute meticulousness. During the sessions some would stay, others would leave and so on. Once issue leaders would have a chance to meet everyone, they would act as delegates over their assigned areas as well as ensure that information flowed to new people coming back, while another wave left. It would work this way for the duration of each conference. Additionally, each of the issue leaders needed someone to record everything and keep the information safe, while disseminating it to the other scribes to be shared with their designated areas. These people were vetted more vigorously than black ops operators, and mainly Derek Holden handled the investigation, with oversight coming from Christian Adams. He and Holden worked together well and made a fine balance of power and responsibility. Trying to keep the information flowing, while also keeping it secure. It would be a monumental challenge but Samantha was confident the process was as foolproof as it could be.

Everyone in AmendX was trusted, but with a degree of skepticism; this group did not get to where they were by trusting people blindly. To mitigate any possible leaks or distrust, certain controls would have to be followed. This would not only protect the ideas but also the people involved. It would go like this: two recorders would be chosen for the initial days, a principal and a backup. The backup would then make sure the information was passed to Jackson Cooper in-person verbally, while the principal stayed in place becoming the backup, bringing in a new principal. The recorders would be given tablet computers that looked like they were straight out of Star Trek. Quinn had been working on these for years and even though what they became were beautifully designed, graphics-heavy computing tablets that could possibly replace laptops, the beginnings were that of this type of data collection and would be encrypted and unable to reach the Internet. When a particular issue had to be passed to Cooper and he was not on-site, the backup recorder would give the tablet to Samantha for safe keeping, and fly to wherever he was to be briefed. This system would continue as the main documentation system for the group. Each recorder would take down the data germane to their area, creating a chronicle that would become the skeleton of a new nation. Working together, Quinn, Kinsey and Nikoli created a system that would allow the tablets to "dump" the data to a secure location in Austin and kept there until needed at a future date.

Many in the group felt this type of slow, precise movement was antiquated, and that plans needed to be accelerated, but some failed to see how far they had come since three college kids started wondering how things could be changed back in 1993. People met, group members planned, land was purchased, ground was broken, and construction began. Life went on, maturing members of the group, even changing some view points, but mostly throughout the years the group became strong, with incalculable resources, and entrenched in almost all of the sectors of power that would allow them to one day, pull the plug and be gone...just gone.

Samantha Sloan was lying on the floor of her living room suite at the resort, giving Oliver love and pets, when her cell phone rang.

"What's up, Mike?" she asked.

"Did I wake you?" Michael Bishop asked.

"No, I'm just laying on the floor with Oliver."

"So Niki told me everyone signed off on the conference process," he said.

"Yeah, no one had any major issues with it, but a few want to come out more publicly now that we have the plan in place."

"Who specifically?"

"God, I can't remember his name, but he spoke for several of the Los Angeles contingent, um, that writer guy, Craig. He said Bilderberg is stealing our thunder."

"First of all, we don't have or want thunder. We actually want to create a paradigm shift that will change our world. Second, according to both Jackson Cooper and Christian Adams, both of whom have kept close tabs on them and have attended several years in a row, they are totally insignificant. They want to be known as a secret organization that holds the strings to our global society. Did you hear that contradiction in terms?"

"Be known for being secret? Yeah I did. I'm just telling you what they told me."

Bishop let out a groan, "They have advanced this cause so much over the years, but it's like they have this piece of DNA that needs recognition. I'm surprised we've kept it quiet this long to be honest."

"It is material to the plan being successful and they know that. That is why they brought it up in the correct arena. Some feel that a leak is destined. We are too close to setting the plan in motion, so in perfect Hollywood fashion, they want to manage the publicity and our message their way. I told them I would let you know, but I also said you were unlikely to change your mind on the topic, nor would anyone else support that."

"Good, we are too close and everyone has been extremely disciplined in this regard so let's get through the conferences and set a date."

Sam rolled over onto her knees and kissed the sleeping Oliver on the head, "Agreed."

Saturday, April 14, 2012 – 7:45am Mountain Daylight Time (13:45 hours Zulu Time)

Minutes before the conferences were to start, Bishop sat quietly in his room. The calm before the storm, he thought. He was very rarely indecisive or afraid to take action, nor did he care about how he would be later viewed, but he allowed himself this moment to reflect. In truth, it was important for him to leave a legacy. One of positivity, ingenuity, and most of all of a producer; there had to be someone who stopped at nothing to get things of value done. He also wanted to show people that change can be made without the use of politics. Just the word politics has become synonymous with inaction and partisanship. How could anything get done like that? No! This was to show that to really change something, one must take action. But in the end he knew that that the actions he was determined to take must be seen as righteous to a broad range of people. Otherwise, he thought, you are just a rebel, a terrorist, or just out there hurting people. Would he be remembered as a terrorist, or someone who didn't love this country? Did he lead all of these wondrously brilliant people down a course that would be misunderstood? He looked out the window, things were beginning to green up after a pretty cold winter, but April was warming up nicely. Maybe some golf in the next couple of weeks to calm his nerves is what he needed. Enough doubts! He was about to walk into a room to start something that he whole-heartedly believed in, and remembering that, the path that got them all here appeared in his mind.

PART 4
FOUNDERS (1997-1998)

CHAPTER 9
VISIONARIES

Thirteen years earlier...

Wednesday, January 29, 1997 – 9:30am Eastern Standard Time (14:30 hours Zulu Time)

Derek King Holden, III was always well prepared for anything that could be thrown at him. He was used to political scrutiny because of his extreme right wing beliefs. But most of all he believed in personal accountability; his father espoused it, being a Navy SEAL further enforced it, and as an adult, he saw it slipping away in the country he loved. His father taught him the work ethic he was proud to have though he credited both of his parents for the man he had become. His father constantly said perseverance, determination and personal responsibility is what made him a man; his mother saw to it that those traits were also imbued in Derek through a kindness and empathy that he wished he'd gotten more of. As far as work ethics went, no one worked harder than his father and Derek learned that having a lot of money wasn't the way to get what you wanted, working hard was. He didn't feel any job was beneath him and he got his hands dirty. His pastor friend Paul always said it took a big person to do something small and he liked that.

Since meeting Bishop, he knew he would be a part of something big. He was in the middle of creating SOURCE and was planning on the company being operational by the end of the year, knowing that one day it might have to champion a new kind of military and protect what he held dear. Meeting Michael Pearson, as Vice Chief of Navel Operations, the man struck him as highly motivated upwardly mobile. He was well educated, but more than that, this man was sharp with common sense, a rare combination these days, he thought to himself. Pearson was strategic and laconic with deeply held values. He was a bit intimidating. Sure, he has been doing work with the government for years now, met the president many times and a trove of other top personnel, but Pearson was someone he also really respected. Holden was used to being approached by lunatic fringe groups because of his wealth and experience, but Michael Pearson was anything but the lunatic fringe. Even if he wanted nothing to do with these guys, he owed Pearson the time to listen to what he had to say.

The name of Holden's company, SOURCE, was an acronym that Holden had developed, and stood for Section One Universal Resource Coordination Enterprises. Holden chose that name based on the double entendre... he wanted to be the real 'source' for supplying governments and private enterprises with the proper personnel, and what they truly did was coordinate resources. Universally. SOURCE had become a worldwide organization, and supplied highly trained operators and support personnel to entities in more than 40 countries. Plus, he secretly liked how 'Section One' sounded. Kind of like a clandestine organization.

SOURCE would be a multi-campus, multi-faceted private military operating facility training military personnel as well as a law enforcement organization. It would also recruit personnel from both entities to be used in private security endeavors from putting staff in place to guard installations overseas as well as dignitaries from the US and abroad. Further elite, small teams were built to be on ready to get jobs done that were covert, dangerous and part of the United States Department of Defense black budget. The people on these teams essentially did not exist and Holden had to house them, keep them safe, trained and occupied when not deployed. SOURCE was an interesting project because for all of its secrecy and truly "unwritten" goals, he also had to put a face on it that the media could tear into without ever knowing its true nature, plus he wanted civilians to be able to come and train on its campuses, so it had to at least look like there was some transparency. That was really the hardest part. How do you maintain the world's most covert facility while training the weekend warriors who might be the butt of many Rambo jokes, real, serious training to make them safer, more adept and experienced with their weapons of choice? How do you do it? Right out in the open.

Landing in Moyock, North Carolina, the home of the main campus, one afternoon to check on the progress of many small upcoming missions, he saw a parking lot full of rent-a-cars and instructors giving orientations to "trainees" of all kinds. These weekend warrior types were wearing t-shirts ranging from UFC, to The Evolution of the Pipe Hitter, to Titleist caps and Doc Martens footwear. He saw this and thought to himself they could be the best secret military in the world. Get a few thousand of these middle-class fashion victim, NRA card carriers and you could invade before anyone had any idea what was going on. He chuckled to himself. Not a bad idea, really. This group cares more about their country than the ones sitting at home watching the desperate housewives of the north shore or whatever these programs are called these days.

Holden, a devout Roman Catholic was married to his wife right out of college and proceeded to have four children. His wife had issues with his time in the Navy but never voiced anything publicly and lived a very upper-class country club lifestyle. Holden ruled the household with an iron fist; he never physically abused his wife or his kids, nor did he believe in such treatment, but they did not test his resolve either. He believed in spankings and praise. His kids excelled in both school and athletics. He was passionate about eating healthy and taking care of one's self. Standing six-foot four and weighing in at two hundred and ten pounds, he was on the lean side and maintained nine percent body fat. He was rock solid and worked hard to keep his body pristine. With greenish eyes, pale skin, and even though he could have a full head of dark blonde hair, he chose the look of bald badass. That further accentuated his intimidating demeanor. Not having a particularly great sense of humor, nor having a large circle of friends, Holden's reclusive reputation only made things more difficult for him in the press and he was regularly crucified. Whether the information was correct or not, he never seemed to be bothered by it and continued on his very carefully laid out plan to build SOURCE and to execute his business plan.

The day he sat down with Pearson and Bishop, Derek really didn't know if he wanted to get involved, building SOURCE since his father had passed had taken almost everything out of him. After they spoke, however, he knew that Pearson wouldn't get involved in anything fly-by-night and he knew enough about him and trusted the things he said to be relevant. Any official contract jobs that he and Pearson found themselves working together, Holden found him to be extremely competent and professional. Pearson had known

Holden albeit professionally for years and they shared a mutual respect. Holden had never heard of Michael Bishop and seemed to have come out of nowhere and as Bishop explained to Holden that he had no ambition to come out of that obscurity. He thought he could do better work as someone no one would ever really know. That was understandable to Holden, as he had seen, many times, the media get ahold of someone and twisted everything out of context, exaggerated and flat out lied, making it impossible to try to get any real work done. The obscurity, though, made it so Holden would likely never have taken this meeting with Bishop. He could see the relative ease with which Pearson and Bishop interacted, which told him that they had known each other for a long time. The relationship between Holden and Pearson allowed Bishop this meeting and the opening he needed to lay out his vision from a high-level perspective. Bishop had a team that he relied heavily on to work out details and this allowed him to be quite laid back. Holden even envied, a little, how easy going Bishop was; Holden never allowed himself to relax and always had full control and a tight grip on everything under his purview.

He set aside two hours for this meeting, instead it lasted eight and he had cancelled his day because Bishop was almost mesmerizing in the way he spoke. He couldn't put his finger on exactly what it was, but Bishop had a gift for being able to explain things in a way Holden could completely understand and get behind. By the end of the meeting, Holden committed his time and his company for whatever this group needed. He'd never trusted anyone like that. After putting everything he had into SOURCE, he was ready for the day he would need to dissolve it, if necessary, or relocate it. He and Bishop would figure out what was best and pursue excellence together.

CHAPTER 10
EVALUATORS

Thursday, March 13, 1997 – 2:00pm Eastern Standard Time (19:00 hours Zulu Time)

Next, Holden met with Samantha Sloan. He didn't know much about her, but Pearson thought very highly of her so he had to give her a little leeway, a little. He would give her thirty minutes max. He had a lot to do; he had just signed a very lucrative deal with the government to provide private security and military enforcement wherever and whenever needed on behalf of, but independent of the US government. He hadn't heard much from Pearson since they had originally talked and he was a bit annoyed that he hadn't been kept in the loop. I guess this woman was here to do just that.

"Good afternoon Ms. Sloan," Holden said putting out his hand to shake hers. Being in his office, he was wearing a dark gray suit; he believed in the old school, that if you dress for success, the success comes more readily. As if it gives you a subconscious confidence that translates into a more professional, successful, job. He always believed in looking one's best. The suit was upper end but off the rack. He noticed what Samantha was wearing right away, a tailored black suit that was taken in at the waist so you could see how small she was, but the pants were wide legged. It was a very nice suit; he liked that she looked professional. Before he could ponder professionalism anymore along side her he noticed a huge Saint Bernard.

"How do you do Mr. Holden?" Sloan properly responded, extending her hand.

Holden shook her hand noticing that she had a strong handshake, but not too strong like some of those women that had something to prove shook hands. "Ah, well how are you?" He muttered with raised eyebrows.

"This is Sawyer, he is totally mellow, but if you don't like slobber I wouldn't get too close," Sloan said smiling.

Just then he did notice what looked like a bit of dry slobber on her pant leg. At that point, she pulled out a monogrammed towel from her bag and wiped Sawyer's face.

"What do the initials stand for?" He asked.

"Sawyer Sigmund Wentworth," she replied beaming down at him.

Again his eyebrows went up in a questioning expression. He told himself he didn't really want to talk about her dog, but then, he did.

"I have a naming convention that I use when I name my fur-babies."

"Fur-babies?" He interrupted, rolling his eyes.

Ignoring his eye roll, she continued, "A name I love, a famous scientist's name and name from a favorite movie of mine from the 70's called High Anxiety.

Holden motioned for Sloan to sit down in the black, Queen Anne, tufted wing-back chair as he sat in an identical one, and scooting it back just a bit so Sawyer couldn't spew anything on him. He was a great looking dog. She sat and the dog lay right down next to her and put his huge head down immediately, nap commencing. "That's funny," he said amused, thinking that the whole dog thing was at a minimum a good icebreaker. Then he got into the business, "So give me the rundown, what have I missed?" He asked.

Sitting, Sloan looked confused, "I'm sorry?" Looking around the spacious office, she noticed the beautiful high-end furnishings. The wingback black leather tufted chairs flanked a black mahogany and glass oversized coffee table. This furniture grouping acted as a reception area within the office just past the office door. The floor being all marble lightened up what could end up being a pretty dark space. Black mahogany bookcases behind the enormous black mahogany and glass desk. Continuing past the desk area was a good-sized rectangle conference table that also appeared to be black mahogany and Herman-Miller Aeron chairs around it. The conference area was situated just in front of floor to ceiling windows that had a spectacular view overlooking the water of Virginia Beach. Owning the entire building, his suite was special. Pearson had told her about the windows; they were bulletproof and by the touch of a button could go from being clear, translucent glass to black. One could see out, but not in. In the back corner was another tufted leather wingback chair with a matching ottoman, a small area for one to sit and reflect, relax or survey the room. Each of the big spaces had white area rugs to warm up the area but not diminish the look of the marble. The office was stunning and yet simple; each space had its own function.

"Aren't you here to give me an update on what the group has been doing? Has the group been doing anything?" Holden asked holding his breath a little.

"No, not really. I mean, no I'm not really here for that, but yes we have all been working quite a bit on our own tasks. It isn't like a secret handshake group that gives directives to report on during secret meetings. You are doing exactly what you are supposed to be doing, building a great company, producing something, becoming an expert at it. Make sense?" Samantha was smiling.

Holden was not amused, "So why are you here?"

"Now that you have committed to such a large role in the group, I thought it might be wise to get to know you, talk values, methodologies, beliefs. Really get to know you." Sloan sat back in her chair and watched Holden for his reaction.

"I'm going to want you to work pretty closely with Jackson Cooper. I think you will like him," said Samantha.

"Why would I like him?"

Sloan laughed, "Well, he's a likable guy."

Holden, annoyed decided to see if he could get a rise out of her now retorted, "yeah, I heard you think he's pretty likable."

"What does that mean?" Sloan looked annoyed.

Not one to care about rumors, but since the comment was successful in getting her smooth demeanor to crack a bit, he continued, "you have to know about the rumor that has gone around, not just this organization, but out in the world that you and he are quite the item," Holden said to her with one eyebrow raised.

"Jackson is married and I don't care what the rumor is, but I do think it is important that our group stays transparent," Sloan said looking annoyed. "Ask me anything and I will answer you truthfully, but shoot innuendo at me and I'll just tell you to fuck off. As we get to know each other, I'm sure we will learn each other's idiosyncrasies, so we'll just call that your first lesson in mine. Jackson Cooper and I are very good friends. He has been a real rock for me in some difficult times. We have not had an affair, to be honest, more because of him than me, but neither of us approves of such a thing, and I would think, Mr. Holden, that with your devout beliefs you would agree. However, what I believe and what I have done in the past have sometimes not coincided, and I am not proud of that. Having said that, Jackson is not one of my indiscretions. If you would like the full run down, I am happy to provide that for you, although I think our time is better spent on other, more practical issues."

Holden's eyes about popped out his head at her straightforwardness and then quickly gaining composure, he said, "No, that is quite all right. I have no desire to hear about your love life but I do appreciate your candor," he laughed, "in fact, that was rather unexpected but refreshing. Let me apologize for the insinuation, it was inappropriate."

"Apology not necessary. There is indeed a rumor so I'm glad you asked and got it out on the table. Now I hope the ice is broken and the air is sufficiently cleared such that we can get started." Holden nodded in agreement and Sloan continued, "You will work very closely with me and Mike obviously. Nikoli is involved in many technical issues and is in the middle of assessing infrastructure in Texas. I don't think there is a need that you two see each other regularly, but if you want to meet him sooner rather than later, I will arrange it. Other than that I will make sure everyone is kept apprised of what other members are doing, but if you ever feel like you want to know about something specific or just that you don't know a member as well as you'd like to, let me know and I will arrange more frequent meetings. With as busy is everyone is in their "normal" lives, it is hard to bring everyone together as often as I'd like. I believe it is important for the smallish group that we have now to know each other as people as well as get to know their personal values. We are working on a scale that makes that difficult but not impossible. Besides the fact that Nikoli, Mike and I started this, those that we consider as much as founders as we are should be able to make the time and work together to get more and more comfortable with each other and what we are going to do. Now, having said that, the other member that I think you should get to know is Cooper, and please feel free to bring up the rumor and see how he responds," she said winking. "Jackson will be the face of the group just because of who he is and the political nature of things. He is ok with that. I don't know how but he is. Your expertise is going to be invaluable when setting up the compounds in Texas, and as you know they are going to have to be strategically placed and virtually undetectable. We, or rather you, will need to be ready to make recommendations on military strategy including defense, security and weaponry to Mike and Mr. Pearson."

"You mean Admiral Pearson, don't you?" Holden asked, sternly.

"Yes, I'm sorry, I have only known him on a personal level to this point, but that is no excuse," Sloan replied a little embarrassed. "Mike will depend on the Admiral as well as a few of the men he brought in to explain your recommendations if he doesn't fully understand them."

"Whom else has he brought in?" Holden asked curtly. He thought he would have known about these people by now.

"Many of the military people that have come on board because of Admiral Pearson have asked to stay unidentified. I would think you would be an exception to that rule, and that we could let you know who they are, but let me make sure with Mike and he will get back to you, ok?"

That was all he could really ask of her, but he was pissed all the same.

"So besides these high-level, obvious issues what is Mike working on?" snipped Holden.

"Besides his 'real-world' work, he has a major interest in getting to know as many of the people in the group that will really become the community and society."

"Is that the best use of his limited time?"

"I think so, if you think about it without them we have nothing. We need a force or a large collection that agree with our stance and take it and make it better. Sound familiar say, from oh, 350 years ago?"

Holden thought to himself for a minute, he was really hoping that there was action behind her ideology. "Yes, I understand what you are saying, but to have the voice of that stance shaking hands and kissing babies sounds like what is happening now."

"He's hardly doing that," Sloan laughed. "He is meeting those that share our ideas and have ones of their own so we can improve while we plan. It is rather simple really."

"Yeah, ok, what else do you have for me." Holden said, ready for the next topic.

They discussed high-level issues, such as regular communication with Cooper and the planning of compounds throughout Texas, training and recruitment of personnel through SOURCE.

"We're developing a plan to secure borders once the state is taken," she said laying out a folder for his review, "and after discussing those let's talk about anything you have for me. The agenda items I have brought to you will have to be followed up with Jackson and then you two will be working directly on them without me. I will be available for any assistance either of you might need. This documentation, "she said, pointing at the folder, "is to be read here and now and then I will return it back to Jack. Once you two start your collaboration, you will be given access the information you need."

Holden was impressed. Sloan was laconic and to the point. Holden was told to prepare a plan for recruitment of personnel as his first task, as this was key for securing Texas. Many currently serving military members would become part of the force, but the reliance on SOURCE would be significant. Far more people were required than could be depended on from military units. Goodfellow Air Force Base would be a central facility for both military and SOURCE personnel, where they would train together, as well as deploy together. This entire movement would be in jeopardy without success in this area, and Holden understood this immediately.

SOURCE had networks of specialized recruiters both in the US and internationally, but they agreed that people would only be recruited from within the borders of the US, at least initially. SOURCE's recruiters would capably screen those that could best contribute to the cause. These same recruiters would later be brought to Texas to continue this process once the movement was entrenched. The biggest mistake that could be made when marshaling a fighting force is to ignore the requirement to sustain the force itself. Things happened to people, and attrition would take place. Those people needed to be replaced, and recruiters would be needed for that. SOURCE's were the best in the business.

The confidentiality around recruiting seemed like an immeasurably large obstacle. How would they ask all these people to join a movement, in a secret way, without word getting out? It seemed impossible, but understandably necessary. Holden offered Sam some methods that SOURCE had used when recruiting from native populations in the Middle East, when even talking to a recruiter could get a villager publicly killed, not to mention having his family tortured and murdered as well. These creative methods were part of the success that Holden's company had earned worldwide. Holden felt extraordinarily confident that he could build this so-called secret army without incident. He even looked forward to the challenge.

Holden did convey to Samantha that, despite his confidence in building the rank-and-file participation in their cause, he was very concerned with how they would ensure that high-ranking military and political figures would be motivated to remain on course, and stay quiet about what they were up to. Holden knew from experience that, when something secret was going on, good operators could feel it instinctively; they could almost smell it. That was a risk.

"Ms. Sloan, from what I've heard here, there will be many people in government who won't be informed as to what we're up to. Many of those people are remarkably smart, in the intelligence community, especially. People will know that something is up. Those people are undeniably good at sniffing out and, through many manipulative means, tricking people into giving up the goods, so to speak. How do you anticipate handling that? Given your complete lack of experience in that world, you can't even contemplate what that's like. You're a lamb among wolves," Holden stated.

Samantha smiled, not offended by his words. She was used to the fact that, upon first impression, they didn't give her the credit that was due.

"You're correct, Mr. Holden, in that there is certainly a risk. I understand exactly what you're saying, and having done substantial work with law enforcement from the psychology perspective, particularly as it relates to interrogations, I have seen exactly what you describe. Because of that, it's important to note that the selection of people that we do bring into the fold takes this into account as a requirement. Belief in the cause, consistency of behavior, a good cover story, and extreme diligence are all parts of what will be required for success. Leave that part to me."

Holden was listening to every word out of her mouth, processing the meaning and implications of her statements, and making judgments as to whether he thought she was credible. Given what he was hearing, he was convinced that her responses were not canned, but rather that she, and others, had thought this out in incredible detail, and that they were properly assessing the dangers. He was satisfied for now.

The two continued to talk about some logistical details, agreed on some future discussion items, and filled each other in on the best methods to get hold of each other. The meeting had taken a long time, and Samantha needed to leave.

"Thank you for your time Mr. Holden, I know how busy you are. The schedule for meetings you've given me will work well. I appreciate your organization. I will be in touch." Sloan said turning to leave.

"Oh," just remembering, Holden said, "I understand a happy birthday is in order Ms. Sloan," Holden said with a hand extended to shake hers. The little homework he did do on her said she was twenty-four years old on this day, but she looked about sixteen. How could this young woman be out of high school let alone be working toward a Ph.D.?

"Thank you Mr. Holden," she said bending down to put Sawyer's leash on, "I've always loved birthdays but don't you think the celebration should be more the mother's than the child's? The mothers do all the work," Samantha said smiling, giving Holden a glimpse into her personal side.

Holden smirked, "I've never really thought about it that way but I suppose you are right. Enjoy your day Ms. Sloan," Holden said ending the meeting and watching her and Sawyer walk out of the anteroom. Again, a meeting that he had planned to be a certain length went all day. But it was different from the meeting with Pearson and Bishop. It was more detailed, frank and to the point. He liked her. She had a process for everything and if she didn't, she made a note to create one. Expectations were laid out, intentions were known and ha, organized is an understatement, he thought. If, for whatever reason, the group fell apart, he was going to grab her up to run one of his companies. She was a true anomaly.

CHAPTER 11
MAGNATES

Monday, May 19, 1997 – 11:15am Central Daylight Time (16:15 hours Zulu Time)

Sitting once again in Derek Holden's office in Virginia Beach, Samantha Sloan brought Jackson Cooper to meet the head of SOURCE and get to know each other.

"How did you two meet? Other than the ridiculous rumor, I don't know your history at all," asked Holden. He wasn't about to poke the stick at Jackson Cooper as he'd done with Samantha Sloan.

Samantha adjusted her chair to make sure Sawyer was lying comfortably on the marble floor. She had put the meeting together as Derek would prove to be one of the "founders" and as they all believed, it was important that they all got to know each other. Everyone in the room knew their roles at a high level, but it had come to the point that in-person meetings needed to begin, so the planning could proceed in earnest. Samantha was once again in a black suit, Cooper also dressed professionally in a black suit, white shirt and red tie with black cowboy boots on. Holden was dressed a little more casually in light gray trousers, a white collared shirt and a dark gray sweater over it.

"This little lady came and straightened up the place at the Office of Agriculture while on break from her school work, and I've got to tell you she really saved the ranch, she really has quite a horse sense," Cooper beamed.

Sloan rolled her eyes. "Don't listen to him, the primary reason I went there was to put some of my theories on organizational culture and group behavior into practice. I was kicking around one of those theories for my Ph.D. I ended up going in a different direction, but the work I'm doing there is great for the office and will be relevant to clinical work," Sloan finished, all business.

"And what about you Mr. Cooper? Before I get in bed with any business partners, I'd like to know quite a lot about them." Holden flushed a little because of the in bed comment and the aforementioned rumor. "Sorry, no pun intended."

"Don't mention it," said Cooper, waving his hand dismissively.
I think is just as important in this case because of what's at stake.
I know Pearson well, and he wouldn't lead me astray, but I still want
to do my own homework," said Holden, way more congenial than
he intended to be.

"First off, call me Jack. All my friends do, and it is important to
me that you and I have a friendship as well as a business relationship.
Second, this ain't just business, this is going to change our way of
life and if we can't get along, then we are no better off than we are
right now."

"Agreed," said Holden, as Sloan also nodded in agreement.

"Where do I start?" Cooper said in a big Texas accent "Been in
Texas and politics all my life. My family has been in Texas for what
seems like forever, my family is just a bunch of salt-of-the-earth
farmers. Did a little work for my dad after college, and the Air Force,
but my family is too nuts to keep up with - a bunch of hillbilly nut
jobs, I tell ya, but who's ain't. And don't mistake me; I love Texas and
everything she stands for. I don't like the word hillbilly but when the
redneck fits, ya gotta wear it."

Holden laughed. This was a likable guy, like Sloan had said
previously. He was a man's man. He reminded Holden of a little bit
JR Ewing from that old TV show Dallas, and of Ronald Reagan; he
even looked a little like Reagan. Cooper went on and talked about
his past and his values. He said the reason he didn't stay too close to
his family was because he disliked laziness and his siblings seemed
to be just that. They would watch their dad work like a mule, he said,
and they would just have their hand out for money, because their car
broke down, because they didn't maintain it, or they lost their city
job, because they called in sick all the time. Nope, he had no use that
kind of lack of ambition; he didn't even want it around him.

When he was done, he said, "I believe in bringing this to Texas,
but no matter what we do, or how we do it, we've gotta respect the
land. It's gonna protect us, so let's do the same to it in kind." Then
his phone rang. It was the Governor, and he had to take the call. He
excused himself and went to the adjoining anteroom.

Samantha continued the background on Cooper. She said he
was loyal to a fault for those he believed in, as evidenced by how
gracious he was to her when they first arrived. He had some issues

with Nikoli because he felt Nikoli was too modern for his tastes, but thought he was young... He would come around. Cooper had said, "Smart kid though, he'll do good for us," she explained trying to mimic his Texas drawl. She said Cooper could be off-putting to people at times because of his relentless sarcasm. She heard he went through multiple roommates during his freshman year at Texas A&M because they couldn't stand the sarcasm and antagonistic attitude he had. She said she had never experienced anything too terrible, so she excused it as them not having their big boy pants on, again mimicking his Texas accent. She did it well.

When Cooper came back Samantha was telling Holden about Cooper's wife and two children. Kate, the oldest, was a lot like her dad. Forest, however, didn't get his dad's charisma. His strength was his even-mindedness, like his mother. Vivian could be a bit timid, but she was also able to stop conflicts in their tracks and Jackson was great at starting them, so her skills came in handy on a regular basis.

"I heard you tryin' to talk like me child...not even close," he said. "The wife and kids don't know about the movement yet, I don't anticipate any disagreement with staying in Texas. Kate will want to help for sure so as soon as we decide to tell our families, we can use her, she's a smart girl." Cooper said happily.

"Well now that I'm filled in, I guess my question is: Why Texas? I mean who came up with that?" Holden asked Cooper.

"Do we need a reason other than it being the Lone Star state, the best-of-the-best!" Cooper said razzing Holden and winking at Sloan.

"No, I didn't mean it that way and no offense to Texas, Jack." Holden said a bit unsure of himself.

"I'm just givin' you shit Derek, you have to get used to my humor."

Holden raised his eyebrows and said "it's only been a couple hours there Lone Star," looking over at Cooper, he could tell that was another joke. "Yeah, I get it." he said smiling, "You're trying to get me again so screw you." He said playfully. He could tell they were going to get along fine.

"But seriously, why Texas? There are a lot of reasons." Cooper was interrupted, as Nikoli Borodin came bouncing in the door.

"What have I missed?" he asked smiling. He was the most casually dressed in the room, wearing a black t-shirt with a molecule on it, and the words "Stand Back, I'm Going to Try SCIENCE" written across the chest. Over the shirt, he wore a black suit jacket. Baggy blue jeans and red sneakers completed the ensemble.

Holden and Nikoli hadn't met yet, and it was important to Holden to get to know the three that started this whole thing. If they ended up being whack-jobs then he was hitting the road. So far they had been brilliant, ambitious, and most of all, passionate for a kind of change that, if it came to fruition, would literally change the way the world looked at the US forever.

"We were just starting to talk about Texas and the reason we chose there," Sloan explained.

"Ya know, I still don't know really why, I mean why not Nebraska or Colorado?" Borodin asked impetuously. "I always get my ass kicked when I go to Texas."

"And we know why," Cooper said and winked at him with a smile. "Haven't you heard of the ole saying Niki? Don't mess with Texas! But to answer your question Derek, if you think about it, it's brilliant. Texas says in its constitution that it is a free and independent state and takes its guidance from only the US Constitution, which by the way speaks nothing about secession for any state. Texas and Hawaii are the only two states that came into the Union as independent territories, and Texas never said that, because of joining, they could never leave. Well I'll tell ya, they did it once, and, in all reality only came back under heavy violence and governmental threat. But we can do it again. Now having said that though, I'm not saying all Texans are ripe to welcome a possible secession. Most are like the rest of Americans and believe incorrectly that Federal statutes, policies and programs automatically supersede any State's rights. But I am a big believer that Texans will be the most accepting of such a movement."

"So you think most will stay post taking?" asked Borodin.

"No, but on a percentage basis, I think more Texans would than any other state citizens. Outside of secession issues," Cooper continued, "Texas also has resources that other states may not have, at least in such large supply. Texas is sitting on potentially the largest deposit of oil and natural gas in the states. We have huge amounts of coal, silver and even gold. The gold will come in handy if it comes down to trade, if US currency is no longer going to be used, but I doubt that will be the case. Biomass and other natural resources like minerals and lumber are plentiful as well. The coastline is another huge resource for us. Being land locked might not be the best security posture for us, even though protecting the coast will be a major priority. Weather in Texas gives us all of the seasons and enough water so farming will be sustainable barring abrupt climate change and if that occurred it would affect all states anyway. Urban development has also always been strong in Texas, with this crappy economy Texas continues to grow at a higher percentage than other states combined, so we are equipped to bring any number of companies and the jobs that go along with them into a robust environment. Bishop did his homework well on Texas and from what I've seen his plan is detailed to the point of multiple contingencies that Texas can handle."

Everyone sat quietly for a few minutes. Nikoli was thinking that Cooper nailed it. He was happy to have him onboard; with a political insider among the ranks so much more could get done while other plans were made and carried out. Cooper was thinking the meeting had run later than anticipated. He wanted to stay and keep talking, but he had to hit the road soon or he was going to be late for his other obligations. Samantha was also thinking along those lines, as she had to get some work done and was going home to see her parents over the weekend. She was happy that Holden and Cooper had hit it off as well as they did. Both men were extremely powerful, smart men that were used to being in charge, and she thought there could have been some ego clashes; there were none. And it would have to continue that way, she thought, if things were going to be successful.

Holden had only one thing going through his mind. "I think I am the only one of the group here that has not seen the detailed plan that Mike has come up with. I mean, he has told me a lot in our conversations, but mostly methodology. What's the chances I can get my hands on it?"

"Having it sent to you?" Borodin asked. "Zero. Even though he knows I can encrypt everything he does digitally, he is super old school about it and has a copy in a safety deposit box somewhere and another copy with him, and I mean WITH HIM. He has it under his pillow when he sleeps, I think," he said with an impish grin. "But if you want to see it, he will come here with it and show it to you anytime... give him a buzz."

"I will, thanks." Holden said.

"And on that note, we need to swap spit and hit the road." Cooper said jumping up.

"Excuse me?" asked Holden with a look of gross on his face.

"Skedaddle, head for the wagon yard," and then in a perfect English accent, "I believe it is time to take my leave of you." Then in his normal voice, "I have a meeting with the Governor in the morning so I best be prepared. Derek, it was a pleasure. I must say even though I was in the military, I never thought of myself as a military man, so I was curious to know how you would be. You surprised me in all ways pleasant."

"Thanks, I try for a nice balance. My wife says I am still too rigid, but that is how I get things done," Holden answered back. They shook hands and Cooper was gone.

Holden looked at Samantha, who had a strange look on her face. Samantha quietly remarked, "He'll be back for them," pointing to Cooper's rental car key, "too much going on in the frontal lobes for them to do anymore."

"Does everything have a brain explanation?" Borodin said sarcastically, knowing that Samantha always justified behavior because of some brain functionality.

Sloan got right in his face and said, "Yep!" with enthusiasm, smiled, curtsied and pivoted back to Holden. Borodin shook his head with a smile on his face.

"Thanks for spending the time Derek, I appreciate your busy schedule. I'll be in touch in about five or six weeks and we'll figure out what's next, but call Mike, spend some time going over the details. You are going to have to flesh out a lot of the military and security stuff with him anyway," Sloan finished.

"Will do," Holden said shaking Sloan's hand. Looking over to Borodin, he said extending his hand, "and it was nice to finally meet you, Nikoli."

"Call me Niki, that way you sound like you at least tolerate me." Borodin said giving him a high-five instead of a handshake. He loved to take Holden out of his military man box whenever the opportunity arose.

"One last thing Derek…" said Sloan, then, looking at Borodin, "I'll catch up with you in a few minutes Niki." Borodin exited Holden's office as Cooper came back in, grabbed his key from Samantha and headed back out. "Derek, I promised to get back to you about the members that Admiral Pearson has brought on board. Mike wanted to tell you but has been indisposed with some stuff at school. It looks like he might be leaving his Ph.D. program to take a research job at MIT, so until he gets that resolved, he has gone underground, so-to-speak."

"I don't care who tells me to be honest," Holden responded, a little annoyed. "I just want to know that everything is as transparent as claimed and if it isn't then I want to know that. I just don't want to be dicked around…and that is not to say that you have. I just want to keep it that way."

"Understood," said Sloan unbothered. "I am sure you will meet everyone individually as you need to, but in the meantime I can just tell you, CIA station chief Joseph Bailey, you already know Harlan Mackay and…"

Holden cut her off, "What?!"

He was shocked. Harlan Mackay? _The_ Harlan Mackay? He thought Mackay was the spook to end all spooks and he was with us. The man who basically built the Air Force's Air Intelligence Agency. He was kinda like Hoover in a way, well except for the lady's dresses, he laughed to himself.

"What? What's the matter?" Sloan asked.

"Sorry, I was just surprised. I have followed his career and yes, I do know him and have a tremendous amount of respect for him. I'm sorry, please continue."

"It is not a long list Derek, but new people will be coming in everyday. The other two are Harris Corrigan who you worked with as a SEAL, I heard, and Dylan Sterling."

"I know Harris well. He is an excellent commander. We had some joint missions with the Marines and he kicked ass every time. I just saw that bastard a few weeks ago and he didn't say a thing."

"Did you?" Sloan asked sarcastically.

Holden grunted, "Yeah, I get it, but how is that going to work, really? Once we know each other is in, how do we communicate?"

"No different than you do now. Harris has known you were in since the day you told Mike, but that doesn't affect how you guys work on the outside, right?"

"That makes sense. I'm still getting used to the secret handshake and all the shit that goes with it," Holden said with a tone of sarcasm laced with a bit of frustration.

"I get it, really. I don't mean it to sound like a secret handshake; it's not. People started listening to Mike's methodologies quite by accident and a few pulled him aside and said if they could help in any way to let them know. So he did. It has happened even faster than he thought it would, and he had a pretty good idea of where everything stands; you know that as well as I do. But until anything really happens and we officially organize, we are just friends talking and any other time; we just do our jobs inside and outside. That is the simplest way, our Occam's razor," Sloan said with one eyebrow raised.

"Nice. And who was the last guy? Never heard of him."

"Dylan Sterling. You've heard of him. Think Reagan days, Gramm-Latta Budget? He is an economist. He has some of the best economic policies that I've ever heard. He is absolutely brilliant."

"Oh, ok, I was thinking military. Got it, that is a bit out of left field coming from Pearson, isn't it?"

"The Admiral is an old friend of Reagan. He introduced them and they have been friends for years. Small world, huh?"

"Christ, it's getting smaller everyday."

"In a month or so it will probably be a good time for you to meet Sakti Sharma" said Samantha. "I'll have Cooper introduce you."

"Say that name again," said Holden.

"Sakti Sharma, he's our energy guy. You'll like him. He is going to need a place to do his research undisturbed and with SOURCE starting the facility in central Texas that might be the perfect place."

"Ok then, bring on Mr. Sharma."

CHAPTER 12
COMMUNICATION

Wednesday, December 3, 1997 – 1:18pm Mountain Daylight Time (19:18 hours Zulu Time)

The three sat around a table, having just finished lunch. The topic of discussion was communication.

Three days earlier, Bishop, Sam and Nikoli had all arrived in Breckenridge, Colorado, for a ski trip, and to iron out some details about the group. The snow had been good, for the first of the season, but after two solid days on the slopes, they were ready to spend the third day on business.

Communication was something that all of them knew would be critical to their success. As the group grew larger, communication would become more difficult as well as riskier, but no less important. In fact, they agreed that they needed to devise a system that would protect the information, as well as the identities of those who contributed. It was a gargantuan task.

The first few methods they had discussed and experimented with over the preceding months were ineffective. They had tried to stay with mainstream technology, and utilize secure messaging technology that already existed on the Internet, and to have the most sensitive information shared between them only via cell phone, which wasn't secure at all. Their paranoia was heightened by stories about Kevin Mitnick, the notorious hacker, who had only recently been sentenced to twenty-two months in prison for illegally hacking cell phone access codes. They were all anxious to have a reliable way to communicate with each other, but previous attempts to do this had been unsuccessful.

Now, here they were, sitting at a round table in the hotel room Sam was staying in. They had knocked back a good lunch of meatball subs, salad, and lemonade, and had brewed a fresh pot of coffee. Both Bishop and Nikoli couldn't understand how Sam could eat like that but still look nearly anorexic. Sawyer was asleep on the bed after having shared in the lunch goodies.

Nikoli kicked off the discussion, "I have an idea. In reality, we don't have to transmit and store massive amounts of data. We have some key information we need to share with each other, but most of it can stay in one place for now."

Bishop and Sam exchanged a knowing glance. Nikoli had the specific gleam in his eye that they had been waiting for. It was the gleam that indicated that he had figured out what they would do. No need for further discussion… they just had to listen and learn. Nikoli's brilliant mind had come up with a methodology that would precisely meet their requirements.

"I'll talk about the stored data in a minute," Niki continued. "As for the stuff we'll send each other, we will use steganography. Basically, it's when messages are encoded within pictures. The greatest part about this method is that people who intercept the traffic don't even know it's a message, so they're not going to even try to break the code. Quinn's stuff is really good, but I think I made it better. I'm sure he'll be pissed, but whatever."

Neither Sam nor Bishop had ever heard of this, so Niki gave them some technical background. He used the example of sending someone an image file, such as a picture of one of Sam's animals. Sam might start with an innocuous image file and adjust the color of every 100th pixel to correspond to a letter in the alphabet, a change so subtle that someone not specifically looking for it is unlikely to notice it.

Nikoli pulled out his laptop to make his point. He quickly showed them how a specific pattern could be used with an off-the-shelf image-editing program to embed the message within the photo. It was brilliant, and virtually untraceable.

"That's excellent," said Bishop. "We'll have to get used to using it before we're all comfortable with it, I'm sure, but it's a fantastic idea, and it looks like it's going to work great."

Niki beamed with pride. He loved figuring out complex technical problems, and his satisfaction was evident.

"What about the rest of the info?" asked Sam.

Nikoli laid out his idea. "Here's where I think we need to use Ford." Nikoli was referring to his old friend, Langley Ford. "Ford's got a huge datacenter, right here in Colorado, that I'm sure he'd be willing to let us tap into. He could carve off some storage for us, and

I've got some ideas as to how to use some high-capability encryption to protect the data."

"OK, that works for me," Sam started, "but I'm not sure everyone will be comfortable with that, and will Ford be okay with storing data that he has no clue about? I'll leave it to you to convince everyone of its security risks and benefits. You good with that too, Mike?"

Bishop nodded. He had spent time with Nikoli and Ford together, and trusted Niki's judgment completely.

They all knew that Nikoli would get Ford to contribute the resources without having to divulge any information to him about the group. Nikoli was constantly working on large-scale technology projects that required a 'skunk works' project to be set up, and he often went to Ford for secure storage and computing resources.

"We also need to talk about just regular old-fashioned face-to-face communication. We are working on a project that is going to take many years to complete. We all have to stay connected to each other and that is going to be hard, considering whom the people are that we are talking about," said Samantha, fidgeting in her chair.

"Don't be getting all restless already Sam. We have a lot to go over," Bishop said warning the ever-hyper Samantha. "We are going to need a coordinator, and I imagined that to be you, Sam. If that is too much to take on with school, let me know and we can figure something else out, but you've met all the players, you know the different schedules and the locations of everybody, and the vision. So?"

Samantha thought about her schedule and tried to figure in the amount of time it would take her on top of her studies to facilitate this process well. She was only consulting at the Office of Agriculture for Cooper so that shouldn't take up too much time so after a cursory review decided she could. "That's fine," she said. "How often should everyone be in touch? I mean, we are so far out from any real action that having structured meetings is going to make people's heads explode."

"Well," Nikoli grunted, "that isn't exactly true. We have to determine each member's contribution both physically, as well as financially, and set up accounts to that end."

"Yeah, I get that Niki, but those are things that can be done on an individual basis, we don't need a scheduled meeting calendar quite yet, right?" Samantha asked, trying to be exact.

"Both of you are right, and I can work with Sam on the financial stuff so that doesn't get too time consuming and you are already managing resource contribution Niki," answered Bishop, relieving both of their stresses.

They spent the rest of the afternoon going over the details, then had a nice dinner at Kenosha Steakhouse in downtown Breckenridge, before Bishop took off towards Denver to play some golf at a nice course he'd heard about in Golden. Even though winter had set in, it wouldn't be the last round he got to play. Colorado weather seemed to be cooperative that way… It was common to be able to ski in the mountains, and do outdoor, non-snow activities down in Denver.

CHAPTER 13
YIN-YANG

Tuesday, February 3, 1998 – 9:30am Central Standard Time (15:30 hours Zulu Time)

It took almost nine months before Sakti Sharma was ready to meet Derek Holden and the other founding members of the group. Sharma was crazy busy with the work he had been doing for NASA, but now there was a lull in the project so he called Bishop and said he was free. Jackson Cooper set up the meeting.

Sitting in Sakti's small home office in Alamogordo, New Mexico, Derek Holden was waiting for Cooper to join them so he could formally introduce him to Sharma, but even though Holden arrived a bit early, Cooper still wasn't there and Holden was annoyed. Sharma had to finish up a phone call and went into his kitchen to do so. Sharma had answered the door already on the phone and gestured to come in and go into his office. He looked younger than Holden expected; he was wearing a blazing orange Cowboys and Indians t-shirt, and baggy jeans. The t-shirt made Holden snicker and in that second, he knew that Sharma had a great sense of humor. The t-shirt had a traditional cowboy on a horse with a lasso and a gun. Behind the horse was not an American Indian but an Indian from India, like Sharma, with the customary robe and turban, riding an elephant. Cowboys and Indians! Holden thought it was great! As Holden was waiting he looked around the office trying to get a sense of what this man was like. The office was tidy and laid out to encourage the utmost efficiency. He had two huge racks of CD's, one for what seemed like data-type things. The other one was filled with music; he had quite a wide range of music, but a good portion was music that Holden recognized, making him think they were close in age. Holden's dad had hated much of the 80's music and had discouraged him from listening to it for more "inspiring" music as he put it. Inspiring meant classical or Christian, and even though he grew to love both, he did appreciate music from the 80's from time to time as a young teenager.

Holden was in the middle of the room at a small round maple wood table that would accommodate four comfortably, five tightly. The table matched the desk as well as the shelving around the room. At the moment, there were only two chairs at it, with another one up against the wall right by the door. The only other chair in the room was behind the desk. It, too, was small and very utilitarian, more like a task chair than a desk chair and nothing like the desk chair that was in Holden's office. His was more like a throne, and he blushed a little just thinking of the contrast. This one was black with rope-like strips as the seat and the back with silver armrests, and finally a middle pole staring out into five legs on casters. There was a plastic mat on the floor to protect the tan flecked Berber carpet underneath. His desk was interesting, stretching the length of one wall with built-in shelves above it. The row of shelves closest to the desk all had doors, those above that were open. Engineering books, technical magazines and other reference material packed them full. The desk surface itself was kept clear. There was a cordless phone base; Sharma was on the actual phone, his computer, and a basket that contained a few pieces of paper in it. Holden thought this was probably his inbox. There was a piece of art at the far end in the corner where the desk met the wall. The art was also a perfect match of the maple wood. The walls were a very relaxing, masculine grey. Holden made a mental note to himself that he wouldn't mind having his office this color. At one corner of the room where the desk and wall met was a black floor shelf that gave the impression of holding up that end of the desk. It too was cram-packed with manuals and reference material. The shelf was the only thing on that wall, besides a small window with white shades that were open, allowing a view of the desert and a rather barren back yard.

Continuing to look around the room, an enormous printer took up the majority of the wall that was on the other side of the desk, and the skinny space remaining held a floor to ceiling built in shelf with flush cabinet doors; a good use of space, Holden thought. Opposite the wall with the desk was the door to the entryway of the house and next to that was a glass cabinet that intrigued Holden. It was filled with G. I. Joe action figures, most of them still in the box. They were the older, full-size action figures; not the cheap shit that his kids played with today, he thought. Sharma had at least twenty different figures and a good number of whole sets. He moved closer so he could read the boxes. He had the Dress Parade Action Pack, a Crash Crew Fire Truck Vehicle Set and even a G.I. Nurse. He chuckled; he remembered playing with these figures when he was a kid, but he didn't remember a nurse. He thought it was very interesting that this engineer from India loved G.I. Joe, but he, the military man actually preferred the Tonka Trucks growing up.

As Sharma returned, another call came in, he answered it and then put it on speaker.

"Good morning, Angels!" came a booming Texas accent through the phone.

Sharma looked confused, and Holden asked, "Where are you Jack?"

"I'm still in Austin. I tried to get a hold of you before you left, but your secretary said you were already on your way to New Mexico so I just figured I could do an introduction over the phone. You two don't want me around askin' all kinda questions anyway - you'll be more productive this way. Sakti, this is Derek, Derek this is Sakti Sharma. He is going to revolutionize the energy industry, Derek, and Bishop got him. So Angels, you have your work cut out for you, I..."

Holden reached up and hung up the phone, cutting off Cooper from making anymore Charlie's Angels references.

"Was he quoting..?"

Holden cut Sharma off, "yes, and frankly I'm not in the mood. I wish he would have at least called me on my cell to let me know he wasn't coming, but it is no use sitting here pissed." Holden extended his hand, "It's nice to meet you."

"You as well," said Sharma in a thick Indian accent.

"So, just to let you know, I really don't know anything about your work, I know you are here in Alamogordo because of a NASA project you are working on, but I don't know what the project is or what you really do. Cooper did say that you will be needing space in one of the SOURCE facilities once they are completed in Texas."

"Do you have an estimated date of completion?" asked Sharma.

Holden grunted.

"The plan is to buy the majority of land starting in early 2001 and continuing through the year. We have already purchased small sites in the Trans-Pecos, high plains area, and Central Texas is underway.

We will then add to them in the bigger purchases, but I felt we needed something in case the shit hits the fan earlier than expected, and it seems that everyone I've talked to wants space already. From what I understand, Bishop bought land under a shell corp. that will be for some kind of ruse down the road that you are helping him with."

"Hmmm," Sharma said wondering what kind of shit would hit what fan. He was not a fighter, in the sense that if they expected him to pick up a gun and go running through some city declaring freedom for all, that just wasn't going to happen. He was an aerospace engineer looking for ways to harness energy to perhaps one day live on another planet. He continued, "Yes, the facility is just outside of Sweetwater, he told me about it a little while after we met. He wants it on the power sensor grid to appear as a nuclear fusion facility requiring a massive amount of power…for some kind of possible event in the future. All I know is that the land was purchased about a year ago…one hundred and fifty acres I think. He wants the build out to look like a multi-building nuclear fusion test and production facility."

"Interesting. I haven't been asked to be involved in its development as of yet, so I am going to stay focused on the SOURCE facilities for now. I am going to need a list of things you will require in a lab and I will have them brought in. I anticipate the central facility will be ready for you in about a year. If you are really pressed, I could offer you something in SOURCES's headquarters in North Carolina, but that is not part of the group per say, that is my private business and I like to keep them separate for now, we only use it when we really need to," Holden explained.

"Ah, no, thank you," replied Sharma. "I don't anticipate needing anything more than I have for some time. My lab at Holloman AFB is quite sufficient and kept under wraps, and I am left to myself."

"Can you tell me what you are working on? I have security clearance if that is the issue, if this group is sticking to those kind of need-to-knows, but there has really never been a need for me to know this side of things," Holden asked inquisitively.

"Ah, I can tell you, it is not a secret as such. NASA, along with the Air Force, has asked me to research possibilities of sustaining life on Mars."

"Interesting," was all Holden could come up with to say. He was actually not interested at all, and he wanted to know what that had to do with why the Xers wanted his expertise, and even that was so far out of his purview that he wondered why they couldn't have just had a conference call. But then he remembered what Sam had said about this group having to build tight-knit relationships, so he tried to have a better attitude.

"Most people do not think so, and I posit you are only trying to be polite." Sharma replied. "I know what you are thinking and no, that is not what we are working on for Texas. The work for NASA was primarily to get enough oxygen supply to live there, but through this research, I have begun a pet project that entails reversing the oxygen process and harnessing natural resources other than fossil fuels to drive higher energy efficiencies. Currently, I'm looking at gypsum sand, which is plentiful here. Depending on the sand's makeup and how powerful the chemical reaction is between it and oxygen, there will be a determination of the fuel cell's strength."

"Ooookay," Holden said hesitantly. "I have to tell you, I understand what you just said but I'm not sure I understand what you just said, ya know?"

"Perfectly," Sharma returned. "The end goal is basically to produce a unit that would allow each home or business to have its own energy source and to lessen or stop altogether the need for the grid for that kind of power."

"The grid?"

"The power grid," Sharma said, and followed up by saying, "Our reliance on a central power grid leaves us vulnerable in many ways, two of which are dependence on a central source that can charge basically anything they want, and the fact that many of these items are built oversees in China and could take close to a month to have replaced. So I do not need to tell you how that opens us up for many other vulnerabilities if a main grid went down."

"Christ! Now I understand. And you think you can do this?"

"I know I can, it is just a matter of time," Sharma said confidently. "It is getting late, how long are you in town? Miss Samantha said we must do our best to know each other, so will you allow me to host you in a dinner out?"

"I leave tomorrow morning, and dinner sounds great." Amazed by Sharma and even more amazed by what Michael Bishop has assembled in people and ideas, Holden was saddened that it took this kind of extremism to make real change. Before they left he had to ask about the collection in the case, "hey Sharma, what's up with this?

Sharma looked back at the case and smiled. "Growing up in India, we did not have this type of toy. We had all kinds of toys and things to occupy our time, but this was special. My older brother caught the collecting bug first and then it just became a competition and I really grew to love the workmanship in the older, full-size figures, but I do have to admit, I am ashamed at what I have paid for some of these."

"Do you mind me asking what something like these goes for?" asked Holden.

"Not at all. This one for instance, the Shore Patrol Set, Hasbro only made a limited number. I got it mint in the box for $3,500."

"Are you kidding me, three grand!" Holden exclaimed. "I played with these too, but I would never have guessed. I didn't even remember there was a nurse."

Sharma stood, "after you, Derek," as they left the room he said, "yeah, she's one of the most expensive in the case, she took me for $5,000."

"Holy shit! That's a woman for ya, huh? That's crazy Sharma."

Sharma looked at him a little baffled.

"I'm just kidding about the woman thing, but that is a high price to pay," Holden said feeling that he came off quite misogynistic even though he wasn't and they left for dinner.

PART 5
CONNECTIONS IN THE COMMUNICATIONS (1999-2001)

CHAPTER 14
A COMPANY IN THE RESEARCH

Monday, August 9, 1999 – 7:45am Pacific Daylight Time (14:45 hours Zulu Time)

It was a pretty typical day for Langley Ford. As he walked from his car in the underground parking garage, he was mildly amused by the fact that one of his senior executives, Nathan, was getting out of his car at the same time but, unlike Ford, Nathan had a chauffeur. Despite Ford's enormous wealth, he still chose to drive himself. The success that had resulted from the technical advances that his company had made were not the result of Ford wanting wealth, power or status. They came from his desire to use technology to make something great.

Born from humble beginnings, he always had to work hard for what he got. His parents divorced when he was 11 years old, and his father had cycled through dozens of jobs throughout Ford's youth. They had lived in no less than 10 cities, as his father decided, somewhat randomly, that it was time to move on again. He laughingly described his father as the consummate gypsy. Oddly enough, for many, this lifestyle would not really provide of a good foundation for children to have any chance to succeed, but for Ford, what he saw in his father was a tremendous work ethic. As the saying goes, "Anything worth doing is worth doing well." He learned at an early age that putting your heart and soul into your work was the minimum standard. He excelled in school and received an academic scholarship to Stanford for his undergraduate work. He continued on for his graduate studies at Stanford as well, and that was where he met Nikoli Borodin.

With Nikoli, he was able to create a successful organization. The two had met and become instant friends. In 1997, they started working together on a research project for Stanford that involved computer databases. They were trying to attach extra information to databases that would allow other systems to better utilize the data. The project gleaned another idea that Ford and Borodin worked on in secret. They had figured out a search algorithm that allowed for super fast searches across databases of all kinds, and it also had the capability to be used on other technologies besides databases.

Both Ford and Borodin decided the new project was more exciting than the current one they were working on for their doctorates, so they dropped out of Stanford and started a company. Before long, it exploded with success, making both of them multi-millionaires and then multi-billionaires. They were taking the computer/technology industry by storm.

Their company, Sensedatum Technologies, was heralded in tech magazines as one of the most innovative companies for five years straight based on their search criteria algorithm that would ostensibly return results from all known data sources, not just ones connected to the Internet. They sold the algorithm to a company called Omnis, which is Latin for 'all-knowing.' So far, the world seemed to agree with the tech magazines, as Omnis commanded about 80 percent of the market share for search engines. Other tech companies created entire divisions with the specific intent of building search engines to rival Omnis.

Ford reaped the rewards of this venture, to the tune of many billions of dollars. Nikoli shared in Ford's passion and enthusiasm, and like Ford, remained heads-down in the business because he loved it. The money didn't hurt, either... They took their money, but didn't run. They used a good portion of it to start a venture capital aspect to the firm that looked for other great tech ideas at first, and then expanded to include any idea that they felt would make the world a better place. They gave grants to universities for research, to small companies to expand on promising ideas, and even individual people as long as they felt the idea was strong enough. The fact that it was a grant meant this was money that would be invested without having to pay it back, in cash, anyway. There were two conditions to the grants. First, Sensedatum got a percentage of the company, patent, idea, etc., if it was successful. In this respect, it was more like a private equity firm than a philanthropic organization. Second, upon that success, they had to take 25 percent of their original grant amount and "pay it forward" to another person or company that the successful company felt worthy of a shot, and Sensedatum then took 2 percent of that new venture as well. This produced superior achievements and staggering profits. Sensedatum invested in ideas that became email services, the first online auction site, Internet radio stations, and what would become social networking sites. One company that they invested in came up with digitally enhanced closed caption television for security purposes and was sold to not only private business but state and federal government as well. They even formed a publishing company for books that focused on higher education and self-taught technical subjects. Finally, they put a tremendous amount of money into finding profitable green ideas and did rather well in that venture too. Both Langley and Nikoli loved the idea of finding great minds and giving them the opportunity to thrive. Not all the ventures came to triumphant fruition, and some of them even drove Nikoli crazy. He wondered how such brilliant minds could piss away their talents, brains and money. It just wasn't in his DNA.

Ford continued his trek towards his office, cutting through one of the many employee break areas, and grabbing a cup of coffee on the way. The break area had fancy coffee machines, but he didn't understand why anyone would want to drink it any way but black. It's not that he was that much of a purist, but why wouldn't they want coffee to taste like...coffee?

Throughout the years of working to build the company, Nikoli and Langley grew closer, and an inseparable bond formed between them. When Nikoli began his work with AmendX, he would often seem to disappear for extended periods of time, citing that he had personal business to attend to. Langley thought it was strange at first, but got used to it after a while. Nikoli was always diligent about company business, and never missed anything important, so Langley never felt cheated or short-changed by Nikoli's extra-curricular activities. The friendship between them was strong enough that Langley never even asked about the other stuff, and Nikoli knew he didn't need to explain. They communicated on a different level. Langley knew that, for Nikoli to spend this time and attention on something, it had to be important to him. Langley was just fine with letting it go at that.

From Nikoli's perspective, he appreciated the fact that Langley didn't press him on the issue of how he spent his time. He thought of it kind of like Bruce Wayne, who was seen by the world as a billionaire adventurer, and let everyone assume that, while in reality, like Batman, he was off secretly doing things that would make the world a better place. The world around him had created this perception and it was in his best interest not to challenge. Not that he was at all like the caped crusader...the thought of that alone made him laugh. Nikoli knew that he had been blessed with brains, seemingly at the expense of brawn. But what little boy didn't want to be Batman!

Nikoli would likely never tell Langley about AmendX. He knew that Langley wouldn't like how he and the other AmendXers were going about it. He had originally intended to tell Langley, but never found the right time. Months turned into years, and by this point, there wouldn't be a right time. Nikoli was content with the knowledge that his friend, partner and confidant would support him, and his desire to do well.

The billionaire adventurer persona was alive and well at home for Nikoli, as well. His girlfriend, whom he had met during his time at Stanford, knew nothing about AmendX either. Even though Samantha and Bishop knew both Haley and Langley very well, it was agreed that nothing would be said until Nikoli was ready. Haley assumed that he was gallivanting around the globe, looking for his next adventure. As their relationship had progressed from knowing each other, to dating, to living together, there was always an intention in the back of Nikoli's mind to tell her. That day had not yet come.

CHAPTER 15
LIFE'S TWISTS FOR THE THREE

May 2000

"Well at least Samantha will finish her education," said Bill Bishop, Mike's father to Pearson.

"It's been too long since we've gotten together for a cocktail," said Pearson sitting on the patio of Michael Bishop's boyhood home.

These two men had been friends for upwards of twenty years. He wondered why Mike didn't want to tell his parents about his plans. Both the plan and Mike were brilliant and his father would understand. Of that, Pearson was sure. But he respected Mike's decision; it would all come in time. But because Mike's dad didn't know of his busy schedule and many pressing tasks, he had to just nod and look as though he understood when Bill Bishop talked sadly of what could have been had Mike continued his work and completed his Ph.D.

"The research work that he has signed on to perform at MIT is not just grunt work, Bill," Pearson said, trying not to sound too defensive of Mike.

"I know, Mike has done well, I would have just liked him to finish what he started."

If only I could tell you how he is doing just that, Pearson thought to himself. Instead he said," you've got to let these kids figure things out for themselves. Nikoli didn't finish school either and look where he is. I heard he is up for Entrepreneur of the Year with Sensedatum."

"I'm proud of all three of the kids, really I am, but there is nothing that beats a good education and they were all three lined up for the best education possible and Sam is the only one that followed through. I know I'm just being a hard ass, but we didn't get that chance, Mike, we did what we had to, and don't get me wrong, I'm not bitchin'… I just want everything for them."

"I know, Bill," but they have to make their own way, and I would say they are all doing it well."

***

Samantha ended up defending her dissertation and receiving her Ph.D. in clinical psychology going into the summer of 2002. She completed the process more quickly than most could. It wasn't necessarily something she chose to do or was even proud of; she barely slept, she loved to study, and felt it imperative to stay busy. The next step was to complete licensure in California as well as Texas. Samantha loved to learn, she was almost sad when her formal education came to an end. She thought of applying to another program to pursue another Ph.D., or look for post-doc work to keep her mind active, but for now, she promised Mike that she would dedicate her excessive energy and brain power toward keeping everyone on the same page, making sure everyone knew and respected each other and, in Mike's words, "be the glue that kept everyone together." She didn't know exactly how she would accomplish it, but she figured everyone was involved for similar reasons and they all believed in Mike. Whatever it was about him, when he talked about future possibilities, some thought Mike was too liberal, while others thought he was too conservative, but all thought his ideas could bring about the kind of change that would mark a new way of life. Having this knowledge, she knew being "the glue" wouldn't be that hard, she just had to keep everyone consistently communicating; she believed that was the key. If someone felt kept out of the loop, that is when problems would start. Not everyone had to know everything, but as it pertained to them, she better damn well make sure they knew about it, and that was how she was going to proceed.

Nikoli's love for education did not exactly match Samantha's. What he did love was his company and all that he was able to create because of it. He learned something every day, and he felt that was more valuable than school, so he left his program a couple of years into it and concentrated full time on work and home life. He remained close with the AmendX initiative as well as Samantha and Mike; he didn't think it was even possible to grow apart from them, so he focused on Sensedatum, Langley, and Haley. He and Haley had been dating since his first year at Stanford. He was in no rush to get married, but he had no doubt that he wanted to spend the rest of his life with her. Not telling her about AmendX was the hardest thing he had ever done; it wasn't that he even meant to hide it. At first, no one was sharing anything with anybody that wasn't already in the group. As the group expanded, Quinn, the founder and CEO of 13-C Computers, insisted that his family not only knew of the project, but also wanted them to be involved. This gave him hope that he would tell Haley soon. Then, one day just turned into the next. When there were concrete plans as to how to incorporate family into the mix, he would tell her and everything would be fine. Since he was working on things that related to Sensedatum tech anyway, he really wasn't even keeping anything from her, so he could continue to work on what he loved and spend time with the woman he loved…life was good.

Not so much for Michael Bishop. He started his graduate work as happily as the other two, but something inside of him just started to feel uneasy. He continued with his diary as he called it; it was really a schematic of basically everything he felt could be improved and simplified about major policies and practices of the country, everything from education to healthcare to philosophical thoughts about entitlement versus earning. His most significant dilemma to date covered the gamut of policy, infrastructure, and even opinion of how life should be lived. On one side he thought that every human being should be able to live without the worry of homelessness or hunger; the fear of the possibility of losing everything, or not being able to provide the minimum of basic survival for their family. He wrote in his diary, asking rhetorically, "wouldn't it be an unsettling factor, one that would prevent us from concentrating on the betterment of society and production and excellence, if, in the backs of men's minds, there was a complete insecurity of what tomorrow might bring? The idea that I have a place to live no matter what, and my kids will have a bed, no matter what seems like a basic tenant of humanity." As he contemplated that utopian thought, the screaming obvious questions came raging into his mind: why should this be? Who is going to pay for it? Who is going to define the basic minimum? Why should you get the bigger house and I get the basic minimum. The American spirit came out of ingenuity and fortitude. Nothing was given to those who first came here; they earned it. They went and worked until their fingers bled, until exhaustion was a way of life. Even though he grew up in a stable, loving environment where money didn't seem to be a problem, he didn't have everything he wanted, he had to earn it. Every dollar he spent since entering college, he earned. Even before that, actually, his parents insisted that he have a part-time job, learn the value of money and the difficulty in making it. If he had been handed the basics, would he have sought for more, or would he have been content with what was given to him? At his core he believed in striving to always do your best and continue to do better, and this new quandary really made him struggle. He understood that some countries provided education and healthcare to their people; these same countries also had enormous tax percentages, one thing this country would never have. These other countries grew, over time, as a communal groups. Over hundreds and hundreds of years that was the way of living. America did no such thing; individualistic personalities founded this country to move away from high taxation and sought an individuals right to accomplish. Of course there were many mistakes along the way, but he couldn't take those back now, nor could he solve them for the future; all he could do was treat everyone fairly now. But the individualistic culture that this country had borne would never give rise to 'for the love of your brother' — it just won't happen. And unfortunately, the individual of time past, one that admired individual ambition, had turned sadly into the entitled of today, and the attitude of 'since he has it, I deserve it, too.'

His coursework was interesting enough, and he did what he believed was his responsibility, his best. When two planes hit the world trade center it would bring back those feelings from 1993 that caused a shift in his thinking forever. It wasn't even the hideousness of the terrorist's actions that struck him to the bone. It was the fact that anyone could stick a poker in our way of life and change it forever. It was too fragile in his mind, and if anyone was going to change it, it should be him and for the betterment of the people, not the death of them. He withdrew from Stanford, knowing he would never return to complete his Ph.D., and took a research analyst job at MIT. This would give him ample time to struggle through the very questions that relentlessly kept at him. This would also mean moving across the country away from his two best friends; his partners in this monumental endeavor.

CHAPTER 16
INTENTION AT THE ELECTION CELEBRATION

Friday, January 5, 2001 – 8:00pm Central Standard Time (Saturday, January 6, 2001 – 02:00 hours Zulu Time)

Jackson Cooper was elected Governor of Texas by a landslide victory. Since Cooper had been acting Governor since George W. Bush had resigned to take on his new duties as President of the United States, it was almost business as usual and the assumption of office in December came and went with little notice, but this was a full-fledged election that Cooper won, so a small faction from the group came to celebrate. Only Nikoli was considered famous of the three and they worried that he might draw too much attention. It was decided that it would seem to be innocuous enough, so he came to celebrate Cooper's win. The appearance of Michael Pearson and Derek Holden, on the other hand, was quite a different story, so they stayed away and Samantha planned another, more intimate and, more importantly, covert celebration later in January. The first week of January is usually a dead time for state government, especially when a 'new' Governor comes in, so Cooper was able to get away under the guise of a family vacation. Similarly, the myriad members who came to celebrate with Cooper were all suddenly vacationing in undisclosed locales that in reality ended up being the Broadmoor Resort in Colorado Springs, Colorado. Samantha and Michael Bishop could come and go as they pleased, as no one knew them, but Mike always did get the looks from the ladies. He came in the mood to celebrate. He wore a beautiful Isaia tuxedo with a crisp white shirt and black bow tie. He had been waiting for some event in which he could wear this new tuxedo. He didn't dress up much, but when he did, he went all out. Isaia is widely available in the US, but while he was in Italy the previous year for a long weekend with a lovely Italian girl, he decided to go to the point of supply. It was a magnificent piece of clothing, and so comfortable. Maybe he would sleep in it that night, he thought to himself. Samantha was also dressed to the nines; Holden couldn't stop looking at her. Not for what one might think: he was perplexed at her dress. He could not figure out what it was made of. It was a black dress with a tank top, but floor length and tight all the way down. There was absolutely nothing she could hide in it. He knew she often carried a concealed weapon, but he knew she wasn't wearing one now. At first he thought it was rubber, which made him shake his head. But on a second look he could see rubber doesn't move as easily as this dress did. Leather? No, still too restrictive. She kneeled down to pick up a pen that an elderly gentleman had dropped and she had no problem bending at the knees, it just looked painted on...it was mesmerizing. He shook he head again and made himself snap out of it. He went and greeted some old friends from his SEAL days that had just walked in.

Upon arriving at the Broadmoor, striding into the ballroom, Cooper was a bit taken aback when he saw how many people actually turned out for this party. A lot of high ranking military officials, both active in the field, as well as retired, had shown up. There was also a large contingent of civilians working for various agencies like the FBI and CIA. Michael Pearson brought Joseph Bailey and Harlan Mackay, both heavy hitters, Assistant to the President for Homeland Security and the Associate Director for Military Affairs for the CIA respectively; both men were not visible in the media and could easily appear in public without being recognized. Derek, however, came with Harris Corrigan, the Marine Corps General who, at that time, was in charge of the entire Southern Command and on track, as rumors were going around, to be Marine Commandant, and the next Vice Chairman of the Joint Chiefs. He was more recognizable for obvious reasons, plus, it wasn't like he could ever appear incognito. He was 6 feet 5 inches tall, African-American, and tipped the scales at 250 pounds. Bald, with a nicely manicured mustache and horn-rimmed glasses, and towering over most men, he tried to look friendly, but had such an intense face and a million things on his mind, he usually failed. If anyone was going to be recognized, good money was on Corrigan.

Anytime the AmendXers came together in larger groups, they were surprised at how the group had grown and delighted to learn who shared their beliefs. Not everyone got along happily however. Holden and Bailey never did get along; each man thought the other was an egomaniac who should be kicked out...as if anyone could be 'kicked out.'

"Bailey is a dick and he's gotta go!" Holden had an exceptionally short fuse, and had never been accused of having a great sense of humor. He raged inwardly against those whose actions were unproductive to what this group was trying to accomplish. This rage, as usual, gave him energy. He was adept at displaying an outer calm, while inside, he had a boiling intensity that drove him along. He cursed Bailey, and his poor attitude. He cursed his inability to achieve his goals faster. He cursed the politicians that had propagated this bullshit way of life. He cursed the terrorists that were hell bent on killing innocents. His blood boiled.

Pearson could see the consternation on Holden's face, and responded to Holden's comment by getting right back in his face. "Deal with it, Holden." Pearson had no patience for drama. And the last thing he needed to was to have these two at each other's throats. Both were dangerous men. Holden could kill a man with both hands tied behind his back, and Bailey had spent his whole career finding new and interesting ways to destroy terrorists, by bringing the fight to them. If Bailey and Holden continued down this path, no good would result.

"You're a dick, too, Holden, and nobody is looking to kick your ass off the team," Pearson continued. "So kick it down a notch, switch to decaf, or do whatever the fuck you have to do to get it under control, but get over it, and march on."

Holden walked away, steaming. He liked Pearson, but despised being talked to like that. The first commander that he had served under as a SEAL had talked to him the same way, and although Holden always toed the line from the standpoint of the chain of command, he always wanted to be the one giving orders, not the one taking them.

The party went on without incident. Holden assessed the situation and realized that Bailey was a necessary member of this group. He had access to places and people that simply no one else had. But how could anyone find him anything but annoying? He was brazen and rude, and...Holden shut his eyes, he was tired. He looked around and saw everyone enjoying themselves while he was in the back of the room brooding. Fuck it. He wasn't going to worry about it now. He was finally among people that thought like he did, for the most part, and he was going to take advantage of it and have a good time. He might even have a glass of champagne. It had been probably ten years since he last drank.

While the party was still in full swing, Cooper met with a small group wishing to talk about next steps now that he was Governor.

"I know everyone here understands this, but I want to have it said so there is never any misunderstanding, I have to do what is right for Texas first. I am a loyal member to this group, and I truly believe that what is best for Texas is also what is best for what we are trying to accomplish…

Nobody in the group was likely to disagree. They all looked up to Cooper, trusted his judgment, and were already used to his style of leadership.

Cooper spoke for a few minutes, trying to put things into perspective for everyone. "The path ahead of us will not be easy, but the world moves on. Some things are within our control, whereas others are not. The earthquake in India that killed 20,000 people is a perfect example of something we can't control, but has an effect on our world. I'm sure everyone saw that, last week; the FTC approved the merger of Time Warner and AOL. These big companies will continue to grow, and great technology will evolve. Another piece of technology news from last week: that Wikipedia thing that everyone has been talking about finally went live. Some say it'll be the next big thing. Who knows. Regardless, look how much technology is changing the world we live in."

A man in a black tuxedo, stylishly matched with a black shirt and black bow tie, spoke up at this point, "Sure, that makes sense, but what does that mean for us? Just look at the news. The 'Texas 7' that have been running amok since escaping from prison down in your neck of the woods were finally caught. Here, right here, in Colorado Springs, just a couple of days ago. How do we get from where we are now, with such a huge disconnect between the highest levels of society and the 'real' people on the street, to where we want to be, with everyone doing their part, and being held accountable when they don't?" The man's voice had grown steadily louder as he spoke, signifying the passion that he had behind his thoughts.

Cooper responded, and even with the deep Texas drawl he had, he commanded respect, "Listen, partner…" He paused, "it ain't gonna be easy. It's gonna take everyone in this room, and many others. You, me, everyone. Like I said a minute ago, I'm gonna focus on Texas, and what's best for Texas is gonna be best for what we're trying to do here. How are we going to get that done, you ask? Let's talk about specifics. My campaign was based on a few key concepts. Those weren't bullshit. They were the real things that we need to do, starting now. All of you know that Sam, Nikoli, and Bishop are where the rubber meets the road. They're the ones putting the structure to the plan, and I've been working with them for a very long time to make this happen. Remember a couple of years ago? I think it was P.J. O'Rourke that said that the Clinton administration launched an attack on people in Texas because those people were religious nuts with guns. Hell, religious nuts with guns founded this country. Who does Bill Clinton think stepped ashore on Plymouth Rock?" Everyone laughed at the comment. "The point is, let's be passionate, and forceful, but rational, and strategic."

Cooper motioned to Sam and Bishop, who had been holding court with 4 or 5 other party guests a few feet away. The whole group came over, and now it seemed like 30 or 40 people, standing in the room, waiting to hear what they had to say. The man in the black-on-black tuxedo was front-and-center, clearly anxious to hear what they had in store.

Cooper put his arm around Bishop's shoulders, and looked back and forth between Bishop and Sam, his eyes holding each of theirs briefly, then spoke, "Sam, Mike, let's talk about next steps, here. Everyone is anxious to start tying all of this together. This election is a major step forward, and we need to keep this momentum. Let's walk through how we do that, based on the discussions we've been having."

Bishop smiled widely. He was incredibly happy to be here, talking about what truly motivated him, and putting thoughts into action. He usually talked to only a few people at a time. His role was not to lead the masses; his was to motivate the leaders to then recruit the masses that agreed with the message. But tonight he knew this entire group was a collection of people that the leaders had already brought in, this group that was vetted, and confirmed as highly interested in this cause. So, a little out of character, he was chatting everyone up. This was great! "Sure."

He scanned the faces in this small crowd, and said, "As the Governor was saying, the election win was huge, and it puts us in a good position to make further progress, without some of the hassles we'd have if we hadn't won. The next steps will involve moving through several aspects of how society should work, if designed properly from the ground up. You'll recognize these topics, because they make up the majority of what Cooper's election platform was based on, as well as subject matter that has been discussed with you individually."

"I was just telling them that," Cooper said. "All this is well planned."

Samantha spoke up at this point, "That's correct. To do this right, we have to agree on many things about how a society should work. We're going to get together and discuss topics, in a particular format, to design and document what we're doing. We will work through things like foreign aid, education, the economy, energy, the Internet, homeland security, and welfare. We'll continue on with the legal system, criminal justice, and healthcare. Finally, who can forget taxes? Gotta get that shit fixed, huh?" The rapid change in character and tone made everyone chuckle.

"I'll be reaching out to some key people to start the planning process," Sam continued, "and I think the expectation goes without saying, but I'll spell it out: We have to have the utmost sense of urgency, while maintaining confidentiality. You have to maintain trust in the leadership here, and do what is asked of you, diligently. We aren't asking anyone to blindly follow. This isn't a friggin' cult, for Pete's sake, so ask questions in order to understand, debate what you don't agree with, and always stand up for what you, as an individual thinks is right, and we'll get it done."

A few people in the crowd nodded their heads as Samantha spoke. She was small and thin, but when she was 'in the zone' like now, she really commanded attention. She had presence.

Cooper made a few closing comments to reinforce key points and then he urged everyone to go enjoy themselves at the party. It would be a long time before so many of them would be able to get together like this again.

CHAPTER 17
RAW MATERIALS IN THE LAND

Friday, June 22, 2001 – 8:30 AM Central Daylight Time (13:30 hours Zulu Time)

Once Jackson Cooper was legitimately Governor of Texas, he was more able to get things done without other watchful eyes. No money, time, or other resources were ever taken from the citizens of Texas to plan and build the compounds that were being laid out across Texas, but it was the kind of project that needed the utmost secrecy. On this day, he was meeting Michael Bishop and Rex Morrison on a more remote part of King Ranch, down South, across from Padre Island. There was an outpost there that had been nearly completed. This would act as a surveillance jumping off point for some drones, and Padre Island would also eventually be utilized for some important strategic maneuverings.

King Ranch was founded in 1853 and covers 825,000 acres in Southern Texas with not all of the land being contiguous, but separated into four divisions: The Santa Gertrudis, The Laureles, the Encino and The Norias. It started as a cattle ranch in the Stanta Gertrudis division, the other divisions became known for other resources. Everything was here, from lumber to precious metals to enough agriculture to sustain Texas in the worst of outcomes, and the amount of planning that was going into safeguarding these resources was extraordinary. Norias, however was where the oil was. Not only would it be the ace up their sleeve for keeping the state up and running, but it also would be a key negotiating topic with the US as it is one of the US's top oil reserves and that is not something they would want to lose. A treaty might be able to be made for the US to be able to have some ownership rights for allowing a peaceful secession of Texas.

Bishop was standing outside of his BMW M5 when Cooper and Rex Morrison drove up in a beaten up pickup truck. Rex had not spent a lot of time with Bishop and thought he was too much of a city kid to understand the true value of King Ranch. Henrietta Chamberlain King was Rex's great grandmother; the land meant something to him. It wasn't just a piece of a complicated puzzle and he needed Michael Bishop to understand that. He, like Cooper, believed in the land for the sake of the land, and if Cooper was in bed with Bishop, ready to sacrifice what he loved and valued, he knew he could hear Bishop out. It was amazing but they were actually close in age. Rex had just taken over for his dad, Rex Morrison senior. His dad and Cooper went way back. Rex figured it seemed he had more in common with Cooper's generation than Bishop's, but he would reserve judgment until after this conversation.

"As much as I've researched this place, it still surprises me to see all the ranching and farming done on this land. I assumed its value was in the oil." Bishop said to Morrison.

"You drove here, Bish?" Asked Cooper, just shaking his head.

"Yeah, I wanted to get away for a while. The weather has been crappy for weeks in Cambridge and my research fellowship doesn't officially start until September."

"You probably want to be available to these people Michael. You were lucky to get asked to do this fellowship since you haven't finished school," said Cooper.

"Thanks, 'Dad'," Bishop said back to him a little annoyed, and a bit sarcastically.

Surprised, Rex asked, "You haven't graduated yet?"

"I haven't defended my dissertation for my Ph.D., and actually don't think I will. There are other issues that I want to concentrate on, how 'bout you?" Bishop asked, deflecting the attention off of him.

"He's a fellow Aggie just like me and his dad!" Cooper exclaimed proudly.

Wanting more, Bishop looked at Rex. "Undergraduate in Agriculture, specifically soil and plant management and masters in Agricultural Business, or what we like to call Agribusiness." Rex responded, feeling a little like he was on an interview. "Do I pass your test?"

"Ha," Bishop laughed. "Didn't mean to make you feel under any pressure. I just wanted to divert attention from my academic failings."

"So how about you, what did you study? Or rather what are your academic failings?" asked Morrison playfully.

"Double undergrad in physics and finance, masters in Physics. I was headed for my Ph.D. in physics, my dissertation being around something like quantum mechanics for small-molecule reactions within a finite space, but I really didn't flesh it out much."

"I don't even know what that means," said Morrison.

"Me either," answered Bishop winking at him. Bishop walked straight up to Morrison, put one hand on his shoulder and the other one out to shake hands and said, "If you choose to join us on a plight that I know you are already struggling with, you are as important as anyone else; school, no school, money, no money, just you, no ranch. I am looking for the people that can make the change and I believe you are one of them."

Shaking his hand, Morrison could feel Bishop's piercing eyes boring into his mind. He could see how genuine he was. Michael Bishop had the strangest way about him, and Rex didn't know what to make of him, but he knew he liked him. At that moment Bishop turned and started walking off. Looking at each other, Cooper and Morrison took that to mean follow him.

The three men walked and talked for hours. Bishop did his regular job of focusing on the new recruit, talking methodology, values, goals, both personal and what he saw for the future of the group. Morrison talked in detail about the four divisions, how they were split up and the resources and what quantities could be expected from each area. Cooper mostly listened to both men and interjected when there was a political question or conflict that might jeopardize Cooper's position in any way. Bishop answered questions, told some jokes, and quoted some song lyrics, which Rex didn't understand until Cooper explained the song game to him.

"I thought he was dumb as dirt with this dang game. I mean, don't we have important stuff to be talkin about?" Cooper said, explaining the concept to Morrison. "But it seems to relax everyone, and this group is so God-dang competitive, we've got an Indian fella listening to music constantly now just to keep up. But who am I to complain? It's fun in the lighter moments, but'cha never do any country so I miss most of 'em."

Bishop was just smiling, watching Morrison for any hints as to how he felt. Morrison was surprised at how much information he had given up. Not that it was a secret, more that he thought he would be more reserved in his decision, but as the men talked, his head and heart decided he was in before the man was conscious of that fact.

"Mike, you know how I feel. Jack wouldn't have had ya come all the way down here if I wasn't serious. I'm in, and anything and everything I can bring is in too. We have thousands of employees that we've managed to make like family and I want them to be taken care of in this. They are the busy, ya know what I'm sayin? They work harder than anyone I've seen for better lives, and they have since this place was founded. They'll see this as no different, something new and better to work toward."

They walked back to where they began. Bishop stopped at his trunk, disappeared behind it and came up with a handful of platte surveys and plans. "This outpost will be done in a few months, and thank you by the way for letting us get an early start on things. I'm thinkin we'll want to start excavating the east side of the Laureles next. I know there is some land that has been marked as unusable for your needs, but Rex if you would take a look at some of the surveys I've got, maybe you can make better sense of them than me. We need between 20-50 acres to do the underground facility correctly. There is some moderately mountainous and rocky areas, but that shouldn't be too much of an issue. It's just that some of the mineral samples are strange."

The men shook hands and Mike jumped in his car and headed off.

PART 6
LIFE AFTER, PREPARE (2001-2004)

CHAPTER 18
ACQUISITIONS, FOUNDATION

And so it began. From the beginning of 2001 to 2004 the goal was to acquire land in Texas while everyone continued their respective state of affairs. It started with the creation of one company: Deciplicatus Corporation. It was a twist on the latin words for 'ten' and 'fold,' and essentially meant that the number 10 would multiply by virtue of itself. It would be the only company used in the secession effort that had a name based on the AmendX movement. The scrupulous leaders of the movement were smarter, and less egotistical, than many others who would have named an empire of companies after themselves or their beliefs. Confidentiality was paramount, and everyone kept to that creed.

Deciplicatus was a classic shell company, designed to do nothing but create other companies. The children corporations that were spun off from Deciplicatus would, in turn, create other companies. This web of organizations was virtually untraceable, crafted by the knowledge and experience of those who had spent decades, even lifetimes, understanding corporate legal structure. Although Deciplicatus started with no assets, the child corporations received capital infusions from AmendX investors, leading to the capability to perform one specific task: purchase land in Texas.

The complex Trans-Pecos Natural Region includes Sand Hills, the Stockton Plateau, desert valleys, wooded mountain slopes and desert grasslands. The Basin and Range Province is in extreme western Texas, west of the Pecos River beginning with the Davis Mountains on the east and the Rio Grande to its west and south. The Trans-Pecos region is the only part of Texas regarded as mountainous and includes seven named peaks in elevation greater than 8,000 feet. This is where the land purchase began. The land was ideal for what they needed, which was mostly two things at this point, covert, strategic military stations to include training areas, and underground facilities to advance Sharma's technology efforts. This mountainous region was perfect because the terrain was often un-passable without knowledge of the area, and satellite surveillance could only see straight down, leaving tunnel entrances completely undetected. The nearly unlimited number of winding canyons and gorges left ample room for SOURCE's personnel to train in relative secrecy, and the disparity in altitudes added to the efficiency of their preparation. The fact that the region receives only 12 inches of rain per year ensured that the weather was almost always cooperative with training efforts, and the lack of precipitation also created subtle variations in ground temperatures, which further diminished use of satellite thermal imaging. The Trans-Pecos region represents over 31,000 square miles, and in the first year of land acquisitions, the Deciplicatus subsidiary companies had silently purchased more than 40% of that land. The acquisition companies used in this particular effort were set up primarily as mining companies, so that the excavation that was visible from above would appear justified.

Jackson Cooper was in charge of finding the land, and other lesser-known members did all the purchases. As Cooper was giving the instruction to buy this unique Trans-Pecos region, he thought of the secret Colorado valley of Galt's Gulch, from the book Atlas Shrugged, and chuckled to himself. He found himself wishing he had that valley's special machine that could hide the presence of this area from a world that seemed to be crumbling around them.

There were 13 military bases in Texas. Of those, six were Air Force Bases, four were Army, and three were Navy. As the land was acquired, the location of those bases was a key factor. Cooper knew that, to be successful, most of those bases would come into play at some point, either for or against their efforts. He preferred to have a plan to influence in the positive direction.

Halfway between Fort Worth and Midland lies Abilene, Texas. Just outside of Abilene is Dyess Air Force Base, home of the B-1B Bomber and the Spectre C-130 Gunship. Dyess housed 5,000 people, of which about 4,500 were military. This base was one of the first to have AmendX members at the top of the chain-of-command. Its 40 B-1B Lancer aircraft performed well as a nuclear deterrent, and upon inclusion into AmendX's plans, they would serve as both a deterrent and a bargaining chip for the group in their treaty negotiations with the US. The fearsome Spectre gunships would be called to use if necessary by unmanned aircraft used to fly air patrol over the Texas border. There is not a ground-based threat in existence that can stand up to the ferocity of its 40mm cannons. Further, the central location of the airfields, and essential security elements, made the base a perfect staging area for the Predator drones that would be used during the evacuation, and further protection, of Texas.

One little-known fact about Dyess Air Force Base is that it is known for being one of the most "green" AFB's in the country, and was the first Department of Defense facility in the country to utilize renewable energy. What made this so effective was tremendously efficient use of power generation technology. In essence, Sharma's technology had already been put to one of its most major tests. Although the base maintained a small power generation facility for the purposes of outside perception, the entire base actually ran on Sharma's boxes.

Cooper directed the Deciplicatus resources to purchase a significant portion of land surrounding Dyess, as well as throughout the entire Abilene area. From Sweetwater to Clyde, and from Stamford to Coleman, land was purchased. Central Texas was quickly and silently being added to the already-vast land resources of the movement.

Next was Lackland Air Force Base. Lackland is home to the lone entry processing station, which is used for Basic Military Training. It is primarily identified for its responsibility of being the only United States Air Force Base for this purpose. Everyone who signs up to join the Active Duty Air Force, Air Force Reserve and Air National Guard, will receive their training at Lackland AFB. This base is often called, "Gateway to the Air Force."

Since all personnel came through Lackland at one point, psychological screenings took place, and all files were stored there. For years, unbeknownst to recruits, the screening were used by key AmendXers to determine who would be the most suitable to participate in the movement, and who would be pressed into leadership positions in the Air Force. In addition, likely antagonists of the movement would be located outside the state at the time of the accident.

***

Other members continued to build their companies and maintain the status quo in their lives. 13-C was always coming up with something new, and 2001 was no different. This time it was some kind of way to track the use of digital music and a music player that was small enough to fit in your hand, and it held 1,000 songs. The day it came out, during a computer convention in California, Sam thought it looked very much like the unit Quinn had given her to transport large amounts of data. Like an external data drive, but different, it encrypted the data making the device very secure. Now it played music too? Nikoli helped a colleague launch a reference website that everyone could access, as well as edit. Anderson Glennis and Ryder Burns held a contest to stimulate interest in privately funded space programs. It was a multi-country contest in which the first person or group who came up with viable plans to launch a manned craft into space would e reviewed and then built by Glennis and Burns would pay for it, as well as make the winner a personal multi-millionaire.

In August of that year, following 43's announcement of federal funding for embryonic stem cell research, the science contingent in the group got into such a huge fight that it threatened to expose AmendX. Matthew Morris and Jason Thomas were the ones leading the scientific research group on many items and took charge when something had to be done within the scientific realm. Both men were extreme right-wing conservatives and often had vigorous debates with a few of the more liberal bunch, specifically Laura Bennett and Kevin Green. Once, when Bennett exploded over the stem cell research announcement, Morris thought having a woman on their side would help sooth the heated emotions, so he asked Ella Clark to join them. She was a Ph.D. candidate working primarily on evolutionary psychology, but her background and undergraduate work was more concentrated on biology.

"What does the bastard think he is doing?" shouted Bennett.

"He is allowing the continuation of a science that has proven to have incalculable benefit to medicine," answered Thomas.

"You guys! I'm so sick of hearing how pro-life you are, but you are all for using and destroying embryonic stem cells," continued Bennett.

"Whoa!" Chimed in Clark. "I hate to be the bearer of bad news, but first of all the stem cells are from discarded embryos and second if abortion were illegal, the opportunity to harvest even these stem cells from aborted fetuses wouldn't be possible anyway, so you can't have it both ways."

"The hell I can't," raged Bennett. "We are talking about two separate issues: a woman's right to choose, and hacking up an embryo to use these stem cells."

"Come on, you are a scientist, Laura. You can't be serious, you don't see how those two things are inextricably linked?" questioned Morris. "Overall, I am against this research, but there is a plentiful pool of discarded embryos that would be destroyed otherwise and as long as abortion is legal, it is nearly blasphemy to not use the byproduct of a terrible situation to help the already living and potentially suffering now. How can you say, 'yeah abortion should be legal,' but throw away everything that goes with it? Canada is already putting systems in place to use embryos from fertility treatments as well as abortions, and they are taking things one-step further. An associate of mine said they are equipped for embryonic cloning. That takes the controversy up a notch, wouldn't you say?"

"You're not a woman so I can't explain it to you. Having to go through an unwanted pregnancy for any number of reasons, I think we all know, is a daily torture in itself," said Bennett in a dismissive tone.

"That's bullshit, and you know it, Laura!" shouted Clark. "Last I checked, I am still a woman and I am whole-heartedly against abortion, period. What I will agree with you on, and there are some women that are far more rigid than me on the issue, some instances of an unwanted pregnancy does take a horrendous toll, but there are things that can be done to protect the biological mother and the baby until he or she can be adopted to a family that will loved and cared for. I am willing, however, to open up a dialog of termination when it comes to incest or a warranted medical reason that would risk the mother's life or the fetus anyway."

"How righteous of you." quipped Bennett.

Kevin Green looked a little embarrassed. Bennett wasn't even acting rational anymore and he was surprised because she was usually a levelheaded, logical scientist. This might have been hitting too close to home, he thought.

"This group will fight 43 on this, I can tell you that much," Bennett continued.

"I don't think so," said Clark. "Overall, the research is the right thing to do."

The fighting went on, back and forth for some time until Bennett couldn't take it anymore. She was overwrought that this group that she had been so loyal to could be this far from what she believed.

"That's it! I'm done. You, and this group can fuck off!" She yelled as she thundered out of the room.

Green stood up and shook a little bit as if to rid himself of the whole conversation. "I will talk to her once she has calmed down. But doesn't this scare you guys just a little?"

Standing up, Morris said, "What?"

"This is a perfect example of something that can polarize this group and if this can, how many other things can? It is issues like this that are causing the problems this country sees today."

Morris, again, said, "Well, I see what you're saying, but we have to act very differently about how things are handled and Laura spun out of control. There was no talking to her. She wouldn't budge from the hardest subject matter, meaning abortion, even when I tried to bring up other issues that we have to take under advisement and be aware of, so she has to be reeled in. But if I had to posit a guess, I would say true democracy will hold out. The group will be small enough that if most people want something one way, say this research for example, then it will have to be agreed upon, ya know? I'm sure this is something that is being discussed elsewhere, but I would also have to think issues like this are only the tip of the iceberg. But Matthew, you bring up a good point. Let's tuck this away to bring up later and find out what the plan is for handling this type of concern."

"Agreed." Concluded Morris, and with that the think tank of scientists took some needed time off.

***

On December 15th Samantha threw a holiday party at her parent's house in Menlo Park to get a few people from the group together, primarily to maintain closeness while also letting everyone interact with each other without it having to seem like they were responsible for deciding the fate of their futures. This night was to drink some champagne, catch up on what everyone had been up to, and to relax. Besides her guest list, her parents invited many people, to include childhood friends of both her and her brother. She was in her usual black, but this dress was really nice. The top was tight with a bateau or boat neckline and long, tight sleeves. The back was open all the way down to her waist in a 'V' shape. At the waist it belled out to an A-line, flowy skirt that stopped right at the knee. She wore her favorite holiday black pumps with Christmas red soles. The only other adornments she wore were a single strand pearl necklace her mother gave her, and a giant crystal cocktail ring on the middle finger of her right hand.

She had been seeing a man, Mason Lane, for a few months, yet he still knew nothing about the group. She met him at a dog obedience class. Her friend Allison decided to get a dog; Riley, a golden retriever and she was unequipped to handle how hyper he was. Years before, she had taken Sawyer for puppy kindergarten classes and he was such a good, mellow dog, he really didn't need much more. Riley had more energy than both Sam or Allison could imagine. Really, in the back of her head she thought, why didn't she just get a Saint Bernard, but not everyone was so enamored of the breed. She told Allison she would go to the first few classes with her to make her feel comfortable, and Mason had been there with his bulldog Angus. He was a really nice man who loved his dog and that really mattered to her. It was also nice that he was shockingly attractive. 6 feet 4 inches tall, good build, dark brown eyes and a bald head. She thought he was going bald, and had chosen to do the right thing, and instead of hide that fact, just shaved it all off. His head was bald, but his chest wasn't. Being Italian, she guessed gave him that machismo chest-wig that she would just have to deal with. If that were the worst of his qualities, she was certainly in the black. He was also not high maintenance. He was totally okay with the fact that she was always traveling around, and she did her best to make time for him whenever she could. He was in sales for a major tech company and his area was hospitality, so he focused on outfitting stadiums and arenas with his company's equipment, which meant he also traveled. At times they would meet up in different cities, but he was mostly the western region so they saw each other in California and Colorado. He was his own man and she got the impression that he saw other women when she wasn't around, but they never talked about it and when they were together he made her feel like she was the only one and that was all that mattered to her. She talked to Victoria about it once and she was more bothered by the fact that he may see other women than Sam was.

"How does that not bother you, Sam?" she asked.

"Why would it?" she answered. "Think about my life, V. It's not like I can expect anything from him. He doesn't know about the group, or about the fact that I just might not be here one day. Or even that when I am driving all over this country, I am actually helping plan a coup. A real relationship can't be built on the kind of moving platforms I am living on right now."

"Well," moaned Victoria. "I didn't think about it that way. I was thinking more like, you are a total homebody in the sense that you don't party, you both love your animals like children, you like a lot of the same things, he isn't clingy, and you love that. I thought he was a pretty great find."

"No offense, but knowing your choices in boys, I should run the other way." Sloan said cynically. "In all seriousness, he is great, but I don't get to do great, so let's say I'm borrowing great for now. With the way I have set my life up, it just isn't possible."

"Tell him about us, about the group, maybe he is one of us and then you can be honest," Victoria pleaded.

Letting out a sigh, "it hasn't been long enough for me to even test the waters of the group, let alone see if he is appropriate to being in. This isn't about me needing a partner. I have three of them, Mike, Nikoli and my sweet Sawyer. I am totally fine with spending time with Mason as it is now. Really, I believe he will be an Xer, but I don't think that has anything to do with the fact that I'm sleeping with him. Once Mike meets him, he will decide if we move forward with that part. Until then and completely separately, I will just enjoy him."

So tonight Mason was meeting Bishop and Nikoli for the first time, which was stressful enough, but also Derek Holden, Michael

Pearson and their spook contingent, who included Harlan Mackay, Harris Corrigan, Joseph Bailey, and William Brahe. She thought he would recognize them for sure and wonder why the hell she was hanging out with major military heads of our government as a psychologist from California. As an explanation, she was going with the story that they were acquaintances of hers through Bishop, and he knew them because of his childhood neighbor, Pearson. All true, she thought. Then she would let Bishop take it from there.

"I always thought you hated him," Nikoli said referring to William Brahe, a career politician.

"No, quite the contrary," Samantha replied. "He is unique in that he has the balls or guts, I should say, to say the things that need to be said. Or he just doesn't care enough to filter his thoughts when he has them and that offers me the opportunity to respond equally as unfiltered. How many times have you sensed a problem and it be pushed just to the edge of blatant but someone is passive-aggressive or unwilling to say what needs to be said and so the conflict just sits on top of every other situation like air pollution, which incidentally, I believe is more toxic than anything Brahe says."

Her brother Stuart was also in attendance with his new wife Camryn. They had been married for about nine months. Samantha attended the wedding and had been to dinner with them a few times since and always had a good time. But it was the same with Camryn that it had been with Stuart; while they were together, it was great, but in the times that they were apart, she sensed that if a get-together was planned, it was out of obligation, and both of them couldn't care less about Sam otherwise. She never confronted either about her feelings, so she couldn't blame them for anything. If it ever became a real issue, she would have to raise the subject. Stuart was in a very outgoing mood, he hadn't seen some of these people in years and seemed to really be enjoying their company, which made her think again...why does it take everyone else to put these functions together? If we didn't, we would never see him, she thought.

She turned around and saw Bishop talking to Mason. Yikes. She hadn't even had time to introduce them and they seemed deep in conversation. Should she walk over and interrupt? Should she walk the other way? She grabbed a glass of champagne and went around the corner of the room to watch, and not be noticed. The two men were dressed almost identically, both in black suits with white shirts unbuttoned with no tie. They both looked really good. Bishop looked younger, but Mason had this magnetism about him that was very appealing. As she was watching, Holden came up behind her and in passing, he said smiling, "It's not nice to spy."

She jumped and thought to herself, how ironic that it's Derek Holden who says that to me. She gave Derek the evil eye and went into another room where her dad had a group around him. He always had a group around him. Being an ex-NFL quarterback and current sportscaster, he had throngs of people always wanting to chat him up.

He saw her come into the room, "Here she is now. Can you believe her favorite team isn't even who I played for?" and, in an exaggerated tone, "She likes the *Patriots*!"

A few people laughed, a few people groaned.

"Yep," she said proudly. "Now that Belichick is with the Patriots, I love the Patriots. I liked the Jets when he was there, the Giants, the Browns...get the picture?"

"That's my girl," grabbing Samantha and giving her a one-armed hug. "She watches more football than my son. She has always loved it. But she likes the strategy and the system."

Sam rolled her eyes, but she had to admit, she liked that her dad was proud of her, even if it was for the wrong reasons. "Happy Holidays, everyone," she said as she walked off.

She knew she could hide out pretty well with Harris Corrigan. He and his wife were talking with Holden and his wife, Marie, as she walked up. They were, not surprisingly, talking politics.

"How's everyone doing over here?" she said, glancing in the direction of Bishop and Mason who were still talking.

"These two are impossible," said Marie, Holden's wife referring to Derek and Harris.

Sloan looked at her questioningly.

"You can't get them to not talk shop," Marie explained.

"We are trying to have a nice time, catch up on what the kids have been doing and what shopping we have left before Christmas and all they want to talk about is that new Patriot Act that got signed back in October," chimed in Lynnette Corrigan.

"Don't let her fool you Sam, she knows more about the intricacies of the act than I do," joked Corrigan.

"Yes, but I don't want to talk about it tonight, and that's the difference, honey."

"But isn't it a great thing to love what you do so much that you even talk about it at parities?" responded Sloan a little sarcastically and a little seriously.

"So true," answered Marie, glancing at her husband, the man who was always working.

At the same time, the group saw Dylan Sterling sitting alone in a small alcove of the house jotting notes down on a legal size yellow pad.

"Sterling is going to have a stroke, I swear," said Corrigan.

"What's the matter with him?" asked Sloan.

"He was asked awhile back to consult on possible illegal acts by Arthur-Anderson concerning their relationship with Enron," answered Corrigan. "He slaved on that gig and no one listened. I don't know the details but he was against some kind of way revenue was being booked, but Anderson said it was fine. All I know is now Enron is filing for bankruptcy and all hell is breaking loose. Dylan sees it as a personal affront to him and the US economy, he said."

"I'll go see if he is okay," said Sloan. "You guys better get these ladies some more champagne."

CHAPTER 19
OUTRAGE, SECURITY

Tuesday, September 11, 2001 – 5:53am Pacific Daylight Time (12:53pm Zulu Time)

It began with the phone ringing. Holden had been working on building SOURCE for almost 5 years, and had focused on international contracts, knowing all the while that it was a domestic incident that would be the growth catalyst for his organization. It was happening.

Grabbing the phone off the nightstand, quickly coming awake, he recognized the number on the caller ID as his VP of Operations, calling from SOURCE headquarters in Texas. "Holden" was all he could get out before being urged to turn on the television and begin following the events that were unfolding.

"This is real," he was told. "Looks like the North tower of the World Trade Center has been hit by an aircraft. The news is going crazy. This is going to be a mess. I'm mobilizing both offensive and support resources, and putting all locations on high alert. I'll keep you posted."

"Perfect. Thanks," said Holden, and hung up. As it would turn out, the senior leadership team at SOURCE would be one of the few groups that immediately understood the significance of the attack, and not be among the masses that assumed initially that it had been an accident. By the time Holden hung up, the calls were already going out to every SOURCE location in the world, using a precise protocol that would make any law enforcement agency in the world jealous.

Most importantly, Holden knew he needed to get back to the Texas headquarters. The plane had hit the first tower at 8:46 am Eastern time. SOURCE headquarters in Texas was in the central time zone, so 7:46am was when the wheels started turning there. Holden had been finishing on a trip in San Diego, where he was meeting with some of his Navy SEAL buddies to discuss a new training facility in southern California, so for him, the event took place at 5:46 am. He had received the call from SOURCE at 5:53 am. "Seven minutes... not bad," he said to himself as he quickly and efficiently loaded his belongings into his suitcase. In that amount of time, the event had taken place, had been identified, verified, categorized, and the notification process begun. He was instantly frustrated that he was separated from the action, but he had a high level of confidence in his team.

He was impressed, but not surprised, by the rapid reaction time that his team had displayed. As his organization had grown over the past few years, he knew that building the information-handling aspects of the business would prove to be equally important as building the military components. To that end, he had directed the construction of a state-of-the-art Security Operations Center (SOC). This facility was equipped with technology and personnel that focused on the collection of specific intelligence data, correlation of that data, and acted as SOURCE's first point of notification for any major incident worldwide. The SOC was tasked with 'command and control' responsibilities, and would be the central point to provide coordination for the deployment of any SOURCE resource. The 7-minute elapsed time from the event until his original notification was less than half of the 15-minute requirement that the government's own intelligence community had as a standard for themselves. To maintain a proper level of collaboration with the government, once an incident was verified and classified, if it exceeded a specific threat level, notification was passed to a group within the nation's intelligence community, a group that would someday become the National Counterterrorism Center (NCTC). This government entity served as the central point to get the information to all relevant government agencies. Thus far, the agency had not reciprocated on this behavior, but that didn't bother Holden, for the time being. He knew it was the right thing to do, and there was an ugly mass of politics to overcome if he wanted a government entity to give SOURCE, a private security firm, access to priority government data.

About 45 minutes later, Holden was in his rental car, headed for Texas. He had correctly anticipated that there would be issues getting a flight, and when the news of the impact of the second aircraft came through, it was confirmed that he had made the right decision to drive. He had 1,300 miles to go, and he wasn't wasting any time.

***

4 Days Later…

Holden had been back in Texas for two full days, and had been given the opportunity to digest all the intelligence data that his firm had to offer. He'd been able to soak in all of the information that his team had gathered about the group responsible, and how the attack had been coordinated. In the hours after everything had happened, the news media had gone nuts, and misinformation was rampant, but what else was new with the media and incorrect information being disseminated to an unsuspecting and oblivious public. Holden had faith that his team was able to sift through all the noise and extract just the information that was relevant and accurate.

He was sitting in a conference room in a local hotel with Bishop and Sam. His team had swept the place for electronic eavesdropping devices, and each of the three AmendXers had arrived at separate times, from separate directions. They knew that it would pay off to have discipline when it came down to operational security of their meetings.

"Tell us what you know," said Bishop. He had been the last to arrive, having been in Colorado when the whole thing went down. It had been four full days, and the FAA was just starting to allow commercial aircraft to fly in the US, so since he had been on a road trip of sorts, having driven to see Rex and Jackson in June, he had driven from Texas to Colorado where he spent the summer. His work, thus his presence, was not required in Massachusetts until later this month so now he would just turn around and drive back to Texas. Sam had been in Colorado as well, but left immediately upon knowing what happened, so she had arrived a few days ago. These days, her animal menagerie traveled with her everywhere, so she could just leave at a moments notice.

Holden jumped right into it.

"There were 19 hijackers, in total. Initial intelligence leads us to believe that these attacks have been in the planning stages for about two years. It's certainly al-Qaeda, if anyone's wondering. We think they only chose these targets a few months ago, though, based on how much time they had to prepare."

"From the hijacker perspective," Holden continued, "it looks like the dirt bags who played the primary roles, like pilot, had been in the US for anywhere from 12 to 18 months, with the others biding their time in Germany before making it over here earlier this year."

"How does this happen?" asked Sam. "It's not like coming across the US border is the easiest thing to do. We check passports. And there's a terrorist watch list, isn't there?" Her face had turned a darker, scarlet shade by this point. You could tell she was getting worked up.

"Complacency," was the only thing Bishop could say.

Holden responded as well as he could to her question, without going into the graphic details about border security. "We don't know yet how they got across, but Sam, you have to understand that to defend our borders properly, it takes an enormous sacrifice as a nation. You know how expensive it is to secure thousands of miles of borders between the US and both Canada and Mexico, as well as both oceans; and every fucking airport, large and small? It's ridiculous." It was Holden's turn to get worked up. "You want good border security? Check out Israel. They know how to do it in the no-bullshit way that I think we should use here by the time we're done. For the people that don't want to go through the hassle or expense of properly defending ourselves, and want everything to be convenient, easy, and cheap, STAY OUT OF TEXAS."

"Alright, you two, let's keep going over the facts and not get pulled into philosophy about border security that we all agree on anyway," Bishop said. "We have to make sacrifices to get to where we want to be, and Sam and I are just trying to understand where we stand from someone that knows the strategic side of something like this, you know what I mean Derek?" Bishop raised his eyebrows and looked at Holden.

Holden looked right back at him, clearly passionate, but totally in control. "Sure, Mike. I get it. The bottom line is that we have to have enough control over our society that we know who we're letting in, first of all. Second, we have to have a rational approach to the right to privacy. I'm the biggest privacy fan here, I guarantee it, but I also understand that there has to be a balance to allow us to monitor and stop this kind of bullshit. Thousands of dead people in a pile of rubble is not something I'm ever going to let happen on my watch. But the citizens are going to have to understand to have the right amount of the kind of security we are talking about, it can be invasive and inconvenient."

"Good," said Sam. "That's why you're here. You're the friggin' expert, for God's sake, and if you can't get it done, nobody can."

Bishop moved the conversation forward to practical matters. "I know there's a ton more information that's going to come out about this over time, but while that's taking place, what are some of the actionable things we can do to positively affect our preparations? I know there are people that are going to want to accelerate the schedule, but I think that would be a mistake. We can learn something from this sick shit and maybe all those lives will not have been lost for nothing." He stopped. Both Samantha and Holden could tell he was crushed by the event. He had the intelligence, surely, to know things like this can happen, but the heart and mind couldn't reconcile any of it.

Holden agreed that the plan should not move hastily forward because of this. He had spent the majority of his time over the past two days putting together just such a list as Bishop was asking about. The three of them took several hours talking about how over the next few years this plan would progress.

**

A month later life had still not returned to normal. Meeting a friend for lunch at the Houston home of fellow Xer, Paul Olson, Holden commented, "I expected people to brush off what happened faster than they have. Everyone is still moving around in a fog. I mean, usually people are in complete denial and just want to forget when something bad happens."

"This isn't just something bad Derek," Olson said. "This country has never seen the likes of this before, but we have to accept what happened and try to heal. It has been overwhelmingly positive at the church. Members are gathering in droves to volunteer and do whatever is needed. That is still the beauty of this country; we band together and it makes us stronger."

"It is just unfortunate that it takes these kinds of thing to make people remember that," Holden said shaking his head. "SOURCE is making sure the families of the fire fighters lost have what they need for now. But they have lost their loved-ones so we end up feeling so useless," he said while dismissing a call from his cell phone.

"You can never feel that Derek. Do you have to take that call?" In response to Holden shaking his head to go on he said, "There is nothing we can do to take away the heartbreak of these families, but what we can do is focus on the positive and the love and show them that we are here. That is all anyone can do."

The cell phone rang again. "Hang on, let me take this really fast, I will be right back," said Holden jumping up and leaving the sunroom they had been sitting in.

Five minutes later Holden returned. "That was Quinn, you guys have met right?"

"Yeah, a couple of times, but I don't know him well at all," answered Olson.

"Well, 13-C, his company is rolling out a new product that is supposed to revolutionize the world with respect to music, a music player of some kind, but the board thinks maybe they should hold off because of everything that has happened. Quinn doesn't want to, largely because I think he has been working on this for so long, he wants to get some closure, also because it allows him to stay busy and not internalize the immensity of it all. I mean he actually got pissed at someone when he couldn't use his plane to get to New York a couple of days after it happened. He needed to get his designer back to California. His wife told me later that if he stopped to really think about what happened she thought he would just collapse."

"Wow, I understand that. He comes off a little harsh anyway, I've heard, so that probably didn't help. But so do you Derek, and I know you and you aren't anything like people think."

Holden smirked, "Part of that is intentional, and the rest is just people assuming things they know nothing about. Quinn can be a real asshole and he doesn't even care, but this...this made him take a pause."

"So why is he calling you about a product launch?" asked Olson.

"Oh, yeah, it is something we've been using for awhile and he wanted to borrow one of my guys to demonstrate how easy it is to use. He is pretty theatrical during his keynote talks I guess."

"You have been using it personally, or at SOURCE?"

"SOURCE," answered Holden confused.

"Why would SOURCE be using a music player?"

"Oh, we've used it in a different capacity."

"I don't get it," said Olson frustrated.

"Let me back up. The device was originally purposed for data storage, making it be able to hold large amounts of data in a small, portable package and easily retrieved by the user, with password protection, encryption and all other kinds of layered security of course." explained Holden.

"And what does that have to do with music?" asked Olson.

"That is actually where it gets funny…I guess an exec blabbed to some low level designer at a company function and the designer goes home and dreams up a music player with the same basic framework and actually got to Quinn to pitch it to him. Quinn hated it at first and threw him out of his office. Two days later, he is tracking down this guy giving him a huge promotion saying it was going to change the world."

"I'm not all that technical but it sounds interesting I guess, I mean, I'm fine with my cd player," said Olson.

"Hmmph, I like music as much as the next guy," Holden said palms up, "but this guy bleeds over this shit."

With a raised eyebrow over the language Olson said, "reminds me of someone else I know."

"I have to be detailed Paul," rolling his eyes, "the equipment I deal with is very sophisticated and requires precision, so the guys I have working on this stuff," he said enunciating the word stuff, "have to be meticulous."

"So does he apparently, just in a different industry," Olson said standing and motioning for Holden to follow him into the house for lunch.

CHAPTER 20
ASSOCIATIONS, EVALUATE

2002 basically didn't exist for the group, or at least very little was done to forward the cause. Everyone focused on their outside lives and maybe tried to convince themselves things were getting better. Samantha's year started out quite nicely. As a Christmas present the previous year, Nikoli got her Super Bowl tickets for the New England Patriots and St. Louis Rams, so with animals in tow, she drove down to New Orleans and spent a couple of weeks doing all the touristy things, drinking Café au Lait and eating beignets at the Café du Monde, she took a riverboat cruise, went on plantation tours, hung out in the French Quarter, and ate like a queen. The game was fantastic. The Patriots beat the Rams 20-17. She had a blast! She could barely talk for a week afterwards because she was so hoarse from yelling. Sharma was assisting NASA once again on work relating to a Mars mission and a malfunction on its imaging probe. As much as he hated the bureaucracy that engulfed NASA, he couldn't help himself, he was always there to help. Many of the members got together in February to watch the Winter Olympics and cheer on the American teams, which brought about much waxing philosophical about how things would be without a country to root for. The common consensus was even though the break would, in fact, make them another country, they would always be Americans and would always be able to root for the teams that they wanted…even the girl that was secretly hoping the Russian skate team would win. The fact of the matter was that those athletes were exactly the kind of people this group did root for, in every walk of life. They were the ones that worked beyond exhaustion for something they really believed in. So much negative was always discussed, sometimes it was hard to keep the original intent in mind. This endeavor was to be able to start fresh with hard work, ethics, empathy and honesty and yes, even idealism. It was to let those weighted down by the fat, lazy grind to shine again. Dylan Sterling was also busy consulting for the Federal government team overseeing the WorldCom Chapter 11 bankruptcy filing. He was so disgusted with what he seeing during this case, it made him all the more zealous in putting together an economy package that would speak to this kind of financial delinquency in the simplest, most straight-forward terms. He would joke that even the top MBA's in the country would be able to understand his package. He was also dead set against the new Sarbanes Oxley Act being signed into law, as he thought it was just another "treacherous bulk of words without masters to confuse everyone it governed." He believed there were more efficient ways of making sure the deleterious acts of these criminals like Enron, Tyco, and now WorldCom could be handled rather than a new set of guidelines to challenge them to try to find a way around.

One short-lived but devastating rumor that swept through the group was whether or not the Beltway sniper was, in fact, a member of AmendX. It was unclear how the rumor got started but the gist was that a decorated ex-SEAL had gone off the rails and was the man authorities suspected of being the sniper that started his killing spree in October. The correct part was the man that the Xers were talking about was an ex-SEAL and absolutely part of the group. The incorrect part was that he had gone crazy, and yet the bigger blunder was believing that he was the sniper. The conversation that ensued quelled rumors fast.

"Alfie Scott? Fucking, please!" Huffed Mackay. "This needs to be shut down right here, right now. If the media gets a hold of this... you know they are clamoring for anything right now. They will print anything and it will fuck us up supremely, not to mention ruin Alfie's life."

"I hate to even ask, but we've known weirder and worse things to happen," Sloan started in.

"Don't," replied Mackay. "He was vetted completely so many times his ass is raw from so many people being up it investigating. I have no idea how this started, especially about Alfie of all people, but it's over, right now. Get the word out."

"Yeah," scoffed Bailey. "Besides if he was the guy, Holden would go end him himself...there is no way." Not one to ever agree with something that made Holden look good or be shed in a positive light, Bailey knew this was as far-reached as it got.

Bishop sat motionless and said nothing. This was not his area of expertise and he knew it. He let the guys that did these kinds of things for a living figure it out. Nikoli's eyes darted back and forth uneasily to the men talking. There were homeland security guys there, NSA, some domestic preparedness guys there that all seemed to never look directly at you. All of these guys were the real deal, he thought and he was glad to have them in the group, but he never wanted to cross them…that part he knew.

"Get ahold of both of them. First Holden and ask if he has any thoughts about how this could have started. Then make sure as shit that they are both safe. Get them to one of the think tank spots for some R & R until this is over. I have a meeting to get to," finished Mackay.

Scott had been Holden's right hand man while building SOURCE. He knew him from his SEAL days. They went through the program one after the other and since the participants usually went from about one hundred guys to about 15, many of the graduating classes got a chance to know each other. Scott was extraordinarily smart and even more so peaceful and patient; two qualities that complimented Holden's strengths because he certainly wasn't peaceful or patient. Once he was in the group he was the second in command when Holden couldn't be two places at once. With the massive groundwork and construction being done, Holden had to have someone he could trust.

The rumor started and ended within the group. It never made it outside to the media or anyone else that could jeopardize the group's security. Two weeks later the real killers were arrested. Samantha didn't like how quickly this rumor got started and took it upon herself to start touring the sites where large groups resided to keep a feeling camaraderie and well-being amongst the members.

***

Unlike 2002, 2003 started up fast and proved that things were changing, but not for the good. Holden was never around, as he was working in underground bunkers and overseeing the manufacturing of the first fleet of drones. Along with the Needham brothers, and Anderson Glennis, Holden had been collaborating for years to have superior surveillance capabilities via the cameras on board the drones, as well as radar for both perimeter detection and target-locking capabilities. Holden's expertise brought weapons and strategies, Glennis' aviation talents were unmatched, and the Needhams manufactured everything everywhere so could easily hide the creation of certain parts to be assembled later in Holden's favorite underground facilities just South of Midland, Texas. It was the second largest facility next to the Trans-Pecos, but it had all the great toys. Antonio Montes spent a good amount of time there as well. He and Sloan worked there occasionally, going over some kind of studies relating to prison inmates and using the Texas inmates in high-risk work capacities. Holden overheard Sloan citing a study that said certain kinds of prisoners could, in fact, flourish and be quite capable given a second chance to work within legal settings. Frankly, it sounded horrible to Holden, and he didn't have time anyway, so when they were around, he went over schematics to improve sight lines of the drone operators to make them as visually complete as they were tactilely responsive. Holden had been in a great mood since late January and the announcement of the creation of the U.S. Department of Homeland Security. He believed it was in direct response to some well-intentioned advice from the group. Others in the group thought it was coincidence. It didn't matter at the end of the day, he thought, because security was finally getting some attention. This country was getting too fat and happy and one day we are gonna get picked on.

Friday, February 1, 2003 – 5:15 PM Central Standard Time (23:15 hours Zulu Time)

Making his way back to Austin from Midland in his car after many planning days with some of the leadership, Cooper was listening to the radio, relaxing and getting some much needed downtime in during the five-hour drive. A somber DJ came on to report like he had done each hour since its occurrence, that the shuttle Columbia had disintegrated over east Texas killing all seven of its crew. The Governor made calls to all concerned and scheduled a call to the President to see how he wanted to handle a memorial and reaching out to the families of the deceased.

Friday, March 14, 2003 – 4 PM Central Standard Time (16:00 hours Zulu Time)

Holden, Cooper and Christian Adams were in the car going to the Four Seasons in Austin for a rare sit-down with Antonio Montes. They were talking about the newly formed Department of Homeland Security and how their friend Mark Gonzales would fit into the new structure. Adams was genuinely in town to have some meetings with the Governor so no bait and switch had to occur. They just made some time to do other things as well.

"The Secret Service is under Homeland Security now, Gonzales just got moved into one of the details. I wonder how this new department will really run," said Holden, thinking out loud.

From the backseat, Adams asked, "how long has Gonzales been with the Secret Ser…" cutting off his question he yelled, "God I hate this song, my daughter is crazy over it and plays it constantly!"

It was a song from Jennifer Lopez that had recently hit number one on the charts. Turning the radio off and annoyed with the distraction, Holden got enough of the question to answer. "Five years, so he is a relative newbie, but real smart and a hard worker… if he does well he might get on a direct detail in a year or so."

"Is that wise?" asked Cooper. "That puts him with zero degrees of separation from the President. Others might think he is the one getting the notes across and put him in a tough position because he knows about them."

"What?!" Holden exclaimed and then remembered. "Oh, that's right. Bishop had a long talk with him and they decided he wouldn't have any contact with us for quite some time, that's why he hasn't been around, plus he never had anything to do with the notes. Essentially since he needed TS-SCI full poly, he couldn't know anything so he could answer truthfully. We are…"

Cooper interrupted, "what in the world did you just say?"

Adams laughed, "it is the level of security clearance he needs. After you say these things a thousand times, you acronym everything. It means Top Secret, Secure Compartmented Information, and on top of that, includes a full polygraph."

Cooper saw Holden looking at him like he was a moron for not knowing this. He let it go.

Adams continued, "Speaking of security, what are we walking into when we meet with Montes?"

"Not much. He is a bit ahead of us with the changes he wants to make in his country, but hasn't started executing them yet," Cooper answered. "He moves around this country pretty much unabated, but that will change soon so he wants to get as much done here as possible before that. He is such a hard worker with an unmatched work ethic, he insisted on coming to Austin to find a way to help the group besides just financially."

"And what does he want to focus on?" asked Adams.

Cooper responded. "His top three are how we are going to deal with Homeland Security, that is why you're here and the agenda for today. You just have to give him high level strategy, no details about your current work, and then you can give him all the information he requires about how we are going to handle Texas. The economy, which he will be working with Sterling and a couple of other folks in Colorado in a few of months, the law/criminal justice type stuff, which he and Sam are going to tackle bringing in whoever needs to be brought in at the time."

They were silent for a few moments while Holden and Adams absorbed Montes support and involvement. "Did you hear they found that Elizabeth Smart girl?" Cooper asked pulling the car over to let Holden and Adams out a few blocks away from the Four Seasons on San Jacinto Boulevard. Christian Adams would likely not be recognized with Cooper but someone was always snapping a picture, so he would valet alone and the others would meet him in the room.

"Yes!" Exclaimed Adams. "That is fantastic news. After nine months I don't think anyone expected her to be found alive. I am so happy for her family."

Once in the hotel suite the men got down to business. Adams had with him a report on defense and homeland security that fully integrated with the package that Corrigan and Mackay had put together to present in preparation for the future conferences. Antonio Montes was polite and offered his guests refreshments that were on a table next to a floor to ceiling window in the main room of the suite, but it was obvious he was anxious to get to work.

Holden poured himself a glass of water and sat down at the table also ready to work. Cooper got off of a call and grabbed a pastry and a cup of coffee. He sat down as Adams floated a copy of the report to him across the table.

"I figured it would be easier for everyone to just read the report and then I can directly answer any questions that might come up," said Adams matter-of-factly.

"That sounds great Chris. I may have to excuse myself throughout this meeting. There are some state issues I have to make sure get addressed today, so please continue on without me if need be," said Cooper looking at each man.

Nodding, Montes said, "That is acceptable. If you need some privacy there is a small workspace we have set up in the second bedroom off to the left that one of my assistants has been using. Feel free to use it."

"Thanks Tony," said Cooper as Montes grimaced. Antonio Montes was a proud Mexican man. He was named with the traditional Spanish naming convention and Tony was not a part of it. In America, he simplified it to make things easier; Antonio, his given name. This also happened to be his father's given name, and Montes, his father's surname or maiden name. His whole name, Antonio Carlos Montez Nieto, confused many, so he shortened it to the more American custom using his first given name and father's surname. Carlos was his second given name from his beloved maternal grandfather, and Nieto was his mother's surname. Cooper loved to shorten names. He understood why; it conveyed a closeness and familiarity, so he didn't protest. Still, he was un-assuaged with it.

The men all got quiet as they read the report:

Defense is run through the government but was created by SOURCE (Section 1) so other military quadrants follow the same naming convention; Army - Section 2, Navy - Section 3, Air Force - Section 4, Marines - Section 5. SOURCE is private, however Section 1 is the governmental arm that oversees Sections 2 – 5 and is the division to which the Chairmen of the Joint Chiefs belong.

There are many facets of security that apply to our new nation. Sometimes we refer to these under the heading of Homeland Security, whereas sometimes we use the term National Defense. We're all familiar with the term National Security, as in, "keeping this secret is in the interests of National Security." Regardless of what term we use, what we're really talking about is keeping the people of our nation safe. This primarily encompasses safety from a physical perspective, but also means safety from cyber threats.

To act properly on these guiding principles, the scope of Homeland Security shall begin with our nation's ability to defend its borders. We're really talking about two borders here: the border with the US, and the one with Mexico. The border between Mexico and Texas is about 1,200 miles long, and has dozens of existing border crossings. The border with the US is about 1,500 miles long, and is shared with New Mexico, Oklahoma, Louisiana, and a tiny bit of Arkansas. There's about 350 miles of coastline that needs to be defended as well. What does that mean for us? The three border regions (Mexico, US, and coastline) require three different strategies. In all, with over 3,000 miles of border, we need to be very creative about how to approach this. We have our standard resources, provided by SOURCE, to contribute to this task. We will also have control of about 10,000 Marines, 100,000 Air Force personnel, 150,000 Army soldiers, and about 45,000 personnel from the Navy that will convert to the aforementioned names. Those 300,000-plus military personnel will be stationed and present in Texas at the time of the event. In addition, the largest joint military exercise in decades will be taking place at the same time, requiring an additional 350,000 troops to be present, headquartered out of Goodfellow Air Force Base. The total personnel in-state will exceed 1/3 of the combined US Military, and due to the nature of the exercise, will incorporate approximately 80% of the military's command structure. Having said that, no one will be held against their will once the proverbial dust settles. Those who want to will be allowed to leave through very small, specific areas of the border.

At present, the US Air Force has about 5,500 aircraft, many of which are deployed for international missions. In Texas, we will have direct control of more than 1,800 aircraft. Although this represents less than a third of the total, it is especially significant in that Dyess AFB is home to both the B-1B Bomber and the C-130 Spectre Gunship. Dyess AFB also has the capability to operate as the command-and-control center for Texas' fleet of Predator, Reaper, and Global Hawk drones. Between the Spectre gunships and the Predators, our military forces will be able to fly extraordinarily effective air patrol of the Texas border, and the shoreline. These forces will leverage Texas' six Air Force bases, four Army bases, and three Navy bases to serve as the foundation of the response capabilities. Finally, the underground facility now in place, and built entirely by SOURCE, will serve as the main Texas command-and-control center for all forces.

Note: With respect to drones, of the approximately 7,000 drones possessed by various agencies in the US, just under 5,000 of these will be located in Texas at the time of the event. More are being manufactured by SOURCE now, as well as new ones being designed and then built. Unmanned Arial Vehicles (UAVs) will be a central strategy for observing and defending the borders. These aircraft will take on full responsibility for C4ISR duties (Command, Control, Communications, Computers, Intelligence, Surveillance, and Reconnaissance), as well as performing key offensive and defensive operations.

Never will so many troops, so much firepower, and such a level of strategic capability be concentrated in such a small area.

The role of specific military bases is critical to the success of the mission. As stated earlier, Dyess AFB is a major player. There is not a ground-based threat that can stand up to the Spectre's 40mm cannons. Also, the B1-B bomber is essential for US national defense, and plays a key role in the nuclear deterrent strategy. This bomber base will be a negotiating point to get the US to the table in treaty negotiations. Of the 450 Inter-Continental Ballistic Missles (ICBM) still currently active, more than 180 are controlled from Dyess. Sharma's boxes are to be used here. Unknown to the general population, this Air Force base's reputation for being green, and the use of renewable energy, is actually based on use of these boxes.

At the time of the mobilization and the staged event to be discussed later, there will be a military joint training exercise in progress. Members of the military will be training with source operators at Goodfellow, and the majority of forces will deploy from this point. Its proximity to the center of the state will serve well as a deployment point.

All Air Force personnel came through Lackland Air Force Base at one point, since it is home to the Air Force's Air Education and Training Command (AETC). Because of this, Lackland is home to the lone entry processing station, which is used for Basic Military Training. Lackland is primarily identified for its responsibility of being the only United States Air Force Base for the enlisting BMT. Everyone who signs up to join the Active Duty Air Force, Air Force Reserve and Air National Guard, receives their training at Lackland AFB. This base is often called, "Gateway to the Air Force." Psychological screenings took place at that time, and *all files are stored there. For the past several years, unbeknownst to new recruits, screenings have been taking place to determine who would be most suitable to participate in AmendX, and who would be pressed into leadership positions in the military. In addition, likely antagonists of the movement would be located outside the state at the time of the event, or held until arrangements can be made to move them across the border.*

With respect to Army bases, Fort Bliss, home to the US Army Air Defense Artillery Center, and also headquarters for the 1st Armored Division, will initially be key to the ground forces available to Texas. This focus will shift to Fort Hood, TX, because of the 1.2 million acres that Fort Bliss occupies, 90% is located within New Mexico, not Texas. Fort Hood, on the other hand, is centrally located. Home to the 1st Cavalry, the AH-64 Apache helicopter, and the M1 Abrams tank, this base will be the central Army installation. Although forces will initially be mobilized out of Goodfellow AFB, this base will house the majority of the ground forces for the Texas military.

Fort Sam Houston, in San Antonio, will contribute strategically. It hosts the headquarters of the Army North and the Army South. The same goes for the Medical Command headquarters, not to mention the recruiting brigades and training schools.

Coastline defense will be headquartered out of the Naval Air Station, Corpus Christi. NAS Corpus Christi is located in the Nueces County, only 10 km from Corpus Christi. It is also referred to as Truax Field. The most important unit at NAS Corpus Christi is the Chief of Naval Air Training. The base is also the home of the Training Air Wing 4. Four squadrons are hosted here as well. Two of them are primary – VT 27 and VT 28, while the other two are advanced – VT 31 and VT 35. Seven associate or tenant units inhabit this station, the Navy Operational Support Center being the most important one.

Beyond just defending the borders, it is important to consider the other aspects of Homeland Security, namely biological and nuclear security, intelligence, cybersecurity, and managing proper security for those traveling to and from Texas. With the huge concentration of military leadership, and the far-reaching capabilities of SOURCE, the load for the remainder of Homeland Security and National Defense will be shared. Intelligence and incident management will be based out of the SOURCE command center in Austin, whereas transborder security will be run from Dyess AFB, along with the rest of the border security functions. Details as to the other auxiliary security management can be found under an appendix at the end of this report with its corresponding name.

Montes sat quietly as the other men finished reading the report, then discussed some of the intricate details. These men would be ultimately responsible for how their new nation would be protected. With Cooper's leadership, Holden's strategy and firepower, and Montes' finances and unmatchable intellect, Texas was in good hands. Adding to this was Adams' extraordinary ability to 'connect the dots' which proved to be a valuable glue to hold the whole strategy together.

Adams looked up and said, "Horrifically difficult decisions need to be made to make this country safe. If the media portrayed the truth about what is going on in these third world countries, the public policy would change so fast on killing 'innocents' it would make our heads spin. These women, children and everyone else labeled 'innocent' know where land mines are, most of them are armed if they aren't actually in Al-Qaida, and the ones that aren't connected hate us! They hate us with white-hot intensity, so they would sooner see us dead than occupy their area. There really are some innocent people that would be killed in the crossfire. But if Yemen was taken out or at a minimum the non-populated hills of Yemen, anti-American terrorists would think twice about attacking this country. They count on us not playing their game. Obviously the goal is never to kill innocents like children, but unfortunately, their parents are teaching them that we are the enemy and they will kill us just as fast as look at us, so it becomes a choice - me or you; that is the disgusting truth about these conflicts."

Holden nodded and continued what Adams was saying, "We *must* fortify our own borders first. We *must* send a message of our strength to our every enemy. And most importantly, it is not a moral issue, it is a safety requirement of our own people; when they fight in the new ways outside of the Geneva Convention and any other compact that restricts fighting methods, we have to fight the same fight. It is not an issue of being better people, taking the higher ground. It is not higher ground to let our soldiers die when they are fighting a war with different sets of rules, and when our men and women die that result only strengthens their cause."

Wednesday, March 19, 2003 – 11:34pm Eastern Standard Time (Thursday, March 20, 2003 – 4:34 hours Zulu Time; March 20, 2003 – 6:34am Baghdad Time)

It had been a crazy week. Quinn was in Washington DC, doing some due diligence research on a small software company he was considering buying, and adding to the 13-C portfolio. He had decided to treat himself, and had booked a room at the Hay-Adams Hotel. It could certainly be seen as luxury accommodations. Quinn loved the history of the hotel and the history made by those staying in it. Built in the 1920's, the Hay-Adams was as much a landmark as the celebrated monuments it neighbored. Upon walking into the lobby one immediately got the sense of grand style and elegance with the mahogany columns buttressing the ornate curved arches and inlaid ceilings. The hotel was not very large like some of the hotels in New York, but it was opulent. His room was on the 5th floor, and decorated with time-appropriate draperies and furniture that befit a king. The room looked across H Street, through the park, directly at the White House. It was a beautiful view, especially at night, with the White House all lit up.

He sat with a glass of cabernet in his hand, feet up on a chair, enjoying the view. He had been working out of his hotel room all day, so he was surprised to see significantly more activity around the White House than he had seen during the day. He wondered what could be going on. There were a bunch of people on the roof that hadn't been there before, and two helicopters had landed on the North Lawn in the last half hour.

He stood up and walked out onto the small balcony. Glancing up to the floor above, he was amazed to see a huge cluster of microphones pointed at the White House, and several cameras. They looked permanently mounted there, in plain sight. The obvious nature of these devices led Quinn to believe that the 6th floor, being the top floor of the hotel, may be used exclusively for media companies. He would later learn that he was correct, and that the floor was permanently leased by major news outlets.

He flipped on the television, and turned to CNN. It didn't take long to find out what was going on. A huge banner across the screen read, "WAR - US INVADES IRAQ." Apparently, about an hour earlier, several countries, led by the US, had invaded Iraq by forming a coalition, and coordinating attacks on Iraqi oil fields, military bases, and were headed toward Baghdad. The shit had surely hit the fan. Now, the activity around the White House made more sense.

As he looked outside, he could see that Pennsylvania Avenue in front of the President's residence had been completely sealed off. Rather than functioning as one of the most popular tourist photo spots in the country, it was surrounded in yellow police tape, and was occupied by no-nonsense looking uniformed Secret Service agents, loaded for bear. It would be a long night for folks in the West Wing, he thought to himself, but certainly not as tough of a night as was being had by our soldiers with orders to find Saddam Hussein.

Tuesday, July 15, 2003 – 7:00 PM Pacific Daylight Time (Wednesday, July 16, 2003 – 02:00 hours Zulu Time)

Away from everyone, sitting outside on the deck Tim Conrad and Nikoli Borodin were discussing the latest news to hit the tech industry. Somewhat good for Nikoli, he wanted to get a read on his competitor, as well as a friend's point of view.

"So what role will you play in the new Foundation since Netscape has been disbanded?"

"I played such a minor role in the company anyway since the sale to AOL/Time Warner. It was really just an advisory role, and now they really just need my name, so frankly it doesn't affect me at all," said Conrad, clearly downplaying the news.

"I'm surprised you didn't have to be there for the announcement," said Borodin, goading him to say more.

"Like I said, not a big role," Conrad replied in amusement, "and I know what you are trying to do Niki, and it's not going to work."

Standing and gesturing for Conrad to do the same, Borodin said as they walked inside to join the conversation, "You suck. What is wrong with trying to get some inside information from the competition?"

Sitting at the round dining room table, Bailey looked directly to Sloan, "Without us taking action, what gives you this idea that things have any chance of getting better? We, as a society, have done nothing to create accountability."

Bishop just sat back listening, Bailey continued, "We have put all our attention on what not to do, and when offenders offend, kids are bad in school, or just about any other negative consequence, that is what gets the attention. If you think there is a version of things getting any kind of better based on that type of behavior, then you are just naive. I didn't join this group to continue with the status quo, and just hope things get better here. I'm sick of it, I'm ready to go."

It was rare that this many of the top leadership of the group were in the same place at the same time. Only today, it was just a think tank tossing around ideas. Just one normal weekend day, the group gathered together at Sloan's vacation home, in Mystic, Connecticut. So much was going on, the military bunch were dealing with a war, others were buried in work relating to the group's building efforts in Texas, while still others were becoming successful in the "regular" world, proud of their efforts and skills.

"Well that actually does make sense, the human brain is geared toward the negative," Sloan said, sitting up in the armchair she was previously lazily sitting in, interested in what Bailey had to say for the first time in a long time. "But why are you directing that at me? What I meant earlier is that things cannot keep going down hill at this rate or frankly there will be a line at the proverbial door of Texas wanting to join us."

"Not everyone knows about our brain chemistry or how it works Samantha. All I can tell you is that we, as a society, put the attention in the wrong place. I don't know how to change it, I'm not even sure that it can be changed, but we need to do something as a species not just a country or we are doomed. And I don't think we should be waiting around for anymore failures, I think we should do this now and ask questions later," retorted Bailey.

"It is always about the brain with Sam," snickered Borodin.

Samantha just looked at him with her famous look of displeasure.

"I have to kinda go with Joe here, but if we aren't ready we aren't ready," chimed Conrad.

From a bar stool across the room, Bishop smiled, "that is why you are in the group Joseph. We need that insight; we need everyone's insight if we are going to make any positive change. But we can't just fly off we aren't ready. There would be way too much blood shed, more than any of us deem acceptable, as if any is."

Joseph Bailey rubbed most people the wrong way. He was gruff, politically incorrect to the point of being rude, socially awkward, and as a rule of thumb, pissed off at everyone. He held a very important position as the Assistant to the President for Homeland Security and the position fit him perfectly. He was hyper-vigilant and he believed most people were out to screw you. He thought the 'youngsters' that started this movement were gullible and accepting at face value what people told them, yet brilliant at the same time. He thought it his responsibility to tell them how the world really works. He was amazed, however, at their success navigating their respective worlds. They were each intelligent, and got the job done at all costs within the confines of integrity. They were puzzles to him that he could not fit together.

Sitting next to Bishop at an adjacent bar stool, Rex Morrison Jr. chimed in in his thick southern drawl, "well I would expect an entire culture shift would have to occur. Americans are the most dichotomous people on the planet. Most would give you the shirt off their backs. They are hard working for the most part when there is a goal in mind, holy moly look at our Olympic athletes. I challenge anyone in this room to find harder workers. But that is the elite, think of the farmers, I've seen some of them work, and they got me beat every time. But then our obesity rate is epidemic, our schools are failing, and the ones that do succeed scholastically seem to make the least. We are not prioritizing the right things. If we could somehow show the kids of today it was cooler to be the star of the science fair instead of just like their heroic, steroid-pumping baseball player, we might get somewhere. If we showed our girls that their minds were more important than their make up, their bodies, and what handbag they carry, maybe that Kardashian show wouldn't be so popular. I just turned on the TV the other night to get the news and saw a commercial for that show over and over. Maybe they would use their energy for something more if we showed them other things to strive for. But until we stop giving mixed signals to our kids, that will never happen."

Michael Pearson was tolerant of Bailey, but sick of his haphazard behavior. Professionally he was concise and methodical. Why couldn't he be that way in his personal life, he thought. Standing between the kitchen and the great room, leaning against the wall,

Pearson said, "Joseph, we aren't even close to being ready. How can we ask a group of people, one hundred or a million to follow us if we don't even know what we are going to do yet? How are we going to fix the problems that Rex just pointed out, and myriad other ones that we haven't even discussed yet? You are making people anxious and I can't have that. Christian called me the other day on his last nerve. He has enough to deal with since the Hussein regime was taken down a couple months ago, he doesn't need you chirping in his ear, and it does no good for anyone else either. Bring some of your professional sensibilities to this and let's start carving out our plans in a more fixed way, and then when the day comes we will be ready, more ready than anyone would have imagined."

Pacing all around the room, "I actually have a different take on all of this," said Nikoli Borodin. "I see a wonderful country, a place with unique opportunities. You've got to understand, people in other countries do not have the opportunities that those in this country have. And the reason I'm in this group is because those opportunities are completely being squandered. People want the attention of fame without having to do anything for it, they want money without working for it, that is where I see the problems stemming."

Bishop loved times like these. There were times and places for planning, executing the plans and working through issues, and this was not one of those times; this was for the visionaries of the this group to butt-heads, get to know each other, and to generally work together. The debates made the group stronger and richer of thought, and it were these times that thoughts and feelings were shared that the group would come up with the answers for decision days down the road.

"There are so many details around every piece of what we are doing yet to accomplish Joseph. And I know you aren't alone in thinking we should move ahead, but that would be a mistake, this administration has been more willing to work with our suggestions than the previous one, maybe, unlikely, but maybe we might not have to take it all the way. The contingencies we have talked about may become more important, but just flying off the handle is not the right approach and you know it. Now you just need to calm your fellow hot-heads down and get back to business," Sloan said rubbing her eyes. She was tired, she was driving from coast to coast, dragging Sawyer and the kitties along with her. Sawyer was getting on in age and she always worried about him. The cats seemed impervious to anything; as long as dinner was at 5 o'clock sharp, they didn't care if it was in San Francisco, Texas, or Connecticut. They didn't love the car, but calmed quickly. Big Kidd was ten and the two Ragdolls she had gotten him as play mates were turning five. She seriously had to research those jet leases, leasing time on business jets might be the way to go if she was to continue this kind of travel.

Jackson Cooper had just been sitting back in a couch in the great room that backed up to huge windows showing the deck outside. He didn't say anything to this point, but he was engaged completely in the conversation. He was always amazed at how many different points of view there could be. He was more used to Samantha, who understood from an intellectual stand point that there were different points of view, but personally she believed that there was only one: hers. She would be happy to try to explain her point of view to anyone to help them see the light as it were, but after that she fully expected them to come over to her side. It was a good thing that she and Bishop, for the most part, always had agreeable points of view. He decided to throw a political point of view out there.

"We've talked about this before, and what I'm hearing are issues that continue to get worse, or more pervasive. Politically speaking, the isle is getting wider and wider; there are no moderates anymore. You all know I'm a pretty conservative republican, but I believe I can see both sides and most of all I want to hear the other side. I probably won't change my mind, but I'll keep an open mind to hearing another side. It allows for a dialog and is what made this country great. Nowadays you won't see someone against abortion and the death penalty, who believes in the right to bear arms, but doesn't have a problem with registering their weapon, who believes in small government and big community. I think that person is getting more rare by the minute, and that is precisely why I'm in this. I mean after the fiasco last May, I felt like Bailey, I wanted to go kick some ass, pardon me ladies, seriously though, you can't just hide out to avoid a vote if you don't want to pass a law. It brought the legislature to a complete standstill and I for one think that was completely unacceptable. If someone just didn't come to work one day because part of their job was unappealing, they would get fired, and that is what should have happened here but the rules for congress and government officials just don't work that way. The partisanship continues to spiral."

Sitting next to Cooper on the couch, Sakti Sharma was, as always, excited to be a part of this group and enthusiastically taking part in the conversation. "But what I think everyone here has missed to this point, and I'm with Nikoli here, not being from this country I think we see the opportunities without the entitlements. But having said that, I think all the negative sides we have been discussing about our society are certainly out there. It is what we are not hearing about that is going to give us a chance to succeed. I think most people are hard working, honest and just struggling to get by for them and their families. They are the ones getting crushed, and it is them that really should be given the opportunity to start again with their ideals in mind. We should stop worrying about all the sloth that is about, that will take care of itself when all is said and done. Who will give them their entitlements when we are gone?"

Sharma looked around. Everyone was silent. Cooper patted him on the shoulder, "from the mouths of babes," he said smiling. Very few people knew Sharma well enough to tease him for his youth; Cooper was one that could. He stood up to stretch and continued, "Derek is getting a little anxious too but he understands the need for strategic planning. After the blackouts in New York City last month, it makes him really twitchy and understandably so."

Bishop sat up straighter, "yeah, that's a problem on many levels and it is one we have to look at as a main issue. If the power grid is compromised, we are screwed." Pearson nodded in agreement as Bishop went on. "Sak," referring to Sharma, "can you do some research on this? I know we've got the units tested out pretty good, but would they compensate with a complete outage? And how exposed are we in the context of the national grid?"

Sharma immediately answered, "250,000 people were trapped in subways for I don't even know how long, but I have done extensive research already on this very issue. I had to for my work and assessment of other resources. I can't imagine it has gotten any better in the last six or seven years, but I do know material sourcing changed in 2001 to have some redundant parts on the ready. Before that, there was just nothing here, all the components were and probably still are made in China, so if something even more significant than New York were to go down, we would have to source it like a dysfunctional supply chain administrator and then just wait."

"Unbelievable!" yelled Bailey, still feeling very tense.

CHAPTER 21
THE ECONOMY, ANALYZE

Tuesday, September 23, 2003 – 11:00am Mountain Daylight Time (15:00 hours Zulu Time)

Michael Bishop stood in the room that had grown familiar. They were in one of the conference rooms of the Broadmoor hotel in Colorado Springs. The faces looking at him had also grown familiar, and he felt privileged to be among these people that were willing to sacrifice so much to work until something changed. The direct messages to the President had proven to be mildly effective. Some reform had come in a few places, but what Bishop had suspected was the problem was the sheer scale of each issue. Even with the help of the administration some of these issues were just too big to be fixed in any conventional way.

The conferences would eventually be held here, but for now the rooms were used for bigger think tank meetings. Today's issue was the economy, and some heavy hitters wanted to be involved. Antonio Montes was making his way around the group and becoming less intimidating by way of his demeanor and quick wit. Ryder Burns was a regular by now and Collin Nelson was always a welcome part of the think tanks even though he stood strong regarding his stance on the group. He would give his thoughts and money, but he would never leave or split off from the US. He believed the problems could be solved at home and that was the crucial difference of opinion. This was the first appearance of Kylie Chamberland. She was a hard-nosed, no bullshit kind of lady that didn't take kindly to wasting resources or money, and she had plenty of both.

"This one's gonna take awhile so I'm not going to waste any time," started Bishop. "Mr. Sterling really thought out-of-the-box to put this plan together. For the past year, under the guise of educational research, he has been consulting with the world's best economists to come up with a package that is, for all intents and purposes, the best free-trade economic package ever written."

Before standing, Sterling looked over to Bishop and said, "What, no song to guess?" He too had been around the quirky game Bishop had been leading for years and he thought it might be a nice ice-breaker, but Bishop just looked at him, that's what he gets for trying to be whacky. Just stick to what you know, he thought to himself, even if it is like trying to drink sand.

Bishop was surprised to see Sterling so playful and then he realized he looked more shocked than surprised because Sterling blanched so he laughed, thought for a second and said, "Way to go, Dylan...nice to see you playin'. OK, new car, caviar, four-star daydream...think I'll buy me a football team." He looked around the room for the look of familiarity.

Holden rolled his eyes. He wasn't too fond of the game. He thought it was a waste of time, but he understood that there needed to be a bit of whimsy to lighten the mood at times. He also had no idea who sang the song.

Cooper finally spoke up, "Most of these guys are probably too young to know it Mike...Pink Floyd, Money!"

"Yes!" Bishop exclaimed. "I gave you guys an apropos one." Smiling but getting serious, Bishop gestured to Sterling, "Dylan, anytime you're ready."

Sterling stood up, cleared his throat, and calmly thanked Bishop for the praise during the introduction. He wasn't a shy man, and had an IQ in the top 0.01% of the population. Regardless, his ego was less than one would expect, and he loathed public speaking. He could pontificate for hours in a budget meeting, as he had to numerous past presidents as an economic advisor or policy director, but standing behind a podium and speaking to a crowd was something he viewed with disdain. At least he could take solace in the fact that, in this room, he only had to stand at his seat to speak, and that he was only speaking to a smallish group.

Sterling started slowly, with the intent of giving the room a basic background on his thinking, and hoping to wrap up within 5 to 10 minutes. Instead, his passion eclipsed his intentions, and he spoke for the better part of an hour. The group paid close attention, and remained completely engaged for the entirety of his informal address.

Sterling spoke on his philosophy for economics, which was based on the cornerstone of personal responsibility. Sterling knew that a core component to a successful economy, and to the American way of life, is the willingness to accept the consequences of our decisions. This translates to taking responsibility if bad decisions are made, and knowing the importance of taking credit for the things that go right. Many people believed that the government would and should be there to bail you out, at the expense of the taxpayers, whenever things didn't go perfectly, regardless of risk. This could not be the case in the new economy they were building. When people, and businesses acting as people, made certain decisions, the consequences of those decisions would need to come to pass. The tax code, the civil code, economic policy, and fiscal policy all needed to work in sync to support good individual decision-making.

He gave an impassioned sermon on these very topics. "It is a flawed view, at its very foundation, to allow home loans to be non-recourse. For those of you in the room that don't know what that means, it means that if someone can't afford to make the payment on the home, they can legally walk away from it, and it becomes the lender's problem. Even though the lender ends up with the property, its value may or may not cover the outstanding debt, and even though the morality of walking away from this debt could be argued, the law shouldn't easily allow the homeowner to walk away. It's complete bullshit."

He had surprised himself by swearing, and a few eyes in the crowd opened a little wider, then smiles ensued. The topic of personal responsibility was a popular one with this group, and his enthusiasm was taken in stride.

He continued in the same vein, "That said, there are other pieces that must be in place to allow for debt restructuring, not forgiveness. I have a friend, Mark Mitchell, who is a professor of government at a Midwest university. He and I share many of the same views, and he articulates one of them well. He says that, in Greek drama, hubris plays a key role. Hubris, he says, is the fatal pride that brings down even the greatest of men, and is the failure to acknowledge limits. It is the failure to live within the bounds proper to human beings. Ultimately, it is a failure of virtue. He goes on to say that when we delay payments rather than our gratification, we reveal our ill-formed character. When our demands for more things are limited only by our insatiable imaginations, vice is running the show. When our leaders tell us that they can solve any crisis if only we grant them more power, hubris has taken center stage."

Seeing Ryder Burns begin to object to that statement, he followed up by saying, "and please do not misunderstand, an insatiable imagination is a wonderful thing, most of the time, but in this context it shows the human frailty of looking outside instead of cultivating one's inside. This is not meant to inculpate or condemn, it is just part of our human condition." Burns seemed satisfied by this.

"There is an another way we can go about this that is based on what we learned from our parents and grandparents. It is based on ideals that every American knows about, but have been drowned due to the need for more. These ideals begin with moderation, and include others such as humility and self-reliance. They may be old-fashioned, but perhaps it is time for us to drag them kicking and screaming back into the present. Our way of life can be sustainable only if we acknowledge that publicly and privately we must be responsible. As Mark would say, hubris is only countered when we recognize limits."

This last comment drove several people to speak at once. Sterling stopped for a minute and let everyone settle down. Many ideas as to how limits could be enforced circulated throughout the group, and not everyone was in agreement as to how to proceed. As Samantha, Nikoli and Bishop looked on, they were all thinking that Sterling had been a great addition to the group. This type of discussion and debate was exactly what they had hoped for. It would lead to solutions. It had to. He wanted to have a discussion, and get some of the group's thoughts, about what should happen in the event that the entire housing market took a dive, unemployment soared, and people got laid off in droves. What then? How would we handle the basic needs of society, such as housing and the other basics described in Maslow's hierarchy of needs?

Once the room settled down, Sterling continued. He wanted to get the conversation headed toward a huge subject not so exciting to most people - a complete replacement of the current tax code. He knew that the majority of the population was too shortsighted to be accepting of a new tax, while being opposed to changes in the existing structure. They wanted it to be painless. It couldn't work that way. A totally new tax code was necessary.

"The new code," explained Sterling, "would be based on a flat tax for all citizens, accompanied by a value-added sales tax." Again, mini-conversations broke out in the room, but Sterling took control and spoke a little louder, demanding attention. "The United States is the only developed country that has not adopted a VAT. It's been clearly shown that resistance to a VAT is low, and if we just took the US debt as an example, more than a third of the budget deficit would be eliminated immediately."

"Further, the other benefits are clear. It's harder to evade taxes using this method, so that saves us all some work as we determine how to handle those that choose to skirt our laws, and it encourages investment, because it doesn't tax capital gains. Don't we want people and companies to invest in Texas instead of outside its borders?" He had toned down, and his lowered volume got the group to lean in, and listen to what he had to say.

Collin Nelson chose to speak up and question Sterling on a big spending topic, the defense budget, by asking, "Mr. Sterling, isn't it the case that introducing limits to defense spending would both decrease the tax burden, and increase the amount we have to assist our citizens in need?" When he said it, he thought that Sterling would immediately agree, and was quite surprised when he didn't.

"On the surface, I can see why one would think that, but from the perspective of defense spending, economically speaking, a decrease in defense spending ends up resulting in a decrease in social welfare. The research on this is relatively easy to understand, given an intermediate knowledge of macroeconomics. The exception is when the threats to our nation decrease so substantially that it overrides the downside of lower defense spending, like what happened during the collapse of the Soviet Union."

"I don't get it." said Nelson, "How can decreasing spending in one area *not* help another area directly? Isn't this what we call the Peace Dividend?"

"It all comes down to what happens with public and private investment opportunities. The price of national security is the loss of production of non-defense goods. If military spending goes down, can the economy be robust and efficient enough to convert that spending to non-defense goods, and subsequently to take advantage of investment opportunities? This would imply that the economy is operating on the frontier of the production possibilities curve, or PPC, macro-economically speaking."

He paused and saw some eyes glaze over; knowing that he had crossed over into economic theory, and not everyone would follow. Leveraging his skills in conveying information, he restated his point in a way that he knew everyone could understand, but kept it from sounding like kindergarten speak or demeaning in any way. Not everyone loved this stuff like he did.

"To get benefit in one area by reducing spending in another implies that the economy is operating at max efficiency. This is certainly not the case today. We're not at full employment, the trade deficit is too high, and we can't seem to balance the federal budget. Don't get me wrong. Defense spending is intricately related to how we invest in social welfare. My plan is to find the *right* level of spending, in every area, to maximize the efficiency of the machine."

There was some spontaneous applause at the back of the room that gained energy for a moment, and then died down.

"Enough about defense for now. The plan for that is a big and complex one, and there will be time for everyone here to consume it, and comment. Let's flip the conversation to social welfare. Thanks, by the way, for your comments, Collin. We need to keep talking through this until everyone understands."

Collin Nelson nodded and smiled. They both knew that Nelson had a better grasp of the topic than he was leading on, but he also knew most of the room didn't and he wanted to ensure everyone understood the complexity of this undertaking. He was certainly impressed, not only with Sterling's aptitude to understand these complex topics, but to distill them down to the essentials, and spend his time and energy on what truly mattered most.

"With respect to social welfare," Sterling started, "emotions tend to get the better of people. Phrases that start with 'we should...' and 'it is our obligation to...' are often used. Nowhere in our government does morality and ethics play a bigger role."

"In this category, there are many topics, such as food stamps, Medicaid, minimum wage, disability, etc. We have to tackle them all, but to do that we need some guiding principles. We're all here talking about this together because we have a shared sense of personal accountability. With that, goes a sense of social responsibility. What

I mean by that is that we all produce to the best of our abilities, and through that effort, we contribute to society's overall benefit. We help each other by doing our individual best. This system breaks down when some members of society are not accountable, and make a decision to live off the efforts of others."

Cooper and Bishop were sitting together, and looked at each other. Bishop leaned over to Cooper, and in a low voice, commented on Sterling's introduction to the new topic, "Dylan summarized that well. He's a quirky guy, but I'm sure he drove the speech writers crazy back in the day, doing their job better than they could themselves."

Cooper smiled, and thought about how much Sterling reminded him of Milton Friedman. Cooper remembered an interview that Friedman had done with Phil Donohue, talking about the virtues of capitalism, back in 1979, and how that interview began with talking about whether the minimum wage should be raised. The topics covered in that interview closely resembled those that Sterling was talking to the group about now. Back in 1979, soon after Cooper had left the Air Force, even though he was working on his father's farm, the nation's economy was something he had always been supremely interested in.

He could hear the interview playing in his head... Friedman had a way of explaining how something that might sound good on the surface, i.e. minimum wage, could, in fact, hurt who it is trying to help. He furthered the example by then going into welfare and why it should be abolished based on not fully thinking through corporate subsidies and paying wages too low to sustain an employee's livelihood. So, according to Friedman in the interview, if corporate subsidies are bad to incent employers and welfare programs keep the working wage too low, both should be abolished.

Then Cooper remembered the real gem of the interview. Phil Donahue was pressing Friedman on why he thought capitalism was good when it showed the distribution of wealth being so skewed to one side and thus showing the greed of capitalism being so in one's face. Donahue asked how that could be a good thing. Friedman was priceless. He started by asking what other societies do not run on greed, then said something that Cooper would not forget as long as he lived; he said the world runs on each individual pursuing his own interests and that the greatest achievements where those accomplished by individuals, not by governmental bureaucracies. When he heard Friedman explain the concept so matter-of-factly, he felt like he figured himself out that day. He never really got along with his siblings because they were perfectly content taking and taking, never contributing anything, and from day one, Cooper felt that was wrong. He was relieved to find that others felt the same way. He made a note to himself to track down that interview and show it to Bishop. It was, by far, the best explanation of why capitalism and free trade work, while other societies departing from it are failing and have failed.

Donahue played an excellent Devil's Advocate, Cooper thought; they don't make them like him anymore, then his attention shifted back to the present. Sterling was talking about capitalism in those same terms, in lock step with Friedman's beliefs. Friedman's final interview comment spoke boldly to Cooper. Friedman had asked who the angels were that would organize society. And here they were. In Cooper's mind, the angels were Bishop and Sloan. Sure, Nikoli had a huge part in it, and they all had their role. But Bishop, especially, was the one with the grand ideas. The vision. The ambition. The capability to communicate, motivate and support others in their combined effort. AmendX, Cooper knew, was that group of angels.

Now the action was taking a turn. While Sterling was speaking, several members of the group made comments to each other, mostly in agreement to what Sterling was putting forth. However, a look of disagreement remained on the face of Antonio Montes. When Sterling paused to collect his thoughts, Montes took the opportunity to stand in place, and speak as though he represented the group. Although he spoke softly, it was with authority.

"Dylan, you are certainly an intelligent and articulate man, and all of us appreciate your perspective. It's very convincing. However, I must say that I can't simply agree with your view on the minimum wage, and the essence of market control. Corporations cannot be given such a level of control as to allow them to pay workers whatever they want to. If there were no minimum wage, then a growing number of our citizens would decline below the poverty line."

Sterling looked ready to reply, but Montes continued, "I grew up without very much. My father's companies did not flourish until I was older. Working with him I have earned what I have now. At

17 years old, I was working for my father's company, for just a few pesos a week. I was fortunate, because I was able to communicate the value of my work, and negotiate a decent wage. Others around me, despite their ambition and productive capacity, didn't fare as well, simply due to their ability to negotiate this wage. What is our goal here? To simply reward those shrewd enough to make the best deal, or to support those that are making true, productive contributions to our society? Not only do I think we need a minimum wage, I think it should be higher in Texas than anywhere else."

Sterling responded in an even voice, with a clinical lack of emotion, and an almost-academic tone, "We've had a minimum wage in the US since 1938. Before that, the Supreme Court overthrew any effort to establish one. Their motivation in doing this was to put the control in the hands of the workers, where it belongs, not the companies, Mr. Montes. Only the Great Depression was the impetus to overcome their resistance. Even then, the intention was that it only be temporary. But I'll paraphrase what Milton Friedman once said, that nothing is as permanent as a temporary government program."

Cooper's head snapped around. He was just thinking about Friedman and now Dylan was talking about him. The others in the group laughed. Even Montes, who had sat down as Sterling was speaking, cracked a smile.

"It's not up to us to inject morality into the economy," Sterling said, "but rather to operate on rational, just, and agreed-upon principles. We don't need to get stuck in a cycle similar to what we're experiencing now, where most of our energy and effort is devoted to correcting the effects of the mismanagement of government."

Cooper loved the talk thus far, and was smiling ear-to-ear. He sat back and listened as Montes and Sterling went back and forth, further debating the topic. Many other weighed in, mostly in support of Sterling's view on minimum wage, but enough that opposed it that Bishop finally decided to table the topic until the next meeting. He didn't want to go so far down a tangent that it affected the momentum of the whole meeting.

Bishop stood in front of the group and made some of his own points with respect to the economy, and especially with respect to investments, where he had a strong background and keen insight. The discussion was very interactive, as Bishop talked about setting a reasonably low corporate tax rate. Almost everyone had an opinion as the subject of capital gains taxes was raised. Bishop believed that there should be no capital gains for the lower and middle class based on the amount invested, which would get them back into the market, encouraging them to invest. Bishop knew from experience that taxing capital gains was an issue. He was able to get the whole room to be silent so he could set the stage on the topic.

"The reason for reducing or eliminating taxes on capital gains, especially compared to ordinary income, is twofold: it is a double tax, and it encourages present consumption over future consumption."

Sterling was nodding his head in agreement.

"First, the capital gains tax is merely part of a long line of taxation of the same dollar of income. Wages are first taxed by payroll and personal income taxes, then again by the corporate income tax if one chooses to invest in corporate equities, and then again when those investments pay off in the form of dividends and capital gains. This puts corporations at a disadvantage relative to pass through business entities, whose owners pay personal income tax on distributed profits, instead of taxes on corporate income, capital gains, and dividends. One way corporations mitigate this excessive taxation is through debt rather than equity financing, since interest is deductible. This creates perverse incentives to over-leverage, contributing to the boom and bust cycle."

Bishop glanced over and saw Colin Nelson looking at him with a look of fatherly pride.

"Second," Bishop continued, "a capital gains tax is a tax on future consumption. Future personal consumption, in the form of savings, is taxed, while present consumption is not. By favoring present over future consumption, savings are discouraged, which decreases future available capital and lowers long term growth."

"Hang on," said someone near the front. "I'm a military guy, not an economist. What you just said sounded like it came right from a text book, and I didn't really follow it, so could you break it down one more step for me, and the folks here that aren't as up-to-speed on finance stuff?"

Bishop smiled. "Sure. Sorry about that. Everyone does need to understand this, because we're building the basis of how we're going to run everything, and it doesn't matter what your background is, your thoughts matter."

The man nodded, and Bishop continued, "What I meant was that, if someone has a choice, such as spending their money now or later, and the government dictates that money that's saved will be taxed, then many people will spend the money now, instead, because they feel they'll get more for their money. The same goes for investing. If a person is choosing between buying a stock, on which the gains will be taxed, versus buying something now that could appreciate in value, they'll choose the present, not the future. Does that make more sense? Eliminate this tax, and that encourages people to save or invest, and not just spend right away. For a healthy economy, we need investment."

Nobody could disagree with that logic. Even those that were somewhat less fiscally conservative didn't speak up. Some in the group were concerned that a potential source of tax revenue would be absent from their economic model, but the dis-incentive to save, and the concept of double taxation were enough to offset these concerns. Once again, Bishop had used his knowledge, experience, skill, and charm to get his point across. Even Sterling had been impressed by Bishop's clear articulation of the issue at hand.

Bishop simply wanted people to culturally think about the future, rather than just the present. The group had talked about how to better engage the people. He knew that, as a country, we have gotten fatter, dumber and so complacent, that the television shows being broadcast were liquefying our brains and our time engaged in the things that really matter was waning. We are in a place where it's cool to waste insane amounts of money on shopping, having multiple nannies, their own private jewelers, and being stretched, injected and siliconed until they don't even look real anymore. That is where our culture was going.

As the meeting continued, many other topics were raised and debated, such as executive compensation, retirement, social security, welfare, and many aspects of tax reform. Bishop wanted to be careful to ensure that the decisions made here were made by the group, not just his personal mandate. The government of Texas would be by the people, and for the people, not just in theory, but also in practice, as the idea had originated two hundred and twenty seven years ago. He respected and appreciated the authority that he had as the leader of this group, but knew that he had to be simply one of the group when it came down to how the government worked. Many people knew the saying about power corrupting, but few knew where it originated. Bishop remembered it from one of his first civics classes in college:

> "I cannot accept your canon that we are to judge Pope and King unlike other men, with a favorable presumption that they did no wrong. If there is any presumption it is the other way, against the holders of power, increasing as the power increases. Historic responsibility has to make up for the want of legal responsibility. **Power tends to corrupt, and absolute power corrupts absolutely.** Great men are almost always bad men, even when they exercise influence and not authority, still more when you superadd the tendency or the certainty of corruption by authority. There is no worse heresy than that the office sanctifies the holder of it." - Lord Acton, Letter to Bishop Mandell Creighton, April 5, 1887 published in Historical Essays and Studies, edited by J. N. Figgis and R. V. Laurence (London: Macmillan, 1907)

As people were filing out of the room, Bishop talked quietly to Sterling when Kylie Chamberland approached. She stood looking at both men. Finally, Sterling decided to speak because he felt the silence had become uncomfortable.

"Well Mrs. Chamberland, what did you think of the whole thing?"

She looked at them for quite sometime and right before Sterling was going to take another stab at getting a response, she said, "well done. Very well done. I hope the research and expertise on this undertaking continues at this level of quality."

"As do I Mrs. Chamberland," responded Bishop. "And by the looks of the way the groups have been developing their areas, I suspect that it will."

"We will keep you abreast of our progress ma'am," said Sterling.

"I would expect that you would," she said and then she left the room.

The two men just stood looking at each other.

Sunday, December 14, 2003 – 9:00 PM Eastern Standard Time (Monday, December 15, 2003 - 02:00 hours Zulu Time)

Holden sent Christian Adams a covert text message conveying his congratulations on the expertly handled capture of Saddam Hussein. It read, "Saw that the turkey got basted, and see you for Christmas dinner."

CHAPTER 22
LATRUNCULUS ACADEMICA PARASITARIIS, TARGET

Friday, April 2, 2004 – 9:45am Eastern Daylight Time (13:45 hours Zulu Time)

Samantha was often invited back to her alma mater, Wellesley, to talk on different matters. Through her undergraduate advisor, she was introduced to some faculty at Princeton who also asked her to speak. They wanted her to be the keynote speaker for a seminar on vision and success, and give her thoughts on what it takes to get both of those things. A committee was formed to vet out the speakers and tie all the talks together. The assistant chair of the committee, Dr. Sharon Ryan, was a lifetime scholar, having never worked outside of academia and to say she was liberal was an understatement; Dr. Ryan was so far left of the left, she had no desire or ability to hear anything concerning individualistic pursuits.

Sitting in a small but warmly decorated office on the Princeton campus, Samantha met Dr. Ryan.

"Dr. Melina asked me to be the assistant chair to ensure the importance of community is discussed in the seminar," Dr. Ryan said with an air of elitism.

"Cooperation with others is an important aspect of success, but when thinking about one's own vision and plan to succeed in any given field, community should not be considered immediately," Samantha responded.

Jutting her chin up, Dr. Ryan spoke quickly, "I completely disagree Ms. Sloan. If how the community is effected is not considered, then only selfish endeavors are pursued and the community gets nothing and thus suffers."

Sloan was in no mood. She had already sized up Dr. Ryan and she could tell this was not going to be a very fun conversation and her energy just didn't seem up for the task. The previous week she had lost her precious Saint Bernard Sawyer. He was almost nine years old, and she knew it was time for him to go, but that didn't make it hurt any less. She was sad and felt a little exposed with her emotions so close to the surface.

"You may call me Dr. Sloan. I hold a Ph.D. in clinical psychology and am considering pursuing a second as a way to keep up-to-speed in the industry as well as stay involved in education. That is the primary reason Dr. Melina asked me to come here and speak. This is not something I am regularly interested in doing, but Dr. Melina was a fantastic professor to me and I owe him a lot. Having said that, if there is a specific agenda to the seminar regarding community-based involvement, I am not your person to speak, let alone keynote it. I believe that the individual pursuit of perfection is what lends to strong communities. If you are a community planner, you clearly have items to take into consideration that I do not. But, I believe I advance many communities' strengths while working individually." Samantha sat back and observed Dr. Ryan stepping up onto her proverbial soapbox.

"Again, Dr. Sloan, I have to disagree." Dr. Ryan said, giving special emphasis to the word 'doctor.' "If you are just out for yourself, what about all those that did not have the opportunities that you or I had? What about those that weren't allowed to be born in this country or that made a mistake in their youth and went to prison? And those are just the major areas to speak of. What about the minorities that depend on welfare programs to sustain their families? If we don't first give to those in need it that weakens the community. Our efforts should be focused on giving back. I'm surprised at you, to be honest, with your psychology background; I would expect that you know that the less fortunate has no choice. It is not their fault. If we don't give our resources to them, who will?"

"They should," Samantha retorted even though she knew the question was rhetorical.

Dr. Ryan continued, ignoring Samantha's comment. "There are no villains, there are no bad or evil people. They are the product of their environment and if we don't make their environment better, it will continue to get worse and the community as a whole will suffer, and as I said, as a psychologist you should know this."

"If that is how you feel, I am the wrong person to give this talk. Why don't you do it?" Samantha asked dryly.

"Don't think I didn't volunteer," Dr. Ryan huffed, "I believe my approach will give these students many more positive issues to think about and act upon, but Dr. Melina was adamant that we talk with professionals that seek independence and individual achievement goals. Personally, I think that is a recipe for disaster. What will happen to all the people that need us? What will…?"

Samantha interrupted her, "They will have to work, get jobs, stop having kids, get off drugs, apply for citizenship and get educated, and above all, do their best. They will have to depend on themselves, not us. In other words, they will have to do exactly what I have to do every day. Listen, I came here to give you a brief overview of what I had planned to talk about, and here it is." Samantha passed a few pieces of paper across the desk. "If you don't think I should keynote or speak to these students in anyway, discuss it with Dr. Melina. I am not going to get into a political debate with you because we are clearly at opposite ends and, in my experience, people like you do not want to see the other side. I agree with you in that it takes many people cooperating, doing their best to create a robust community, but handouts and no work for welfare programs are only going make community worse, it is an economic no-brainer. The more people work to give up what they have earned to give to another person who has done nothing, will not only affect the feelings we have for humankind, but it also discourages the people that are working. Put simply, why should I break my ass, when someone else will do it for me? The more people that come to that realization, the more will stop working, put their hand out and at the end of the day there will be more hands out than hands to give. No one will be working or producing anything. Then what? What do you propose the community do for each other then?"

"Well!" Dr. Ryan gasped indigently. "That won't happen. I will always have a job and you would never stop working."

Samantha interrupted again. "Don't be so sure of that, people will get sick of working to pay for someone else, people are already sick of that and let me tell you there are absolutely villains of all kinds. There are bad, sick, predatory people in this world and we have to figure out a way within our *community* to make people accountable. But if you don't even want to make the ones accountable that aren't breaking our laws and social contracts, what makes you think we are going to be able to do it with the worst-of-the-worst? You've spent too much time in this plush little office, Dr. Ryan. If you want to see the damage that a lack of accountability has gleaned, take a trip around some cities; take your head out of the sand. Not only have the welfare programs not worked, but the incarceration and punishment programs are ineffectual as well. You've been in your ivory tower too long. Down there they will kill you, rob you, rape you, just as soon as look at you. Obviously, that is a huge generalization, as there are people everywhere just trying to survive, but I hope they know enough to get out of these wastelands and go anywhere else. Furthering that kind of community is creating a war zone and by definition it will only spread." Samantha stopped, shook her head. "Well, I didn't want to debate this, but you insisted. Good day, Dr. Ryan. Have Dr. Melina call me to discuss my speaking at the seminar. Otherwise I will assume I have been removed from the speaker list."

Samantha was calm in the short amount of time it took her to rise and exit the room, but she was seething inside. Latrunculus academica parasitariis she said to herself...the looter academic parasite. How sad, she thought. Dr. Ryan on the other hand looked like she had been slapped across the face for several moments after Samantha's departure. As Sam walked to the car, she thought about how this exchange exemplified what was wrong with this country. It wasn't just academia, this idea was pervasive. Through Bishop, Samantha had learned to hear all sides of an argument, and not jump to judgment. But this kind of thinking was just plain dangerous. She had no understanding how intelligent, rational beings could advance this mentality. Consuming everything without generating or producing anything cannot last in any scenario. Niki always said these people that talk like this weren't about sustaining anything, but gaining power...those who hold the limited resources and the power can dictate everything. Sam couldn't imagine that this country was headed that way, but after this conversation, she certainly had a better understanding of the road to get there. She had to put this out of her mind, she had a meeting with Harris Corrigan, Antonio Montes and Vassily Novikov in DC next week to discuss the criminal justice system and miscellaneous law issues to prepare for. Novikov had asked to be involved in a few topics but hadn't shown up to two of them. He was a bit of a partier and was using the world as his personal playground, but he always got the job done; he put his money where his mouth was, so she was curious to see if he would show up for this meeting.

***

Sloan hated being in DC; it made her jumpy as though she was wearing a sign saying, "secret meeting happening here, follow me." She was getting paranoid and she knew it was ridiculous...who the hell was she, she thought, some socialite traveling around with her dog? Well, used to travel with her dog. She missed Sawyer so much! She didn't start crying, but a giant tear rolled down her cheek. She wiped it off and shook her head and if to shake the idea that he was gone loose. As far as people noticing anything, people were just as unaware as ever, but she was still paranoid nonetheless. She had listened to Holden, though, and hired a security detail that mapped out methods of circumventing tails and other modes of surveillance, just in case. Being this close to the inner workings of the machine put her on high alert. She understood that Harris had to be in town and available at a moments notice. To make matters worse, she wasn't staying where she usually stayed while in town. The Ritz-Carlton was fantastic with regard to customer service for those traveling with pets and when she had Sawyer with her, he always loved it there. She felt so heavy every time she thought about being without him, like a weight pulling her to the floor. Again, she shook it off. The cats were at her parent's house in California. With the crazy traveling she had been doing, it was just getting unreasonable to keep moving them, and cats liked being in the same place. Since Sawyer's passing, the Four Seasons would be fine. It was a great hotel. She liked the Mandarin Oriental for pet care, too, but Montes wouldn't stay anywhere but the Four Seasons. An Xer from the CIA told her that he had struck some major security deal with the hotel. His rooms were like fortresses with small armies around him, and you would never know it just walking around the hotel. It looked completely normal, just another upscale hotel with people wandering around.

By way of getting the meeting started, Sloan asked that everyone introduce themselves and give them a chance to get comfortable. There were about 15 people in the room. She started in, "has everyone read the report from the researcher and professor from Baylor?"

Everyone nodded his or her heads in the affirmative.

I think you would all agree he has done some really fascinating work. It is really controversial, so please let's keep emotions out of it. Today is about bringing up as much as we can think of for the later conferences where we will nail down specifics. But for now, this is all very preliminary."

"The criminal justice system is so complex that we couldn't possibly get to everything here today. So as you can see from the agenda that you all received, I want to cover two main things and keep those things high level. First is the Baylor research, and how some of what came from that can dictate new thoughts on jurisprudence in general as well as individualized law. Second is how we can reduce the time it takes to get someone through the system or even if that is necessary."

"That is apropos actually," quipped one of the lesser-known group members. "It took nine years, I mean *nine years* to convict Terry Nichols for his involvement in the Oklahoma City bombing. The verdict came down this past March for an action nine years ago. Now that certainly has to change. Everything from the land of law suits and tort reform to speedy trials means less than nine years. Let's put some common sense back into the judicial system."

"Exactly, nine years seems excessive to me. But, I don't have a law degree nor am I an expert on constitutional law, so we have to have this conversation with the understanding that these are lay ideas. During the conferences, we will have many people involved with the law, judges, lawyers, law professors, and so on to help us out and really mold something new. This meeting is to bring new thoughts to them; rather, we need to give them the version of what the everyday people might be thinking," responded Sloan enthusiastically.

"But what about things like ambulance chasers and everyone being sued for everything? Tort reform is needed. That is a huge topic and I, for one, would like to see that completely overhauled when we go," said a lady that was part of the small group that had been chosen to prepare for this meeting.

Sloan started to speak, but Montes spoke up with an astonishing lack of Spanish accent, "Understood and agreed, but there will be a time for that meeting and today is not it. If we let ourselves run off topic we won't get anything done and this particular subject is one that we have to get right. Not that I'm minimizing any other topic, but today we have specific things to accomplish. I'm sure tort law will have its own meeting,"

"Indeed," said Sloan. "Tort is something that many of us have much interest in cleaning up and I can promise you, you will be involved in it as well, ok?"

Looking a little defeated, the lady nodded in compliance.

"Now, what I thought might be prudent since we read the Baylor research, was to bring in the man who oversaw it. Keep in mind; he is not a member of the group. He is under the assumption we are a group of concerned citizens, who want to learn more about his field of work. I know you all know this, but please refrain from any specifics as to how this information would pertain to Texas while he is here."

Again, there were confirmative nods.

As the professor came into the room Samantha thanked him for making the trip to DC. Many people were shuffling papers around and before he could even sit down, they began spitting questions at him regarding his research and conclusions.

"How can individualized law not cripple the justice system with regards to resources and time and can you define neuro-law?" said the man concerned with the sluggishness of the trial system.

In the back of the room, someone that was clearly a student asked, "why should it matter with regards to punishment if disease or trauma was a cause of the crime? Isn't the crime the same regardless?"

"Can it even be determined who is ill from disease versus just a sicko or a "healthy" criminal?" retorted an older man and lawyer putting his fingers up in the quotes motion, "and if so, can it be "cured"?"

In trying to get the group to slow down, Sloan asked, "besides the research this group read, can you talk a little about your background and how you came to be interested in these topics?"

Not to be assuaged, another woman, sitting next to Novikov, asked "would the biggest changes be in how criminals are punished or would laws be written differently in the first place?"

Another woman, wearing the strangest yellow suit Sloan had ever seen asked, "well, wouldn't that have to do with behavior and motivation and how to tap into those things?"

A woman and mother of two young kids that Sloan knew from the Austin group, who was also particularly interested in this topic asked, "do you believe that juveniles should be treated the same from what you know about the brain, brain chemistry and crime?"

Then Corrigan said, "I would like to get your thoughts on where rehabilitation and recidivism come into play."

After he spoke, the room became still. Corrigan was a very intimidating man and the group forgot, for a second, that he was in the room. Montes didn't ask any questions, but it appeared as though he was interested in the ones being asked.

To the group's astonishment, in order, the professor went down the list answering the questions, at least partially to each member who had asked them. As he spoke to the first question, he jotted down several different symbols vertically on a piece of paper as if creating a list of the questions with one or two symbols. It was the strangest and most efficient short hand Sloan and the others had ever seen.

He spoke quickly answering the questions. Looking directly at the man who posed the first question, the professor said, "that is the question for the ages, it really is, but truly some of the research shows that the system, or more to the point, the process can be the same while the justice is individualized."

The man started to interject, but the professor cut him off, "I know what you are going to say, how can there be different justice for different people for the same crime?"

The man sat back in his chair, raised his eyebrow and motioned for him to continue. Clearly the professor did indeed know what he was going to ask. "To do it, we must get over the mentality of equal justice for all and that is a tough pill to swallow. If you let me move on to some other answers, this is certainly one I'd like to come back to and answer in more depth, plus the topic will flesh out a bit more."

The group nodded in agreement.

"As far as defining neuro-law, that is easier, although even it is ever-changing as the interdisciplinary fields change. But basically, it is how the discoveries we made in neuroscience affects crime, the law, policy, social control, and anything else that fits within the scope of subject matter. The different interdisciplinary fields include social psychology, criminal justice and law, of course, cognitive neuroscience, even politics to a certain extent, although I have stayed away completely from that part of it so I really can't speak to questions on its influence. My sweet spot is more brain imaging. Imaging helps us detect areas of the brain responsible for actions as well as identify disease and/or trauma related to a specific action."

Directed to the student, he said, "and the reason we would want to individualize punishment or jurisprudence in general based on disease is because the underlying factors are so different. One person may be able to be cured," he said looking at the lawyer. "Consider a tumor sitting on the amygdala in one individual, while another person that committed the same or a similar crime is tumor-free. If we can remove that tumor and return the diseased brain to a healthy one, should the punishment be the same? The victim, and the relationship between them and the offenders, comes into play here, and it gets very complex. I'm sure the victim of the crime would say the punishment of those two in question should be the same, but for the sake of argument, let's throw out victimology for a second and look only at the brain as a separate entity and the logic of curing the one versus delving into why the so-called healthy brain committed that same crime. The 'cured' offender might then be able to go on to become an advocate or contribute in other ways, while the healthy brain that just chose for whatever reason to commit the crime, it is so much more complex than that, but for the sake of the answer today, needs rehabilitation or simply to be removed from society. Plus, and this is another touchy subject, but the diseased person's brain caused the actions of the person. Is that his fault? Just like the victim didn't do anything to cause the action against him or her, neither did the diseased brain."

Seeing everyone start to rustle around, the professor quickly continued, "truly that is just a question that needs to be raised. I may or may not have an opinion on it, but this is not the time to state it, nor is it appropriate when researching the subject. We just have to attempt to think of as many of the questions as possible to understand the breadth of the problem. So short answer, yes, in many of the cases we can tell a diseased brain, depending on the disease or trauma, from a healthy or non-damaged brain, and as I said before, sometimes it can be cured," he concluded nodding to the lawyer.

"As far as your question regarding my background Sam," he continued, "my father was a psychiatrist, and my mother a biologist so I've been exposed to these kinds of questions my entire life, and you can obviously see the biological and the unseen consciousness blending that was the status quo in my house. My specific interest in the brain came out of my need to know 'why' for everything. If we can drill down to find concrete answers to the 'why' questions, I believe many different, other problems can be solved. So, I had a very clear path early and I was able to pursue it undistracted. I got my Ph.D. when I was twenty-four and concentrated on research and writing until I was old enough to at least pretend I was older than many of the students I was teaching," he said smiling. Everyone knew he still looked younger than the average graduate student.

"To answer your question," he said looking at the woman seated next to Novikov," that is where politics come into play so the answer is I don't know exactly. But, I believe it is both. The entire jurisprudence system will need to be overhauled and most importantly money will have to be diverted from the prison system to areas more equipped and experienced to handle the mentally ill. And don't think I'm not saying take the valuable money away from areas to protect and keep our citizens safe, quite the opposite in fact. In many of the cases, just diverting the money to other areas within the same purview that it is being controlled now, just spent differently. That diversion could go towards detainees with special needs and specialized employee training. Then to your point, that follows almost perfectly," he said looking toward the lady in the yellow suit, "starting earlier on acceptable behavior is key to really changing our society. It would be behavior modification to those old enough to know the differences now. It would be tapping into proper motivations and encouraging our young to do whatever we deem are the 'right' things."

The group looked confused. "Ok," he said," societies, for the most part, follow whatever creed is set by the larger. Of course there are exceptions, but let's just stick with larger group for a minute."

"You mean the cattle," said Novikov in a very thick Russian accent.

The professor hesitated, "yes, kind of, but it isn't as derogatory as it sounds. Of course, not thinking for yourself isn't a good thing and just following the masses means cattle, but also when you do think for yourself, you can agree with the masses on appropriate actions and you follow those actions, that can also be cattle, so using that for an example, currently young kids are interested in trying drugs. Why?" He stopped and actually wanted someone to answer.

Corrigan gave it a shot. "Because their friends are doing it and peer pressure is almost impossible to compete with at certain ages."

"Excellent," said the professor, "plus our kids see their parents doing them in many cases, or they just see them coming home and having a few cocktails every night to dull-away the day. We have made the idea of tuning out, and not just from drugs or alcohol, a not only acceptable practice, but an encouraged one, both implicitly and explicitly. Now let's skip ahead one hundred years, enough time that all of those who completely rejected the new idea are gone, but not so long that the new population have forgotten what it was like when we killed our brain cells on a daily basis. Now it is cool to reject anything and everything deemed able to kill brain cells and limit plasticity...the ability to organize and reorganize neural pathways in the brain. You brush your teeth with your right hand every day; there is a very deep pathway for that action to the degree that you don't even have to think about. Then you try with your left hand and you stab yourself in the gum immediately. You have to think more about what you are doing. But if you keep it up, you can lay down a deeper and deeper pathway for brushing your teeth with your left hand. Incidentally, if you do many different things like that, studies have shown, it keeps your brain more plastic than if you don't. But back to life in one hundred years... now that the "cattle" believe this new way of living and it is pervasive in society, fewer young people will head to the fringe. Another example, over time, our kids have stopped believing in hard work or they think work is beneath them. An ill-fated consequence, albeit a magnanimous goal, of our parents and our parent's parents wanting an easier life for their children. Many…most of these offspring have not learned the incredible results of self-reliance or felt the increased self-esteem from earning what one gets."

Montes got up and very uncharacteristically shouted, "Bravo!"

This made the group laugh and lightened the mood a bit, but everyone was in total lockstep with what the professor was saying.

Looking at the clock, the professor knew he was running out of time, so he grabbed his backpack and pulled out a pile of papers. "I thought there might be questions about juveniles and crime, and just as a side note, going back to our example of youth and drugs, we know the brain isn't fully formed until as late as twenty-four years old in males, so the idea of young kids doing drugs and impairing what isn't even fully developed yet is a scary proposition. That topic, plus some other information, is in this paper that a colleague wrote on juvenile crime and punishment. I think it will answer your questions much more thoroughly than I can." He passed one directly to the woman that asked the question, and left the rest of them on the table for those that were interested to grab one.

"Finally, to your question on rehabilitation and recidivism Mr. Corrigan…"

"General," pointed out the lawyer.

"Oh sorry, General."

Corrigan waved it off and listened intently to his answer.

"Once again, this is a tough pill to swallow, and depending on the crime. I'm not talking about the crimes that require immediate and long-term banishment; I'm talking about those crimes that are not a serious threat to society. But we as a society don't want to work with, live around, or be involved with criminals. We poo-poo them, and rightfully so, as we work hard and do what we are supposed to, so why should they get a second chance, right? It is an understandable mentality, but when we do that, we make it impossible for that person to get a job, work legally and integrate back into society so the recidivism rate goes up. They believe they have to turn back to the one thing they know they can still do. We have to have a mechanism to show they have done their time, learned from their mistakes and are ready to change their life. Otherwise, we might as well not even look toward rehabilitation programs. Then there is the whole issue of rights while being detained. Do we want them getting law degrees to fight us or be with us again? Or do we want them learning more crimes versus learning how to reintegrate into society? All tough questions, so we have to be able to think through the different outcomes to be sure we are getting what we really want, not what we think is justice, just because someone needs to be punished."

Novikov quoted Truman Capote, "The problem with living outside the law is that you no longer have its protection'. I say once you decide to break the law, you don't have rights."

"Well that is all well and good, but are we cutting our nose off to spite our face?" said the professor. Is cutting them out of civil society going to benefit society in the end? We have to be smart about it and figure out what is the most beneficial to the largest group of people. If someone committed a crime against my family, or me, I would certainly say 'off with their heads' or lock them up forever, but who is really paying for that? We, as a society take on that burden and I can't imagine there is benefit to that for the largest group."

"And what about the falsely accused, Mr. Novikov? Isn't the whole point of this country's justice system to prove guilt?" said the torts girl.

"Well," snipped Novikov, "I'm talking about the open and shut cases, those with DNA evidence or something else that proves guilt. Save the money of trials and lawyers and time for those."

"There seems to be easy answers for me," Sloan added. "There is no gray with me; there is right and there is wrong, yes or no. For example, to me, it is our right to own a gun, it is also completely okay to register it. It helps if it is stolen and used in a crime, the information can be helpful within a gun database, and so on. Then if a load of guns ends up on the street illegally, they are much more easily narrowed down. But gun rights people say it is a slippery slope. I say don't worry about the slope until it starts to slip... meaning if those who have registered their guns start to get harassed, it is, once again, easy to me, the harassers get prosecuted. But that is making one large assumption that the system isn't corrupt in the first place, and what we are organizing and building I know isn't corrupt so the simple works best. If corruption is discovered, there has to be a means of reporting it and getting it reviewed so the corruptors go down, not the system itself."

The professor spoke up, "Agreed. There has to be a check and balance system of power that is sustainable. So, the easy answer is also quite complex. To your point Mr. Novikov, if anything were that conclusive, I would agree with you in the murder and more horrific cases, but even then to get to the point of behavior modification and rehabilitation, we have to delve into why the crime happened in the first place. Even for the murders and hideousness, we have to learn why to change things."

Everyone was exhausted, the topic was exhausting and they had many things to think about, but they still had to get through some other work. Once the professor left, many said he should be recruited for the group. Sloan had already made a note to talk to Bishop.

The torts girl summed up some of the other work the project group had been working on. She passed out reports and recommendations on how the civil social contract might work versus actual written laws. She wanted to meet with the sub-committee again to amend this recommendation based on what was said about behavior modification and social engineering. The lawyer distributed materials and talked about what he had on the legal system and how law review would be done and potential changes that should be made in it. He also wanted to amend some things based on the conversation today.

Finally, and surprisingly, Novikov stood and passed out a booklet entitled Civil Rights. Stunned, Sloan asked, "what is this?"

"Antonio and I had a chance to work on this and I think today is a good day to show it to everyone," he said with Montes nodding. "Antonio and I come from countries with very different civil rights than Americans have and that is good for the most part, but in having all of these fantasticheskiy rights comes pravo and Ya, we think that is wrong."

It was hard for the group to understand him and were straining to do so. When he spoke fast, he inadvertently spoke most words in English and some in Russian, and all very quickly.

"Ok, wait, say that again slower Vassily, I missed half of it," said Sloan.

"We come from countries that do not allow such great rights to citizens, and where that might be good for most part, we want to avoid it getting entitled."

186

Antonio said, "there are many things in this report, but basically one of our main concerns is that these rights pertain only to those who are citizens and chose to be. Not who snuck in, or was born here illegally, things like that. But that is not to say they should not have any rights, we as a people are trying to ever-evolve, there are some rights that all humans should have. And that rights are not given forever, they can be lost in our opinion."

"And animals! I believe you can tell everything about a person by the way they treat an animal. But this is incredible and a great start, thank you!" said Sloan, leafing through the report. "Unless anyone has anything else, let's call it a day. Because we got so much information that we have to process, I think everyone would agree that amendments to their reports should be done and we should reconvene when appropriate?" Sloan said asking but really telling.

The majority nodded in agreement. Novikov shook his head, "no, ours is fine as is."

Sloan smiled, and Corrigan laughed. "Must be nice to be so sure," he said.

"It is." Novikov answered aware of the rhetorical nature of the statement, but answering anyway. Sloan wished she still had the balls to answer as Vassily had.

Friday, June 11, 2004 – 11:01am Eastern Daylight Time (16:01 hours Zulu Time)

Harris Corrigan sat in his office and reflected. It had been more than a year since the Iraq invasion. Almost two years before, in July 2002, the real invasion work had begun when a CIA team, part of the Special Activities Division, had entered Iraq. Shortly thereafter, joined by US Joint Special Operations Command (JSOC) special operators, the teams laid the groundwork for the mass invasion. The coalition eventually invaded on March 20th, 2003, and subsequently took Baghdad on April 9th. The whole invasion was wrapped up on April 15th. By that time, the US had lost 139 military personnel. Conversely, the coalition had brought massive firepower to bear, and had managed to kill 9,200 Iraqi soldiers and 7,300 civilians. And those were just the official estimates. Some analysts within the administration claimed far higher numbers.

This weighed heavily on Corrigan. More than 16,000 people killed? For what? All the work that had taken place with AmendX had been balanced by the time and effort it took to run a foreign war. The effort was evident in his physical appearance. He had lost about 15 pounds, but as a larger-than-average man, it was barely noticeable to others. The more prominent change was in his face. His face was gaunt, and had a somewhat haunted look. His extraordinarily dark skin accentuated this appearance, and others around him had noticed. The stress was taking a toll.

It was taking a toll on everyone, though. Corrigan had an inside view to the President's team, and everyone's perspective. The mess in Abu Ghraib had been in the news for about six weeks now, and public sentiment was turning sharply against the administration. Corrigan had always been a vocal advocate of protecting the innocent, and this situation was difficult to navigate. His views differed from many in the administration, a few of who believed that the US had no role in protecting Iraqi civilians from the insurgents that had risen up so strongly this year. Corrigan believed that every US service member had a duty to protect civilians from inhumane treatment, to intervene, and stop it. But these weren't civilians. They were Iraqi combatants. What respect did they deserve? Public sentiment said that the prison guards crossed the line by a large margin. That called into question every activity that the military participated in. It made Corrigan a mainstay in the media spotlight, because his Marines were often those in the most hostile situations versus the insurgents, and he couldn't lift a finger without the public scrutinizing his every move, often without any of the context. The media often showed what looked like innocent civilian women, robed and looking vulnerable, but once the camera panned off, it was a regular occurrence to have them wielding a weapon from under those robes. The point was our military never knew what to expect; no human being should have to be in that situation, much less be constantly criticized about it from the media. Especially because they were in Iraq fighting to ensure their way of life stayed intact for those exact people.

So, the administration was divided. The public was in an uproar. It was easy, though, to have a discussion with his fellow Xers. Rational dialogue was a basic premise, and he was often able to get his mind back on track through those conversations. It had been a couple of weeks since he'd had one of those talks, so he decided that now was as good a time as any. He pulled his BlackBerry 7100t out of the small safe that was part of his desk, and turned it on. It returned a series of beeps that represented the extra security steps that had been integrated into all the Xers phones. He was able to browse the directory on his phone, and see that Bishop, Sam and Sharma were all offline, but Holden, Cooper and Nikoli were showing active. He decided to call Holden. Corrigan got used to calling Holden when things started getting overwhelming or things stopped making sense. They had great debates and he really enjoyed their talks.

Holden's phone was sitting on his oversized walnut desk next to his laptop. The top of the desk was sparsely populated with his essentials, which were neatly organized around the thick glass pane embedded in its center. He had just finished logging the data from his morning workout, and the recovery meal he had devoured afterwards. He was obsessed with logging his data, and that obsession seemed to keep him focused in many other ways. His BlackBerry buzzed loudly on the glass pane. He saw that it was Harris Corrigan calling, and punched the green button to answer. There were two beeps, and a brief delay, and then the call was connected.

"Good morning, Harris," Holden said.

"Hey there," Corrigan responded. "How are things?"

"Good," Holden replied. "Nice day here in Texas. You in DC?"

Corrigan said, "Yeah. This week and next, then I'm headed to Geneva to meet with leaders in the coalition. It's been a bit hectic around here. Is now a good time to talk?"

"Sure," said Holden, "I was just about to jump in the shower after my run, but I've got plenty of time. Pretty predictable day today. Famous last words, I know… anyway, I'm free for a while. What's up?"

"It is disturbing, it really is," said Corrigan as if they had been in the conversation for a while.

"What is?" asked Holden.

"Everything from basic day to day living, to how we prosecute criminals, we are going the wrong way."

"Oh man! You're starting to sound like Samantha," sighed Holden.

"It's true Derek." Corrigan's voice elevated. "Minorities get higher sentences than their majority counterparts. Actually, Samantha told me this...symmetrically faced or rather prettier faced offenders get shorter sentences than those with asymmetrical features. That cannot be our jurisprudence system. It certainly wasn't when this country was founded. I wasn't raised with money and I know first hand how minorities can be treated. It isn't an excuse it is a reality, but there are ways of getting out from under that life and I've shown it can be done."

Holden responded, "Since you are interested in the criminal justice side of things, you should talk to Sam and I'm not being sarcastic, she is working on planning some sort of meeting or conference for us to talk about just those kinds of things."

"I have been talking to her, but sometimes when I read her binders on all of this stuff, it just makes me sad...Sad and tired."

"I get what you're saying," comforted Holden.

"Plus, I just wanted to get your thoughts on a few things. You and I have seen eye-to-eye on most things since we met. Common backgrounds help, of course, but I wanted to get your perspective on the stuff that's been going on in Iraq, and what you think the others are thinking." Corrigan paused for a few seconds, and Holden could tell he wasn't done, so stayed silent. Corrigan continued, "I have seen public sentiment spike up, then crater, then spike up again. When we captured Saddam at the end of last year during Operation Red Dawn, nobody was even thinking anything bad, much less saying it. Those who disagreed with our involvement in Iraq were drowned out by the victorious cries of those who thought we were on the verge of final victory. When this Abu Ghraib crap hit the fan, now the opposite is true. When one soldier from the other side gets killed, it's front page news, and a leading story on CNN."

"Sure," said Holden, "par for the course."

"I know it is. I was just wondering what your personal view is, and whether other Xers agree. We're doing this thing with Bishop for our own benefit, but more so, with the idea that it will benefit everyone else in the long run. As things become public, people are going to say a lot of things. Similar things to what they're saying now, about the US Government, that the government has no right to be doing what they are. They'll say the same things about us, even though we're in it for them, largely. In the end, I'm not really worried about what the public may know or think, but I just want to make sure we're on the same page, and that we're approaching it the right way. We have to minimize the possibility of innocent people being negatively affected."

"We will, Harris. We will. You know that a price has to be paid to get us where we need to be, right? Undeniably, some people will get displaced. Others will get hurt. Some will get killed...fact of life, brother. I could say some stupid shit, like to make an omelet, we have to break some eggs, but you know what I'm saying. And yes, to directly address your statement, the others are on board. Minimize the collateral damage."

Corrigan sighed. Holden was saying exactly what Corrigan thought he would, and it's what he wanted to hear, and at some point, he'd feel more comfortable, but he wasn't there yet.

"We need someone in charge of this," said Corrigan. "Someone who eats, sleeps, lives and breathes the thought that some people need to be protected."

"No offense, Harris, but we all have that principle firmly in mind. To put someone in charge of the anti-victim-hood seems a little over-the-top. Seems like we're slipping into the area where government's role is to protect everyone from themselves, and that builds bigger government, and costs more money. I don't know, but that seems like what we're trying to avoid, not what we're trying to establish." Holden leaned back in his chair, and waited to see what Harris would say to that.

"Sure the way you just described it, but sometimes I get the feeling like the general public needs to be protected from themselves. The level of stupidity is growing everyday."

"Harris, I get what you're saying, most people are stupid."

"I didn't mean that, Derek. You and I have seen some ferocious stupidity, so in some things, I agree with you. There are smart individuals, stupid people as in any group of people. Did you know most people don't even know the tremendous history of this country anymore? And I'm talking about high schoolers and college students, who are just getting out of school...forget about those who have been sitting like vegetables in front of a television for 20 years. So, when I think about that, I think those same people need to be protected from themselves."

Derek leaned his head into his hands, elbows on the desk and thought how sad that sentiment really was. "Have you read Atlas Shrugged, Harris?"

"I thought that was required reading to be in this group," Corrigan responded, chuckling.

"I love the book as much as anyone in this group, but I can tell you there is a fatal flaw in it that I hope we will avoid. Waiting until the engine is stopped isn't the answer. All through the book, the doers, the producers say that it is enough to work harder and produce for themselves, and ignore the fact that those not producing should be dealt with then and there. Remember the part that Dagny has to remove herself from her position at the railroad to go finish a line because it is built on the metal that is not looked upon favorably? That's bullshit. If she would have stopped right there and said, it either gets done this way or no way, what? The board is going to let themselves go out of business? I don't think so. There are a ton of examples of that throughout the book. My point is this…if someone isn't willing to put their big-boy pants on and do their part for themselves, why the fuck should we help? If they are then there is a mutual cooperation among men, yeah, yeah…and women, I have no interest in helping someone with their hand out, that isn't willing to help themselves. When the shit hits the fan, I'm sorry to say Harris, you are going to be looking over an onslaught of those kind of people wondering where their entitlement is…it is pervasive in our day to day and our lives in general."

Harris thought about Holden's point of view for a moment and said, "I always looked at it like the producers can and will get something done at all costs, despite the hangers-on, plus it made for great drama. But you're right."

"Yeah, I get the drama part. I think we are getting a bit off-topic," said Holden, shuffling the papers on his desk for the third time. "But I can tell you, Harris, those are precisely the reasons we are doing what we are doing. And it isn't about protecting people from themselves, it is about transplanting those that want to live a better life to a place that allows for that."

"No, we didn't get off topic. You gave me precisely what I needed. Thanks, brother."

PART 7
DELIBERATE, PLAN, ACT (2005-2011)

CHAPTER 23
DEVELOPMENTS & TO WIT A LIFE

January 2005

Over the course of six years, the group operated like a machine; members conducted their lives as normal, functional, contributing members of society. But all the while, they were getting closer to other members, figuring out complex, and always tough, decisions. Bishop often wondered if The Framers of The Constitution had such a difficult time, or if they knew that getting specific was so complex that it was better to leave issues open for interpretation. Years and years had gone by, and Bishop was as torn today as he was when the effort started. Should rights and responsibilities be lines in the sand? Could The Framers imagine these masses living by and twisting the great words of the Constitution to serve their purposes, or was it just that no one, not even those great men, could see the future? Now with all the problems, it had gotten so convoluted that spelling things out seemed necessary. Or was this group falling into a trap that The Framers knew to avoid? Trying to create such detail around rules might just be impossible. It was such a complex quandary. What Bishop did know, though, was the "social contract" was all but ignored, obsolete, or unknown.

The spirit of what this country was built on certainly wasn't forgotten; he had met so many people that were now in his life, willing to sacrifice and contribute their time and money to fight for that essence of what once mystified him. Yet, the direction the country was going was just wrong. He didn't necessarily believe it was the masses because he would often meet people randomly that had nothing to do with the Group and their views were much like his own. Inevitably, most would become members, but often, for whatever reason, some people just stayed out there on their own, doing their own thing. There was, however, a contingent that had the country by the balls, and it was a truly painful experience. The partisanship has gotten so bad, the only thing left to do besides their plan was to split again like the civil war days. The Right wouldn't do anything that the Left wanted, out of what they *thought* was principle at this point, and the extremes were even worse; there were no real moderates anymore. And if there were, they weren't pulling their heads out of the sand to be squashed. Honestly, he thought he could talk through anything with anybody, but lately things were so out of hand and some of the opinions, policies and ideas were so insane that the Group's idea to split was the only thing, in his mind, that could save any shred of what this country once was. He also had to let go of his idealized notion of what this country was in the past. He had to move forward and fight the fight based on what he and the group thought was the right way to be, to lead, to live. Let the two sides split off as peaceably as possible and see which side comes out successful. Successful, in this case, meant lower debt, more accountability, more integrity and a clearer picture of every other policy that the Group had laid out to the past administrations and gotten nowhere.

Success, failures, celebrations, and tragedies had happened to the AmendX members, making many from this group bond like steel. It's what happens when people get together that have similar passions and that can all learn from each other over time.

The progress in Texas was astounding. There was more going on underground than above. Thanks to some very deep pockets and the work of some incredibly brilliant minds, military-like compounds were being built along all of the borders. The land purchases went completely unnoticed and the construction was shielded with radar and surveillance jamming equipment, making it impossible to detect any action from above. One thing learned from the US military over the years was that to evade detection from above, whether from aircraft or satellite, a combination of technologies is required. From the 'dazzle' camouflage developed for ships in World War 1, to infrared LEDs that confuse sensors, the Xers used a multitude of technologies to create an amazing level of invisibility to their operations.

The techniques employed used temperature sensors, and accompanying heaters and coolers, to eliminate any measurable temperature differences between the ambient environment and the equipment operating in the facilities. The same was done on the infrared spectrum, so the temperature and infrared radiation sensors used in the satellites that operated above these locations were all but useless. To add another level of protection, in key places, special camouflage netting was erected above construction sites. Electricity was channeled through the netting, acting as a Faraday cage, and thus was impenetrable to microphones, cameras, and other sensors. The end result was an external static electrical field that protected the Xers site from electromagnetic radiation. However, it was designed not to block static or slowly varying magnetic fields, like the Earth's magnetic field, so compasses still worked within the site.

SOURCE was becoming huge on both sides, the Xers for obvious reasons, as well as in the government's arena. The line between the regular military and Holden's contractors was blurred, to say the least. He was doing all he could to do the right thing. If the Xers needed something, he was there with no questions. When a division of the government needed his services, he was also there, and that was getting him in trouble. One division of the government asked him to deploy people and supplies, which meant everything from guns to transportation vehicles, at a moments notice, while another was fining him, or had him before congress, for violating some obscure rule buried in an old private military code of conduct reference. Because of confidentiality and contractual obligations, he couldn't tell the left hand what the right hand was asking him to do. It was taking its toll, but Holden never faltered. As long as he believed it was right, he tried to be there for everyone.

During a meeting regarding how changes in the Internet would be developed, free speech and privacy-versus-security came up. It was an old debate for the US, and now even this group, was used to talking about it.

Holden decided to get involved in more than just the security and military side of things for the group. He wanted to support many facets of the group's initiatives and he believed he could contribute some value. He looked at the reports for education and submitted his thoughts to Samantha. He agreed with much of what was already down on paper, and he had some additions. He was also interested in healthcare. His wife had a lot of cancer in the family and he wanted to do what he could because it was of primary interest to her. The Internet and privacy, first amendment type of policies, were the topics that he wanted to be involved with in person. He knew all to well what it was like to be hounded in the name of freedom of information and speech, and although he believed strongly in what the Founding Fathers were attempting to attain, he also believed those measures were being abused.

Standing and chatting with a fellow Xer who was also on this privacy committee while they were on a break and new committee members came in while others were finishing up and leaving, they watched Bishop with some other committee members. Bishop was his usual self: unpretentious, humble and easy to talk to. He looked at his watch and both men heard him say that he was late for a tee time and had to leave.

"He certainly isn't the man you imagine when you hear all of the ideology. He has become almost a myth," said the man standing with Holden.

"Don't fool yourself. He works really hard to come off that way. He is the most complex, complicated, and intelligent man I have ever met. He might look like he is just off to a golf game, but he also works harder than anyone I have known. I work about a hundred hours a week, although I'm trying to spend more time with my family these days, and I think he works more than I do," replied Holden.

Bishop walked past the two men and stopped. "Derek, it's great to have you here," he said shaking his hand. "And Heath, I loved what you wrote about privacy-versus-security and the differences between privacy from the government, the media and other lay people. The part about the media's responsibility and flagrant abuse is going into the report everyone will read. I hope you will be on hand if anyone has any questions."

"Of course," said Heath shocked.

"Well, I'm late so I've got to run. I will see you guys soon," and with that he was off.

Looking at Heath, Holden said, "What's wrong?"

"I've met the man once before when he came in to talk to a group of us about his original goals. The group was already basically in, but we all wanted to hear it from the horse's mouth, so-to-speak. Since then I've only worked with panel leaders, thus the 'myth' comment I just made... and he remembered me?"

"I don't get it either. I have never seen him off his game. It is freakish," answered Holden.

***

Renting a house on Lake Travis just outside of Austin, Sam tippie-toed to the kitchen to get some coffee. She had not slept much and it had been a long night; a new puppy will do that. She missed Sawyer so much and was feeling so down and depressed that Mike and Nikoli showed up with an eight-week old Saint Bernard puppy. From the minute she saw him, she knew she was never going to let him g, or at least until she couldn't lift him anymore. She had realized, with Sawyer, how fast they grow and she promised herself if she got another Saint that she would squeeze, hold and hug one until he or she was full-grown. In this puppy's case, he didn't want any part of that. He was way more hyper than Sawyer ever was, and had these rambunctious brown/amber eyes. She named him Oliver Newton Thorndike, using her regular naming convention. In this case Thorndike fit both the scientist and the movie, but she wanted a first, middle and last name, so Newton it was. She couldn't have been more pleased. The boys knew her so well, and knew she needed to move on. He could never replace Sawyer and she wouldn't want him to. She would always have her memories of that big block-like head and loving expression. She would have thought she needed to pick a new dog out herself, but they did a fantastic job, Oliver was perfect! He was, however, a puppy, having to go outside every couple of hours and making his puppy pouts and cries, and she couldn't fall asleep until she heard that deep sigh, which indicated Oliver's comfort and that he was sleeping soundly. The cats were in full revolt and had completely cut off any love-giving to Samantha until the dog was removed, or at least until they wanted dinner. Big Kidd and Oliver soon became friends. The other two kitties took a little more time to warm up to him.

In addition to AmendX work, she was in Austin doing consulting for Cooper, and seeing some clients that a colleague had asked her to take over while he was on sabbatical doing research. She was in a nice, comfortable routine, and it was times like these that it was hard to see all the problems that were driving the group to leave. Day-to-day seemed quite nice sometimes, but she did isolate herself from the things she didn't want to hear or know about. That was her M.O., especially when she and Mike weren't around each other that often. She could almost bury her head in the sand when he wasn't around to obsess about everything, every detail, and the complete confidence that everything could be fixed. She knew he was right, of course, but sometimes she liked to be lazy like everyone else.

With cup of coffee in hand, she opened the front door to get the newspaper. With everything going to on-line formats, she wondered how long it would be until newspapers just went away entirely. She liked to read the newspaper, the feel of it in her hands, the smell of the paper. As she turned around she remembered the door automatically shut behind her quite loudly…she stood still. Within a few seconds Oliver came hopping out like a bunny and she had to smile. Baby dogs don't have a good working knowledge of their back legs so they hop like bunnies…so cute. She put the coffee and newspaper on the table, picked Oliver up and took him out to do his business.

Getting him some breakfast, and settled back in with some new puppy toys, she sat down at the table to finally read her paper with a fresh cup of coffee. In a small headline toward the bottom of the front page, it read "Wife of Mercenary Billionaire Dies in Tragic Car Accident." Samantha choked on her coffee and read the article as fast as she could. The article basically said that while driving home from a church function, Marie Holden, wife of Derek Holden III, was killed when her sedan drove off the road, with no apparent reason for the loss of control. She hadn't seen Derek in almost a year. They had spoken pretty regularly, but with as busy as he was, it was quick, concise, almost coded messages about work for the group. Over the years, she had gotten to know Derek Holden pretty well and appreciated him for his quirky personality. Like many of the chosen leaders, he knew his shit, truly. He was an expert in his field, and she trusted him completely. He was also a quiet man that liked to fly under the radar, which was practically impossible. Some writer or media person was always trying to pry into his affairs. SOURCE was under constant scrutiny with innuendoes and half-truths, as well as out-and-out lies about the private military contracting business and the slant was that they did not have to obey the laws that our military did. Now this! The article said that police were investigating the car accident, as there were suspicious circumstances and Holden was asked to come in and speak to police voluntarily. He had not obliged.

She dropped the paper and went to the phone. First, she called Mike Bishop. He had been just about to call Sam. He already knew and had spoken to Derek. Derek was distraught, of course. He was trying to figure out a way to tell his four children. They were with the nanny for now, but he couldn't keep them there for long, she wasn't full-time, and Derek always thought she was too young to manage four kids. He asked that the nanny have her mother come and help for the time being. Bishop said it might be nice for Derek to hear from a woman, and Sam would know how to assess his well being at the moment and to report back if Derek needed anything else. He then explained exactly the time and place the accident helped with precision detail that made Sam understand. It meant that Derek did need something from her and that she should get on it. She ended the conversation with Bishop and immediately called Derek. He answered the phone with less than one ring.

"Well?" he asked.

"Well, what?" Samantha replied.

"Oh...who is this?"

"It's Samantha, Derek, what's going on?"

"I was expecting a phone call from a friend of mine looking into this fucking mess. You know I always knew this would happen, I just expected the bastards to whack me, not Marie, what the hell am I going to tell my kids, Samantha?"

"Hang on, calm down. Whack you? You need to back up a little bit and catch me up," Samantha said.

"Fuck, I don't have time to go over this again Sam, and besides, I have a dick-tective waiting for me to go down to the goddamn police department because I have not given them an alibi...as if I have to, like I would have my wife killed. Really?!" Holden screamed.

Samantha immediately knew he was in trouble. "Just tell me, what do you mean, whacked?"

"Killed, Sam. Killed. The things that I have done in my life certainly made enemies over the years. I just never thought they would go for my family." Holden said, sounding a bit calmer.

Knowing what whacked implied, she ignored Holden's definition and asked, "you think this was a hit? Why? Why now? Did you get any warnings or anything?"

"No, that is a bit strange. You would expect some kind of ransom, or even if it was just to kill her, I would imagine something a bit more gruesome, not a car accident. I gotta go, this jag off is wanting me off the phone."

"Don't do anything to piss them off, Derek, they are just doing their job and it will only make things worse for you. You might have to admit your time with Allison, and that you are actually human, and you messed up. You know I'm here to help if you need me." This was her code for understanding he needed something and that she would do what she could.

He knew she was trying to tell him something, but he didn't understand and didn't feel like analyzing it right at that moment. "Thanks Sam, you get it and I appreciate it. I'll keep you posted."

There were no goodbyes; they both just hung up the phone. The third call was to her good friend and fellow Xer, Allison Myers. Allison lived in Virginia Beach, not too far from Derek. Sam knew Derek would say nothing to police regarding an alibi; he hated having to answer to anyone, plus she knew he had other reasons to stay quiet. He was a retired Navy SEAL; they understood how to be questioned. She also knew he wouldn't be particularly happy with her solution, but she wasn't a SEAL, and she didn't know how to be all that covert. She was all about "full disclosure" so she sent in Allison, and within the hour Derek Holden was an adulterer, but not a murderer. From the two conversations with Bishop and Holden, Sam deduced that Derek couldn't tell the police where he was because he was doing something for the group, and part of the promise they all made was that nothing could lead any authorities back to a person, a place or even a project that could expose the group. So once she figured out that Derek would say nothing, she had to provide an auxiliary location for him to have spent his time, and with someone during the hours leading up to the crash and the time of the crash. That was where Allison came in. The police would have to stop the interrogation with Holden. Allison did fantastically well and Holden was released.

***

About nine months later when Sam and Holden were together, he really laid into her about the whole adulterer story. It made her mad because she had about a minute to figure out what was going on, what could be plausible, and get the resources there to help. Now he was lecturing her on what a pillar of the community he was.

"Why would you think I would cheat on Marie?" Holden asked irritated.

"Which one?" Sam replied snappishly, leaning down to calm Oliver. Every time there were raised voices, Oliver would snap to attention to make sure his mom was okay. Not that he had a mean bone in his body... He might drown a perpetrator in drool, but Sam didn't like him getting all riled up.

"Touché" Holden said back, rolling his eyes.

Turned out that Holden's new wife is also named Marie, and that she happened to be the mother of that all-too-young nanny, Sarah, that was now the full-time nanny.

"Well, seriously, I take marriage and the vows very seriously. I am Catholic and have always considered my religion, as you should know by now, to be very important."

"I know Derek, and I'm sorry for snapping. But I didn't have a lot of options that day, and had I known you were into this Marie..."

Holden cut her off, "I wasn't! I barely knew her then. She has been living at the house helping Sarah on my request, so we started spending time together and it just happened!"

"Ok, I don't want to argue. I'm sorry I mistook the situation. Congratulations, really, Derek. I am really glad something good came out of all of this." Samantha replied genuinely.

Looking at Derek, Sam could tell that wasn't the end of the story. "What else?" Sam asked reluctantly.

"There is one more thing I should tell you...you'll find out about it sooner rather later anyway, and this is just going to make you believe me less, but it is what it is. Marie is pregnant. It is not something I'm proud of, it happened really quickly. She is at the end of her second trimester. That was the reason for the quick marriage, but I wanted to marry her anyway. She is also Catholic, and Marie Samuels would have wanted me to move on." Derek used Marie number one's maiden name to make things less confusing. I loved her, but she died. My kids need a mother, I want a wife, and may she rest in peace, it is time to move on."

Thinking his time to move on was quicker than hers after Sawyer died, but she wasn't there to judge and she felt in her gut that Derek was, in fact, a good man. "You don't have to justify yourself to me Derek. This is your life and you have to be okay with it, not me." Samantha said, falling into her clinical voice.

"Ugh! Don't shrink me, but I get it, thanks."

"Someone should, Derek, but it is not going to be me," Samantha replied with a grin, "but before we get to work, did anything ever come of the investigation?"

"The police said it looked like she fell asleep at the wheel, but I just don't believe that. Toxicology showed no drugs in her blood stream, but they did find an unusually high amount of the hormone melatonin. I still think there was some kind of foul play. My P.I., Gunner, found out that someone she didn't know was trying to feed her some cake during the church function, but the police questioned the person Gunner spoke to but said there wasn't really anything to go on."

"Gunner? Perfect name for a P.I.," snipped Sloan.

"He's good, I'm tellin' ya. Anyway, after that there were no more real leads. Gunner is staying on the case and if there is anything to find, he will find it."

Knowing Holden was done talking about his personal life, she switched gears, "ok, we have a lot to cover, one priority is that equipment we talked about. We need to get it purchased, tested, and hidden in the outpost outside of Dyess."

CHAPTER 24
A BOX OF SAND & A BRAIN

Friday, March 25, 2005 – 9:30am Central Standard Time (15:30 hours Zulu Time)

"We've got so many people on board, it is starting to feel a little eerie. I had a long conversation with Reagan Mills about how she could help and who she should stay in contact with." Pearson said while flipping through the channels of a television in Jackson Cooper's home office.

"Reagan Mills? I thought she was a model." Cooper asked confused.

"Can't models be a part of trying to make this a better place and bring world peace to all?" Pearson replied sarcastically.

"That's not what I meant...actually I don't know what I meant," Cooper said, rubbing his eyes, "I'm so tired, I don't know if I'm comin' or goin' anymore. It will be nice to get away for a couple weeks," he said, referring to his upcoming vacation.

Just then, his personal assistant came in, a young man with a slender frame, who was a hard worker and had principles. He had worked for Cooper for only a little while and knew nothing of the group. But Cooper had the feeling he would be one of them, or rather he was one of them, it just wasn't official yet. Cooper read a piece of paper the young man handed him. He looked at him and said, "take this back to her and ask for at least five possible consequences of this policy. I want to see forward thinking and some solutions, not just an update of problems." The young man nodded and quickly turned around and left the room, closing the door behind him.

"You know that no matter where you go, we'll need you for something," said Pearson in response to Cooper's vacation comment. "Every time I try to get away from everything, I get a call from Sam or Bishop asking if I can just do this one little thing, and then of course regular work is always there."

"So tell me about her, is she really that amazing looking in person?" Cooper asked.

"Oh, yeah, and bright as hell. Can you imagine what those board meetings are like? Her dad is the president of one of the biggest investment groups in the world. She sits on the board, comes into a meeting and surprises the shit out of them. She has her MBA from Tulane and she knows her stuff. I'd pay money to see that." Pearson chuckled as he said it.

"Speaking of money, do we know how much she is bringing in?"

"Not exactly, but she alone, not including daddy, is worth about $11 billion."

Cooper gasped. "I will never get used to figures like that..."

Pearson cut him off, "Here it is." Turning up the television, both men sat and watched Sakti Sharma get interviewed by a business correspondent for a news channel.

The interview, recorded the previous month, was about an idea for clean energy that Sharma's new company, Sativan, was working on. In truth, Sharma had been working on this fuel cell for some time and had test units working in different locations and outposts for the group, but he also wanted to roll it out to the country, and to the world for that matter, as a clean energy alternative to fossil fuels. Using elements from everyday sand and rocks, as well as a patented, secret engineering process, Sharma managed to turn around a process that he had been working on with NASA's space program officials for energy usage on other planets. These small fuel cells would be able to reduce greenhouse emissions, as well as, provide cost-efficient, reliable power to the masses. Sharma didn't want to give anything away, so he just told everyone what day it would be shown.

"You know Sharma is going to have a tougher time now. He is recognizable," said Cooper with a look of concern on his face.

"We're used to it, so we will have to help him navigate the celebrity. But Coop, this is his life's work, the thing he is most proud of, so we couldn't deny him this. Whether the world takes full advantage of this or not, we wouldn't have wanted Sakti if he didn't want to produce something for the world to make it better," Pearson said with an equal look of uneasiness.

"I know...I know. There are just risks that come with it that are dangerous for us and for Sharma and I don't want him to get hurt. He is a good kid, and this zeal he has for his work blinds him sometimes. Sometimes he doesn't see the true nature of why we are doing what we are." Cooper said, shaking his head.

"I think he understands more than you think he does. His passion makes him look more naive than he really is. I'm proud of him. The work he has done could be world-changing as it relates to energy. It is fantastic really." Pearson said smiling.

Just then the phone rang. It was Sharma.

"Well? What did you guys think? I think it went really well. The show decided to use Ed because he is also an engineer and he could ask and explain the concepts to the general public more easily than the regular correspondents. He did a good job. It was fun. Do you think I looked fat? TV is a weird thing...my face looked bloated or something." Sharma was talking a mile a minute.

"Got some adrenaline pumpin' there, boy?" Cooper asked laughing. "You are the only man I know who would ask if he looked fat."

"You looked great, son," Pearson interjected. "I think it went perfectly. Good job."

"Thanks, I just wanted to appear well, you know? Hey, did I tell you I've made the cell even smaller than the one I showed."

"Whoa, Nelly! What phone are you talkin' on, Sharma?" Don't let the wheels come off the wagon, now!" Cooper warned.

"Oh yeah, but that isn't a big deal, all versions are only in the testing phase...anyway, I just wanted to hear what you guys thought. I will be back home tomorrow to start the agenda for the energy talk."

"When is that scheduled for again?" asked Cooper.

"Later this month."

"Shoot me a secure email once the agenda is fleshed out, ok?" Pearson asked.

"Ok, will do, bye guys." Sharma said disconnecting before he even heard a reply.

"These kids. I can't even imagine what it is like to have a mind like that," Pearson said.

"I know," agreed Cooper. "Some of these guys astound me. I mean I know Bish had to go back to MIT to continue some physics research, and that is his day job... It's crazy!"

Pearson clarified, "it's not just physics work, it is particle physics looking into how the world became the world. Some of his team are delving into questions like what happened right after the big bang, and will time end. Stuff like that keeps me up at night. Do we really need to know? It is mind-boggling, but we need all kinds."

"God bless 'em," said Cooper.

***

During the lion's share of 2005, Michael Bishop was working with a theoretical physics team on questions relating to the expansion of the universe and inflation modeling, something that if the lay person were to hear, their eyes would just gloss over as if another language were being spoken. He found the research compelling, but his work with the group took so much time that he barely had time to complete research the team lead asked of him. He always found the time. If he gave his word that he would do something, he did it. So, he bounced back and forth between MIT and to the places that people asked to meet with him. He relied on his partners to fill in when he couldn't be in two places at once. He took some time to visit the girl he was seeing on and off named Annabelle Ellstin. He was introduced to her by Jackson Cooper about a year before. She was originally from Kentucky but moved to Texas when she was young. Her mom worked for Cooper and when Cooper became part of the group, he knew the Ellstin family would fit perfectly. Annabelle though, was special. Cooper used to tell Mike she looked sweet enough to give you a cavity, but to beware; she was tough as nails and could take care of herself. Others said she reminded them a lot of Samantha, just without the neurotic quirks that Samantha had. The first time Bishop met her was at King Ranch where she decided she could be of most use. She came riding up on a horse with a Weatherby rifle on her back and dirt all over her face. Bishop liked her but he also knew that because of his relationship issues, someone else would come and snatch her up and be right for doing so.

As far as the other two in 2005, Samantha and Nikoli knew they were not as effective as Bishop when explaining the vision.

After all, initially it wasn't their vision. They both agreed with it whole-heartedly, but it was Bishop that saw what needed to be done and they were just his lieutenants to help carry it out. Samantha balanced her work pretty much fifty-fifty during 2005. Having her own practice allowed as much flexibility as she needed, so when someone from the group needed something, she was always able to comply. Nikoli, in contrast, was barely around for the group physically, but he was always there in spirit. He checked in when he could, but he had, with his business partner, taken their company public and made a killing. They were the toast the of the tech world. The success was bittersweet for Borodin. It was everything he ever wanted and that he knew he could do. He just thought it would be with Michael Bishop and Samantha Sloan. He always thought they would create a company together. But as close as they were, they had such different interests. Now as an adult, he could see this was the only way it could go. He loved Ford like a brother and the work they did together was astounding. He felt energized after several eighteen or twenty hour days.

The other big event in Nikoli's life outside of AmendX and Sensedatum was finally asking Haley, his long-time girlfriend, to marry him. Haley was a pillar of patience. Most women would have given him the marriage ultimatum years ago, but Haley was happy in their relationship and knew his commitment was to his company first. She could see the change on his face after it went public. He had accomplished what he had set out to do, and now he had a look of serenity and maturity. A month later he proposed, and now that money was not an issue, he wanted her to have the wedding of her dreams. They would be married in Napa Valley on September 16th, 2006.

***

Flying from Austin back to San Jose, the lead individuals working on the energy component of the group's most critical list were Michael Bishop, Randall Quinn, Tim Conrad, Rex Morrison, Sakti Sharma, who was the real leader, and a rare appearance from Nikoli Borodin. Nikoli wanted to be involved in every item on the list, but time just didn't permit such a commitment so he had to pick those areas that he could be most useful. Technology, of course, energy and education were those areas. Morrison was intrigued with Bishop's 'real-world' research, so following the meeting, they would continue on to Boston and work together for a few weeks. Dean Kinsey couldn't be at the meeting but would meet up with Nikoli and Sharma to be briefed once they arrived in San Jose. Adam Edelstein put his money where his interests were, and he knew that he would lock horns with Quinn, as they did in almost everything, so he bowed out of this one and would work on some economic research with Dylan Sterling. The group literally consisted of hundreds of people working in different ways: research, implementation, reporting, et cetera. This meeting was a recap of action items that had recently been prepared.

"Ok, since we last made our list of items, our contributories have compiled the following report on current and expanding energy resources in Texas," started Sharma, in his now familiar Indian accent. "Prior to anything we have augmented, Texas was the top crude oil producer in the country, and with the new find at King Ranch, that production capacity has doubled. We have sent some people down to Texas City to find out how bad the refinery explosion really was and what the impact will be since it known to be the second largest refinery in Texas. From what I heard, it's a mess down there. We won't know how any of it affects us for a few weeks at least. Other non-renewable fuels that we are working to expand on include natural gas, coal and nuclear energy, although I believe nuclear energy should be on the renewable list instead, but that is a debate for another time. Renewable sources that exist in Texas include solar, geothermal, hydropower, and wind. Wind is the only one we have done nothing with. Currently, all of our facilities are functioning on either solar, geothermal or my fuel cell."

"Are the facilities running solely on those, or are they supplemented by any non-renewable fuels?" asked Conrad.

"Wholly," answered Sharma. "Each facility, depending on need, is running completely on one of the three. And keep in mind, these are also running completely off of any energy detection devices, with the exception of the nuclear facility, which we want to be observed by the sensor grid."

"Yeah, I saw that on one of the reports that we got earlier, what is that about?" asked Quinn.

Sharma looked at Bishop to answer that question. "That is a nuclear facility we want on the grid for the planning of the event down the road. Since we are talking about something to happen at a much later date, I recommend we skip that piece for now and talk only about what has been developed with regard to the renewable energy sources," answered Bishop. "Except to ask, what is currently being detected?"

"Two mid-sized reactors, one with fusion capabilities, the other being fission, that is what is reported to the applicable agencies," answered Sharma. "We will discuss this more at a later date, as Bishop indicated, but what I will say is that it's located in Sweetwater, which is in central Texas. The two current operating nuclear power plants in Texas, Comanche Peak Nuclear Power Plant and South Texas Nuclear Generating Station, are both a good distance from this plant. We have to remember that the Nuclear Regulatory Commission defines two planning zones for emergencies around plants like these: a plume exposure pathway zone, which is about 10 miles, and an ingestion pathway zone, which is at least 50 miles. Chernobyl was a Level 7 event, which is the biggest. On that day, workers 680 miles away had radiation detected on them. Based on our event, the levels will show the same level of exposure, leading to evacuation of essentially the 90 percent of the state."

"I don't even know the difference between fusion and fission, much less understand levels of nuclear accidents," said Nikoli.

"Irrelevant, since they aren't really there," said Bishop. "But if you want to know, as I said, I will explain it later."

"I thought everything was going to be run off of the sand cell," said Morrison.

Sharma grunted, "My fuel cell can run most things, but there has to be diversification and redundancies to ensure success. Incidentally, that brings up another point. The cells running in Texas have an additional piece to them. Within a specified distance, they will also emit a pulse, similar to an EMP, which will shut down any electrical system not fitted to detect it. Horst, a friend of mine who is working on a fully electric car helped me work on it. Once he joined the group, he made it more efficient and more powerful."

"Are you saying that it will shut down everything near it unless it has this bypass?" asked Conrad.

"Precisely," answered Sharma. "It will basically scramble electrical signals, shutting down a device."

"And this is good…why?" continued Conrad.

"If any move is made to deploy an attack, electrical systems will not work, thus be stopped via both land and air. Air systems will get a warning, but if it enters Texas air space, it will shut down." Sharma answered matter-of-factly.

Bishop interjected, "these are things the spook team is working on headed up by Pearson. But since it is energy related Sakti and Horst have had a lot of input. But Sakti's main priority was looking at the different resources and figuring out which ones could be enhanced or left alone."

"So, have you enhanced other energy methods or are they good as-is?" asked Nikoli.

"Oh yes, we have," said Sharma proudly. "The progress we've made in geothermal has the most impact. We are able to heat and cool any facility or home completely without the use of standard electricity or natural gas. These guys don't know what they have. We keep relying on other country's resources when we have everything we need and more here at home, and as far as Texas goes, we have plenty."

"We will have to be ready for some kind of consideration once this happens regarding crude oil," announced Morrison. "The US isn't just going to leave a quarter of refining capacities behind, and that is just what they know of. Bishop and I have talked a little bit about it, but I want it written in the whole package because that is what wars are about and we don't want to go down that path, right?"

Nodding, Bishop said, "Correct, Rex and I were thinking of a buy-back or trade agreement of some kind centered around making it easier to get those who want out of the state out and those who want to join us in. We have the housing dilemma pretty much well in hand, so we just have to make sure that the actual people swap does not become violent and I think the oil will make much of our requests more tolerable. Also, Cooper is going to need to know what energy is going to go where and what is being utilized now in our facilities. Rex, beam him the map from your tablet when you get back to Austin. Aren't you seeing him and Antonio again when you get back from Boston?"

"Yeah, Antonio wants to talk about border issues and how King Ranch will be fortified. Really, he has organized a monthly thing with everyone I think, right?" Morrison looked around the cabin as most men nodded in the affirmative. "He is one brilliant guy. I don't know how he does it all. I know we are all busy and I am often mystified at all ya'all, but he is ridiculous! And about that border control, he and Sam have some pretty radical ideas about how we are going to use some of our more problematic citizens."

"The gang thing, huh?" asked Nikoli.

"Yeah, what do you think of that?" replied Morrison.

"If what she is saying is true, and I'm sure she's got the research to back it up, and it goes into effect I think it will be great. I mean what a way to turn things around to the positive, right?"

"It is way too pie-in-the-sky for me, but I'm trying to keep an open mind. I will be interested to hear all about it when they release their recommendations on the subject," said Quinn.

"Do we have things pretty well wrapped up?" asked Bishop. "Between our discussion and the report, I think we all have what we need and we are starting to move off-topic, so unless anyone has anything else..."

"We have made huge strides on a lot of these resources. If anyone has questions or wants to add anything, send me a message or come see me. I will be at Sensedatum this week with Nikoli then back to my scary underground lab," said Sharma making a scary face. "Don't tell Derek I said that. He thinks it is quite palatial, and it does indeed have every comfort, but it's nice to see the sun once in awhile."

"You don't always have to be at that lab, Sakti," said Quinn. "Don't you have like five? One here in California, in fact."

"Derek says the only time he knows I'm completely protected is in the lab at the facility under Midland, or rather just outside of it."

"Oh, Derek is being too protective. Get Mackay to talk him down, he listens to Mackay...or Pearson. You'll start getting weird if you stay under too long with those of the black ops variety," Quinn said winking.

"I'm sure you can spend some time at any of the labs you feel desirable," said Bishop. "Oh, good we're landing. I have a tee time." "Are you going down to watch the Masters again this year?" asked Conrad.

"Of course, every year. Wanna join me?"

"I may take you up on that. I have to see what the family plan is and I'll let you know."

Wednesday, June 1, 2005 – 8:15am Central Daylight Time (13:15 hours Zulu Time)

Just as Samantha walked through Jackson Cooper's office door with her six-month-old Saint Bernard, Oliver, she knew the plans they had to go over the education agenda was out the window.

"Well find out about injuries or deaths for Christ's sake and get whoever the hell runs that gas company on the horn. I want details damn it!" screamed Cooper, slamming down the phone causing Oliver's head to snap up.

"What's the matter Jack?" asked Sloan, almost afraid to hear the answer, patting Oliver gently.

"There was a goddamn natural gas explosion last night in Crosby...Holy Moly, he's gotten big. You know back in March that refinery exploded in Texas City. At least that was just a refinery; we aren't talking about our resources just leaking out of the land. These idiots don't know how to put it out... they're saying three to five days, like that is even remotely acceptable. Oh, and no mention about the people there...no, no, the Governor doesn't need to know this shit. Can you believe this?" Cooper went on ranting and pacing around his office. "First, Texas City, then the hand grenade and now this. What the hell next is gonna happen?"

"What?" asked Sloan trying to stay with Cooper's rant. "Hand grenade?"

"You heard about that, right? The Armenian that threw a..." Cooper's voice got low and he sat down at his desk and leaned into it. "Fuckin grenade about fifty feet away from 43."

Nodding, Sloan knew what he was talking about.

"Didn't go off, how lucky is that?" he said.

"Maybe I'm just being thick here, but what does that have to do with the refinery and this new explosion?" asked Sloan.

"Can you imagine the shit we would be in after having a president assassinated? We, I have enough to worry about with just the shit going on here in Texas. An assassination would set back our efforts in a major way if not completely derail them!" Cooper answered, pushing himself away from his desk exasperated.

"Well...I'm not sure that is true, but these recent happenings are certainly making things harder. Did anyone die from the explosion last night?" she asked.

Cooper grunted, "I wish I knew." Then in a much louder, so as to let the anteroom hear him, "the information I have coming in is, well let's just say, is a bit sluggish."

Sloan was seated in a chair across from Cooper's desk. He reached across the desk and put out his hands. She was a little confused and paused for a second before putting her hands out to meet his, and he grabbed them.

Letting out a deep breath, "what do you want your legacy to be Samantha?"

"That is big question Jack. I mean..."

Cutting her off, he sat with his arms stretched out on his desk, holding her hands and said contemplatively, "I always thought being a part of this group and accomplishing something, anything that we are setting out to would be my swan's song. But sometimes I feel like we will never make it. There is too much to battle against, too much lethargy and waste, not to mention incompetence."

"We all feel like that sometimes Jack, and you have so much to do while planning all of this, I'm surprised it hasn't hit you sooner," she said, not sure how much counsel he wanted.

Staring down at his desk, still holding her hands, he said, "Really, though, what do you want to be remembered for?"

Taking her hands back and readjusting in her seat, "I haven't really thought about it all that much...being remembered? I just want to get some things done first before I start thinking of that. But you know, coach Bill B. says he tries to give back to football as much as he has gotten out of it. How about using that in life? I mean we could look at all the shit, and there really is plenty of it, but why not look at the good. Look at what we are doing, look at the amazing people we have with us, contributing, giving so much…let's see if we can give back as much as we have gotten."

In his Texas drawl he said, "There just has to be more 'want-to' out there."

"Hmph," she said. "If we keep waiting on those 'out there' then we will be waiting forever. That is why we are taking the ball, ya know?"

"Yeah, you and your football analogies," he laughed.

"I just love good coaches and teachers. You can learn so much from what they do, and it makes me feel like I have a purpose; without one life wouldn't look all that great. You can tell a good teacher really easily because they make you want to do well for them and that transitions to wanting to do well for yourself. My Russian teacher in junior high was like that."

"You took Russian?" Cooper asked off point.

"Yes. I wanted her to be proud of me before I understood the importance of doing things well for yourself. I just didn't want to let her down."

Cooper's admin came into the office after a quick knock on the door. "Shelby's got the gas company President on the line for you, Mr. Cooper," she said.

"Thanks, Cindy," he answered.

Sloan got up from her seat; "You are going to be busy with this for a while, Jack. Call me later and we will reschedule."

"Thanks Sam, I'm sorry for…for all of this."

"No worries, talk soon," she said getting up with Oliver in tow.

As she left she thought, at least they talked a little about education, from a philosophy standpoint anyway.

CHAPTER 25
DRAMA, WINE & DOGS

Monday, February 6, 2006 – 1:30pm Eastern Standard Time (18:30 hours Zulu Time)

Flying from Detroit to Boston, Michael Bishop and Samantha Sloan were talking about a wide range of topics. Light-hearted things like the results of Super Bowl 40, which they just attended and more serious matters like the decision to try to take children to Texas when the couple is divorced.

"The Stones were good, don't you think?" asked Bishop.

"I'm kinda over the insanity at halftime. The hype is so huge about the game in general that nothing can stand up to it and there is an automatic let down when it's over. Unless of course the only reason you want to celebrate is to get completely tanked and not remember it anyway. I'm glad the Steelers won though..."

"You were screaming pretty good during the game, and yes, I know you've always been AFC-biased," snickered Bishop.

"Don't get me wrong, I had a great time," Sloan said. "Thanks for taking me. But I miss Oliver and the kitties. Unless it is New England or Denver I could watch the game from home and be just as satisfied."

"Why can't you be normal and like the 49ers, or even the Raiders?"

"Well, the Raiders are East Bay shit and I can't even believe you asked me that...you hate them too, and remember, I am AFC-biased. I just think my teams have more class. It is about the competition and athleticism, not the 'roid rage meat head B.S," answered Sloan.

"Ok, you tell yourself whatever you have to...SF is back on track but it will always be Candlestick to me, not that Monster crap...I mean, what is that? Do you think they made a dollar from changing the name? I think so many people were pissed that it actually hurt them."

"I totally get it...the stadium in Denver will always be Mile High stadium to me."

Bishop changed the subject. "Let me get your thoughts on something else. I was having a conversation with a member who does IT consulting. He was doing security stuff at MIT when we first met. He is really struggling with the possibility of leaving his kids behind when we go. He doesn't live with them because he divorced his now ex-wife, like five years ago, and she insisted on custody. Since he traveled for his job he thought it was best."

"And he wouldn't want to tell her about the group and have them all come?" asked Sloan.

"Oh, no way. I guess from what he has said about her, she is a real piece of shit. He said 'she is my kids' mother, I have to keep it respectful, especially in front of my kids.' He's a good guy and he's told me stories of the trash she talks about him in front of the kids and if he dates anyone, the mom says the girlfriend is a whore or something even worse, even having never met them."

"She sounds lovely," Sloan said sarcastically.

"So I guess since he is in Boston pretty much without travel, he had his oldest daughter come live with him for a while. It seemed good at first and then she up and left with a weeks notice, just saying she was ready to go home. Come to find out, she was stealing from him, wrote really nasty emails about him to her mother, that he recovered and about a friend of his that happened to be a woman. His daughter was doing drugs even after he explicitly talked about it with her, letting her know it was not acceptable while living with him...bragged to her boyfriend that she got away with it and how stupid he was."

"How old is this girl?"

"I'm not sure, he told me I think...I'm thinking twenty-one."

"He should have sent her packing," said Sloan in a definitive tone.

"He found all of this out after she was already gone...but it gets better. Part of the reason she was living with him was to try to go to school, better herself, all of that. He said her vocabulary was that of a middle school student. Her food choices were hideous; I guess the mother very rarely cooks and eats complete junk herself. I mean, everything he said made me glad I don't know this woman, or the daughter, for that matter. He said the daughter ended up being two-faced and wickedly manipulative. He was really hurt by this whole thing, and was wondering that if he took her to Texas, could he get her to change?"

"No, is the short answer. How old are the other kids?" she asked in disgust.

"Quite a bit younger," Bishop answered.

"If the kid is of age, it is too late for her in the sense that forcing her to go somewhere else will only make matters worse. She will grow up mentally and emotionally some day and realize her mother is complete trash and that her father was just trying to get her out of an environment that was not conducive to growing as a person and give her some opportunities she would not have had otherwise. But for now, the daughter is as much trash as the mother so he has to let that ship sail. As far as the younger ones, if they were younger than eighteen, I would get them for the 'weekend' and never look back. It will be really hard for him, almost like deprogramming them from a cult. They will believe life is supposed to be one way based on how the mother parented them, or rather un-parented them, but unless he wants to leave them completely behind, it will be a long hard road. Being in the environment we are trying to set up will make things a little easier if it is any consolation. The kids will only be around others that share our philosophies, and they will soon come to see them as their own."

"Do you think I should give him advice either way?" asked Bishop.

"No, he has to make the decision himself. He already made the tough one to join us. Once people see us out in the open, many will want to join us because that is the life they live anyway and are getting beaten down and frustrated because of it. It is just too bad his ex-wife is so selfish or bitter or whatever her pathology is to actually let it hurt her children."

"Agreed," said Bishop. "Maybe that is why I haven't had kids… it seems like every minute you interact with one, you could be screwing something up."

"That is not the reason you haven't had kids. You are in the middle of changing a societal paradigm, and even more importantly, I think you might need a girl for that." Sloan quipped light-heartedly.

"Hmmm," Bishop said nodding. "How long are you staying in Boston?"

"Like five days I think. Cooper wants me back to join him at Fort Hood. We have been profiling for a while now but I have about thirty psychiatrists and psychologists there now really ramping up. Reports have been fascinating."

"How so?"

"So many of the soldiers, and even the command, love this country so much but feel outside of society, like general society pushes it out of mind, which in and of itself is natural, but the way they are reporting back is more like a refusal to believe there is a problem in this country and if they stick their heads in the sand long enough it will go away. But the reports are promising in that these are the ideologies we want. They are not reporting anger, but sadness, need to step in and improve, not create violence, and that shows sound psychological health."

"That is great news. So let's grab dinner if you can a few nights before you leave again."

"Sounds good."

***

When Sloan was due to leave six days later, most northeastern airports were shut down due to snowstorms. The news reported New York City was due to get a minimum of two feet of snow. She was going to be there for a while and she was pissed. She missed Oliver and called her mother, who was taking care of him and the cats, for an update everyday.

"How is he doing?" she asked.

"The same as he was yesterday...happy running around in the yard and eating like a king. I can't believe what you feed him Samantha," answered her mother.

"He eats some kibble, which is good for his teeth. Plus, studies show that by eating animal protein like real chicken, his bones, hydration and weight all stay healthier," she responded agitated. "I will be on the first plane out of here, even if I have to fly privately."

"Oh, really Sam, that is such a waste of money. He is fine. A neighbor down the street loves Saints and asked if her daughter could come play with him so he got all kinds of attention this morning, and he loved it."

"Ahh!" said Sloan brightening up. "He loves kids. I miss him so much!"

"I know you do dear. He is here, happy, eating better than us, so just get home safe and keep me posted so I know when to expect you. Oh and your car got dropped off with the new tinted windows."

"Excellent, how does it look?"

"Your father thinks it is ridiculous that you needed a new car in the first place, let alone having to have the windows tinted."

"With as much as I drive, I think I nearly had a hundred thousand miles on my last Cayenne. It was time for a new one. Did they put the new dog cover on the back seats?"

"I didn't know to look. I'll take a look in a few minutes, and when you call to check on the animals tomorrow, I will let you know," answered her mother in that motherly tone.

"Thanks mom, really. I appreciate you caring for them like I would, even though you don't believe it should be that way."

"Well these animals are probably going to be the only grandkids I get out of you, so I'm glad to do it. Be safe."

"Talk to you tomorrow," she said, and with that, hung up.

***

September that year was wrought with drama, both bad and good. The bad being a death in the group of a disgruntled member, and the good being Nikoli's wedding to his girlfriend, Haley. The beginning of the month brought a lot of scrutiny, criticism, and distrust among the group members. An unknown but rather wealthy member had been openly unhappy with the lack of action in the group. At first Bailey agreed with him, but after awhile, he saw that it was ego and instability that drove this man. He had given millions to the cause and felt that because of this, he should also be calling the shots single handedly. Many members tried to intervene with no success. Sam and Bishop both worked with him to investigate his ideas and endeavor to use them if appropriate. None of his ideas were appropriate; what he wanted was strictly action for action's sake, and that usually ended with a violent plan to hurt people. This was never a goal for the group.

After some time, Samantha concluded that he should leave the group and that they should part as friends, while keeping the secrecy and integrity of the group intact. One of the group's initial requirements was if any money was put into the cause, it was spent and not available to be returned. It was completely acceptable to not put in any money and provide sweat equity instead. This was an idea and a group that shared ideals and ideologies, so in 99% of the cases, this was not a problem. This man turned everything on its side. He threatened to go to the media if his plan was not put into action. He threatened other group member's families. The situation got so bad that a meeting was called to discuss options. Because Holden and Mackay were both out of the country, it had to wait until the second week of September.

Before the meeting took place, the man was found dead in his home in Austin from an apparent heart attack. The toxicology report would find, many months later, cocaine in the man's system, and evidence of prolonged use. But prior to that information being available, it was just too mysterious to not raise the eyebrows of some of the members, and per the usual... Bailey.

"Another mysterious death? What the hell is going on? You can't leave this group without dying?" Bailey fumed.

"You should try and see," Holden sneered. He was in no mood, he came straight from the airport with no sleep and he wasn't about to put up with Bailey for one second.

"There have been members who have left and they are all still living happy, healthy lives," Sloan responded.

"What the fuck, really? Are you kidding me? You don't think this is odd at all, Samantha?" screamed Bailey, almost panic-stricken.

"Stop, Joseph, just stop. If you always look at the weird stuff, this might seem weird, but you have been working with the same people that freak did, and you have had none of the problems that he had. You have made progress where he made none," Samantha said stretching her neck side to side clearly stressed out.

"And where were you the night he died?" Bailey asked whirling around to Holden.

Derek Holden had had enough, standing as he started to talk, but was interrupted by Harris Corrigan, who was much larger than both men and very commanding.

"Derek, wait. Getting in each other's faces for the tenth time isn't going to solve anything," Corrigan offered.

Sitting back down, Holden asked staring right at Bailey, "do you really think I would do it myself, if I did it at all?"

"That is not helpful Derek," Bishop said rising in a relaxed and nonchalant manner while leaving the room to take a call, not stressed at all.

Much around Derek Holden seemed mysterious. Many members often wondered if he was capable of the things Bailey kept insinuating about him, or was it just coincidence? Most decided they didn't even want to know. Derek, on the other hand, didn't make it easy for himself by saying the things he said. He almost got off on the mystery.

"We need to stay away from this one, and I mean far away. We have some members in the Austin PD that can report back when all is said and done, but until then, it is what it is. I've done some checking, and other than our regular interactions with each other, he wasn't close to anyone, so there shouldn't be any questions asked of any of us. But if for some reason there are, answer them truthfully. You knew him in an acquaintance sort of way. Originally, you thought you had a lot in common with him, but he ended up being unstable and you distanced yourself from him. Is that not true?" Samantha asked looking around. "Ok, then, pass it around and we are done." She finished, and then shrugged in her chair.

Saturday, September 16, 2006

The drama around the wedding was wholly different from earlier that month. Nikoli wanted to give Haley everything she wanted, and that was the best part; she wanted only Nikoli. Haley didn't come from money and it didn't impress her. Obviously, money offers security and when talking about the sums that Nikoli had, it offered opportunities and conveniences that very few were given. She loved wine, but one of her favorite things was to find wines that didn't cost a lot of money; these treasures that almost anyone could buy. She also didn't have the time or desire to put on airs. She and Nikoli loved to grab a yummy bottle of wine and some really spicy hot wings or pizza and picnic in their backyard while watching the sunset. She would pick that over a fancy restaurant any day. When Tate called Nikoli to let him know he could use the Bravium land, he was ecstatic. It was Haley's favorite wine and she loved to visit the winery whenever possible. Tate Hendrix was a marketing executive turned venture capitalist by trade, wine maker by love and passion. He brought successful IPO's from some of the most promising tech companies in the business. He did his work well and with integrity, and he followed those same guidelines when making wine.

Self-described oenophiles, Hendrix and his wife grew close to Nikoli and Haley. Unable to tell Haley about the group, he didn't want to recruit Tate either because he was so close to Haley, and didn't want to put him in a bad position. Over time, Nikoli realized that his day-to-day life could not mesh with his life with the group, unlike Samantha and Michael. It often troubled him, too. Tate was a poster child for the perfect Xer. He held strong beliefs but mostly all moderate. He wasn't fanatical about anything except striving for perfection. After years of success, his venture capital company basically ran itself, allowing him to focus solely on the love of wine and wine making. He started Bravium with a little bit of land and a huge passion for wine making. His college education was in environmental science, which ended up working well for him when he went back for a Masters in Viticulture and Enology at UC Davis. He worked endlessly on figuring out how wine was made; what role the land, weather, and the process played from delicately bringing up the grape, to the harvest, to the bottling and aging of the wines. He decided that he wasn't out for mass distribution. His land purchase was large enough to focus on the types of grapes that thrived in the area. For other grapes, he would buy from other wine makers and grape growers in other parts of California. Over the years, he became better and better, cultivating wonderful boutique wines and an extensive following. There were waiting lists to be able to order his wines, which was never his intention. His intention was to make enough wine that he was able to control all aspects of the process resulting in a wine that met his high standards. One of the wines, a red blend, became so sought after, that he finally conceded and doubled the yield.

Nikoli and Haley supported his ideals and convictions and were ready to help in any way they could, and the only thing they wanted in return was to always be able to get his wines. Nikoli used to joke with him, that he was not beneath bribery for a case or two. Having the wedding at Bravium was an honor. The event was tastefully done; there were no extravagant requests of the couple or obligations of Hendrix. He had an idea this day was coming so he even made a special white wine for the occasion and called it White Wedding. The red blend would also be served. Tate's wife would not be partaking in the wine, however, as she was six months pregnant with their first child, a son. The wedding party consisted of the groom, and his best men, Nikoli's two best friends Michael Bishop and Langley Ford. Haley asked Samantha to stand with her to be nice, but Sam knew she had two ladies in mind to walk with her on her special day so she thanked her, but told her to have the most important people in her life be with her on that day. She had her best girlfriend growing up and her mother. Her father wasn't really in the picture; he and her mother had been divorced since she was a young girl. He was alive and would be at the wedding, but he was too self-absorbed to even notice she hadn't asked him to walk her down the isle. Instead, he and her fourth stepmother would be guests only. Her mother would walk with her down the isle and join her best friend as a bridesmaid. She wasn't all that sentimental about the whole wedding thing. It wasn't until Samantha, of all people, pointed out what a special day it really was did she get all mushy inside.

Interestingly, Rex Morrison was well acquainted with Tate Hendrix. They were both involved in responsible agriculture and green groups. Not the kind like save the thorn-mint leaf, but real practices that might cost a little more, but would sustain the planet, while still making quite a profit. Both men believed that those endeavors were not mutually exclusive. Since Samantha was not dating anyone at the time of the wedding and Bishop was, she asked Rex if he would accompany her as her guest. He was an invited guest, of course, but this worked out well. Bishop's date, on the other hand, could have missed the whole event and it wouldn't really have mattered to either of them. He was in an off period from

Annabelle and she was busy doing what she loved, being hands on at King Ranch. He and this new girl were in the third month of the relationship; right about where the girl realizes it is going nowhere and where Mike got bored. He tried his best to keep her with him while mingling and talking with other guests, but she had no interest in the conversations he was a part of and decided to go to the bar and talk to a few other girls that she had met in the last couple of months and had more in common with.

The ceremony was short and very sweet; the whole thing lasted about twenty minutes. It had no religious underpinnings even though both Nikoli and Haley were raised Christian. It was important to Nikoli to have traditional vows read and they each said words from the heart to each other as well. A judge friend of Nikoli's and fellow Xer conducted the ceremony. Following the ceremony was a simple but elegant dinner, dancing and the traditional reception. Many conversations were happening all around the valley floor adjacent to the vineyard. This area usually hosted wine tastings and was furnished with giant long refectory tables under an enormous pergola with soft white lighting for ambiance. On one side was a fire pit with stone seating all around it. There Samantha saw many people engaged in a conversation that looked heated, yet Bishop was as calm as ever. She walked over to listen.

"This administration is totally ignoring the social needs of the country. Hot spots in metropolitan areas are worse than ever, education is only for the rich; public school has essentially been left to rot, and will we ever get some sort of healthcare system that takes care of all of our people?" Said a handsome man in a tuxedo that had one day been really nice; but with time looked a bit worn and the pants were slightly too short.

Michael Bishop stood and walked closer to the man and offered his hand to shake it, "I'm sorry, I didn't catch your name."

Taken a bit off guard at Bishop's cordial manners, as they had been essentially arguing for the last ten minutes. He returned the outstretched hand, shook his hand and said almost stuttering, "Martin. Martin Harrison."

"Michael Bishop, it is nice to meet you. I very much enjoy speaking to people with very different views than mine because it helps me see many sides of extremely complex issues. There are no easy answers and unless all sides can come together and really hear each other, no compromises can be made." Michael said returning to his seat.

"That's the thing, there shouldn't be compromise. If you know you are right, why compromise?" Harrison sneered back.

"Hmm," said Bishop looking thoughtfully. "The only time I liked the idea of no comprise was the gun company Heckler & Koch's No Compromise slogan," he said raising an eyebrow. He said this specifically to get a rise out of him because he knew people like this who were ready to spend everyone else's money on social well fare programs usually weren't so much the NRA type either.

Bishop got the look of shock on Harrison's face that he intended, yet Harrison felt the need to continue, "Social reform does have to happen in this country, but not in the way you are saying. We need more programs to help the less fortunate, we need to give those who have not gotten a fair shake a leg up." Harrison went on to say that money needed to be put into research to stop things like global warming, stem cell research, and fossil fuel consumption with the use of newer technologies like fracking.

"You know we are not as far off as you might think, but it is how you expect the process to start that is the problem," Bishop said in earnest trying to make Harrison understand. "You are saying few rich have to take care of the many. That model is unsustainable; it encourages the needy to remain needy because if they start making anything, it will go to other needy, discouraging any individual success. If the model flips, it gives everyone equal opportunity to succeed and be valued, obviously with exceptions that must be reviewed on an individual basis. If you and I both produce something of value, we do not need the handout. Now multiply that by six billion. Those are high functioning societies with the ability to help those in need for short periods of time when needed. But we aren't teaching that now, we are teaching entitlements and laziness and by saying we should be helping those less fortunate, you are right, we should be helping them work to produce and live for their own value and find their own purpose. That helps us all and self efficacy is an extremely powerful drug, my friend."

Harrison continued to argue many points, but when asked about details in any of the subjects he raised, he was unable to speak intelligently.

While several people were listening intently, Sam sat down near her friend Victoria who was sitting next to Harrison and motioned for her to scoot over a bit towards her. "You brought this guy? Total idiot," she said with disgust. "Where did you find this one?"

"I met him online. He seemed great. He has a good job, he is divorced but is amiable with the Ex, and he takes good care of his kids. He certainly doesn't look like the enemy," Victoria said exasperated.

"What the hell do you think the devil would look like Victoria? All gross and ignorant? He would be beautiful and smart and totally able to sway you! How can you be so smart and so stupid at the same time?" Samantha got up, rolled her eyes and said, "you better save him before he says anything else stupid," and she walked away.

Bishop was saddened by the beliefs Harrison held, but he was more distressed at the idea that he felt he could not be wrong, and was unwilling to discuss compromise or even learn more fully the ideas he claimed to support. This guy's unwillingness to support enthusiastic debate was different than Sam's inability to understand how someone can think so differently than she does. On the surface, it seemed the same, but Samantha truly didn't understand how someone could be a criminal if she herself couldn't be one. In other words, she had great difficulty in her practice when during pro bono work she had to counsel someone like a convicted rapist. She couldn't fathom how someone could think that behavior was acceptable. But she could understand someone who stole something like food to feed his family. She did not condone it, but she understood it, and she was always willing to hear both sides of an argument. She felt it gave her insight that could, probably wouldn't, but could change her mind. This Harrison guy was just self-righteous and for the wrong reasons. Bishop thought he could always at least try to see other people's side of things. He couldn't understand what this guy was trying to accomplish.

Bishop continued, "By not letting someone produce, you take away something from them and yourself. The person feels no internal value or self-efficacy and taking that away is savage to me. Then on the other hand you lose a contributing member of society that can work alongside you and contribute their different values and the mixture creates something great. Without it, you are stuck with an entitled dependent. These are topics scientists and philosophers have been struggling with for centuries and without healthy debate and the desire to understand the other side, we will never come to a solution. But we are at a wedding, a time to celebrate, so let's do just that." With that Bishop stood and went to find his soon-to-be-ex-girlfriend.

Those around listening seemed confused, but couldn't help feeling a sense of hope or confidence. Everyone had a different bone to pick with the world; for some it was politics, others argued for overhauling whole areas of interest, like taxes or the criminal justice system, while still others just wanted to work on their own community problems. But they all walked away with the feeling of promise, and a willingness to work a little harder for whatever was to come Monday morning. Harrison sat there brooding.

Later, while dancing with Sloan, Rex said, "How are we even supposed to tell who's in and who's out? There are so many of us nowadays."

"It shouldn't matter, it isn't like we are going to make public service announcements to only those AmendXers out there," Sam quipped. But he did bring up a good point actually, and she felt bitchy. "I'm sorry, that sounded crabby."

"No worries," Rex responded in his sexy Texan accent, "I know that is just you."

Snap! She was just put in her place and he had a sense of humor, she thought. Sweet!

As the song ended and they were walking off the dance floor, he said, "I know I'm going to catch hell from you for this, and I don't mean like a secret handshake, but maybe we should wear something unique so we can identify each other easily."

"Hmm, you know, that isn't a bad idea," she said.

***

228

Within a few weeks Samantha and Victoria researched items that the group could use to identify other members. It was decided that a specific metal, rhodium, would be used in the form of an X. It was chosen for a few reasons. First, because of the tremendous amount of platinum found and mined in the Laureles Division of King Ranch, the group held the market on these rare and valuable metals. Since rhodium is a minor constituent of platinum, its value depends on the quantities of platinum being mined. The major, and accidental, platinum find in the Laureles in 2005, when the group was excavating for an outpost, was able to be kept secret, and also added to the already tremendous wealth of the group. Second, with that find, Texas would become the second most abundant source of platinum next to South America. Finally, the X fit the group obviously, but it could also be disguised or even indistinguishable as to portraying any kind of symbolism. Victoria thought of the way they would be presented; lapel pins for men in suits, an X pendant for women that wanted to wear a necklace, and for those more casual times a Road ID-like bracelet with a rhodium plate that had an X badge on it seemed to work perfectly. There would be times that large groups would get together and security would need something easy to identify guests. It would also be great, albeit a rare event to see a fellow Xer at the grocery store or restaurant and be able to recognize them.

CHAPTER 26
FUZZY, A FIGHT & A PIECE OF PIZZA

Tuesday, January 9, 2007 – 10:00am Pacific Standard Time (18:00 hours Zulu Time)

Everyone in the group was curious to know what these 13-C conferences and product unveilings were all about so many chose to attend. Quinn was less-than-ecstatic about the proposition, because his paranoia told him it was reckless. Nevertheless, Elam got them tickets, and Samantha, Bishop, Nikoli, and even Cooper and Holden came to the event. Other techie guys from the group went, more for practical professional reconnaissance of real-world jealousy than for Xer group support, but Kinsey, Dani and Conrad had come in unannounced. The Needham brothers came and that caused much melee. Media asked why they were there, if they were going to purchase 13-C stock, or did they already own it. Their presence took much attention away from the product Quinn was so excited and proud to announce. The brothers simply answered that they were huge 13-C fans and wanted to see first hand what the new beautiful device would be.

No one was disappointed: a smart phone so thin and designed so beautifully. But this smartphone was like no other; it could play music, sync one's calendar and email, it had more stock applications on it to include games, productivity tools and could even be configured to be completely voice activated. Samantha was like a little girl at Christmas. Her enthusiasm for Star Trek often made her talk to air like she was talking to the computer on the Enterprise. Of course nothing responded or carried out her commands. But now, now her phone could. To make it even better, downloadable voices could be purchased…the Star Trek voice being one of them. She wondered why Quinn had not given the group these devices the minute they were available.

She sought out Elam to find out when she could get one, but he had left the country on 13-C business, so she tracked down Quinn. He told her she would simply have to get on the waiting list with everyone else. Later that night most of the same group went to

Bishop's for drinks before each went their separate ways to home and work across the country. Everyone was talking and laughing and having a great time just being with each other when the doorbell rang. It was a messenger delivering about twenty phones. What a wonderful asshole, Sam thought of Quinn while digging into the box to make sure hers was black.

Friday, February 9, 2007 – 5:30pm Pacific Standard Time (Saturday, February 10, 2007 – 01:30 hours Zulu Time)

Samantha had dinner just outside of Menlo Park with a childhood friend that she had kept in touch with over the years, despite the fact that they really had nothing in common anymore. She had just returned from her fourth Super Bowl. The Indianapolis Colts beat the Chicago Bears 29-17. She was wearing black jeans and a black t-shirt with white lettering that said 'Peyton Rocks!' on it. It was rare to find her in clothing that said anything, but she was a big fan of Peyton Manning and loved the shirt. Tiffany, her childhood friend, was a recovering alcoholic, and a super-liberal that never learned personal accountability. She had no self-worth, thus didn't understand the idea of self-efficacy and what real work did for the spirit, the mind, the wallet, or life. But she believed through her own attempts at recovery that qualified her to work with and try to help other addicts. Sam applauded the effort, but believed one's own house must be in order prior to helping others. Tiffany was at one point a beautiful girl and was always very outgoing. Now she looked bloated, over-weight and old. The time they had met previous to this dinner, Sam had offered to work out with her when she was in town, or go to a gym with her, or even do something else that Tiffany could think of. Tiffany had several excuses as to why she couldn't or wouldn't take Sam's offer, so Sam stopped offering. It was disheartening to see someone who had so much life in her at one point stripped down to this. Her parents were wealthy so Tiffany never had to work and although her parents loved her to bits and thought the money would offer her security to take the time to find her purpose, it actually caused her to float aimlessly through life never really engaging. It could have been her parent's fault when she was eighteen. It was most certainly Tiffany's own fault in her thirties.

They got into an argument on a couple of topics during dinner. It started because Tiffany was talking about a man, who she thought she loved, that didn't want to see her while he was in town, or rather said he didn't have enough time. Tiffany said that it didn't bother her. Sam just shook her head and told Tiffany that she thought she was delusional. What was it with these women that were doormats for men? Maybe she was just lucky and didn't have to experience that herself to learn from it. Sam thought to herself that her other friend, Victoria, was world class, had a work ethic and IQ comparable only to the best in the world, and she did the same things as Tiffany. The second argument was, as they were walking out of the restaurant, Tiffany wanted to give her doggie bag to a homeless person across the street.

"Absolutely not," said Samantha.

"I paid for it, I should be able to give it to anyone I want," snipped Tiffany.

Samantha wanted to say, "No, your parents paid for it," but didn't want to start a whole other argument. Instead she tried to explain that by giving anything away for nothing, it diminishes the value of what you are giving, plus it takes away and personal value within the person. Tiffany was having no part of that.

"I hate money, I would rather be poor than have to deal with money, it makes me feel weird," she said.

"It doesn't have to be about money, Tiffany," Samantha started. She went through her whole self-reliance speech to no avail.

"I just wanted to give a couple of slices of cold pizza to that guy. It felt right, and I go by gut."

"It isn't just about giving a piece of pizza away Tiff. Did you see the guy with him? Why wasn't that guy helping him? He had a brand new sports cap on and was clean-shaven with clean clothes, unlike his pal. So what is he doing with him beside waiting to try to bilk you out of money and your pizza."

"I just want to help people... call it the hippie in me."

"Great," grunted Sam. She had had enough. "It's the hippies that ruined this country. If it was just about a piece of fuckin' pizza, that would be that, but you are totally missing the broader implications. And what?! You would rather be poor? You or I don't even know what that means, so how can you even say that. Your parents have bailed you out your entire life. You can't keep a job, you haven't even been able to stay sober, you smoke pot because you have to be altered, and don't you see that is the same thing as drinking? You say you aren't ashamed to be doing drugs but still at thirty-two you won't tell your parents. Except you don't smoke enough pot to pass out and fuck strangers like you do when you drink. You can't even stick to the accountability that will save your life, so how can you try to help anyone else? You are in no position to. Fix yourself. That is what will help other people. Because your mom won't have to plan your funeral, fix yourself, so you can graduate from school and accomplish something big, fix yourself so you can stand on your own two feet and see what it is that I've been talking about all night; what it feels like to know you are strong and worthy and able. Handouts and entitlements do NOT do that."

They sat in silence for the rest of the drive home. When Tiffany got out of the car, Samantha knew she wouldn't hear from her for a long time, if at all. But she couldn't go on anymore letting her believe that her idea of help was in any way beneficial to this world. Her idea was sweet but didn't help anyone or anything. To make matters worse, Sam had to meet with Ryder Burns and a few others the next day to review the education points for the conferences, and then a larger group in Colorado later that year. She was done with her points, and she was sure Victoria was because she had called her about a hundred times to 'peer review' her thoughts before she presented them. So, it was going to be a late night.

Monday, September 17, 2007 – 1:30pm Mountain Standard Time (19:30 hours Zulu Time)

She and the animals were in Colorado again and Sloan was happy to be out of California. The group researching education was large. Sloan split it up into two groups to keep it manageable, K-12, and higher education. Oliver was more high strung than Sawyer was so he stayed at home when larger groups met and had a dog babysitter come in and visit and play with him while Sam had to be away for excessively long hours. During one of the discussions on higher education, with about twenty people in the room Sloan asked an older lady to explain what she had written with regards to her higher education experience.

"Nicole," said Sam, "you made mention here the inadequacies of standardized tests and admission processes for graduate school. I personally have always found them to be lacking. I would like to hear how you came to that same conclusion."

"Unlike you Ms. Sloan, sorry Dr. Sloan, I was not a natural student, or rather my educational interests fell to the backseat at the tail end of high school because I was highly immature, and I felt that other endeavors were more fun at the time."

Almost interrupting Nicole, Sloan said, "but that is 98% of kids that age, don't you think? And please call me Sam."

"Of course, thank you," Nicole replied. "The biggest difference, I would have to guess, is these kids still go to college and either blow off their classes, but still manage to get through, or gain that maturity during college and pull their lives together. My immaturity was quite prodigious because I didn't see the error in my ways and start to understand the value of education until I was in my mid-thirties. Getting into my undergraduate studies was not hard, and I excelled. I not only excelled, I loved it. I realized the gift that an education is. It enriched every part of my life and I only wanted more of it. Graduating with honors with two undergraduate degrees with a GPA of 3.8, I was still unable to get into any graduate school."

"What?" exclaimed Sloan. "How is that... Ah standardized tests?"

"Either that or age, which the school can't come right out and say they don't want older students, but with that high a GPA, a mediocre GRE score and my age, I have two things batting against me."

"Why didn't you just take the GRE again?" asked Sloan.

"Because I am stubborn, Sam. I wanted to study forensic psychology and then move onto a Psy.D."

"What is that?" asked Rick, another participant in the group.

"It is a Doctor of Psychology, very much like the Ph.D., but not as research-based. As far as I know there is no dissertation involved. Is that correct?" answered another participant.

"Precisely, the Psy.D is more professionally focused and getting directly to clinical work, although when I was applying I noticed that you can now obtain a Psy.D in more than just clinical psychology.

But to your question Sam, I didn't want to waste my limited time and energy on studying for something that I believe has little or no probative value as to what my level of success as a graduate student would be. Don't get me wrong, though. If I had not been able to answer one statistics question, or failed the test completely, I get that, but my scores were average. So, with an exceptional GPA, great recommendations, even alumni recommendations, I thought that would be enough. I was wrong. And I was wrong multiple times."

"That doesn't make any sense to me," said Sloan.

"Let me put it this way. We want to educate the masses, and that is a good thing, but the real individual suffers... And by real individuals I mean the individuals that really don't fit anywhere get lost in this dance where they can't make themselves follow the steps."

Sloan sat thoughtfully, as did most of the group for quite a few minutes, while others talked to each other softly.

"That actually makes perfect sense, Nicole. I didn't fit in with the popular girls in middle school or high school so I turned to my studies as an escape. I was always a bit socially awkward so I didn't rebel or go party, so I was lucky to find education and it accepted me. I really never thought it wouldn't except someone that wanted in though," replied Sloan.

"I've never fit anywhere, really. I was social as a kid, but left of center for sure, so the popular kids thought I was a bit freakish, the freaks thought I was too conservative and my parents just thought I was too wild, but I think most parents think kids are too wild. So, once I did get interested in something, chasing a rock group to try to attain a long lasting friendship with them, as if... I put everything I had into that."

Another attendee said, "How did that end up?"

"It ended up well, I guess. I got to know them, and we did become friends. It was unique in that they weren't out for the groupie thing... oh, I mean I'm sure they had them. But they tried to instill some kind of good experience in what was going on. One of them used to always get me to go to the museums they went to, or other places that I could say I got more than just hundreds of sound checks out of. And in the end, that meant more to me than anything. But really, if I look back, it was me just trying out different things and bouncing off different ways of life that I didn't fit in."

Nicole gave many examples of her own experiences of not fitting in in different areas of social groups and life events that were relevant to the discussion of educating the individual. Many people spoke and told similar stories. Through those discussions new items were added to the project list that would be helpful in developing education-related policy.

Toward the end of the day Sloan ended the conversations. Even though we totally got off the subject of today's meeting, I think it shows that we need to think about how we want to construct the higher education policy. Nicole already pointed out how standardized tests, to put it bluntly, screwed her. But at the same time, it isn't possible to personally interview each and every candidate for every school for every program. It might be at first, but if our nation grows like we think it is going to, that will quickly become unmanageable. We also have to have a way of turning these policies over to free enterprise and private business because the said government will not be ubiquitous. Let's adjourn for today and think about those new items and if everyone can, reconvene tomorrow."

Most nodded in approval, and the meeting ended.

"Nicole, could I have a moment?" asked Sloan.

Nicole sat down in the seat next to Sloan.

"I pride myself on being able to see many sides of any topic," Sloan started, "with the exception of anger, I am not very overtly emotional sans anger, but I'm working on that piece. But I really missed this. I have never thought for a minute that there are people that want to be educated that are rejected by institutions for, what... gray-area reasons?"

"I don't know, really. I'm from here in Colorado, and I just wanted to be able to continue my education here. The thing I have had the hardest time with is the fact that I would do anything to excel in any program I have applied for, yet I don't get in. I know someone who did get in to a program I applied for at DU and she quit after her first two quarters to get married. That is fine and I'm glad she is happy, but once I start something I finish it, period, and that has to be what the school's goal is, right? For the student to complete the program?"

"Well yes," answered Sloan definitively. "In the short time we have worked together, I can see that about you. But, not to defend the school, I think the Xers misrepresent that quality to a large degree. This group has made a commitment and changed their lives around an ideal and is willing to push it until it happens. Other than those who are left in Texas when it happens, our society will be tiny relative to the rest of the US, and I know it will grow, but I am willing to bet you right now, and this is a sad fact, that most will be too lazy to come. Some will be ambivalent, most will be apathetic."

"Do you really think that? What happens if many think they want to come and then they aren't willing to do the work? That is what scares me," Nicole shivered as she spoke.

"That is something that Mike Bishop has thought a lot about. Almost every time we talk, he has something to say on the subject. But, we aren't taking prisoners. Getting in will be much harder than getting out, of that I am sure."

"I have to admit sometimes I feel like this is futile. I try my hardest and my hardest isn't enough."

"How many committees are you on?" asked Sloan.

"Just this one, but if anyone needs anything else, I can make myself available."

"See, you just answered your own query. You are willing to put more and more and more in. Usually I would say win at all costs, but in this case trying your hardest is winning. Can you look yourself in the mirror and know you put it all out there most days?"

"Yeah."

"I do, too. Nikoli and Mike do, too. As long as we are doing that, we are going to win. And on the days my best isn't enough, you will be here to help, and vice-versa. But the first premise has... *has* to be we are putting our best out there."

"I'm glad we've spent time together. This is the first place that I haven't felt like I'm either invisible, or at least that I want to be, ya know what I mean?" asked Nicole.

"Completely. I feel like I've known you for a long time. I don't make friends easily, but with this group, it is easy and I think we know why."

"Now we better get our shit together tomorrow. Mr. Burns will be here at the end of the week to talk K-12 and we better have this part wrapped up," said Sloan chewing her nails.

***

The next day, the group talked about the agenda items missed from the previous day. But the hot topic was by far whether or not higher education should be offered like public school K-12, and the benefits and disadvantages about keeping higher education facilities as private businesses.

"Yesterday was very valuable. It exposed a hole that I had not thought of before. After speaking with Nicole, her experience might be more relevant than mine. I mean, I know mine was more unique in the sense that I didn't need loans and didn't have to work, etc., but the exclusionary factors had not occurred to me. She might better speak to these points," said Sloan, gesturing to Nicole.

Nicole turned beet red.

"Are you ok, Nicole?" asked Sloan

"I'm fine. I've always turned bright red when attention is placed on me unexpectedly...even when it is expected, sometimes," she laughed. "Correct me if I'm wrong, Dr. Slo.., Sam, but as I see it, we are looking at how higher education can be attained by most if not all of our society, who pays for it and how admittance is gained?"

"Precisely," answered Sloan. She looked around the room as if to say does anyone have any suggestions.

A man across from Nicole said, "Are we assuming everyone wants to go to school or are we going to try to force the issue?"

"I don't think we are going to force any issue," answered Sloan, "and that brings up another good point. Higher education is one type of education. I think we have placed too much attention on this need to be college educated especially if you want to be an electrician. I mean, I want my electrician to be an expert in his field, not in anthropology. What I'm trying to say is that it takes all kinds and in my perfect world, those practicing in their desired fields are good at those fields. So, can we agree that trade work schools also be included?"

The group nodded in agreement. After a 16-hour session the group looked like a train had hit them. Much debate over how higher education should be funded took most of the time, but there was agreement on changing how admission is gained acknowledging higher enrollment numbers make it more difficult for smaller programs to allow everyone in. Suggestions that seemed the most viable were to change how programs were taught from one professor to teams allowing for double and triple the admittance and the expansion of online programs that do not require a high level of lab or research work to be done. This solution was offered with the understanding that the onus is placed even more firmly on the individual to learn from the information being offered to him, unlike a classroom environment, where more collaboration and motivation can come into play instead of staring at a lecturer for hours. Finally, how trade schools can be de-stigmatized and placed on the same level as universities was discussed.

Sloan asked Nicole and two other committee members to help summarize the session and prepare for the K-12 committee meeting to be held later that week.

***

As Ryder Burns walked into the room, many of the ladies and possibly some of the men got a bit star struck. Even though the man had billions of dollars, he appeared to be a real world kind of guy; outdoorsy, athletic and ridiculously outgoing. He could talk to anyone, and his lack of ego made it easy to talk to him. He wasn't hard to look at either. He was in excellent shape; longish blonde hair and something just past a five o'clock shadow gave him the look of nonchalance and ease. He really could be the most interesting man in the world, Sloan thought. He was, however, not interested in talking about himself, he was interested in figuring out an educational system that could both keep students interested, and help those who struggled, and it wasn't just his money that he brought to the table, he also conducted research and had a lot to say on the subject of academia.

One of the women sitting next to Nicole was quite taken by Burns. "Man, oh man," was all she could say.

"He's one-of-a-kind, for sure," said Sloan's friend Allison, who had been working one-on-one with Burns on many of the educational agenda items.

"For some reason I always thought he looked more Australian than British, but I'm not even sure what that means," said Sloan, "but he is quite good looking, regardless of where he's from."

Sloan cleared her throat, "We should get started. We have spent the better part of this year really focusing on how we would want to change the educational system to better benefit our citizens. Allison Myers and Ryder Burns then went and compiled the data and prepared the reports each of you got last week. Since we hadn't wrapped up higher education, we discussed that this week, but I wanted to get those involved in spearheading this project together to talk about anything that may stick out or need more attention."

This man whom everyone called Fuzzy, though Samantha didn't know why and didn't want to, slapped his palm on the table and said, "I want to talk about the tenure piece of the report. I can't believe that everyone came to the conclusion that it should be eliminated."

Samantha hated this guy. He was loud, annoying, and worst of all smart. It was one thing for someone to just be belligerent, you could easily ignore that, but this guy had some substance behind him, and that drove her crazy. He actually made her like Bailey.

"Shouldn't this have been brought up at the beginning of the week?" asked Sloan.

"I wanted Mr. Burns to hear this," he snorted back, obviously with something to prove.

Burns, who had seen guys like this a million times couldn't have cared less. "I have no problem with talking about tenure. I have always disagreed with it and after doing more research and learning more about it feel even more strongly against it." He said in a faint British accent.

"So what protects researchers in university settings from giving their research to the school and then getting dumped?" Fuzzy asked.

"Well, first we have to ask," started Allison, "why are they getting dumped, Fuzzy?"

"Who knows, but the point is what protects their research? These universities are given tons of money based on the research they do, not how well they teach," replied Fuzzy.

Allison stared to answer, but was interrupted by Fuzzy, "I want to hear the answer from him," pointing to Burns.

With an airy wave, Burns said, "it's ok, Allison." He looked directly at him and said, "Fuzzy, I don't know what your problem is with me, but that could be better settled between us down at the pub after this meeting. Clearly, you have done your work on the subject, so I want to hear what you have to say. So for the time being, can you set aside your issue with me and work together on more apropos subjects?"

Fuzzy flushed. He didn't realize how much of a putz he was coming off as. He nodded and Burns continued.

"Now, as to your point about protecting one's research, tenure shouldn't be put in place to protect one's intellectual property. That should be worked out separately from their teaching job at the school, which you also pointed out is not the reason they are primarily employed. I think this is a problem in and of itself in that the reason I thought we were going to school is to learn. Adding the fact that we go to these schools with great reputations, to be taught by a professor who would rather be in his lab than with his students. My good friend Malcolm Gladwell, who, by the way helped me understand the complexities of this because he has been researching the topic for years says that you are more likely to be taught better by professors more interested in teaching students in non-Class One research universities. Class One research facilities get dollars to do research not teach, and results are expected. What that means is those universities you dreamed about going to all your life doesn't care about teaching you a thing, and tenure only makes them shittier teachers. Intellectual property is by definition property of the mind...doesn't research start that way, a question in one's mind? There are many ways to protect intellectual property and then extend that protection to the level to which you can prove your progress during your research. At no time should anyone be granted a job for life. Keeping a job should demand being the best at it."

Samantha loved that Ryder shut Fuzzy up. He was on her last nerve and she was about to lose it.

"Now, unless you have anything to add Fuzzy, should we move on to K-12?" asked Allison.

Fuzzy nodded in the affirmative that he was done.

"I guess where I am tripped up the most," said Nicole, "is in pay. Pay attracts better people to the jobs."

"That's not necessarily true Nicole," said Sloan.

"After a certain amount," replied Nicole. "Is it seventy thousand depending on geographical location and cost of living? Something close to that, in any case most teachers are well below that and we are asking them to do it out of the kindness of their hearts...and insanely, most do. But when a football player makes like five or six hundred thousand dollars as the league minimum and a teacher makes forty-five thousand dollars, there is something wrong with that."

"Hey don't be messin' with my football players," said Sloan in a joking manner.

"I love football as much as you do, except I don't get to go the super bowls," Nicole winked and turned red again. "I want them to get paid and be safe and whatever else, but the discrepancy is absurd. We want our kids to be well educated and want that to be free, but will pay thousands of dollars for a ticket to a football game. Something is amiss. I don't want to talk about how to take money away from football players, I want to talk about how to put our money where our mouths are when it comes to the value of educating our people."

"That is, by far, one of the biggest quandaries," said Burns. "And that is why we have to look at complete privatization. If I am the best teacher and you want your kid to be taught by me, then you pay the price."

"That, then might start the income discrepancy for lower income families," said Sloan.

"The whole write-up about scholarships and privately funded grants shows how that can be successful on a small scale. Certainly, small like the way we will start out, but we still have to do projections for larger growth," said Allison.

"What about self-paced individualized learning?" asked Burns.

"Now that is my favorite option here," said Sloan.

"Have we seen this in action anywhere…this Kahn Academy?" asked Fuzzy, while the man sitting next to him nodded, as if he had the same question.

"I would have to say Kahn Academy is probably the closest to what we are talking about. Ours, of course, would be much more concentrated," said Burns.

Sloan added, "I think Kahn has only been around for a year or two so I can't speak to the success, but this type of learning has been kicked around since the 60's from B.F. Skinner. Individualized learning and self-paced programs have a great deal of potential."

"Ok, then according to this report, there is someone there, a teacher, to help when the student is confused or needs further explanation?"

"Precisely," said Sloan. "Just like with any curriculum, the teacher would be qualified to teach the range of what is on the computers and jump in where needed. This would allow for larger class sizes, or multiple grades in one classroom, etc. There are many ways to organize such a practice. Some could even be done at home with the support and help of the parents, and this comes back to what do we as a society think is valuable and how are we going to spend our time? What we have to make very clear is that people that are unwilling to work for the things that they profess to value, education or anything else for that matter, will have no place in Texas. Just because you think you deserve something doesn't mean you do."

Other agenda items were discussed and debated like taxation versus tuition, and another discussion around standardized testing, and whether or not to use it, but as a means to determine quality in teaching methods and progress being made.

As the education discussion ended, an acquaintance of Samantha's, and someone that contributed much valuable material on several different topics including education, sat down next to Sloan. Melissa McCann was an executive at AOL. She frequently popped in to work with the tech guys on countless different projects, and they all loved her. Even though she was absolutely beautiful, she was like one of the guys, they would often say. She was old-school tech, she knew the origins and kept up on new stuff as well. She was a great asset to have.

"Fantastic start!" said Melissa.

"Agreed. Largely due to the research you amassed," Sloan answered.

"Thanks Sam, it's been fun. But I have a favor to ask you."

"Shoot," replied Sloan.

"I'm sure you've seen the AOL announcement earlier this week."

"Yeah, I did. What impact does that have on you, or does it?"

With a deep sign Melissa said, "that depends on how you look at it I guess. I could continue in much of the same capacity I am in now, but it isn't the AOL I joined. When I came in we had such a fantastic group. And I know, things change, so as they do I just think it is time for me to move on."

"Ok…" said Sloan, wondering about the request.

"I have no ties. Of course I have my friends, and Alan, but we're not married and I don't have kids yet…actually most of the people I know are within the group already. I am pretty well settled so I don't need to work for quite awhile. I was wondering if I could dedicate myself full time to helping out around here?"

"Are you serious?" Sloan exclaimed. "That is the favor you want from us? That would be a favor to us, not from us!" she said.

Melissa laughed. "Then I guess it is win/win. How do I start? And David may be able to help with education too. He is the guy that was walking in and out. I know he was vetted awhile ago to work on some other things, but he might have time for this as well."

"You know Victoria, right?"

Melissa nodded in the affirmative.

"Call her and she will pass a ton of work to you. I will call her right now and let her know to expect your call. You might have to work with her for a bit to get up to speed, but she is overwhelmed in a major way. I've got some stuff for you too that I can send to your tablet. Mike will be so pleased, really, thanks. As to your friend, what is his name?"

"David Wallace, I've worked with him for about five years and I believe he feels the same way as I do about things."

"What is the relationship, if I may ask?" asked Sloan.

"Strictly friends. I have been dating Alan for, God, seven years now and he is already in, so…anyway David is a bit of a loner, I don't really know a ton about his personal life except to say he has no romantic interest in me." answered Melissa.

"And you say he was vetted already? Oh, Victoria has been in New York a lot. Will that be a problem to go there?"

Melissa laughed again. "That is where I live, and yes, when he became involved he was asked to help someone who was completely overloaded to just help out where he could."

"Really?" Sloan said looking confused. "I know a lot of people are traveling for these, but you never even mentioned that you came all the way from New York."

"Why mention it? You do what you have to do, right? How many miles have you put on that car of yours?"

"Well…" Sloan said letting out a small stymied grunt. "That is my fault with the animals."

"Nevertheless," replied Melissa.

"This is really great. Victoria will be ecstatic! Let me know if you need anything, and in addition to the stuff I'm sending to your tablet, I will also send the updated meeting schedule of the small group of us that disseminate out to everyone else. Please feel free to join in."

"Oh, it's so 'Bohemian Grove.' Sounds good."

Sam laughed, "Just wait, there is a secret handshake, too."

Monday, December 24, 2007 – 5:30pm Pacific Standard Time (Tuesday, December 25, 2007 – 01:30 hours Zulu Time)

It was weird to have Christmas Eve on a Monday, thought Sloan. She was glad that her parents were hosting dinner on Christmas, so she told Bishop she would host a Christmas Eve dinner if it could be at his loft in the Noe Valley neighborhood of San Francisco. He had bought the place several years before, and because he knew he liked to live in nice spaces but had no eye for design, he had a very reputable designer completely renovate the fifty-four hundred square foot home. Bishop was great at finding real estate. Both of his homes were essentially city center, but boasted unique, large lots that made one feel as though they were in the 'burbs without actually having to go through that sacrifice. The top floor had an incredible view of Treasure Island and the Bay Bridge. Modern decor filled the open floor plan, and a glass floor bridged one side of the loft to the other. Sam loved it, Oliver, hated it. He always walked really fast and low as he crossed the scary overpass to get to the expansive patio where he loved to lay, because it always offered a cool breeze. Sam often stayed at the loft when she was in town if her parents were entertaining guests at the family home. Bishop was rarely there and she hated for the space to lay empty.

With the holiday arrangements as is, Bishop could go be with his perfect little family on Christmas Day, Nikoli and Haley could fly off to some secret, romantic location for newlyweds, and she could go to her parent's house. It always bothered Samantha that her family wasn't as close as, say, the Bishops. She always wanted those huge family get-togethers, but since both of her parents were only-children and her only sibling was Stuart, that wasn't going to happen. Then, to add to that, Stuart didn't share the same familial yearnings, at least not for his side of the family, or he didn't act like it. Even being a therapist, she didn't know how to bring it up, because rare is the person that freely admits, 'Yes Sam I would rather be close to my in-laws than my family and here is why...'. So, she just let things go on the way they were and when tense issues arose, like when Stuart's wife Camryn dictated a holiday menu based on her vegetarianism, she just stressed out about it for a few days until the event passed and went on about her business. Even the closeness of the three didn't make up for what she always felt she was missing, but not everyone gets that, she thought. That was another thing that she and Victoria shared. They were both a bit awkward with most people so the few friends they had needed to be special. Plus, with moving around all the time, Sam couldn't get as close to Victoria as she would have wanted. But, they both shared the same desire to stay connected and they both worked toward that end.

Victoria had news to tell Samantha so she came early while Bishop and Sam were preparing dinner. She came into the loft and climbed the stairs to the main floor and kitchen. She heard Bishop and Sam laughing and playing around like kids. As long as they weren't working, they reverted back to being teenagers almost immediately. It was fun to see. They saw Victoria and greeted her warmly as she sat on a stool at the island.

"Merry Christmas Eve!" said Bishop.

Pouring a glass of wine for Victoria, Sloan said, "I can't believe you wanted to come help. You hate to cook."

"So do you Sam," answered Victoria, laughing, and taking the wine. "And Merry Christmas Eve to you too," she said looking at Bishop.

"I do," said Sloan. "But I love bugging Mike."

"So what can I do to help?" asked Victoria.

Swinging around to place an appetizer plate in front of Victoria, Sam said, "Just sit there and relax, and tell me what is really going on."

Just then, they all heard Oliver start barking.

"You have got to train that dog not to bark when he is here," said Bishop. "I have already gotten in trouble with neighbors twice."

"How do you train him that at home it is ok to bark at squirrels, but at Mike's loft it isn't?" Sloan snippily responded.

"You don't. You train him not to bark at all," he said back.

"Yeah, you go tell him that," replied Sloan.

Bishop went to the patio to get Oliver and Samantha looked at Victoria. "Out with it."

"Ugh, you don't make it easy Sam. Do you remember Mason Lane?"

"Of course."

Mason Lane was the guy that Samantha dated on and off for a couple of years, never getting serious and eventually falling out of touch with. She met him while assisting her friend Allison with her puppy at dog obedience school.

"Well, I bumped into him about six months ago at a restaurant here in San Francisco and, well..., we..."

"Yeah?" asked Sloan.

"Well, we, kinda just..."

"Hit it off? Is that what you are trying to choke out?" Sloan said laughing, taking a sip of wine.

"Yes, yes, we hit it off and have been seeing each other ever since. Are you mad? I totally wanted to tell you right away but then I thought you would be mad, but then I realized I really liked him and then I just kept pushing it off. Are you mad? I mean, our friendship means so much, but you know how I am with men...I never find a good one, and then you did and then he was gone..."

"Stop," she said laughing. "Jesus! You are giving me a headache. No, I am not mad. I knew you had an interest when you met him at that one holiday party. No sweat. Actually, I think you two might be good together."

"And you have no residual feelings for him?"

"Mason is a great guy. But like I told you before, my life isn't set up to have a permanent guy."

"Is it weird that we both have, ya know...dated him?"

Sloan scoffed. "No. Think about it, V. We are interested in many of the same topics, are ideals are similar. The things we find compelling in life are too, so why would it be such a stretch that the men we find interesting might also be similar or even the same?"

"Well, that is truly a logical statement, but feelings get in the way of logic more times than not Sam," said Victoria.

"How do I say this...you are right, feelings get in the way of many things, but as time went on and I realized what we were up against with regard to the group, I made quite an easy decision to sacrifice the relationship to not get in the way of our goals. Like I said, he is a great guy, but not worth it to me to get in the way of the work that I'm doing."

"And that doesn't make you sad? And after all, you do have Mike!" said Victoria in a playful way.

Ignoring what she said about Bishop, "on the contrary. It makes me satisfied. Romantic love is full of distress as well as elation, but I don't want those crazy ups and downs. When I made the decision, I realized how happy I really am and I am singularly focused on forging ahead with that ideal. I was watching TV the other night, which I haven't done in a long time, but I just needed some real good old-fashioned down time. The guy on the show said a line so great, I'm trying to remember...something like, 'we are engaged in creating a world worth living in, one directed specifically on giving us what we need entirely and removing all things extraneous'. That IS us. So if I can't live it, how can I ask anyone else to?"

"That is quite severe, Sam."

"What a great quote," said Bishop entering the kitchen with Oliver in tow. "Sit," he commanded. Oliver sat and was rewarded with a nice big piece of chorizo.

"Don't give him too much of that or he will get a tummy ache," said Sam in a baby voice rubbing Oliver's head. "It is severe for you to live the way I live, but I think that line refers to what is extraneous to me. What is to you might be a little different, so in that sense it isn't all that severe."

"Hmmph," Victoria muttered, pleased. "Would you mind if I called him and asked him to the party?"

"Yeah I mind, we don't have enough food for another person," snipped Sam winking at Victoria.

"Funny!" said Victoria, getting up to go call Mason.

CHAPTER 27
KAI, GREEN PASTURES & CHRONIC DISEASE

Tuesday, January 15, 2008 – 10:00am Pacific Standard Time (18:00 hours Zulu Time)

The year started off like many other years for 13-C - a huge announcement followed by the stock skyrocketing. This year however, Quinn had been executing on a plan to buy back 13-C and take the company private again. Through several discreet organizations, all owned by Quinn, he had already amassed control of more than 75% of the outstanding shares. This would reduce complications once the company just disappeared from California. Point-and-Click commerce was the new big thing at 13-C, and the company had been developing it for three years.

Today was 13-C's keynote presentation and product announcement, and it was kicking off precisely at 10am, as it always did. For Randall Quinn, this level of precision wasn't simply a goal, or even a requirement. It was an obsession. Quinn strolled out onto the stage to a roaring crowd. He waited for at least five minutes, letting the very last person stop clapping, then waited another minute in silence just watching the crowd, and then started the keynote speech.

"Put people around you that are smarter, faster, stronger..." he started, "Don't be afraid of being with the best. That will only improve you! The idea that one man can be the reason for success is very popular today, in business, sports, even the government. But I'm here to tell you it is the balance of striving to excel personally, and working within a team, that makes you better."

Dean Kinsey was in the audience. All he could do was roll his eyes. The two had been competitors for years and it was only the Xer group that made them come together at all. He thought Quinn was an egomaniacal narcissist that believed it was his way or no way. So this speech was making his stomach a little sick, but he also had to give credit were it was due. The man built 13-C with a level of fanaticism that few had. He also had good luck along the way and was in the right place at the right time, as was himself and Tim

Conrad and all the other tech geniuses that made it huge, but Quinn was also able to make everyone around him feel that anything was possible and that was what made him so successful among the Xers. He told them a story, they believed it and then went out and achieved it. It was his gift. He still rolled his eyes at the self-deprecating man that was speaking now.

"I need the best around me to create the beautiful products we put in front of you, just as a quarterback needs his team to move down the field and score. Today, I do not bring you a new device – I bring you the future of online commerce. Ladies and gentlemen, let me introduce you to KAI, your own personal shopper for finding anything you like while you are watching television."

The crowd clapped wildly, but also looked a little confused, but before the confusion set in too deeply, Quinn continued.

"Let me show you.," he sat down on a couch that was put there specifically for this part of the presentation. In front of him a small coffee table from which he grabbed a remote control that controlled a television that was also relayed on the huge screen above. "I am at home watching one of my favorite shows, Entourage, and Vincent Chase walks into the scene wearing the coolest black shirt." The television showed the actor just as Quinn described. "Now as you all know, I'm keen to liking only one kind of black shirt," he paused to let the audience laugh, "but this one really stands out, so I pull out my controller," he said holding up the remote control, "and aim it at the television until I can see a cursor appear on the cool shirt in question, then I click on it. KAI goes and links to a database, and as you can see, on the bottom of the screen is the shirt, where it can be purchased, the cost and a 'More' button. The 'More' button takes you a space that allows you to save for later or to purchase directly from your cloud account. This purchase took me less than a minute and that cool new shirt is on its way to me."

Now the crowd really erupted with applause.

"Now let me bring on the chief engineer for KAI to tell you all about the back end, and the timing of the rollout."

Point-and-Click commerce caused the entire industry to shift. The technology was incredibly intuitive, and Quinn made its creation look easy, as he did with most things. The extraordinary effort and complexity were masked by the natural way technology worked as it rolled out of his organization. This huge leap in technology was a catalyst for people to realize that, from Randall Quinn, the best was always yet to come, and to confirm how much of a visionary he really had been.

Sunday, February 3, 2008 – 5:42pm Eastern Standard Time (22:42 hours Zulu Time)

During some time off, Samantha took her animals to her parents' house and went on vacation away from everyone. With her interest in guns, shooting and safety she decided to check out SOURCE as client and participant. A few years back, SOURCE opened up their facilities to civilians to train them on everything from beginner handgun safety to advanced tactical training for the weekend warriors. She was concerned, however, because she knew the reputation SOURCE and its employees had; wrap-around Oakleys, desert fatigues and huge egos - a whole group of egomaniac, bully pricks…not the kind of group Samantha suffered gladly. But she had known Derek Holden for years now, and that just didn't jive with what she knew about him. There were always the doubts as to his squeaky clean demeanor, but it never really showed any cracks. He was always above board, respectful and above all dutiful.

She didn't tell anyone where she was going except her parents. If anyone needed to get hold of her, they would have to contact her through them. She told everyone else that she needed some alone time, and headed to SOURCE's remote south campus. The class agenda said the group would be firing four thousand rounds of ammunition over the course of the five days. The facility offered the opportunity to buy the ammunition at cost instead of trying to bring that much along with you, so she took advantage of it. Since she didn't have her animals with her, she flew to the facility, which involved checking her handguns in with TSA prior to boarding the plane. That was a joke because the agent knew nothing about handguns and had no idea what to look for. She was also told that all of the shooting would be outdoors and to dress appropriately. She brought two pairs of BDU pants, long underwear, a few tactical sweaters, a gun belt that provided a holster, magazine pouches and a pouch for a small flashlight. At the last minute it occurred to her that loading eight hundred rounds a day into magazines was not going to be fun and most likely painful, so she threw in her speed loader, and a pair of tight shooting gloves.

Upon landing she rented a car and headed to the facility. She was driving rather fast because she wanted to get there and check in before the Super Bowl started. Her favorite team, the New England Patriots, was playing the New York Giants. She had been to several Super Bowls in the past and now her favorite team was playing and she books her vacation at the same time. Big miss. In her haste to get there quickly, she missed a turn and got lost. She called the facility but her cell phone had crappy coverage and the call kept dropping. She was tired, frustrated and hungry. She just wanted to get there so she could relax, have a glass of wine, eat and watch the game. Finally, she came into the tiny town that skirted the facility from the north. She followed signs for several miles and came to a check point where she met an armed guard, who stepped out of a guard shack wearing, of course, desert fatigues. It was dark, so no wrap around sunglasses and she couldn't see anything in front of her.

"Are you lost?" asked the guard.

"No, I am supposed to start a tactical shooting course here tomorrow," she replied.

With a raised eyebrow he asked, "Your name?"

"Samantha Sloan."

He went back into the guard shack, called someone and came back out after about a minute.

"Ok, proceed down this road. It will fork in about a mile... take the left fork. You will briefly cross a helicopter-landing zone so make sure not to stop there. Continue past and wind around about another three miles. There you will find the lodge to check in and they will get you to your bunk house."

With that the guard walked back into the guardhouse.

She took off driving, thinking to herself, why would I have to cross a landing zone? Weird. Before a mile was up, there was a chance to take a left, but it looked like a neighborhood of about five houses. Weird again. Why would there be residential houses right in the middle of the facility? She kept going and the fork barely seemed like a fork, and she was getting irritated not knowing if she was going in the right direction. Then she saw the landing pad the guard must have been talking about, but instead of it warning against stopping, it said to stop for all incoming aircraft. She looked up, saw nothing and gunned it across the landing strip. She kept going. On the right she saw a warehouse-looking building with a huge SOURCE logo on it. Beyond that it was too dark to see anything. Finally, she saw the lodge that had a sign welcoming visitors. A little late on the welcome, she thought. It looked a little bit like a ski lodge with a huge fireplace at the front desk.

She walked up to the front desk and someone greeted her.

"Good evening, name please?" the receptionist asked.

"Samantha Sloan," she replied.

"Ah, Miss Sloan, how are you this evening?"

"A little frazzled actually, it took me longer to get here than anticipated so I just want to get to my room, grab something to eat and watch the Super Bowl."

The receptionist looked concerned. "Well, I can get you to your room, but we don't have network television out here, nor do we have after hours eating facilities."

"What?" Sloan exclaimed.

"We are in the process of switching over our satellite television systems, so we do not have any television coverage and the only food that is available is served over at the mess hall and it closes at five."

With a huge sigh Sloan asked, "So where can I get food, and is there somewhere I can drive to watch the game?"

"Actually yes, some of the gentlemen who are in your class left about an hour ago to do the same. You will have to go back off the grounds the way you came but there are a few places in town. Here is a map of the town and the circled establishments offer food. Let me direct you to your room. Most of our rooms are group bunk houses, but since you are the only female, we have you in a private room in the newer building adjacent to this one."

The receptionist explained how to get to the room and Samantha went back to her rental car. Once she found her room in a newer bunkhouse, she just threw her bags in it and turned around to find the game. She knew that it had started already and she didn't want to miss anymore than she already had. She wound all the way back around to the guard stand who was outside talking to another employee. They both nodded their heads at her and she kept going. Not the greatest start to her vacation, she thought.

She stopped at the first restaurant she found. It was in a strip mall of small shops and she prayed they served at least a decent bottle of wine. She walked in and the place basically stopped and stared at her. It was a little bit more rough-and-tumble than the outside indicated. She found a server and asked if she needed to wait to be seated. The server laughed and said, "Where do you think you are, Honey? Find a place that suits you and I'll be along in a minute."

She sat down at a booth away from most of the people, but then realized she couldn't see a TV, so she got up and sat at a table with a perfect view. She glanced behind her and saw about five guys in a booth. That was the perfect place to sit, she thought…back to the wall, comfortable booth. Hmm, she would just have to deal. A couple of the guys saw her looking at them and they said hi. She nodded at them and turned around. The server came back and asked what she was having.

"Do you by chance have a wine list?" She knew that was a dumb thing to ask as soon as it came out of her mouth.

"We have a house red and a house white, oh and a white zinfandel," the server responded, as Samantha winced.

"House red and a menu would be great," said Sloan.

One of the guys behind her asked, "Whom do you want to win?"

"New England," she answered.

"You from Boston?" another one asked.

"No, went to school out there," she said, trying not be rude, but also trying not to invite more conversation.

Soon her wine came, she ordered her food and sat back and watched the game. After she got some food in her, and a second glass of pretty terrible wine, she felt better. The Patriots were winning and she was happy. There was a good mix of Patriots and Giants fans so everyone was cheering and hollering. She talked to the a couple of different groups and loosened up. The Giants came back to win the game at the very end of the fourth quarter, though, making Samantha forget where she was and scream expletives at the television. When the game was over, she paid the bill, said goodnight to the group behind her and left.

The next morning, she got up, got dressed and headed out. She had a protein bar in her bag, so she skipped the mess hall experience as a trade off for some extra sleep. She stepped outside and in the light of day she could see the campus and was surprised by how beautiful it was, and how green. The campus was surrounded by what looked like farmland and pastures. There were also many more buildings, a crashed plane that looked like it was from a movie set, a house-looking thing with no windows, a school, a driving area with faux police cars for high speed driving training, and a small park with what looked to be grave stones and a path. Down the road a bit was a small lake with part of boat and more training areas. She could see that the big warehouse building she saw the night before made big armored vehicles. A few of them were parked by the side of the warehouse. She loved them and wanted so badly to drive one! She later learned that the little neighborhood she passed coming in was housing for top executives. They chose to live close and be available at all times. She had heard that one was Derek's as well, although he never mentioned it.

The directions to the classroom were confusing and she got lost again and was late. She hated walking into places late and she wasn't used to feeling so out of control of the situation. She was thinking maybe this wasn't such a good idea. She walked in and saw the group of men from last night sitting in single student desks. They waved at her and smiled in surprise. There was a half-day of classroom instruction and then out to the first target range, following picking up pre-purchased ammunition. The campus was huge so one had to drive from the different training areas, myriad shooting ranges, and classrooms. The bunking areas and mess hall were close enough to walk. There was also a pro-shop that offered all kinds of merchandise with the prolific SOURCE logo.

Once on the range, some of the guys came up and introduced themselves. Bill was the most outgoing. He was an investment guy from Florida who knew his way around a gun. He was there with his father-in-law. Samantha had to laugh. She was dressed in all of her tactical gear, and although Bill was also in BDU pants, he wore a yellow Hermes sweater and SOURCE golf hat. Then there was Bobbi, this awesome redneck hunter that owned a gun shop in Georgia. He was there with his friend Ed. He talked tough, but he was a super sweet guy that was ready to help anyone. Everyone was curious about Sam, but they were also respectful and treated her as an equal, including her instructors. One guy claimed he was special ops from New Zealand and he instructed everyone to not take his picture. She just stared at him. Why would he be in a civilian class and why was a special ops guy taking a beginner's tactical class? What a douche, she thought. The head instructor was also named Bill and the other one, Woody, had just returned from Iraq from his last tour of duty and was now transitioning to a new lifestyle as a SOURCE instructor. Woody was not his real name, and she believed this guy was more special ops than the Kiwi. The instructors were tough, and they took their work seriously. They were extremely intelligent and skilled at their craft. If someone wasn't listening or joking around too much, they took professional, courteous control. When the situation was well in hand and all was safe, they could loosen up and be engaging both men had a great sense of humor.

Samantha kept keeping her finger on the trigger of her gun prior to shooting and even sometimes accidentally pointing the loaded weapon in the wrong direction, which was not like her. She was a bit intimidated, which took the form of looking more like a novice than she was. Woody corrected her about twenty times. Finally, he said, "Next time you do that, I am gonna revoke your shooting privileges and you will have to do all class time."

Sam, trying to use her girly wiles, "Come on, I know I'm not going to pull the trigger."

He was not having any of it. "It is too dangerous to take that kind of risk, Sam, and I'm not joking, one more time and you are done. Last month we had a female officer here who also kept her finger on the trigger and she accidentally shot the ground," Woody explained.

"Do most of the girls that come here just screw up?"

"No, not at all, and in most things you are doing, you are doing well, but here you have to do everything well. Some of the guys are complete screw-ups. It is our job to guide and correct."

Samantha was so surprised at these guys. Their reputation was unfair and more importantly untrue. You could tell both had seen action in different wars and had defended our country. But there was not even a small part of them that wanted to go hurt or bully people in the name of the big bad military machine. They were soft-spoken, against violence and most of all respectful and professional.

By the third day, all the tough guys were running to her to borrow her speed loader because everyone's fingers hurt so bad. Her hands were sore just from squeezing the trigger so many times. But from the time Woody gave her that last warning, her finger stayed off the trigger and her weapon was either holstered or facing down range. They were in the middle of an exercise when the sound of a bomb went off. Samantha hit the deck almost simultaneous to the sound. Looking up, she saw that everyone else was still standing and looking down at her laughing.

Instructor Bill walked over and said, "This is a training facility. I think you are ok and can get up." He put out his hand and pulled her up.

A bit embarrassed, she didn't look around, and the class continued.

A couple of ranges over, a group was apparently training bomb squads on first response initiatives and emerging threats. Sam's new friend Bill came over to her, still laughing, patted her on the shoulder and said "good one," giving her a hard time.

"At least she reacted quickly, some of you would have been dead if the threat were real. Always, always be aware of what is happening around you," said Instructor Bill.

On her last day, she took the time to walk the memorial walk. It was still under construction, but it already looked beautiful and did what it was built for, to give tribute to the fallen men that had been so misunderstood, because of the media always having to find a way to shock the public for more ratings. As she walked the path she thought of Derek and how important this must have been to him to build. She looked at him differently yet again. She had gained even more respect for him, just from the smallest sampling that she saw; this place was no joke. She, as a gun owner, was more confident, more learned and certainly safer with her weapon. She could just imagine how great this was for our military, our police, our rescue teams and any other organization that came here to train. This was a vacation she would never forget. She also made some new friends, two of whom would come into the group not soon after that February.

Friday, March 7, 2008 – 2:00pm Central Standard Time (20:00 hours Zulu Time)

During the annual psychology conference, Sam was asked to speak because of a paper she wrote during graduate school on the ethics of patient rights. After the last debacle at Princeton, she originally said no, but after having thought about it, she thought she could get some good, real-world information on where the industry stood on mental health care, the stigmas and how far the country has come in removing them. She had empirical data from reviewing research, but as she learned over the years, that doesn't always tell the whole story.

A not so pleasant part of going to these conferences was that of the colleagues that knew her; not many liked her. She had a very unorthodox approach to treatment, which statistically was very effective. But her cohorts thought it was reckless and ego driven. She believed it to be the opposite. She, believed in getting to know the patient in the first couple of sessions and once she had an idea of a diagnosis or treatment plan, she jump right to the last chapter so-to-speak. She told the patient what she thought the problem was and then laid out a treatment plan, or the rest of the chapters. Colleagues said patients had to come to many of these conclusions themselves over time, and it wasn't up to Samantha to "tell" the patient what to do, thus the ego. Sam believed patients were coming to her for expertise and exactly to be told what to do, and sitting discussing issues shadow boxing was not going to change the treatment plan, only extend it and the billing process. She didn't flat out say their way was wrong, she just didn't like it for herself.

Her patients didn't seem to mind. She had a waiting list to get in to see her. With the advent of video messaging she could continue her practice and her work with the group. She also had a collection of psychiatrists and psychologists, who all agreed to her methods with regard to treating her patients in case they needed emergency face-to-face time.

One of the touchy topics that were to be discussed in the upcoming healthcare meeting was the idea of forced care for mentally ill patients. This was something Sloan was often very contentious about. She could not understand how letting mentally ill patients be homeless could be seen as a solution in any way. She reviewed her paper's synopsis that she would have to discuss later that afternoon: One would naturally think quality of life was the goal for these patients and working back from there. She likened it to not letting a child eat too much candy or doing something else that was not good for them because as children they do not know any better. The mentally ill also cannot always know what is best for them, so by saying it is inhumane is not seeing the whole story. Newer drugs mitigate side effects and negative symptoms that have driven many off their meds in the past. Although not a perfect solution, not everything is perfect. Type 1 diabetics have many side effects in taking insulin but they must maintain an insulin regimen if they want to live. There are those who believe forced treatment is against their civil rights. However, forcing meds was a better solution than letting them wander the streets becoming a potential threat to someone else. Not every homeless person is mentally ill and not every mentally ill person is a threat to someone else. But, instead of diverting money to shelter programs and victim care, using the money for facilities and staff to treat those that are forcibly committed, the quality of life that they couldn't get anywhere else can be ensured. Further, they can't harm anyone else outside.

It was a very unpopular, hard line to take but someone had to. She wasn't looking forward to the symposium, and it went pretty much as she had expected. Many civil rights extremists who thought they were acting in protection of something or someone ignored the fact, as they mostly did, that the regular person out there was the only one getting stomped on when other's rights were so grossly taken out of context. The argument went on and on.

Frustrated, Sloan said, "I know it sucks that they have this illness, but you can't give them rights on both sides... you can't force medication, then when they do something illegal because they were left out on the streets on their own, because God-forbid, we wouldn't want to impinge on their rights. Then, because of that, created another victim, you can't make them take responsibility for it because they were off medication... that can't happen. It cannot be both ways. They are either responsible or not."

The symposium concluded in silence. Samantha saw that she had allies, but those who would not budge just gave up and sat and stared at her. Clearly nothing would be solved today in the outside, real world of mental health care.

Thursday, May 1, 2008 – 8:12am Pacific Daylight Time (14:12 hours Zulu Time)

Over breakfast, preparing for one of the hardest issues to cover, healthcare, Sloan, Borodin and Bishop all got together at Nikoli's house in San Francisco. It was rare when all of them were back in California. Since getting married, Nikoli sold his San Francisco loft and bought a house on Baker Beach in the Sea Cliff neighborhood. It was pretty ritzy, and although that didn't matter to him or to Haley, he did love waking up and seeing the ocean right outside his window. The house was built in 1932 so even though it had gone through a couple of renovations, it still needed a lot of work. No matter how much money he made, he still thought it was ridiculous to buy a fixer-upper for several million dollars. But it was what it was.

Bishop's theoretical physics team had concluded their work and disbanded. A couple of the members had gone to Geneva to become part of an enormous scientific collaborative undertaking at the world's largest particle collider called the LHC. Bishop was asked to join them and he found the work as interesting and challenging as anything he had come across in his life, but under the circumstances, he obviously could not leave. It was the first time since the 1993 bombing that he felt the sadness that came with the awareness and feeling of obligation to change something that feels wrong down to one's soul. Sam often voiced the realization that they were different in that they existentially couldn't make things easy for themselves. There had to be a peace in blissful ignorance. In any case, he would spend a few months in California, and a few with Sam in Colorado and Texas, getting things done. He wondered if he had done the last of his 'real-world' activities.

Sitting down with a fresh cup of coffee and settling Oliver down, she said, "We've got most of the reports in, and from what I've seen, your Annabelle put together one hell of a package, Mike. "Her group's ideas on health insurance being brought down to the original catastrophic and chronic care are brilliant the way they laid it out. Plus, it would certainly reduce premiums, administrative costs, not to mention transactions alone. I can't say it will work, but it warrants giving it a hard look. Under the research tab, she goes on to explain things like having to have multiple tests just for correct billing. The example she used was an MRI. Did you know you can't get an MRI on two areas, say your back and hip because they have to have separate billing codes to the radiologist gets paid to read two? That is absurd! Of course the radiologist should be paid for his work but to duplicate efforts, make the patient go through two MRI's just to accomplish that is the height of inefficiency."

"Like I've said, take it down to the simple and build from there. That way we won't miss anything. And if you think I am oversimplifying things," Bishop shuddered, "Annabelle is a real fire-cracker. She strips it down to nothin' and then says 'tough it out until there is a fix, otherwise, stop bitchin'.'"

Sloan laughed. She could picture Annabelle saying exactly that.

"Not to change the subject, but I think it is time to start preparing another note. We haven't sent one in over a year. Thoughts as to what this one should cover?" asked Nikoli.

"I'm done with messages, policy recommendations, and advice," Bishop said looking up inquisitively to gauge his friend's response.

"What?!" Sloan said. "Those have been our benchmarks to indicate if anything is going to change."

Sloan was defending something she never particularly liked. She always felt uneasy each time correspondence was sent to an administration. She was concerned that the likelihood of getting discovered would increase, while at the same time, having the idea that nothing would really ever change reinforced that nagging feeling of the nebulous. But the group decided early on to give each administration as many opportunities as possible and she also liked the thought of that.

"What do you think of this Niki?" she asked exasperated.

Nikoli was silent.

"Have you talked with anyone else about this?" She asked.

"Not yet, but there really isn't anything to discuss or to try to convince anyone of." Bishop was frustrated for the first time since this began. This was his ideal and everyone had always been on board, so he didn't much care for Sam asking if he discussed this with anyone. Not in the sense that he needed permission, but more because he knew she was right. Before any major change in strategy, an idea should be discussed to make sure everyone was in agreement or at least on the same page. This group certainly wasn't making decisions with everyone in a circle holding hands, but he wasn't spouting rhetoric slamming his hand down on a soapbox either. He continued, "We have had moderate success with some of the different administrations, some sympathizers, and some that were ready to back most of our policy ideas, but the same thing happens repeatedly. The problems are too big, the system is too big and there is too much bureaucracy to be effective in anything. It is time we realize that and start making plans associated with the smaller community model. The political structure is excellent for creating a society, but is too convoluted to save one."

"I have talked ad nauseam about the fact that we can't change anything with new laws or new policies but no one wants to hear that," added Sloan. "It is much easier to have concrete, black and white rules, and I, for one, am one of those who would appreciate that. But humans just aren't built that way. If we truly want to change something we have to change the culture, we have to change individual behavior, and sans that, nothing is going to change."

"What do you suggest?" Bishop asked intrigued.

"I don't have the answer Mike, I don't think there is one, to be honest." Sloan paused. "Don't look so disappointed. What I mean is there is no one way to change behavior. If we are talking criminal justice, we have to look at motivations, deterrents, and when or when not to think rehabilitative actions might change criminal behavior. If we are talking about education and the lack of interest in really changing it, we have to look at the motivating factors around that. But if you want one single thing to start from I think we need to focus on what motivates people and once we home in on that, then we can make a plan around that...And for the record, I believe that is what we've been doing for oh...the last five, six years." Sloan finished and watched Bishop contemplate what she said.

Several minutes passed and she could tell what she said hit a nerve. It hit a nerve because this was the closest thing to a fight these two had been in in a very long time. Bishop wondered to himself if they thought he was getting unapproachable or too much the vision of the operation.

"You guys know that I'm on the ground working with everyone and am willing to hear everything, right?"

Samantha sighed and stretched her neck, "yeah, Mike, we do. This has a lot of legs that require very precise timing."

Nikoli was still quiet, and neither Sloan nor Bishop could get a read from him. He was never this quiet.

"Ok," Bishop started. "You know that changes the conferences, right?"

"Only a little," said Sloan getting right back to work, "we can't rely on something as vague and soft science as motivation and behavior. We still do need action items, policy adjustments and rules and laws to govern a society. But it is at the onset of a new community that behavior becomes key. The conferences will glean the actions as well as give us a clear view of the acceptance of behavioral leanings," she said, the most confident she had felt to date about what the group was really trying to accomplish.

"I still think we need to revisit the size of what we are taking on. If we don't scale this correctly, nothing will succeed." Bishop insisted.

"Agreed," replied Sloan. "It should be the first talking point at the conference."

Nikoli nodded in agreement, then said, with a tone of well-intentioned sarcasm, "Can we finally talk about healthcare?"

"He speaks!" said Sloan sarcastically.

"Actually, do we need to?" asked Bishop, ignoring Samantha completely. "From the reports that you," looking at Nikoli, "and the Tim Conrad, Kevin Needham and the Kylie Chamberland groups have put together, the only thing that is really missing is mental health, right? And Cooper and Sam are dealing with that one later today."

"Uhm, ok…you read through all of that?" asked Nikoli.

"Yeah, it was fascinating, the range of the different perspectives were massive at first, not to mention I think more people wanted to be a part of this topic than any other. Yet, in the summarization, most opinions came together," answered Bishop.

"We are still wildly apart on who should be footing the bill for it, which is what this country is struggling with, too," said Nikoli sadly.

"With one huge exception, my friend. We aren't acting like children refusing to play with each other, filibustering each other, nor will we bankrupt ourselves in the process."

Nikoli and Samantha both nodded in agreement.

"Was David Wallace on any of the committees?" asked Sloan.

"Yeah, I had him," answered Nikoli. "He's weird. One minute he is disagreeing with everything, and I mean *everything*... Poke, poke, poke..."

"Worse than Bailey?" asked Bishop.

"Way worse, but then ten minutes later he is like a yes-man. I don't get him."

"Derek said he was pretty erratic when he saw him too, and insisting to be involved in everything. Derek thinks some red flags should be going up," said Sloan.

"Let's keep an eye on it, and him," answered Bishop.

"Just to let you know mental health might not be the final issue Mike," said Sloan, "Cooper says he is bringing someone with him and they have laid out some other things to talk about that he says he wants amended into these binders, so that may change the summary somewhat, but all the heads will have the chance to review and rebut," said Sloan, speed-reading a particular page in one of the three binders on the table. "It is so hard to not make this too complex."

"Just like the tax code had to be," said Bishop. "Strip it down to the bare essence and add later...don't make it harder than it has to be. We are only following the original intent of what we had in the beginning. The difference is, we know the scalability issues now and we will also remove what becomes antiquated and redundant, and that seems to be the only thing that is left in some of this country's policies anymore."

***

A few weeks later, Michael Bishop walked into the end of an agenda meeting, or rather a follow up meeting with a group of individuals that had been working on the economy. There had been many people talking of late of the country becoming more and more polarized taking only one point of view or perspective and the group thought that if the administration switched parties in the next election it would get worse.

"It all boils down to this: I believe working together is key to our survival, but when we look across the aisle and there is no more compassion, or even common ground with those we see on the other side it is time to pull away," said Gannon.

Seth Gannon had been a member of the group for many years. He was a low-level analyst of the NSA when he joined because he was frustrated with his job prior to September 11th. He knew that so much more could be done to secure the country yet no one would pull the trigger, so-to-speak, and do what was necessary to really protect this county. He left the NSA in 2006 to join his brother Benjamin at Bear Stearns. His brother was an investment banker and he asked Seth to come aboard when a restructuring of the IT department was being done. Seth knew nothing of investment banking but he did know computers.

By the beginning of 2008, Ben had lost over thirty pounds and the stress was killing him. He finally confided in Seth and told him what was happening and how bad he thought things were going to get. He told Seth that he couldn't watch the improprieties anymore, and the behavior that ranged from immoral to nauseatingly close to criminal. Ben was quitting the next day.

Once Seth realized the extent of the negligence, he had also quit, and had brought Benjamin into the group. Ben had not had the privilege to hear Bishop speak that often. The group was huge and busy. Both Seth and Ben decided to dedicate their time to working within the group for a while to feel good about what they were doing and have some focus and pride, while Benjamin regained his health. If they had to find jobs again, they would, but for now they were within the confines and security of only X members. It felt like when they were boys, safe in their parent's house, and the only thing they felt was the promise in the world.

Seth loved it when he heard Bishop talk. It reminded him of the first conversation they had together. He often wondered how Bishop's other conversations with other members had gone. Seth was ready to sign up after only a short time talking with Bishop. He wondered if it had been that way for everyone.

"Ronald Reagan gave a speech in 1964 that I would like to read for you now, because it is the true heart of what I believe," Bishop began. "It is the piece that has gone missing that I want to bring back through this group. If I had to say what one main point of what our ideology is in one moment in time, it is this speech," he said, and then began the speech.

"Thank you very much. Thank you and good evening. The sponsor has been identified, but unlike most television programs, the performer hasn't been provided with a script. As a matter of fact, I have been permitted to choose my own words and discuss my own ideas regarding the choice that we face in the next few weeks.

I have spent most of my life as a Democrat. I recently have seen fit to follow another course. I believe that the issues confronting us cross party lines. Now, one side in this campaign has been telling us that the issues of this election are the maintenance of peace and prosperity. The line has been used, "We've never had it so good."

But I have an uncomfortable feeling that this prosperity isn't something on which we can base our hopes for the future. No nation in history has ever survived a tax burden that reached a third of its national income. Today, 37 cents out of every dollar earned in this country is the tax collector's share, and yet our government continues to spend 17 million dollars a day more than the government takes in. We haven't balanced our budget 28 out of the last 34 years. We've raised our debt limit three times in the last twelve months, and now our national debt is one and a half times bigger than all the combined debts of all the nations of the world. We have 15 billion dollars in gold in our treasury; we don't own an ounce. Foreign dollar claims are 27.3 billion dollars. And we've just had announced that the dollar of 1939 will now purchase 45 cents in its total value.

As for the peace that we would preserve, I wonder who among us would like to approach the wife or mother whose husband or son has died in South Vietnam and ask them if they think this is a peace that should be maintained indefinitely. Do they mean peace, or do they mean we just want to be left in peace? There can be no real peace while one American is dying some place in the world for the rest of us. We're at war with the most dangerous enemy that has ever faced mankind in his long climb from the swamp to the stars, and it's been said if we lose that war, and in so doing lose this way of freedom of ours, history will record with the greatest astonishment that those who

267

had the most to lose did the least to prevent its happening. Well I think it's time we ask ourselves if we still know the freedoms that were intended for us by the Founding Fathers.

Not too long ago, two friends of mine were talking to a Cuban refugee, a businessman who had escaped from Castro, and in the midst of his story one of my friends turned to the other and said, "We don't know how lucky we are." And the Cuban stopped and said, "How lucky you are? I had someplace to escape to." And in that sentence he told us the entire story. If we lose freedom here, there's no place to escape to. This is the last stand on earth.

And this idea that government is beholden to the people, that it has no other source of power except the sovereign people, is still the newest and the most unique idea in all the long history of man's relation to man.

This is the issue of this election: whether we believe in our capacity for self-government or whether we abandon the American revolution and confess that a little intellectual elite in a far- distant capitol can plan our lives for us better than we can plan them ourselves.

You and I are told increasingly we have to choose between a left or right. Well I'd like to suggest there is no such thing as a left or right. There's only an up or down: [up] man's old -- old-aged dream, the ultimate in individual freedom consistent with law and order, or down to the ant heap of totalitarianism. And regardless of their sincerity, their humanitarian motives, those who would trade our freedom for security have embarked on this downward course.

In this vote-harvesting time, they use terms like the "Great Society," or as we were told a few days ago by the President, we must accept a greater government activity in the affairs of the people. But they've been a little more explicit in the past and among themselves; and all of the things I now will quote have appeared in print. These are not Republican accusations. For example, they have voices that say, "The cold war will end through our acceptance of a not undemocratic socialism." Another voice says, "The profit motive has become outmoded. It must be replaced by the incentives of the welfare state." Or, "Our traditional system of individual freedom is incapable of solving the complex problems of the 20th century." Senator Fulbright has said at Stanford University that the Constitution is outmoded. He referred to the President as "our moral teacher and our leader," and he says he is "hobbled in his task by the restrictions of power imposed on him by this antiquated document." He must "be freed," so that he "can do for us" what he knows "is best." And Senator Clark of Pennsylvania, another articulate spokesman, defines liberalism as "meeting the material needs of the masses through the full power of centralized government."

Well, I, for one, resent it when a representative of the people refers to you and me, the free men and women of this country, as "the masses." This is a term we haven't applied to ourselves in America. But beyond that, "the full power of centralized government" -- this was the very thing the Founding Fathers sought to minimize. They knew that governments don't control things. A government can't control the economy without controlling people. And they know when a government sets out to do that, it must use force and coercion to achieve its purpose. They also knew, those Founding Fathers, that outside of its legitimate functions, government does nothing as well or as economically as the private sector of the economy.

Now, we have no better example of this than government's involvement in the farm economy over the last 30 years. Since 1955, the cost of this program has nearly doubled. One-fourth of farming in America is responsible for 85% of the farm surplus. Three-fourths of farming is out on the free market and has known a 21% increase in the per capita consumption of all its produce. You see, that one-fourth of farming -- that's regulated and controlled by the federal government. In the last three years we've spent 43 dollars in the feed grain program for every dollar bushel of corn we don't grow.

Senator Humphrey last week charged that Barry Goldwater, as President, would seek to eliminate farmers. He should do his homework a little better, because he'll find out that we've had a decline of 5 million in the farm population under these government programs. He'll also find that the Democratic administration has sought to get from Congress [an] extension of the farm program to include that three-fourths that is now free. He'll find that they've also asked for the right to imprison farmers who wouldn't keep books as prescribed by the federal government. The Secretary of Agriculture asked for the right to seize farms through condemnation and resell them to other individuals. And contained in that same program was a provision that would have allowed the federal government to remove 2 million farmers from the soil.

At the same time, there's been an increase in the Department of Agriculture employees. There's now one for every 30 farms in the United States, and still they can't tell us how 66 shiploads of grain headed for Austria disappeared without a trace and Billie Sol Estes never left shore.

Every responsible farmer and farm organization has repeatedly asked the government to free the farm economy, but how -- who are farmers to know what's best for them? The wheat farmers voted against a wheat program. The government passed it anyway. Now the price of bread goes up; the price of wheat to the farmer goes down.

Meanwhile, back in the city, under urban renewal the assault on freedom carries on. Private property rights [are] so diluted that public interest is almost anything a few government planners decide it should be. In a program that takes from the needy and gives to the greedy, we see such spectacles as in Cleveland, Ohio, a million-and-a-half-dollar building completed only three years ago must be destroyed to make way for what government officials call a "more compatible use of the land." The President tells us he's now going to start building public housing units in the thousands, where heretofore we've only built them in the hundreds. But FHA [Federal Housing Authority] and the Veterans Administration tell us they have 120,000 housing units they've taken back through mortgage foreclosure. For three decades, we've sought to solve the problems of unemployment through government planning, and the more the plans fail, the more the planners plan. The latest is the Area Redevelopment Agency.

They've just declared Rice County, Kansas, a depressed area. Rice County, Kansas, has two hundred oil wells, and the 14,000 people there have over 30 million dollars on deposit in personal savings in their banks. And when the government tells you you're depressed, lie down and be depressed.

We have so many people who can't see a fat man standing beside a thin one without coming to the conclusion the fat man got that way by taking advantage of the thin one. So they're going to solve all the problems of human misery through government and government planning. Well, now, if government planning and welfare had the answer -- and they've had almost 30 years of it -- shouldn't we expect government to read the score to us once in a while? Shouldn't they be telling us about the decline each year in the number of people needing help? The reduction in the need for public housing?

But the reverse is true. Each year the need grows greater; the program grows greater. We were told four years ago that 17 million people went to bed hungry each night. Well that was probably true. They were all on a diet. But now we're told that 9.3 million families in this country are poverty-stricken on the basis of earning less than 3,000 dollars a year. Welfare spending [is] 10 times greater than in the dark depths of the Depression.

We're spending 45 billion dollars on welfare. Now do a little arithmetic, and you'll find that if we divided the 45 billion dollars up equally among those 9 million poor families, we'd be able to give each family 4,600 dollars a year. And this added to their present income should eliminate poverty. Direct aid to the poor, however, is only running only about 600 dollars per family. It would seem that someplace there must be some overhead.

Now -- so now we declare "war on poverty," or "You, too, can be a Bobby Baker." Now do they honestly expect us to believe that if we add 1 billion dollars to the 45 billion we're spending, one more program to the 30-odd we have -- and remember, this new program doesn't replace any, it just duplicates existing programs -- do they believe that poverty is suddenly going to disappear by magic? Well, in all fairness I should explain there is one part of the new program that isn't duplicated. This is the youth feature. We're now going to solve the dropout problem, juvenile delinquency, by re-instituting something like the old CCC camps [Civilian Conservation Corps], and we're going to put our young people in these camps. But again we do some arithmetic, and we find that we're going to spend each year just on room and board for each young person we help 4,700 dollars a year. We can send them to Harvard for 2,700! Course, don't get me wrong. I'm not suggesting Harvard is the answer to juvenile delinquency.

But seriously, what are we doing to those we seek to help? Not too long ago, a judge called me here in Los Angeles. He told me of a young woman who'd come before him for a divorce. She had six children, was pregnant with her seventh. Under his questioning, she revealed her husband was a laborer earning 250 dollars a month. She wanted a divorce to get an 80 dollar raise. She's eligible for 330 dollars a month in the Aid to Dependent Children Program. She got the idea from two women in her neighborhood who'd already done that very thing.

Yet anytime you and I question the schemes of the do-gooders, we're denounced as being against their humanitarian goals. They say we're always "against" things -- we're never "for" anything.

Well, the trouble with our liberal friends is not that they're ignorant; it's just that they know so much that isn't so.

Now -- we're for a provision that destitution should not follow unemployment by reason of old age, and to that end we've accepted Social Security as a step toward meeting the problem.

But we're against those entrusted with this program when they practice deception regarding its fiscal shortcomings, when they charge that any criticism of the program means that we want to end payments to those people who depend on them for a livelihood. They've called it "insurance" to us in a hundred million pieces of literature. But then they appeared before the Supreme Court and they testified it was a welfare program. They only use the term "insurance" to sell it to the people. And they said Social Security dues are a tax for the general use of the government, and the government has used that tax. There is no fund, because Robert Byers, the actuarial head, appeared before a congressional committee and admitted that Social Security as of this moment is 298 billion dollars in the hole. But he said there should be no cause for worry because as long as they have the power to tax, they could always take away from the people whatever they needed to bail them out of trouble. And they're doing just that.

A young man, 21 years of age, working at an average salary -- his Social Security contribution would, in the open market, buy him an insurance policy that would guarantee 220 dollars a month at age 65. The government promises 127. He could live it up until he's 31 and then take out a policy that would pay more than Social Security. Now are we so lacking in business sense that we can't put this program on a sound basis, so that people who do require those payments will find they can get them when they're due -- that the cupboard isn't bare?

Barry Goldwater thinks we can.

At the same time, can't we introduce voluntary features that would permit a citizen who can do better on his own to be excused upon presentation of evidence that he had made provision for the non-earning years? Should we not allow a widow with children to work, and not lose the benefits supposedly paid for by her deceased husband? Shouldn't you and I be allowed to declare who our beneficiaries will be under this program, which we cannot do? I think we're for telling our senior citizens that no one in this country should be denied medical care because of a lack of funds. But I think we're against forcing all citizens, regardless of need, into a compulsory government program, especially when we have such examples, as was announced last week, when France admitted that their Medicare program is now bankrupt. They've come to the end of the road.

In addition, was Barry Goldwater so irresponsible when he suggested that our government give up its program of deliberate, planned inflation, so that when you do get your Social Security pension, a dollar will buy a dollar's worth, and not 45 cents worth?

I think we're for an international organization, where the nations of the world can seek peace. But I think we're against subordinating American interests to an organization that has become so structurally unsound that today you can muster a two-thirds vote on the floor of the General Assembly among nations that represent less than 10 percent of the world's population. I think we're against the hypocrisy of assailing our allies because here and there they cling to a colony, while we engage in a conspiracy of silence and never open our mouths about the millions of people enslaved in the Soviet colonies in the satellite nations.

I think we're for aiding our allies by sharing of our material blessings with those nations which share in our fundamental beliefs, but we're against doling out money government to government, creating bureaucracy, if not socialism, all over the world. We set out to help 19 countries. We're helping 107. We've spent 146 billion dollars. With that money, we bought a 2 million dollar yacht for Haile Selassie. We bought dress suits for Greek undertakers, extra wives for Kenya[n] government officials. We bought a thousand TV sets for a place where they have no electricity. In the last six years, 52 nations have bought 7 billion dollars worth of our gold, and all 52 are receiving foreign aid from this country.

No government ever voluntarily reduces itself in size. So, governments' programs, once launched, never disappear.

Actually, a government bureau is the nearest thing to eternal life we'll ever see on this earth.

Federal employees -- federal employees number two and a half million; and federal, state, and local, one out of six of the nation's work force employed by government. These proliferating bureaus with their thousands of regulations have cost us many of our constitutional safeguards. How many of us realize that today federal agents can invade a man's property without a warrant? They can impose a fine without a formal hearing, let alone a trial by jury? And they can seize and sell his property at auction to enforce the payment of that fine. In Chico County, Arkansas, James Wier over-planted his rice allotment. The government obtained a 17,000 dollar judgment. And a U.S. marshal sold his 960-acre farm at auction. The government said it was necessary as a warning to others to make the system work.

Last February 19th at the University of Minnesota, Norman Thomas, six-times candidate for President on the Socialist Party ticket, said, "If

Barry Goldwater became President, he would stop the advance of socialism in the United States." I think that's exactly what he will do.

But as a former Democrat, I can tell you Norman Thomas isn't the only man who has drawn this parallel to socialism with the present administration, because back in 1936, Mr. Democrat himself, Al Smith, the great American, came before the American people and charged that the leadership of his Party was taking the Party of Jefferson, Jackson, and Cleveland down the road under the banners of Marx, Lenin, and Stalin. And he walked away from his Party, and he never returned til the day he died -- because to this day, the leadership of that Party has been taking that Party, that honorable Party, down the road in the image of the labor Socialist Party of England.

Now it doesn't require expropriation or confiscation of private property or business to impose socialism on a people. What does it mean whether you hold the deed to the -- or the title to your business or property if the government holds the power of life and death over that business or property? And such machinery already exists. The government can find some charge to bring against any concern it chooses to prosecute. Every businessman has his own tale of harassment. Somewhere a perversion has taken place. Our natural, unalienable rights are now considered to be a dispensation of government, and freedom has never been so fragile, so close to slipping from our grasp as it is at this moment.

Our Democratic opponents seem unwilling to debate these issues. They want to make you and I believe that this is a contest between two men -- that we're to choose just between two personalities.

Well what of this man that they would destroy -- and in destroying, they would destroy that which he represents, the ideas that you and I hold dear? Is he the brash and shallow and trigger- happy man they say he is? Well I've been privileged to know him "when." I knew him long before he ever dreamed of trying for high office, and I can tell you personally I've never known a man in my life I believed so incapable of doing a dishonest or dishonorable thing.

This is a man who, in his own business before he entered politics, instituted a profit-sharing plan before unions had ever thought of it. He put in health and medical insurance for all his employees. He took 50 percent of the profits before taxes and set up a retirement program, a pension plan for all his employees. He sent monthly checks for life to an employee who was ill and couldn't work. He provides nursing care for the *children of mothers who work in the stores. When Mexico was ravaged by the floods in the Rio Grande, he climbed in his airplane and flew medicine and supplies down there.*

An ex-GI told me how he met him. It was the week before Christmas during the Korean War, and he was at the Los Angeles airport trying to get a ride home to Arizona for Christmas. And he said that [there were] a lot of servicemen there and no seats available on the planes. And then a voice came over the loudspeaker and said, "Any men in uniform wanting a ride to Arizona, go to runway such-and-such," and they went down there, and there was a fellow named Barry Goldwater sitting in his plane. Every day in those weeks before Christmas, all day long, he'd load up the plane, fly it to Arizona, fly them to their homes, fly back over to get another load.

During the hectic split-second timing of a campaign, this is a man who took time out to sit beside an old friend who was dying of cancer. His campaign managers were understandably impatient, but he said, "There aren't many left who care what happens to her. I'd like her to know I care." This is a man who said to his 19-year-old son, "There is no foundation like the rock of honesty and fairness, and when you begin to build your life on that rock, with the cement of the faith in God that you have, then you have a real start." This is not a man who could carelessly send other people's sons to war. And that is the issue of this campaign that makes all the other problems I've discussed academic, unless we realize we're in a war that must be won.

Those who would trade our freedom for the soup kitchen of the welfare state have told us they have a utopian solution of peace without victory. They call their policy "accommodation." And they say if we'll only avoid any direct confrontation with the enemy, he'll forget his evil ways and learn to love us. All who oppose them are indicted as warmongers. They say we offer simple answers to complex problems. Well, perhaps there is a simple answer -- not an easy answer -- but simple: If you and I have the courage to tell our elected officials that we want our national policy based on what we know in our hearts is morally right.

We cannot buy our security, our freedom from the threat of the bomb by committing an immorality so great as saying to a billion human beings now enslaved behind the Iron Curtain, "Give up your dreams of freedom because to save our own skins, we're willing to make a deal with your slave masters." Alexander Hamilton said, "A nation which can prefer disgrace to danger is prepared for a master, and deserves one." Now let's set the record straight. There's no argument over the choice between peace and war, but there's only one guaranteed way you can have peace -- and you can have it in the next second -- surrender.

Admittedly, there's a risk in any course we follow other than this, but every lesson of history tells us that the greater risk lies in appeasement, and this is the specter our well-meaning liberal friends refuse to face -- that their policy of accommodation is appeasement, and it gives no choice between peace and war, only between fight or surrender. If we continue to accommodate, continue to back and retreat, eventually we have to face the final demand -- the ultimatum. And what then -- when Nikita Khrushchev has told his people he knows what our answer will be? He has told them that we're retreating under the pressure of the Cold War, and someday when the time comes to deliver the final ultimatum, our surrender will be voluntary, because by that time we will have been weakened from within spiritually, morally, and economically. He believes this because from our side he's heard voices pleading for "peace at any price" or "better Red than dead," or as one commentator put it, he'd rather "live on his knees than die on his feet." And therein lies the road to war, because those voices don't speak for the rest of us.

You and I know and do not believe that life is so dear and peace so sweet as to be purchased at the price of chains and slavery. If nothing in life is worth dying for, when did this begin -- just in the face of this enemy? Or should Moses have told the children of Israel to live in slavery under the pharaohs? Should Christ have refused the cross? Should the patriots at Concord Bridge have thrown down their guns and refused to fire the shot heard 'round the world? The martyrs of history were not fools, and our honored dead who gave their lives to stop the advance of the Nazis didn't die in vain. Where, then, is the road to peace? Well it's a simple answer after all.

You and I have the courage to say to our enemies, "There is a price we will not pay." "There is a point beyond which they must not advance." And this -- this is the meaning in the phrase of Barry Goldwater's "peace through strength." Winston Churchill said, "The destiny of man is not measured by material computations. When great forces are on the move in the world, we learn we're spirits -- not animals." And he said, "There's something going on in time and space, and beyond time and space, which, whether we like it or not, spells duty."

You and I have a rendezvous with destiny.

We'll preserve for our children this, the last best hope of man on earth, or we'll sentence them to take the last step into a thousand years of darkness.

We will keep in mind and remember that Barry Goldwater has faith in us. He has faith that you and I have the ability and the dignity and the right to make our own decisions and determine our own destiny.

Thank you very much.

"As you know, Goldwater lost that presidential election to Johnson, and I think that loss was one of this country's miscues that has led us to today. I have never heard more resonating words that are relevant today, right now, than those of determining our own destiny. I appreciate your time," Bishop said, as he finished.

The room was so quiet that you could hear individual's breaths. Everyone was completely lost in thought. How could it be that a speech that had been given in 1964 could be as relevant today as it was then, and maybe more so? Voices began, and then more joined. Everyone was asking Bishop the same thing. Could they get a copy of the speech to circulate around the group?

***

A few days before leaving for Colorado, Samantha attended a healthcare meeting. Samantha Sloan and Annabelle Ellstin were rarely in the same place at the same time. Annabelle stuck to working on her focused items, in her small area, geographically, as well as subject matter that she was interested in, while Samantha was all over the place, literally and figuratively. When they were together in the same room, they looked like they could almost be sisters. Annabelle was taller, and her blonde hair fell below her waist, but it was always braided down her back and out of her face, whereas Sam's was shorter and messier around her face.

Nikoli represented his tech group, and was probably the most liberal on the subject. He and Sam were also happy that they got to spend more time together, being a part of this think tank.

Randall Quinn wanted to be involved because he had had a cancer scare that made him think twice about western medicine versus alternative medicine, and decided to be more aware of what was going on with respect to how the group was structuring the topic. This was clearly out of his expertise, so he would just hang back and listen to what was being said.

All of the non-US citizen leaders wanted to be involved, had a lot to say on the subject, and had a lot of experiences to share regarding how the countries of their origin handled things. The opinions and disagreements started flying almost immediately. Antonio Montes was on one side of the argument, while Vassily Novikov was on the other. Ryder Burns and the people from other countries were somewhere in between. But, when it came down to it, they were all saying basically the same thing: healthcare should be affordable to everyone but not given to anyone.

"Y'all keep tearing strips off each other and nothin' is gonna get done up. The reports y'all brought make more sense than what is bein' said here," Ellstin yelled out after about an hour of the back-and-forth.

Samantha was thinking she would let them burn each other out, but she was glad when Annabelle spoke up. "Let's look down the listed items that are still left open. One of the biggest problems we have discovered in mental health is not having enough professionals in the field to do required work...Sam?"

"I have been studying different parts of the field since college and if I would have believed the only way to be of value was to become an MD and practice psychiatry I would have. Psychiatrists are very valuable... don't get me wrong, but having said that so are psychologist. Teamed up appropriately the two specialties could work in tandem to facilitate recovery while also being efficient. If there is a shortage of psychiatrists, then let clinical psychologists do some of the heavy lifting...there must be at least fifty psychologists to every psychiatrist. If one psychiatrist oversaw the meds and did check-ins to evaluate how patients were doing with the combination of the medicines and the work the psychologists were doing with them, a practice could be highly successful. I'm sure this is being done already, we just have to make it more efficient for our needs down the road as Texas grows."

"Long gone are the real efficiency experts," said a fellow psychologist sitting next to Quinn. "Now it is about billing by the hour and sucking as much time out of someone or something as possible. In the old time and motion studies of the Taylor and Gilbreth team, they tried to find new, innovative ways of making a task more efficient. Now Business Process Managers have to get a certification first, then go and follow a process, to show a business whether or not its process is productive or not. Do you see the convolution?"

"We do," said Nikoli. "and I can tell you things like that will stop in Texas. They have already stopped as much as possible in my company in what we call the 'real-world'. There are just so many people doing the same things, or *trying* to do the same things, there has to be a measuring stick and then I go back to the scalability problem again. When you have one hundred people, it is easy to see who is special, who stands out, etc., but when you have hundreds of millions, you can't easily see anything about anyone and unless you have a tool with which to even start to measure something, you will fail…not that we aren't failing even with tools, but that is what we are trying here to address."

No one could argue the logic, but everyone was frustrated.

"I see where you are comin' from Nikoli, but how do we stipulate needing the measuring stick at the same time as try to send it on its way in Texas?" asked Annabelle.

"Well that is the million dollar question, right?" answered Borodin.

"Since the can has been opened, let's eat the meal, I think it will be a worthy exercise" said Annabelle. Samantha had to laugh at her very southern monikers. Annabelle ignored her and continued, "This can be used in other areas, but for the sake of focus, let's keep our eye on healthcare and talk about how we can both use that yard stick and evaluate something outside of it too."

The group talked about different ways of identifying good ideas, capable people, and even treatment methods that might fall outside of a typical litmus test. The room sounded like undistinguishable shouting, but much was accomplished.

Cooper then spoke up and introduced a man he was with. "Wes is an athlete who is type 1 diabetic," started Cooper. "I met him at a charity event for getting kids outdoors to play outside more, and spend less time on video games and the like. I want him to share some experiences of hardships he's gone through to stay relevant in athletics even though he is also struggling with a lifelong disease."

Wes just looked at Cooper. They had not talked about him sharing anything. He was an Xer, but he wasn't exactly the type to talk about his personal trials. He was hoping Cooper would give him a little bit more as to what he was looking for him to talk about but got nothing. So he started with the difficulty in maintaining a blood sugar when the body is doing something particularly strenuous. "We have trainers, nutritionists and devices to help, but at the end of the day, you have to know what works for you."

"Outside of daily struggles and probably huge individual costs associated with it, what are your thoughts on the idea of healthcare for everyone and the cost being shared by everyone?" asked Sloan.

"In fantasy land, I love the idea, but I don't believe it is sustainable economically," answered Wes. "Being diabetic has been more expensive for me that you can imagine, and I understand that. My personal belief is that health insurance should be a little like car insurance. Your health is how great your car is, so how much insurance do you want to cover it? And based on how many tickets you get, diabetes, high blood pressure, obesity, etc., that equals how much you have to actually pay for your insurance. The healthier you get, say for example someone that is or was obese loses weight and gets on a healthy eating program and gets healthier from blood pressure, blood sugar, heart health etcetera, his premium is reduced versus someone that does not choose to do those things, his premiums will stay higher. Lifestyle should matter. I know I didn't ask for a disease that I will likely have for the rest of my life and it isn't fair, but you shouldn't have to share my expenses because that isn't fair either."

"I wish I had you with me at this conference I was at last month, Wes. I brought up Type 1 diabetes in a different context, but it certainly would have been nice to have someone that knows all about it first hand," said Sloan smiling.

Others were nodding in agreement as well. The idea was a good one.

"What about those who can't afford their own insurance?" asked a friend that Montes brought.

"We are going in with the goal that that not be the case. If we structure it correctly and not have the overhead and redundancies we currently have, there should be plans that everyone can afford.

But, we will need a contingency regardless," answered Borodin. "We don't have to have all the answers, we just have to have better ideas to try."

Sloan chimed in, "Based off empirical data that we have been combing over for years, we will be uniquely positioned to be able to try things that might not work based on a larger population. Then when something works well, we continue with that research and figure out its scalability."

Once again, by this point in the conversation, everyone in the think tank was spent. Annabelle had rubbed her eyes red, Nikoli's hair was messed up from him putting his fingers nervously through it all day, and Sam kept tilting her head back and forth trying to loosen her neck and shoulders.

Still looking as crisp as when the meeting had started in his black suit and pressed white shirt Montes said, "I think we have hit a stopping point. We have some answers and many plausible ideas, at least enough to take to the conference, if not diminishing the need to have this be an agenda item at all."

"Agreed," said Borodin. "Samantha and I will disseminate the information and we can determined the need to continue the discussion at the conferences at a later time."

CHAPTER 28
ONE VERSUS MANY, ANONYMOUS VERSUS
CONFIDENTIAL & THE DOWNWARD SPIRAL

A change was represented in the relationship with AmendX and the governmental administration in 2009. 44 got sworn in and they had to continue to try to build some kind of communication with him. They had continued the letters to show that they could get to him at any time. It was more to prove the point that many people were out there that were unsatisfied with the way things were going. They had such huge numbers within the ranks of the government that now they could use myriad ways to communicate and let him know they were serious. Bishop had hoped to get more done with 43, but although he was willing to hear them, the bureaucracy was so bad only the smallest of items could even be attempted. He also knew that, even if 44 was willing, and few doubted that, he would also be ineffective. But Samantha and Nikoli convinced him to keep sending the communications at least through 2009 and then reassess.

The year was busy for Bishop. His did continue his work outside of the group and it gave him great pleasure, but he also knew he was the vision behind AmendX, and there were always people to talk to. No conversation was ever the same; each was unique. The conversations were private, individualized and always authentic. He wasn't talking to people to sell something. He had a gift for knowing when someone was at the point of looking for answers and that was when he spoke to them. He had been there himself 12 years ago, and even though his friends were around to help, he struggled through what he called his 'head explosion' mostly by himself. It was then he had the idea that the problem could be defined as a scalability problem, and might be solved by starting over in a smaller, more manageable environment, and each year, he became more convinced of it. At first, he thought a civil war was the answer...not so much the answer, but the inevitable. More and more every day factions were becoming less and less tolerant of each other; the line in the sand becoming deeper and deeper. Then he thought of one of his favorite books, Walden Two. B.F. Skinner's contributing idea to behavioral and social engineering. It was the thousand-person experiment in search of a utopian society. Ok, he wasn't going for a utopian society, what he was going for was an accountable society that found the balance between cooperation and competition. Both were required for man to be at his best.

He knew that Cooper was ready to go from the last thing he said to him "It isn't about you versus us, it is about building a 'we' and this country is so split by partisanship, I think we have forgotten that. If we don't tear off and show them that, we might as well split the country in half, we'd do better by the people that way, instead of being dead-locked, refusing to cooperate with each other."

But he also knew that Cooper would wait until the plan was ready to be executed, which, for the most part it was. There were a few odds and ends to be completed, but the conference agenda had been nailed down, resources were about as strong as they were going to get physically in Texas, and financial resources were only climbing. The group's leaders were doing well, the only negative that he saw were many were getting edgy. More and more he heard that many of them were ready to start the conferences and nail down final plans, and Bishop agreed.

He was a bit concerned about Nikoli and wondered if he was pulling away from the group or just him. After a confidential meeting with the NSA Nikoli seemed distressed. All he said was that he was conflicted about what was happening. Bishop didn't know if this meant between Sensedatum and the group or Sensadatum and the government. He was under strict orders to not discuss it and Bishop knew that Nikoli would never break that gag order, nor would he want him to. But something just wasn't right. They hadn't seen each other in a couple of months and Bishop thought maybe the time and distance could be part of the problem. On the phone that day Bishop was concerned about his friend.

"You just haven't seemed yourself lately Niki. Is everything ok?"

"When did everything get so complex Mike?"

"I know what you mean, but I think it was before we had any idea that it was. I don't expect you to talk about the meeting you had but it clearly upset you."

"Yeah I can't talk about it, but I can say this, I feel torn on both sides, between the government and the group and then there is the company that I built that could suffer and I can't have that. I can't expose my company's reputation based on my personal beliefs."

I'm at a bit of a disadvantage not knowing what you are talking about, but you know this group would never ask you to choose between your company and us."

"That's not really true Mike. We decided that Sense isn't coming because of Ford so at one point I had to choose. But I did and that's that. At least I know it will carry on and not die. I know you are at a disadvantage and I don't want you to worry about what is going on. It's fine."

Bishop could hear in Nikoli's voice that things weren't fine. "I'm just worried about my friend. You know if you need me for anything...inside of the group, outside of the group, or just best friends, I've got your back."

"I know comrade, I know. I'll keep you posted once we've had the first run of Internet meetings."

"Talk to you soon Niki."

***

After the conversation with Nikoli, he also remembered a conversation he had with someone outside of the group a year or so earlier. He recalled this man coming full circle after going through a bit of a personal dilemma. Maybe Niki could too. That man had said that killing your competition was the only way to succeed in business, and life in general. The gentleman had just read Walden Two, based on Bishop's recommendation. He was saying how a place like that could never survive because in fighting would most certainly start as soon as someone tried to do something better than his neighbor. Bishop was trying to explain that while Walden Two did seem to skim over our competitive nature, plus the book made little mention of working with communities outside of the utopia, both cooperation and competition are needed to succeed and Walden Two made great strides in showing how in that the cooperation part was obvious. The competition element was more veiled, but as

Bishop interpreted it, it was simply when one is striving for his best beating the competition showed excellence, not destruction.

"You do not perform these gestures out of the goodness of your heart," Bishop started, you do them for some kind of payment that shows your gesture or work is valued. For example, let's create a hypothetical experimental community, like Walden Two, but instead of behavioral conditioning, let's talk about efficiency and value, and let's reduce the number from 1,000 to a neighborhood. There are twenty households in the neighborhood, with some married couples that both work, and have some stay at home spouses. Throw in some single parents, and some roommate situations. They each bring a different set of skills to the table. Instead of paying a ludicrous sum for daycare, maybe one of the stay at home spouses or singles takes care of the children that are too young to start school. This person also makes sure the school-aged children make it home safe and watch them until their parents arrive home. This person does not do this for free. In exchange, this person gets paid money to use outside of the neighborhood, and if money is not what is needed, barter can be done. One of the households that take advantage of the childcare owns a landscaping and lawn care company, so their company takes care of the person's lawn and outside maintenance. This is just off the top of my head and is a very simple example, and obviously cannot be done on a huge scale. Well, actually it is being done on a large scale, but unfortunately costs have gotten out of control and bartering could be considered illegal in some cases because taxes cannot be assessed. But for the point of this example, let's skip that part. The point is to take advantage of the community's strengths and resources, one never has to lose individual value."

The gentleman Bishop was talking to didn't agree at first, but he had come back and seen Bishop recently; he said he tried some of the things Bishop used as examples in his own neighborhood. They had managed to organize a neighborhood watch of sorts to make sure the children of parents that worked made it home from school safely. One neighbor with land that was just open space allowed others to build and fence an area for the kids and neighborhood dogs to be brought to play, all within safe sight-lines of parents and sitters. One neighbor owned an asphalt company and added a walkway that had been needed for years, but since they lived in an unincorporated part of the county, it was not the county's responsibility. Living in an unincorporated area was good for the neighbors because they paid less tax, but the downside was fewer amenities. But as a neighborhood, they pulled together their resources and determination and got things done. He was astounded how, while everyone remained individuals, so much got done with a little cooperation. The man, and his entire neighborhood, joined the group not soon afterward.

Recruitment was almost scary. Bishop doubted that these numbers could remain a secret much longer. When the actress came into the group, she was married to a famous singer from Australia. He had some friends in Aspen, a model and real estate mogul, whose sister was also an actress. She was connected to a super-famous director who knew everybody in Hollywood, and soon a new contingent of the new recruits were the who's-who in Hollywood, which Bishop tried to avoid at all costs. His very limited experience with the entertainment business people was that they had big hearts; bigger check books and no attention span. The director was cut from a different cloth though. Then there was the young actor who was doing everything he could to talk to kids about the evils of entitlement and the benefits of having a job. He was certainly getting some eyebrows raised from others in the field because the way he spoke was that from another time and as young as he was, it didn't make sense to the star-makers and the propaganda machine. He was preaching about having a job, and that building something was a path to a happier, more fulfilled life than any of the getting famous for fame's sake, and having money that you didn't earn. His message was so on-point with what Bishop believed that they became fast friends. He was the first entertainment industry Xer and he had no interest bringing others in. But when they started coming, he helped Bishop vet them for fitness with the group. Before Bishop revealed anything significant, the current mode of recruitment was that of concerned citizens lobbying for change. He had a sit-down with the director, and his also famous wife, and explained his dilemma. He thanked them for their interest, but couldn't afford a flight of fancy for this was a project that would take an enormous amount of time and planning. By the time the conversation was over, the director not only committed to the group, but also promised to weed out those who were in it for the quick gratification of the charity-of-the-week mentality. Some fell off, most didn't and to Bishop's surprise many were helpful as well as had many ideas to contribute. The key to the secrecy was that these were just projects that people who believed in them were working on. Bishop knew ideas, projects; concerned citizens were probably working on theses kinds of issues as well outside of this group. The only difference was that they didn't have plans to invade a state and make a new frontier. But for now most of the Xers were content just working on their individual projects and living their own lives.

When a famous producer was having lunch with Samantha in San Francisco one afternoon, he asked about several famous people and their involvement in the group. Sam was there to introduce him to a group with whom he would start working. It was a policy that a newer member would be placed with a group that shared common interests and, from there, they would split off into other committees and think tanks.

"I don't really keep track of famous members versus the not-so-famous members," she said.

Speaking about the media mogul turned philanthropist, the producer said, "I don't know her personally but I have many friends that do. I was surprised to hear she isn't one of the group – I don't even think she has been asked, or the whole story, but I just wonder why she wouldn't want to be a part of this. She is and will be, however, one of our strongest allies on the other side. Like I said, I don't know her personally so I don't know how she chooses to live, her politics or how she treats others. What I do know is what amazing work she has done with her network and her money. She is interested in putting on smart programming and not mind-numbing "reality" television that has young girls wanting to look like sluts, carrying $1,000 handbags when their parents can't even afford the mortgage. And the sad part is that the parents acquiesce to keep up with the Jones'. This segment of our population have become empty vessels that do not want to produce, they are fat and lazy and poor, financially, morally and emotionally."

"Jeez, don't hold back Marc," Sloan said. She had become very aware that when people first became involved their adrenaline seemed to spike for several months. The excitement of working toward something that you believe is going to change things does something to your stamina for a while, she thought.

"I'm sick of this," he said. "We have to be so careful not to offend anyone, but what I just said is true. People are famous for being famous and you know whom I'm talking about. We do not need another clothing line or fragrance or hipster boutique. We need some intelligent programming, smart commentary and groups of think tanks trying to solve our problems…NOT burying our heads in the sand, watching brainless 'scripted-reality' shows to find out who's design gets eliminated, denied the rose or kicked off."

"Just take it down a notch," she said smiling. "You are going to have plenty of time to help form new ways of doing everything we can think of. But take it from me after doing this for more than a decade, it is exhausting and you have to pace yourself."

"Yeah, you're probably right," Marc said, tapping his fingers on the table.

***

A week later in Austin, reading the paper waiting for a group to arrive to discuss final recommendations on healthcare, Sam read about an insurance company canceling care for a believed-to-be schizophrenic. The guy had hit his limit of mental health visits, but despite his therapist pleading with the insurance company, coverage was still dropped. That same week he opened fire at his school campus when he was kicked out of a Ph.D. program. One person was killed, and eighteen were injured. All Sam could do was shake her head.

Nikoli Borodin was the first to arrive. Samantha had been working on about three hours of sleep the night for the last week so her nerves were raw. Nikoli sat down.

"Our health care system sucks so bad we have no idea the level of sickness that we are flat out ignoring," said Sam explaining what she had just read.

"It is a matter of cost/benefit. I would have to imagine that the numbers say that is a rare instance," replied Nikoli.

Throwing the newspaper directly at Nikoli, Sloan said, "What are you talking about Niki?!?! You have no clue what the numbers say, and should it matter? There are so many easy fixes that we just ignore because of stigma or just plain ignorance it makes me sick. Don't fucking side with them Niki, you have no idea what you are talking about."

"Sam! Calm down, I'm just saying..."

Interrupting Nikoli, "I know exactly what you are trying to say, and you are wrong. The answer is a plain-and-fucking simple brain scan as a part of a general physical and no one is even close to doing that. That way we have a baseline and can measure changes."

"And what does that do?" asked Nikoli.

"It does everything! It can throw up red flags with regard to schizophrenia, which in some cases may be preventable, plus we can see disease as it occurs if physicals are done regularly, and the cost is nothing compared to what it is when we are paying out victim's families when the horrific happens. If we don't shift fast, God! It seems like a plot, like they want the mentally ill to take out the regular citizen and that makes no sense."

"You aren't making any sense Sam, I mean you are, but you are almost manic at this point."

"You don't know what that even means!"

"I don't want something else thrown at me, but really you are over-reacting to this Sam."

Taking a deep breath and rolling her eyes, "I can't do this today. I just need a God damn minute." A tear rose up in her eye. She rubbed her eyes quickly.

"I got this, go. Do what always makes things better for you. Sit in the backyard with Oliver and just breath. You haven't been like this in a long time," Nikoli said with a lot of concern. "And you are of no benefit to this conversation today."

Sloan shut her eyes. She felt terrible losing it on Niki, but if she thought about anymore she would totally break down. It seemed like it was always a fight and she was worn down. Plus, he was right, that an afternoon with Oliver and a good night's sleep would recharge her and make her smile again. She felt like it has been ages since she had. She walked up to Nikoli and just put her forehead in his neck and gently nudged him.

"I'm sorry Niki."

"No worries. Get out of here."

As others were arriving, they looked confused as she was walking out. She didn't make eye contact, she couldn't. She just needed to get out of there.

***

A month later back in San Francisco, throughout the Internet meetings that Nikoli held there was much debate. The small committee was comprised of mostly techies who had not only the specialized expertise, but also the pragmatic experience that could lead to the best outcome. Randall Quinn was originally involved, but because of 'real-world' conflicts, he just couldn't see eye-to-eye with his competition outside of the Xers on this one. He recused himself and let them fight it out amongst themselves. Nikoli spearheaded the effort, while Nadal Dani did most of the work, organizing meetings, preparing research and seeing that it got disseminated to those outside of the committee for any thoughts they may have. Dean Kinsey didn't do much from a task perspective, but he was a fresh set of experienced eyes. David Wallace also asked to be a member and was always jotting notes down in cryptic writing that no one could understand. He was not given a tablet because he didn't head any committees, which infuriated him. So, he took it upon himself to record the meetings, as he felt necessary. Kylie Chamberland was older, and she acted as the moral compass of the committee. So many moral issues arose early on about the Internet because it was something that was in the private homes of citizens, and that privacy had to be a topic of conversation. Joseph Bailey was not a technical person but his work with Homeland Security offered an exclusively qualified opinion from the other side. There were many other technical advisors that were Xers interested in the topic that came and went over the year or so that the committee met. Nikoli was surprised actually, thinking that other topics would generate many more disputes than the Internet, but he found that many of the Xers felt the same way about this as they did about the economy or education, even healthcare. No one really thought about how pervasive the Internet had become in everyone's life, thus didn't think about all of the implications surrounding its use. Many believed that it should be left alone, especial Nadal Dani. He had worked in tech all of his life and because of the email service he created, he believed that the current, basically anonymous, manner in which the Internet lived was the best course of action. Others believed the opposite, and cited accountability as the reason.

"If something is anonymous, it removes any personal accountability from the originator," said Chamberland.

"But if it isn't anonymous, it removes the privacy that it was built on," replied Dani.

"I have to agree with Kylie here," said Bailey. Over the years Bailey had worked very hard on his abrasive personality and many around him saw the improvement. "There is a difference between confidential and anonymous. Anonymous, to me, encourages only those that want to get away with something that they aren't supposed to be doing, while confidential protects them from backlash of their opinion."

"Also," added Chamberland, "if Internet accounts are allowed to be created anonymously, that just adds to the ability to stalk, bully and generally persecute without any reprisal, not to mention such a waste of abandoned accounts."

"Ok, first," started Dani, cleaning up abandoned accounts is very simple."

"Waste is waste," answered Chamberland. She was a woman from a time when wasting was not an option.

"Second," continued Dani, "you don't get Internet accounts..."

Cut off by Borodin, "For the sake of this conversation, we don't have to go into how accounts are made and the definitions surrounding the Internet, we are here today to try to decide whether or not we should allow certain things via the Internet to come into the new community, and if so, do we filter it by subscriptions, or opting in, leave it the way it is, or figure out something else, yeah?"

Dani continued, "I remember that New Yorker cartoon where the dog says, 'On the Internet, nobody knows you're a dog.' That basically sparked the controversy about privacy. What we really have here is a multifaceted discussion that encompasses privacy, confidentiality, and anonymity. Breaking it down, we have to decide what we're trying to accomplish and protect, and whether government has a role in that protection."

Chamberland re-stated her point, "We're protecting individuals. Like I said before, being anonymous means you can say anything without fear of reprisal."

"What it comes down to, "Dani said, "is that people should be able to speak their mind, state an opinion, write a review, or whatever, without being attacked if, for some reason, the subject of that opinion or review doesn't like it. We have the technology to prevent Internet anonymity, if we want. We just need to decide, philosophically, how far we travel down the continuum from complete attribution, i.e. no privacy whatsoever, through confidentiality, and finally to anonymity. How do we keep accountability as part of the equation?"

"But that is my point exactly," Chamberland said. "You are looking at it from the opposite side as I am in this example. You are saying someone should feel free to say anything they want without fear of being attacked. I am saying if they knew they might be attacked, or at the very least held accountable for what they say, they might choose their words more carefully and more respectfully."

Bailey spoke up, almost under his breath. "Not to mention all that marketing crap. Without good tools for privacy, just trying to do some shopping online means that you'll get a billion ads and spam email sent your way. That shit has to go away. Does that crap even work?"

Dani, ever the professor, laughed, and then took the opportunity to lecture for a minute on the subject. "Advertisements will likely be a major source of revenue for companies in the future, and will create massive valuations for organizations that don't actually produce a product. Look at what is already happening with Facebook, and other ad-supported sites. They're making tremendous revenues from advertisements. And yes, it does work, despite your hatred of it." Dani was smiling as he finished his brief monologue.

"Again, I have to say," Chamberland piped up, "these things should all be controlled and the user should either be able to opt in or out of such ad onslaughts. If they aren't controlled, then it will get out of control like it is now."

"But we're getting off track, here," Dani said. "As all of you know, I am a huge proponent of privacy. I believe this protection is necessary. However, everyone makes valid points, so here is what I would suggest..."

Dani went on to describe an environment where accountability would be the basis for decision-making. They had the technology to track people, companies, etc., so they would put rules into place that penalized those who would deliberately use the Internet to harm other individuals or companies, and there would also be penalties for individuals or organizations that carried out retribution where it wasn't warranted. It echoed their beliefs in every other area, privacy and confidentiality, with accountability. Essentially, 'trust but verify' for Internet traffic. Everyone seemed to like the basis of Dani's plan, and they all got to work on the details. The opt-in philosophy was also embraced and needed further exploration.

"In wrapping things up," Nikoli said. "We also need to say whether these policies and protections are coming from the government or should they be regulation type of things instituted by individual companies?"

"I think most of us would agree individual companies should be tasked with running and regulating their own businesses, don't you Niki?" asked Dani.

"In most cases, I would say I agree, but how do we ensure the practices are being followed by all the companies without a governmental presence? Even though now that certainly doesn't work either."

"Correct," said Bailey. "When we rely on the government to make things right, we are doomed."

"This is actually an easy one to see if it is being followed or not. If something is completely anonymous, we know something isn't working as designed," said Nikoli.

Thursday, April 9, 2009 – 1:54pm Mountain Daylight Time (19:54 hours Zulu Time)

During a routine get-together in Colorado, just outside of Denver, Dean Kinsey was pissed and wanted to get some things off of his chest. He wanted a group formed to discuss ways to identify and change poor habits when they start, especially for those in the group that were old enough to know the 'old' ways. Down the road, when all of this would be in their rear-view mirror, younger kids would, by culture, act the new way, but for now, he had some issues to discuss. Nikoli was running the meeting as Sam was in Austin and Bishop was called back to MIT for some work issues.

"Parents hand their kids different forms of media, like video games and movies, so they don't have to have interactions with them. They do this because interaction is more difficult, but it is resulting in these kids lacking any kind of pro-social behavior. Kids end up isolated, lonely, ultimately and ironically, more dependent on their parents. I'm the first guy that will tell you how beneficial technology is, but when you can't even have a conversation with your kids in the car because they have to watch a DVD, we are too dependent on technology. Furthermore, parents tune out so they are robots, going to work, coming home, doing the grind of a dance that could be rewarding, eye opening and fulfilling. Instead they think they are too tired, annoyed...just blank. If they spent even a week interacting with their family, I bet you any amount of money, they would have more energy, they would be happier and they wouldn't give a shit what the idiot on television is wearing...sorry." Kinsey said looking at a man at the table who happened to have been a famous television star.

"No, I get what you are saying, and that is largely why I'm here," said the actor. "Don't get me wrong, I love what I do and I can't imagine doing anything else, but true artistry is falling by the wayside just for celebrity. I try to hone my craft everyday and become better at what I do for my sake and those that watch what I do. But I get what you are saying, the priorities are wrong. There is room for entertainment whilst having a full, aware and conscious life. I believe that anyway."

"Totally agreed and well said," said Kinsey. "I just didn't want you to think I hate all of you," he finished, a little embarrassed.

The actor smiled. Nikoli looked at Kinsey and said, "you had a conversation with industry group – Sterling and that bunch, right?"

"Yeah, we talked through regulation versus free markets and just setting rules in general. It was a fascinating conversation really. It amazes me how someone I really respect can think so differently than me even when we are both in this group for very similar reasons."

"Ok," Nikoli said. "Can you explain that and fill us in on what action steps came out of conversation?"

'Well," Kinsey started, "Some think that all these rules need to be made, while others believe that regulations and the hindering of free enterprise is what causes the problems. Really, the end result was that both sides are right. The larger group mainly believed free-market economics and minimal government interference was the one hundred percent way to go, but then a small group explained that the reason rules need to be made are because people are too lazy to do, generally speaking, 'the right thing'. Let me give an example that means nothing in the bigger scheme of things, but is relevant to understanding my point. I use this because I know we don't have time for a large-scale debate on the matter and these issues are, and have been, being researched by Sterling and his bunch since the introduction of the economy talks in the first place, so I know the issue is being handled well. The example I use is public dress."

"Public dress?" asked Borodin.

"Yeah, the way you dress when you go out in public," answered Kinsey. "It used to be suit and ties for men in the workplace... not so much a rule, but what we knew was the 'right thing to do'. Then casual Friday came into fashion, excuse my sarcasm, now... I can't tell if some people are going to work in their yards or their office. There has to be some business decorum! Sam showed me research on comparisons between people that dress appropriately for work versus those who don't. Results are, to me, as expected. Those that wear cut-offs to the office are significantly less efficient and successful than those who dress in business attire. I personally dress the way I want people to view me... successful, confident, and competent. I went to pick my daughter up from school the other day; she is living on campus this semester to get the 'college experience'. I was against it, but her mother won. Anyway, I was appalled seeing the kids coming and going. Some looked like they had actually gotten out of bed and left their rooms to go to class, still in pajamas. Girls are walking around in t-shirts, pajama bottoms and slippers for Christ's sake! How can they be taken seriously like that? I am one of the anti-rule folks, but if these kids are too stupid to know better, I see where rules need to be put in place. If I was these kid's professors, I would send them out of my class to go change their clothes. It's that simple."

"I can't speak regarding college kids, Dean," Nikoli said, looking annoyed, "but I have to say you don't have to be in a tie to accomplish great things. There is no dress code of any kind at Sensadatum and look at what has been accomplished. In the ten percent of work time we let them work on what they want, more has been done to improve efficiencies and create new technologies than in one hundred percent of other companies, and these guys are in t-shirts and flip-flops."

"I knew you would have an issue with this Nikoli, and in your case, you are right, but you have the cream of the crop of a group notorious for being social... let's say... outsiders. Plus, this is an industry where that might be appropriate. They are sitting in front of computers and other devices and interacting with their peers brainstorming. They aren't going to meetings with investment capitalists. I'm sorry, if every company let their employees decide what they should work on ten percent of the time, it would be a disaster. It took your employees blood, sweat, tears, clawing, finagling, and manipulating anything they could think of to get a job there. So you think they are going to fuck off with that time? Hell no. But not every company has that culture, let alone the popularity to work there that drives these employees to do their best."

Nikoli only nodded, conceding Kinsey's point, but still not fully agreeing with him. "And as far as your rules and regulations potentially hindering free markets, Sterling more than cleared that up for us but you are forgetting one thing: we all want the same thing. We are starting anew just because of that. Haley had a TV show on the other night in the background while she was getting some work done and I just flopped down on the couch and ended up watching it. I can't remember the name of it but it was a cluster to say the least. One kid with Asperger's literally pushed a lady out of her chair to get to a computer to use it and his parents were pissed at the lady because being at this place... some art studio, was super important to his social development. Then other kids of the same extended family, cousins of the Asperger's kid, came to a family function high, and yet another cousin is screaming about her parents getting a divorce because of the kid they adopted, and that everything was great in their relationship before that."

"It sounds like a terrible show," said Kinsey.

"Well it was all quite dramatic and beyond liberal, but here is where my problem lies: the bar keeps getting lowered to accommodate those who don't want to put in the time or the work until we are a society of barely functioning people with nothing but entitled attitudes. If it is so important that the Asperger's kid is socialized, which I'm sure it is, then how is it acceptable that he is violent in the process? And if the parents weren't there, how can they say it was the lady's fault? This is one of those times you wonder if the kid is going to come back with a gun or go to his school with one. The parents are law-abiding, sweet-looking people, but completely repudiate any responsibility regarding their kid. He should have been shut down, calmed down and spoken to with or without professional help and told that behavior absolutely doesn't happen, and if it does, he doesn't go where he wants to go anymore. Period! Next, about the kids that show up high to dinner… you can believe what you want about pot, but the fact remains, that it, like other drugs, and even alcohol, kills brain cells when used in excess, and to be high is excess. So, I certainly don't get drunk because I want every cell that I have to work *for* me, not *against* me. And for all those people that are becoming vegetables, who is going to have to take care of them when they can't take care of themselves? And for that dumb girl being allowed to spout off and say mean things and hurt others, with no consequences to her behavior, it shows a complete lack of empathy on the kid's part and total cop-out on the parents' part for not shutting it down."

"Those are not people I would associate with Niki. What is your point?" asked Kinsey.

"You just made it for me, answered Borodin. "We have been working our asses off for years, bleeding to find the right people, and by that I mean that we share our desires and goals and foundations for how to start society again. Having that in the beginning will serve us better than rules and regulations, and as new generations within that society see and live by the standards we establish and stop at nothing to protect, then we have made it. What changed here is we all let the standards be lowered and over time we now see what happens."

***

While that conversation was going on in Golden, Samantha was sitting at an outdoor cafe in Austin with some friends and some friends-of-friends, many of them not Xers, just having a light conversation. Oliver was at her feet. They were talking about old Star Trek episodes and Samantha said how much she liked to watch them.

Kami, a friend of Samantha's said to her, "You don't really seem like a Trekie to me."

Sam laughed, "I watch them in my down time, plus there are always such good messages in them, that it gives me a sense of hope every time I watch one. They solve problems and act humanely and they explore new places and new ways of doing things."

Someone else, someone Sam didn't know said in reply, "Yeah but they never say how they solved a problem. I think they are dumb, like oh, in the future everything is great, just automatically."

"That isn't true at all." Samantha responded annoyed. "Think of the things Star Trek had, years before something similar was invented in real life. Tablet computers are one example I can think of off the top of my head. Plus, Rodenberry was a genius. Listen – really listen – to the science and cosmology of the show. Many times you will see it is quite accurate. In times for drama there are made-up mysteries, but most of the periphery is completely accurate and you can't tell me crime or medical shows on now are accurate even a little."

"But, like I said," he continued, "they don't say how they solved world hunger or bad weather disasters. I used to watch it all the time and wonder well, if it is so great that you solved it, tell us how, I mean to say the future fixed something is one thing, to say how they did it is another."

"Does everything have to be handed to you?" Sam spouted even more annoyed at the laziness, causing Oliver to whine a little.

Whenever Samantha became agitated, Oliver could tell and would sit up or whine in response. This would usually cause Samantha to notice, take a deep breath and relax again. "Use that thing on the top of your neck and try to solve something for yourself. Everyone can come with problems, but very few can think of solutions. You just sit back wait for a solution to every problem… maybe someone watching that show as a kid said to himself, the weather stuff interests me, maybe I can be the one that comes up with how they solved it in the future. That is what gives me hope," she finished with the deep breath and gave Oliver a love tap on the head.

The guy clearly wasn't hearing Samantha, or what she was trying to suggest. He was, however, picking up on her annoyance, and that made him press even further. He continued with the air of arrogance that comes only with people unwilling to hear any other side of things, and obtuseness in those that are often wrong, but will never see it. "It is a dreamland and it is supposed to be a dreamland. Everyone loves each other, a human goes to a blue barber and they just love each other. No one has an issue with the fact that he is blue; there is just no racism anymore. And religion is never even mentioned so it is never even made available to debate. It's called drama."

Sam was done with this talk. "It amazes me that we watch the same show yet see such different things. The only thing we agree on is that it is quite idealistic, or in your words a dreamland. But Rodenberry is offering us something to strive for. As far as blue guys and religion, there are plenty of reasons to dislike someone besides those things if you take the time to get to know people beyond those things. Take you; I thought you were fine until you spoke. Now I can be annoyed that you're breathing my air because you are a belligerent, ignorant asshole."

She didn't even raise her voice while she said it, but everyone at the table gasped anyway. She took some money from her wallet, laid it down on the table and stood up. She looked around, and everyone was still quiet, wondering if she would say anything else. She put her hand on Kami's shoulder and said, "It was great seeing you, and we shouldn't wait so long to do this. I leave for Denver tomorrow, but I'll call you when I'm back."

She said individual goodbyes to those she knew, smiled genuinely and waved to those she has just met, "It was nice meeting everyone," and with that she grabbed Oliver's leash and they left.

***

A few weeks later, Bishop was headed out to play golf at the Broadmoor and decided to stop in and see if Sam was around. He knocked on her door, but there was no answer. He could hear music coming from inside so he knocked harder. About a minute later, Sam appear at the door soaking wet with black surf shorts on and black t-shirt that had a yellow face frowning with a plus sign, then a white coffee cup followed by an equal sign and finally a happy face, also wet, and a towel in her hand.

"Yeah?" she exclaimed.

"You ok?" Bishop asked.

"I'm fine, it's Oliver's bath day and he is being a butt!" she said as he trotted across the big room to greet the visitor with a towel on his back and head.

Bishop laughed out loud. "You know, I could help you with him when I'm here."

"Then I would just get used to help, it's actually easier this way," she said turning and grabbing him and the towel. "Where you off to?"

"I'm gonna play a round with Dean and two others he brought up for a meeting."

Just then Oliver shook, spraying the residual water from his fur around the room putting spots on Bishops white golf pants; Samantha sighed.

"Well have fun. I have to get him blow dried, then clean up the mess he just made and then I'm going to head for the patio and get some work done."

Bishop bent down and let Oliver kiss his face and headed out to leave. "I barely recognized you."

"What?" she asked confused.

"Your shirt. It has yellow and white on it. That couldn't be Sam, I thought." He said walking out the door smirking.

Sam grunted and yelled, "Bite me!" to his back.

Once she got cleaned up she headed out to work from a patio overlooking one of the golf courses with Oliver in tow, she reviewed some research reports on education from Elam Highfield. She felt tired, and not just from the doggie bath. She had been contemplating too many issues for too long. This week's dilemma was education and the one-versus-many approach. She was totally on board with the idea that psychology is the view of one, whereas sociology is the view of many, but she hated the fact that education was taking the many and standardizing everything to the eventual demise of the one. She was so proud of her education and felt that everyone should have the opportunity to have what she had, but academia was successfully weeding out many great candidates by standardizing any uniqueness out of everyone. From elementary school on up, the problems ranged from lack of individuality, to programs being cut that lend to an individual's growth and possibly the ability to learn other, more black and white topics like the hard sciences. It was all mass and no distinctiveness being taught or even encouraged.

Then to top it off, Victoria called. She had to tell Sam about the conversation she had with her cousin Dawn the day before while getting her hair done. Victoria had been going to her cousin for years, and Dawn was known as one of the best hairdressers in New York. While the color on Victoria's hair had been processing, Dawn was cutting a gentleman's hair and was explaining that, later that night was back to school night for her boys, who were going into the third and fifth grades. She listed off the items she was told to bring: Folders of every color, blue, green, yellow, pink and white, Kleenex, red marking pens for grading, reward stickers, markers, pencils... those kinds of things. Victoria didn't think much of it but the man commented that some of the supplies sounded like supplies for the teacher and Dawn remarked that because teachers get no money from schools for anything, they have to buy everything that they want to use in their classrooms out of their own pocket, so instead, they just add those items to the school supply list.

"It's crazy," said Dawn, "I mean, I don't want these teachers to be penniless because they make shit for wages, but I think there should be some kind of budget for these items in the school money...oh, but wait, what money? Schools have less and less each year and a lot of times have more and more kids."

The man agreed that is was crazy and told another story of what he had to provide for his kids after school athletics.

Then Dawn said, "Wait, it gets better. None of the supplies I will take to school tonight are JJ's or Joe's, they are all put into a pool and shared."

"What?" Victoria asked picking her head up from her phone. "What do you mean, the supplies are shared? Like they are expected to share their stuff with the other kids?"

"No, the supplies I bought are not JJ's or Joe's, they belong to the class." Dawn answered with an eyebrow raised.

"So you get to buy it, but not own it?" Victoria asked incredulously. "That sounds a little socialist to me."

"A little?" said the man getting his hair cut. His sarcasm was clear.

"We just have to make sure that doesn't happen Sam," said Victoria.

"It won't, not by a long shot, V. Talk to you later."

When Sam got off the phone with Victoria, she called Ryder Burns who patched in Adam Edelstein. The two men had been working with Highfield on the education initiative for the group. She didn't anticipate being on the phone long, she really didn't appreciate it when people had full conversations on their phones in public places just raving on and on about whatever personal dilemma they had going on for the whole world to hear. Luckily, she was the only one on the patio, it was October and brisk, even though the sun was shining, most people were inside eating.

"I'm reading this education report and it is pretty sad." She started. "What else do we know about the benefits of education from a many standpoint versus trying to individualize education?"

Edelstein misunderstood her question and started in, "it is pervasive, not just education. I mean education starts it and it continues into the workplace."

"No, what I..."

Edelstein cut her off and kept talking, ah the beauty of cell phones, she thought.

"The biggest thing is office space, and something everyone is trying to get me to do is this shared workspace crap. No one has their own offices or even cube and there are just workstations for groups to collaborate. The open/non-cube environment is the worst idea I can think of. Let's talk about private conversations for a minute... a merger talk maybe, or mentoring or disciplining someone. Where is a CEO that has bought into this "I have no office" bullshit going to have these conversations? His car? So now do you want to talk about distracted driving and all that comes with that? That was rhetorical Sam, before you start in with studies about distracted driving. Or are you telling me this is such a great idea that we will never have to discipline an employee again?"

Burns jumped in, "if you are going along those lines, I would have to say, it isn't that you won't have to discipline an employee, you won't be allowed to because it might hurt the employee's feelings. That is where all this group work, group hug thing is going."

"That is, I guess a little bit about why I called," Samantha said noticing a group that had just been seated on the patio, but just far enough away, she thought she could finish up her conversation. "The group mentality is certainly a cause for concern, but I am really wanting to nip it in schools. Have you guys looked at ways to include collaboration and team work within an individualized, one-to-one system?"

Burns answered, "We have, Sam. Elam has the beginnings of a great plan in the works, it works off something Robert Gilbert stumbled on... damn, I can't remember the name of it, but I'll get back to you after I talk to him next."

"It's Kahn Academy that you are talking about, and Elam took that idea as inspiration with regard to how one student can progress at his own speed, but it is a lot more complex than that. How much time will we have at the conference to discuss it?" Asked Edelstein.

"Gosh, I don't think we are restricting anything with regard to time. It will take as long as it takes, but I want to hear more about this approach. It has made my day. Everything I was hearing and reading today wasn't looking too encouraging. But speaking of private conversations in offices, I have to go, I am on a patio that is filling up and I hate it when people do exactly what I am doing." Sam said watching another table get seated. "When is Elam going to be available? I would really like to have a sit-down with him as soon as possible."

"13-C is getting ready for a huge launch of the tablet, finally," smirked Edelstein. "I don't know how much you can change a product from the original design, much less the tweaking that has gone on."

"Stop, Adam," said Sloan in a warning sort of way.

Grunting Edelstein said, "Elam will be unavailable for awhile, but I will be in Colorado tomorrow, I've got some meetings at the Broomfield offices. I can extend my trip a couple of days and come your way."

"No, I can come down your way, is there some space we can steal for a day?"

"Sure, I'll be done with my meetings by Thursday. You wanna come down Friday?"

"Sounds great, I'll call you when I'm leaving the Springs. And thanks Ryder, talk to you soon." Sloan said, ending the call.

CHAPTER 29
STATED RECOVERY, ENVIRONMENTAL
DISASTER & RECRUITMENT

January 2010

The economy continued to pull itself out of the recession that had hurled so many people into hardship, despair, and distrust of 'the system.' The government was saying that recovery was just around the corner, while people were still losing their homes because of overextension, and banking errors that ranged from bad process to full-blown banking fraud. It didn't matter, the single homeowner had no voice, all they could do was wait and hope they could stay in their homes...many couldn't, and it was the only time in US history that the middle class found themselves homeless, jobless and desperate. Much of the group felt that it was time to act, time to go. Because of the housing situation they felt that once Texas was taken, the discharge of non-Xers and those still wishing to leave would be a much smaller minority then if they waited until recovery really started to happen and could be more fully demonstrated. Bishop knew they were ready from a process and resources perspective, but something in his gut told him it wasn't yet time. Even he had wanted to spark the event by now, but he just knew it wasn't time.

Wednesday, January 27, 2010 – 10:00am Pacific Daylight Time (18:00 hours Zulu Time)

In a written press release, 13-C unveiled the tablet device called Tabella Nunc, that included what everyone was expecting, e-books, but it was capable of so much more. Building on the efficiency of the tablet Quinn created for the group many years before, 13-C worked to make this tablet more entertainment friendly with video capability, photos, email and gaming. Further, Quinn wanted to broaden the music store into an application store that would allow developers of all kinds to contribute to the myriad potential this hand-held tablet could become. Quinn also knew this would be last release before he took the company from being a publicly traded company, to being private again. The big keynote speech and demonstration of the device would come later that year during a developer's conference. Not that the device would need further boosting; pre-orders were off the charts and like the smartphone, people were standing in line at stores for days to get it. Per the usual, Quinn was not available the early part of the year because of his fanatical control over these gadget releases. He would calm down sometime late February, get a lot of work done for the group and ramp back up to a frenzy for the developer's conference in June and the mania would start again.

***

Samantha sulked around after Super Bowl forty-four. She very rarely wanted an NFC team to win and this year was no exception. The New Orleans Saints beat the Indianapolis Colts, 31-17.

Early in February, she was asked via email to consult on a school shooting that happened on a college campus in Huntsville, Alabama. She immediately started thinking of why kids are thinking, more and more, that this is an acceptable way to deal with their frustrations and life problems. Even though she was often asked to consult on forensic psychology cases that did include this type of tragedy, she certainly was not the level of expert on child and young adult psychology to justify being asked to come down to Huntsville. She clicked on the provided link and went into the digital case file. To her surprise this was not the case of a student opening fire on the campus, but a professor slaying three other professors and injuring several others, all because she was not granted tenure. Sloan couldn't believe it. The more time went on, this kind of violent display was becoming more and more prevalent. True, one had to see that these situations were still rare and the general public still hand a handle on reality and what was, and wasn't acceptable behavior. But, we were hearing about them more and more often. Was mental illness rising that quickly? Was the idea of right and wrong or what you could or should do being forgotten? Or, was it simply the fact that populations are growing so the problems, big and small, were going to grow too? She didn't want to go Huntsville, but she knew she had to. After a few hours of research on the case, she learned that the professor in question had a history of violent outbreaks and instability. She kept having to remind herself of that hindsight maxim but she was having a really hard time with the fact that this woman had slipped through the cracks. Over the years, when she would get to this level of confusion as to how a person could think, act, or react in certain ways, she would calm herself by saying that they would not be allowed in Texas. She knew it was silly, but somehow it helped anyway. It was about a 13-hour drive from Austin, so she called Kate, Cooper's daughter and asked her to watch the kitties, packed her bag, loaded Oliver in the car and headed out.

During the drive she listened to a few lectures she had on her mp3 device to brush up on many of the pathologies that could lead to the kind of break that this professor potentially could have experienced. Since much of Sloan's past dealt with academia, and professors specifically, she couldn't imagine how they couldn't have seen some kind of signs. She new all kinds of professors and even the oddest of the odd would never have done something like this. But then again, she thought, so many other tragedies occur when there was no sign of them coming. Plus, there were really no reliable reporting mechanisms for this behavior within schools or even psychiatric practices. If someone calls out a patient for a particular perceived threat, and they are wrong...their career is over by means of the litigious society we have become. But, if they don't, and they weren't wrong...this is what we end up with; a bat-shit crazy professor that was pissed that she didn't get tenure so decided that if she killed others that did have tenure, everything would even out. Are you kidding? The pendulum should swing the other way, meaning that if red flags are raised, and it turns out that the person in question is not a threat, there should be no harm, no foul on either side. But is that even possible once the cat is out of the bag, so-to-speak? Her head was spinning different theories until thankfully she got a call from her friend Allison, and Dylan Sterling. They were working with their group on some ideas around taxes and they wanted to get her thoughts. While she was on that call, another call came through from Antonio Montes. He wanted to let her know the documents they had been working on related to the prison population in Texas and what to do with them post take over would be delivered to her encrypted tablet that evening. She was glad to have that piece of the puzzle done was well. A lot of theories had been considered. She loved his ideas on converting their status to public works projects for the ones that wouldn't be transferred out of Texas. This was a pet project of Antonio's, as he believed, as she did, that not every criminal is beyond redemption. There had to be a way to get them back into the workforce without the risk to the employer and the stigma to the felon once his time and debt was served. But with that label comes the responsibility and consequences for knowing you are starting over from a deficit. There should be no society willing to 'give' you a second chance. That second chance must be earned, and Antonio's recommendations provided that second chance, while also protecting the society in general. While the two were talking, Oliver let out his Chewbacca-like moan, signaling it was time for a bathroom break.

Tuesday, April 20, 2010 – 7:45pm Pacific Daylight Time (Wednesday, April 21, 2010 – 02:45 hours Zulu Time)

Sakti Sharma wasn't usually at the Sativan Energy offices in Sunnyvale on Tuesdays. He liked to be in the lab going over data and trying to bleed out just a little more efficiency from the unit. His Board thought he was crazy, and they always told him that now was the time to sit back and relax. The discovery had been made, tested and was now rolled out to customers in many states. This clean energy fuel cell was his life's work. What they didn't know is he had, in fact, made the unit more efficient; he made it smaller and doubled the kilowatts per hour from the unit that was being sold now. But he was holding the latest and greatest back. He had been working on this since the SOURCE facility in Texas provided him a lab to work in back in 2003. He wanted everyone in the world to be able to have this energy source, not just those lucky ones in the US, but it was the US market that had soured him. Not really the US market per se, but the energy monopolies that had resisted this new technology for old, expensive and CO_2-emitting energy, just to continue to make a buck. These companies were closed-minded and hungry for power – bad combo, he thought.

When the Xers came calling he felt guilty for feeling that sense of hope again because he worked hard to become an American. Once he moved from India in the 80's, to work toward his Ph.D., he knew he wanted to make his home in the US. He loved India and his family, but neither understood what it meant to try to change the world. India, he thought, needed this unit more than anyone. With the sheer number of people there, it was easy to see the need, and eventually the unit would be installed in every household there, and everywhere. The Xers were a group that believed things like he believed them, and he knew this would force people to see what changes were so essential, and to see them faster than what was currently happening.

Through a mutual friend, Dean Kinsey, he met Nikoli Borodin and his life's course changed forever. Dean was so taken by the group that Nikoli was part of that he offered up his giant computer company's resources almost immediately. The Colorado based entrepreneur also offered to invest in the Sativan energy unit. Dean knew what worked and what ideas were good. He wasn't the computer geek that Nikoli was but he could talk that language. Similarly, he could talk the language of business, economics and even dabbled in a bit of engineering and that was how he and Sharma became friends. After a year or so of hearing about the group that Nikoli was a part of and meeting Mike Bishop, he was unabashedly a devotee. He remembered how, in school, a professor could be explaining a complex engineering problem and Sharma thought he understood it because of how well the professor explained it. But then hours later while studying the concept, it was a muddled mess. He would then go back to the professor and have it explained again and he would have a better handle on it. That was how Bishop was; he had this clear view of the balance between community and competition, so much so that during a conversation with him, Sharma would leave fully understanding how things should rightfully and righteously go. Then in the morning he would wake thinking that brilliant balance was a dream. He would have to go back to Bishop for another conversation. But he could never quite hold the complete picture and he gave up trying; he knew Bishop had it and he had faith in Bishop. In fact, going back to Bishop for those wonderfully complex and even chimerical conversations were one of things he looked most forward to these days, besides his work, that is. He had never met someone like Bishop, and he understood how he managed to get the many successful, brilliant and altruistic group of people to follow his vision. He was proud to be one of them.

Eyeball deep into stacks of paperwork that he was catching up on, a newsbreak caught his attention.

Tuesday, April 20, 2010 – 9:49pm Central Daylight Time (Wednesday, April 21, 2010 – 02:49 hours Zulu Time)

Breaking news: The oil rig Deepwater Horizon has exploded 41 miles off the coast of Louisiana and remains in flames. Of the 126 crew members, 11 are currently still missing and presumed dead.

Sharma dropped what he was reading and sat shocked, listening to the horrendous news.

Transocean's semi-submersible drilling rig exploded last night around 10PM. BP, operating the license on the rig, was drilling an exploration well and released a statement in full support of Transocean Ltd. and was working closely with them offering help and logistical support. Leading the emergency response, is the U.S. Coast Guard.

The news report went on to charge sealant issues and a mechanical breakdown as the main cause of the accident. Further reports exposed lack of inspections as the reason why this disaster was not avoided. Sharma sank in his chair. He knew, if he knew anything, that short cuts and bad politics would come out as the primary reason human beings and the environment had to suffer another huge loss.

***

Watching the coverage, Sharma got a call from Jackson Cooper. This can't be good, he thought to himself.

"Jack, how are you?"

"Have you seen the news Sharma?" Cooper boldly yelled into the phone.

"I am watching it now."

"I wonder if this is going to accelerate any plans?" Cooper asked, clearly upset. "When are you leaving for Colorado?"

"My flight is late tonight, I wanted to get in a little early to get settled and help Sam if she needs it." Sharma answered. "How about you?"

"I'm not scheduled to arrive until Monday morning, I ended up being there longer than anticipated in March when we all got together the first time, so I don't think I'm really needed for this little pow-wow." Cooper in his more typical, calmer southern drawl replied.

Sharma carefully stated, "I don't think we need to circle the wagons for this one. I mean, I am sure it will be an item discussed in detail, but I've got some friends at BP, I will give some of them a call and see what I can find out."

"Listen to you Sharma... 'circle the wagons...' soon you'll be talkin' like me." Copper said feeling better, and glad that he had called Sharma. "But you know the drill, don't give away too much."

"No pun intended Jack?"

"That's kinda not funny in this case Sak," Cooper said sadly.

Agreeing, Sharma said, "I know, and don't worry, I won't give anything away. We energy geeks just try to figure out how these things happened anyway, so it is not even out of the ordinary that I will call," answered Sharma. "On a more fun note, when I'm done in Colorado, I am headed to Austin to give Sam a surprise. Did Bishop tell you?"

"No, what is it?"

"You know my friend Horst works at Tesla, and I really love what they have done so when I asked him if they were ever going to do an SUV, he said they had one just out of concept. They will be testing them for a couple of years before they go to market and he asked me if I wanted to be one of the testers. I have the sedan. You really should order one. But I thought Sam would be perfect to test the SUV lugging around that giant dog all the time."

"Oh she is gonna love you for thinking of her Sak," said Cooper. "But it better be black. I can't wait to see it."

"Sometimes they are wrapped so you can't tell anything about it, but this one is totally black...she'll love it.

"But why you waitin' to give it to her in Austin. You will both be in Colorado tomorrow. Have it brought there so she can drive it back to Austin. Does it have the range?" asked Cooper.

"She'd have to stop twice to recharge. Certainly no more than she would for gas. That is a good idea; I'll call Horst and see if I can make it happen. Talk to you soon." Sharma said and hung up the phone.

***

June 2010

Holden knew there was no way he could recruit enough men to fortify the border the old-school way. He set his sights on acquiring the latest military technology around. A small group of highly trained men and women from a control room could surveil the border using drones and other covert aircraft. That had been a main focus but he also wanted as many trained bodies as possible.

In the Marine Corps, the number of marines assigned to a particular group depends on the mission, but is organized within a structure called the Marine Air-Ground Task Force (MAGTF). Within this structure, marines are organized into groups of various sizes, such as a Marine Expeditionary Unit (MEU), which has about twenty-two hundred Marines attached to it, a Marine Expeditionary Brigade (MEB), which is comprised of between four to sixteen thousand, or a Marine Expeditionary Force (MEF), which is the largest of the groups, coming in with between forty-six thousand and ninety thousand Marines.

Working with the Marine Commandant, whole MEBs had been recruited, with about ten thousand marines each, and were ready to take their posts on command. How hard that decision must have been for some of these men and women, especially the ones that had spouses that didn't agree. They either couldn't tell them or lied to them and told them the idea had passed. They were told they were under strict orders not to talk to the outside about the mission. How many divorces happened over the years, how many broken families? With Holden's strong Catholic upbringing, there were sometimes tinges of doubt; it just was not right to be divorced. True, he had been remarried, but it was not because of divorce, his first wife had died in a car accident and knowing what she would have thought of what they were all trying to do made his mind always come back to the righteous answer; he was doing the right thing!

Another challenging part of this process was that in building this private military, the members had to believe in the cause: they weren't just hired for a job. Holden had to ensure the commitment and loyalty of thousands, if not eventually hundreds of thousands of men and women. No one could talk, and if they did, there had to be a mechanism in place to silence them or discredit them. He knew he would be in front of many a panel before all of this was over. Using SOURCE, created after his father passed and the family business was sold, as a screening device over the period of 10+ years proved successful in his endeavor. Aside from the bigger picture he was proud of what he had accomplished. Named after his grandfather and father, Derek King Holden the first and second, respectively, he wanted to do as much good as possible and, heck, it might possibly be enough to not to have to carry out the full plan. But he was ready to go if it came time.

Training was structured with case studies and scenarios designed to build and protect a new nation. He spent so much time at these evaluations, in fact, that he could tell within minutes if the person was right for the group.

Monday, June 14, 2010 – 9:00am Central Daylight Time (14:00 hours Zulu Time)

Later that month during a status update meeting that joined the most Xers together ever, both in person and, Samantha was asked to give the opening speech. She was right in the middle of seeing patients in her regular practice and what came out as a glaring problem among many of them was depression and isolation, so she wanted to address that with the group.

"Are we really happier than our parents or our grandparents? Each generation wanted "more" for the following generation, but each generation's definition of more is different. Do you need more clothing to be happier, a nicer car, or more money than your friend? Are we really happier? I don't think so. Our lives are more convoluted, complex and competitive for the sake of competition, not accomplishing anything... not to bring out the best in us, but just to butt heads. We are more depressed, searching, and lonely with more medication, technology and social networking. I asked a patient the other day when was the last time he had been out with his friends, he actually said he was too busy with work and besides he didn't need to see them anymore to keep in touch, he saw pictures of what they were doing on social networking sites. People pass each other on bike rides for a year and never talk, or park next to the same person at work for years and never talk, and then we say that social media is bringing people closer together? That is a crock of shit. People have NO idea how to be social anymore. They can't make eye contact or even have a simple conversation without their cell phone on the table or in their hand, and I've got to tell ya, there are very few jobs that are so crucial that one must have their cell phones out constantly. Further, if you are out with a friend and have your cell phone in your hand waiting for a text from another friend, you have just defeated the purpose. We no longer engage with those we are with."

"The simple key is loving and respecting yourself, and no one does anymore. I felt a bit of it when Niki and Mike went away to college. I knew I would be close to them, but it was the first time I didn't have constant access to my best friends. I was a little isolated and I started letting myself decline into mediocrity and excuses. I didn't try hard, and I didn't have passion and excitement for anything. And, incidentally, there is nothing that can pull you out of something like that, except YOU. Once I started at Wellesley, I just naturally started to be interested again and it made me realize that the harder we try, the more passion we have for life, and that the more we contribute, the more we earn, the better we feel. From that day on, I look around me and I try to see beauty in everything, be grateful, and do the best I can at anything I am willing to try."

"Of course there are days that suck, times that you just wake up down. If I'm a little low, I go stand outside and I look at the sky, or the mountains or the beach or of course, take a moment with my animals and know how powerful life is, and what a gift it is, too. So why waste it on the pursuit of what your neighbor has or the stuff someone on TV has, or cooped up inside watching TV, wasting your life away on other people's stories...go out and make your own. I love TV as much as anyone, but too much of it makes you forget that you are the most important actor there is, so go live your own story. Work your hardest, love the most, smile a lot, by the way, research shows that if you smile, your brain cannot stay sad, and most of all, respect yourself enough to not take second best for anything. Also, I have to throw out the caveat that what I have just said pertains to those "healthy" individuals. Unfortunately, there are major depressive illnesses that going outside and breathing fresh air will not cure, but having said that, it can't hurt either."

"When we really start to look at people and the dynamics of human nature, one sees that a community is made up of individuals and we've talked richly of how those individuals should perform. But that may be premature. Has anyone thought of the individual as many within himself? We all have those inner voices, some are more selfish or aggressive, while others want what is best for humanity or endeavor to explore their altruistic nature... we are communities within ourselves before we can truly merge with a community of our fellow residents. So can you see the challenges? We have to try to fully know ourselves before we can venture out into our external community and be able to blend harmoniously with others."

"I know this isn't our typical start to an update meeting, but I want everyone to think about these things while we endeavor to create a new culture, so when you are dealing with each other or even outsiders in your day-to-day, see if you can mitigate these walls and ways to isolation."

She stopped, shuffled some pages and without missing a beat moved onto the updates she was in charge of, but was interrupted by a blast of applause. She was caught off guard and even blushed. It showed these people were really becoming that culture they were inspiring to build. Bailey and Holden didn't agree on much but they did agree on hating this kind of psychobabble, as they called it, talk. They looked at each other several times and rolled their eyes at first but, even they couldn't stay cynical about it and Holden caught Bailey clapping as well.

When the meeting was over, Bishop, Cooper, Holden, Corrigan and Pearson stayed behind with some other commanding members to discuss recruitment numbers in more detail. Recruitment was becoming the wrong word. Initially, the military side of things run by Pearson and Holden mostly had to be done by recruitment. Cold, hard numbers were required. Now there were so many members, both military and civilian, it was really more about keeping a lid on the different goings on, so it became more talk of memberships.

"So I heard there was an incident at the Pentagon, Derek. You telling a guard you were gonna, and I quote, "put him down," said Pearson inquisitively.

Holden snickered. "It was more like in the parking lot. I was getting my jacket from the backseat after being checked through and a guard comes up to me and asks what I'm reaching for. I say my suit coat, is there a problem, Private? He actually had his hand on his service weapon."

"And?" said Cooper.

"And nothin, this guy had a hard-on for me, obviously, so I jerked his chain a little and said, as they say in the south, you pull on me, I'm gonna put you down."

"Really? Is that what they say?" asked Cooper in a sarcastic tone snickering.

"Hell if I know," said Holden as Pearson just shook his head. "I heard it on a show once and thought it sounded cool."

"My Lord, this coming from an ex-SEAL," Cooper said, shaking his head too.

"What about the drone program? Are we ready and have we hit our number?" asked Corrigan.

"Almost. Everything is done except the unmanned surveillance only drones. The simulation exposed a software glitch and I'll be damn if these things are going to fly over my heard unmanned and something go wrong," answered Holden.

"So will they be field tested like we talked about?" asked Pearson.

"Yeah, it's a great idea," said Holden. "They all look like hobbyist planes, helicopters and birds. It will appear as a regular day out with fellow remote control users. About three hundred will be tested but we will have thousands by the end of the month."

"What is their altitude capability?" asked Corrigan.

"Most of these will have just over one and a half kilometers…a few will have more," Bishop interjected. "These are just surveillance detection and notification units. These aren't the ones that will have any weaponry or other tactical enhancements, and those are all manned."

"Did you see that show on drones and privacy?" Cooper asked.

Holden sighed, "don't even get me started, Jack. The whole thing was about people saying, 'oh poor me, I'm growing drugs in my back yard and now I'm going to be caught'…there is no expectation of privacy once you are outside!"

"Not entirely Derek," Corrigan said. "Curtilage has often been considered part of the home."

"Curtilage?" Holden asked, tilting his head.

"The area of land attached to a home, forming one entire enclosure." responded Corrigan. "That does not mean open space. Also, there is much case law to indicate that if a person willing and knowingly puts something illegal within the curtilage that can be seen by the public, it is not a violation of the Fourth Amendment. For example, if a typical aircraft can see a marijuana field, which is considered public view. Drones are causing quite a controversy but I suspect they will fall under that purview."

"How about this?" Holden remarked, "don't fucking break the law. I heard Vassily say something like once you break the law, don't expect to have any rights of it, and I like that."

"He quoted Truman Capote, I think, and it wasn't quite that aggressive, but I get what you are saying," said Pearson. "Drones bring up a lot of issues. A lady at a neighborhood pot luck said she couldn't sun bathe naked anymore because of all the drones, and I'm thinking, 'you are worried about drones, when the Wagner's house backs right up to your backyard.' Then her husband says 'Good, no one wants to see it anymore anyway. I almost shit. It was hilarious."

"It all goes back to privacy, security and safety," said Bishop. "And these are all things we are ready to come to the table with. There has to be a balance between surveillance and privacy. It would be stupid to say there won't be crime in Texas and I, for one, want the latest technology to help us catch the perpetrators. But then again," he said, smiling, "I don't sun bathe naked."

"What are the latest thoughts on the trade policy that the Merchant group has been working on?" asked Holden. "How hard of a line are we expected to take with the US and other countries?"

Bishop began by clarifying the difference between trading with the US, and trading with other foreign countries, "Remember, Derek, that although we'll be trading across borders with the US, it's not the same as, say, trading with Mexico, or even Europe. Trading with the US has two purposes. The first is common to our trading goals with everyone: We need to import the goods and services that make sense, where we either don't have some resource or product, or where some other entity can produce it drastically more efficiently than we can. We need to position ourselves to export goods and services using the same rule, and drive demand for the things that are 'Made in Texas' so we can have the best economic opportunities for our citizens. Like I said, that's the same for anyone we may trade with. On the other side of the coin, trading with the US is different because it's not just about the best economic outcome. Trade with the US is a diplomatic tool, and a negotiation about things that go beyond just where we should buy a TV. We will trade goods and services with each other in exchange for enhanced national security, protection, etc. The US Government certainly wants us to act nicely with the massive array of military hardware and human resources we'll have. We want them to do the same. A good trade policy can truly help to make that happen. The last thing we want is economic sanctions against us, or to get put into a situation where someone believes a use of force is necessary. We want to be seen as an extension of the US in some ways and split off in other ways and the trade policy will define at least some of that. The best outcome is to be seen in their eyes as a large-scale research program."

"Thanks, Mike. That makes sense." said Holden.

Tuesday, November 2, 2010 – 11:36pm Central Daylight Time (Wednesday, November 3, 2010 – 04:36 hours Zulu Time)

Jackson Cooper had been on the phone for the past three hours. He was exhausted and his back was killing him, but he felt nothing but joy. He had just won a remarkable third term to the office of Governor of Texas. He was so proud of his state and all the hardworking people that believed in him. He was never shy about touting Texas as the best place to live and work, even before becoming an Xer. He made it his mission to get companies to move to Texas with incentives and support to help build them into bigger, more successful enterprises. He was blessed to know that the Xer movement would keep him at home in the place he had always loved.

As another call came in, this time on his personal, secure cell, he leaned against his home office desk. "Cooper," he announced to the caller.

"Congratulations Jack!" a group of people yelled into the phone.

"Thanks everybody," he replied.

"By the skin of your teeth, huh?" poked Holden.

"Piss off," he said while laughing. "Fifty-five percent is pretty definitive to me."

"Really, congrats Jack. This shit doesn't happen," said Holden. "A third term? They love you."

"Yahoo!" yelled Sharma. "We're all toasting you here, man."

Pouring a small glass of single malt scotch, Cooper replied, "Thanks kid. It's fantastic isn't it? And it will really help the cause too."

"Don't even worry about that tonight Jack," said Bishop. "Just soak it in and give that wife of yours a huge kiss from all of us too. Have you talked to Rex yet?"

"Yeah, he called me a couple of hours ago. Said he would be in Austin day after tomorrow so we'll raise a glass then. Viv went to bed about an hour ago. She has been a machine, I'll tell ya. She sure has got some snap in her garters."

"You should be doing the same," said Victoria. "You have been running crazy for too long now."

"Agreed!" shouted Sloan from far away from the speakerphone. "Get your ass to bed."

"Ok, Mother. I am spent. I feel like chewed twine, but I needed a minute to wind down. When y'all get down here, we'll go out and shoot out some lights." He said as he hung up the phone.

"What?" asked Holden.

"We'll celebrate," answer Bishop.

"Please tell me we won't have to talk that way when we are down there?" asked Holden, dryly.

Bishop laughed. "You don't like Texas-speak?"

"I think it's great!" Victoria jumped in. "It seems more polite somehow."

Holden sighed, "It's a different language."

"Ah, not your wheelhouse Derek?" asked Sloan sarcastically.

Sitting on the couch, wishing these guys would bid him goodnight, Holden just put his head in his hands.

"I'm sorry, I was just kidding," said Sloan sensing the humor was being missed on Derek.

"No, it's fine. I would be more playful if I wasn't so damn tired. You know that tomorrow is the day, right?" he asked.

"Tomorr...oh crap, I forgot. You ok?" Sloan asked sitting down next to him.

"I'm fine. Most of the work is done," he replied.

"Yeah, the rest is ceremony really, right?" asked Bishop.

"What is going..., what?" asked Sharma confused.

"With all the congressional bullshit lately, the "execs" at SOURCE thought it best that Derek step down."

"What?!" exclaimed Sharma.

"Yeah, so first, I fired the fucks, then I sold the company."

Sharma just looked around the room totally confused.

Holden let out a little whimper, a little grunt of a laugh. "Don't worry. Most of it is for show. The company was sold and all of the jagoffs that did want me out are gone. But the new parent company is mine too, but nobody will be able to figure that out and I will maintain complete control. This way though, I'm out of the public eye as the mercenary owner and I can actually get some work done."

"So..." questioned Victoria. "You seem down about it. If nothing is changing, why be down?"

"Oh, things are gonna change," he said. "I'm still just pissed that any of my guys would cower to that kind of pressure and ask me to step down. I'll get over it...maybe, but right now I'm still pissed."

"It's more of a loyalty thing," said Sloan.

"Exactly!" Holden responded. "You know in your heart you are doing the right thing, but someone else can see the same thing and spin it that they are the injured party when you have years and evidence to the contrary. People are blind."

"So what happens tomorrow exactly?" asked Sloan.

Holden looked at Bishop, who, as was his usual custom, just sat back and listened to everyone with the most placid look on his face. He should have been a rock star or something, he thought to himself. "Just a press conference with the new leadership and the boilerplate script they will spew about how SOURCE is in the game to support and back our government and law enforcement communities any way they can."

"Who will run it?" Sharma asked.

"Do you know Christian Adams' brother Keith? He will. He is old Navy and a great guy. He helped me with about eighty percent of the original military recruitment."

"What then?" asked Sloan.

"Then I work from the office complex in Austin," he said.

"Cooper will love having you that close," offered Bishop. "Ha! You might even pick up a little bit of that new colorful Texas language." he said, smiling at Derek.

"'Rumor spreadin' around, in that Texas town 'bout that shack outside La Grange...just let me know... if you wanna go... to that home out on the range." Bishop sang, snapping his fingers to the beat.

"I don't even want to know," said Holden.

"ZZ Top! Why does the Indian have to get them all?" said Sharma smiling.

"Hey, Sam how is that electric contraption you've been driving?" asked Holden to change the subject.

"It is the best thing I've ever driven and I thank Sakti every day for thinking of me," said Sloan, winking at Sharma. "The weirdest thing is getting used to how quiet it is. I was used to the vroom-vroom of the Cayenne's engine. This is nothing like that. The back doors go up so Oliver just steps in and the seats fold flat so he can just lay down and enjoy the ride. Plenty of room for luggage, and handles great. I love it."

"Hmm, I'm gonna go take the sedan for a test drive and see what all this is about," said Holden.

"Any, any amount of money, you will buy one after the test drive," said Sharma wanting to bet Holden.

"We'll see kid, we'll see."

CHAPTER 30
THE LEAK, SERENITY
& THE PHILOSOPHER KING

Thursday, July 21, 2011 – 4:34pm Central Daylight Time (21:34 hours Zulu Time)

In an office building that looked like any other in Austin, the group had built a control center allowing members to come and go as their schedules allowed. Holden built the building in the initial phases when the group got started with infrastructure. But, when he saw the writing on the wall with regard to the media turning on SOURCE, and insisting on a scapegoat, he created his own personal section in it. He willing took on the scapegoat role, and once the effigy burning was done, reclaimed SOURCE command from this building. The building was just off of South Congress Avenue on Cesar Chavez Street, and a smaller version of the giant triangle-shaped buildings familiar in downtown Austin. It was leased mostly to other legitimate companies, but under the parking structure was a SOURCE surveillance and strategy center, and on the 7th floor was a faux atrium and AmendX office space. Christian Adams could be out of Army uniform, dressed like a civilian businessman, head up to the offices in the elevator, and pass completely unnoticed.

On any given day there were between forty and fifty people working in the office. Today, there were about thirty and everyone was busy. There weren't many private individual offices, but there were some for the times that individual work was necessary. There were many conference rooms so groups could get together and work without bothering other groups like the recent bullpen style work that had become popular.

Samantha was doing some research for Cooper on the reduction of bureaucratic bottlenecks...bureaucracy, in the real sense of the word bureaucracy, not the more urban dictionary term for red tape and stonewalling. This was more about business process enhancements and abatement of measures that are no longer necessary. She got an urgent message from Melissa McCann to look at a website. She did as asked and suddenly screamed "FUCK!" and jumped up and ran out of the room.

Michael Bishop was down the hall working with Bailey, Holden and Mackay.

"What the hell is the matter with you?" asked Bishop.

"Go to Wikileaks... I knew it... the son of bitch leaked us to Assange... God damn it!" exclaimed Sloan, pacing around the room.

Mackay typed in the web address, Bailey was reading madly, as was Holden. Bishop was waiting for his chance.

Mackay pushed himself back, away from the computer, and gestured for Bishop to read as he bent down in front of the screen and skimmed the report.

There was a partial document on their energy and solar conversion process, but it was the old version and almost the entire education recommendation for the conference. There were also a few pictures, one straight on of Melissa McCann. Someone is definitely going to track her down, thought Bishop. Two more group photos of Samantha, but you couldn't see her clearly, Nicole, the woman Sam had met that day, Allison, and a couple men that thankfully obscured Ryder Burns. Ryder was extremely famous and recognizable.

"Who took these?" asked Mackay.

"I'm guessing Wallace. I saw him walk in and out but that Fuzzy asshole was driving me crazy," answered Sloan frustrated. "I asked if he had been investigated and Melissa said yes. It makes sense why an energy document is up there. He was the guy we gave Sakti to help him just get his shit together when he was so freakin' busy. The guy was an environmental engineer before he went into Internet marketing for God's sake. We thought he would be perfect for Sharma!" She was nearly yelling at this point.

"Calm down, Jesus!" said Holden, and he didn't often use the Lord's name when cursing. He cussed with the best of them, but chose not to include his Lord when participating.

"Well this has got to get fixed. I'm going to go call Mike Pearson and see if he has any suggestions," Mackay said leaving the room.

Bishop started to convince the others, as well as himself. Looking at Sam said, "You've got no real holdings anymore, and what you do have is under umbrellas, I've moved all of my real-estate outside of Texas into a trust for my sister and her kids. In case we have to leave quickly, and I'm not saying that we do. We need a lot more information first. Nikoli has complete plausible deniability...with as big as Sensedatum is; he has nothing to worry about.

"That is really premature Mike," Holden said. "We can get that removed within a day with our tech guys. That jag off Assange thinks he knows computers, he doesn't know shit."

"I've heard about this guy, hacker from way back...he's good," said Sloan.

Bishop laughed. He looked at Sloan, "what about Gram-ma?"

"That's a great idea!" exclaimed Sloan.

"Who's Grandmother?" asked Bailey irritated, watching as Mackay came back into the room.

Sloan snorted, "Gram-ma is a nickname of a computer genius, hacker we kinda know."

"He is another 'hacker from way back' but now he uses his powers for good. He's in the group, but isn't really all that involved. He knew Niki somehow and hit it off with Sam...he's a different kind of guy." explained Bishop as he started dialing Nikoli's number.

"Hey what's up?" said Borodin is his regular jovial manner.

"I just sent you a link to go to. We've been leaked. I'm putting you on speaker," answered Bishop.

Nikoli quickly scanned the page. "Shit," was all he said.

"We are thinking of getting some help from Gram-ma. What do you think about that?" asked Bishop.

"I think that is a great idea if you can get him to do it," answered Borodin.

"What does it mean? His name is Gramma?" asked Bailey.

"It is some kind of acronym against Big Brother type of stuff... Guarding against, no that's not it. Do you guys remember?" Bishop asked Sam.

I can't remember," said Sloan. "It's just been Gram-ma forever.

"Oh man, it's been so long," said Borodin. "Guarding and Repudiation Against something," he said.

"In any case, Mike, you think getting a face-to-face with this Assange guy might help?" asked Mackay.

"Gram-ma could find him," said Sloan.

"That's what I was thinking," agreed Bishop. "Then you two could go see him. You could use logic with him and Gram-ma could, without saying much, let him know, he's met his better. Guarding and repudiation against malicious malfeasant authorities. That's it! That was driving me crazy!"

"That just sounds weird," said Bailey.

"That's Gram-ma," said Sloan.

"Well, however you decide to 'fix' this," Bailey said putting his fingers up to quote the word fix, and looking at Holden, "I'm behind you."

Holden was silent.

"Now you're behind him?" Mackay said to Bailey disgusted at the implication.

***

During a press conference the day after the leak, the President was asked by Rebecca Rolstad, the media contact for the New York Times, about the rumor on Wikileaks that top entrepreneurs and business people of the world, and especially the US, were planning a secret revolt. 44 heeded 43's advice and said nothing. "Rumors circulate every day in this town, Rebecca. You know that better than anyone. Some viral email got its 15 minutes of fame," then turning to face another reporter, he pointed and said, "What do you have for me Greg?"

Greg Banter of the Chicago Tribune tried to press for more. "But Mr. President, there are two documents and a few photos that show the planning of some kind of coup. Shouldn't we take that seriously?"

"That is so dramatic Greg," responded 44 in his most calm demeanor. "From what I saw, I believe it was a group of people discussing ideas to better education, most of which we are already doing, and some people having coffee or drinks at a hotel resort. First, I welcome anyone that has the wherewithal to want to better themselves, education, and this wonderful country of ours and second, since when is having cocktails with friends a coup d'état?"

Before 44 could motion to the next member of the press corps, Greg followed up with, "Where are we doing those educational initiatives discussed in the docu…"

Interrupting Greg, 44 pointed to Leslie Miller of the Associated Press. "Leslie, please tell me you have something worth asking?"

Leslie knew this was a story, but she also knew she wasn't going to get anywhere with it today, so she asked another question relevant to news of the day. "With the successful landing of Atlantis yesterday, will there be any second thoughts on ending the space shuttle program, especially with the backlash the decision has brought?"

"That is a great question Leslie. Let me first say it is great to have the team home safely. Secondly..."

***

Harlan Mackay was also interviewed regarding the leak on this website. As a former head of the CIA and NSA getting an interview with him was a coup all on its own. It did put him in a strange position though and he didn't want to address questions about the group, for fear of body language giving something away. Mackay was an old pro at keeping secrets a secret, but as the years went by, he had felt saved many times knowing the group was there and he didn't want to give the slightest hint that he may have known about them. He was out of service for the government, but it was reasonable that he be interviewed because of all the positions he held in the past.

Interviewer: "Do you believe there is a secret conspiracy from certain individuals to plan a coup against this country?"

Mackay: "Do I believe that there is a conspiracy? No, I do not."

Interviewer: What do you say about this leak then?"

Mackay: "I believe this website has an agenda that is equal to a real conspiracy. You should be talking to them."

Interviewer: "What do you know of the website?"

Mackay: "I just know they have a misguided sense or belief in what the masses should know."

Interview: "So you believe in keeping secrets from the American people then, General?"

Mackay: "I absolutely do. That is what keeps us safe. If we publicized everything we were doing, our general public might not be of immediate threat, but everyone else, outside of our citizens will be. Secret plans; missions and investigations are just that. Secret."

Interviewer: "Governmental agencies have been criticized for having too heavy a hand in that area. What are your thoughts on that?"

Mackay: "Simply this: I'll give you the existential complaint of the American intelligence community. Here's how it works living inside our liberal democracy, and we in the intelligence community Do live within it too Sherry. American political elites feel empowered, and remember that word folks; in all our talk about entitlism this will come back to haunt us, they feel empowered to criticize the intelligence powers that be that they aren't doing enough when they feel threatened. But once we have made them feel safe again, they turn the tables and feel empowered once again to complain that we are infringing on civil liberties... that we are doing too much. You can't have it both ways."

The interviewer was shocked. All she could mutter was "Thank you for your time General."

Mackay nodded.

A few days later Bishop asked, "Are you sure it was a good thing to say so bluntly?'

"Yes and no," he responded. "Knowing it will go nowhere with regard to the minds of those I was speaking about and the average US citizen, I should have kept my mouth shut. But, knowing what we will do in Texas and how things will be built and displayed differently, it had to be said."

"Okay then," said Bishop smiling. "Speaking of which, with the Internet backbone changing and having to have our own cell towers and channels, have you and Nikoli completed the assignment?"

"Yes, it is very similar to the original 215 program with some enhancements."

"Great, thanks, H."

***

Max James, AKA Gram-ma, was a computer hacker turned computer security researcher, specializing in software architecture, and authentication systems. He was also the head of a company that provided services for other companies that relied on technology that identified whether or not their company had vulnerabilities from a technological perspective. He looked at everything from bringing down a security system so someone could walk in to a brick and mortar building, to the famous penny skimming banking scheme. And it wasn't just about money; he was also very adept at figuring out how to find exposure points in individuals with all levels of security clearances. When certain agencies didn't believe him when he identified a problem, he would just walk in to a top-secret area in his tight black jeans, black sweatshirt and long, disheveled hair. No one stopped him though…he had all the clearances. That, coupled with him being right, all of the time, tended to annoy the different governmental agencies that didn't heed his earlier warnings.

When meeting the second wave of the technology geeks that Nikoli brought in, Samantha could see that Gram-ma was different. He didn't try to one up every guy or girl he had a conversation with when he met someone in his same field. He would stand around and watch the group trying to better each other and she could see he knew the answer before any of them did. When Gram-ma realized Samantha understood he had no interest in the 'my brain is bigger than yours' game and Sam knew his brain was the figurative biggest, but didn't care to brandish it, they became friends. She wished she saw more of him, but besides the fact that he wasn't too involved in the group's activities, they didn't have a whole lot in common. She suspected they were close in age, but she could get zero in the way of information out of him. When they did see each other though, she enjoyed their conversations immensely.

Gram-ma found Assange in about a minute. In reality maybe a half-hour. He was holed up with some woman who was helping him 'fight for complete transparency' against the oppressors. Gram-ma agreed, begrudgingly, to meet Sam and fly together to London to talk to him. Bishop agreed to watch Oliver and the cats, so off she went. While they were waiting for their flight, Melissa McCann called Sam on her cell phone.

"I am so sorry Sam," she said.

"For what?" asked Sam.

"I feel responsible for this. I brought David in," said Melissa.

"This is everyone's fault Melissa, but we aren't about assigning blame. We vetted him and when we saw some red flags, we should have done more, but even we got sloppy. I guess it can happen to everyone," answered Sloan.

"I guess he is bi-polar and went off his meds. I worked with the man for five years and never knew a thing about it."

"Why would you? People don't just come into the office and announce their mental conditions. There is still so much stigma around mental illness, hell, mental health, let alone illness…that is why we find out too late about this kind of thing. Had we known, we could have taken measures to make sure he was taken care of. David is a smart man with a lot to offer, but off his meds, he is a liability for sure, and in this case it really bit us in the ass…shit, we are starting to board."

"Oh, I'm sorry I caught you at a bad time. I just wanted to ask you what will be done with him now that he has been picked up?"

"Picked up?" Sloan asked.

"Yeah, didn't you know? Some doctor claiming to be his psychiatrist checked him in to New York Presbyterian psych ward day before yesterday. Since I didn't know he was bi-polar, I didn't know he was seeing anyone. Then today, the same guy met him, and David voluntarily checked himself out against his doctor's advice, got into a black town car and drove away."

"Holy shit! I didn't know any of this," Sloan blurted out while handing her boarding pass to the boarding agent.

"Sorry," she said to the boarding agent," crinkling her face in an embarrassed, shrugging look.

"How did you learn this, Melissa?"

"David's sister called me and asked me if I knew where he was because his doctor called her, asking. I thought for sure one of our people picked him up."

"Stop talking. We've probably said too much already. Everyone is going to know who you are if they don't already, and you are going to be surveilled." Sam had stepped off to the side of the jet bridge, out of hearing range of anyone, but knew she was pushing it by having this conversation in the open. She decided to finish this conversation now, and try not to say anything else that may sound suspicious to anyone within earshot.

"An old neighbor of mine works at Grand Central. I came here to make the call and then I'm out of here under a different name to Austin for good." said Melissa.

"I hope that is enough. I hope you make it out, Mel, and you remember what you've been told to say if you don't. You haven't done anything wrong or illegal. Answer whatever you can without giving up any names. If you do make it to Austin, I will find out what is going on and meet up with you there. You might find out before me. I am turning around to come back as soon as we've talked to this guy, ok?"

"Thanks Sam. I'll see you soon."

***

Assange was fresh off of the biggest leak releases in his website's history, having to do with US military involvement in Iraq and Afghanistan, as well as sexual improprieties of his own with two women while in Sweden. Sam and Gram-ma went directly from Heathrow to an Internet cafe just outside of Brixton. It was more of a small club and flophouse with a surprisingly fast Internet hub. There were many kids on computers and even more kids on drugs. Even though Gram-ma had money, he could blend in. Samantha was in black suit pants and a black sweater but you could tell they were expensive. People all snapped their heads to look at her and Gram-ma immediately wanted to change the plan.

"This is stupid. If this guy is even here, he's not gonna give you anything. I can find a way to get in and take it down. This is a waste of time," he said.

"We're here. Let's do this." Sloan responded, even though she believed that Gram-ma was probably right.

They went upstairs and it wasn't hard to find him. It was like there was a sign 'I am here behind all of these adoring kids that know nothing'. He was sitting in a corner table with a blue hat on, and black jacket with his laptop on the table and backpack on his lap, as if ready for a quick getaway. There were two boys and four girls sitting around him squeezed in around the table as if to block anyone's view to him and protect their leader.

One of the girls knew Gram-ma. She gestured to Julian and he rose and went to the table just next to the one he had been at.

"Are you one of the revolutionaries?" asked Assange.

"I do not characterize them that way, but let's just say I'm acting as their representative until I know more about how you plan to deal with the information you get," answered Sloan.

The conversation went back and forth about the need for transparency versus the need for security and privacy. Assange blathered on about transparency along with a couple of the girls chirping what they had heard from him, memorized and repeated it over and over until it came down to his dealings and his personal life and then he was quite tight lipped and deflective.

"I assure you, Sam, that we keep our sources anonymous always so if there is anything you want to tell us, you needn't worry about that," he finally said after a few moments of silence.

"Do you even investigate the information coming to you? Because I can tell you some of what you got from David Wallace," Assange looked up quickly with a surprised look on his face. "Yeah, I know who sent it, was inaccurate and those pictures, those pictures could be of any group of friends doing basically anything."

"But they aren't. They are of a group planning something," answered Assange.

"Planning what?" Sloan asked.

"You tell me," he said back to her quickly.

"Listen, you have to see the hypocrisy in this... you think the world should have all this information and be transparent, yet it should come from an anonymous source? And fuck others that this anonymous source hurts? Have you even thought that information about Iraq and Afghanistan is classified for a good reason, and it usually isn't to hide all kinds of secret handshakes from its fellow citizens? If it broadcast everything to its citizens, others would see it too!" She said her voice rising. "Joe America doesn't need to have the missile codes to know they are there, but if gets them, so does Joe Afghani, and that is just one tiny example of why private things should stay private."

"I know the point you are trying to make but when there is carte blanche trust, these black budgets and every objective within them are open to abuse, and it is my responsibility to make sure those things do not happen."

"I never said anything about carte blanche trust, but you might find this hard to believe but this isn't at all about you or your misplaced ideology. I came here to tell you that you have inaccurate information. So you're telling me you won't take it down?' asked Sloan finally.

"No. I love the idea of a rogue group of radicals operating out of the US right under the nose of that smug administration," replied Assange.

Shaking her head in utter disgust, "You have it all wrong, Mr. Assange. There simply is no group of radicals. There might be a group of people trying to find answers to hard questions, and you make things dangerous by putting ridiculous ideas like that out there. We will get it down."

Assange looked at Gram-ma as he stood. He said nothing the entire time but he felt pretty confident in his assessment of the situation and motioned Samantha to go out ahead of him.

As they were walking out Gram-ma leaned down and said, "You shouldn't have said 'some of what you got'...that implies that other stuff he got was true."

"I know," she replied shaking her head. "I thought of that as soon as I said it. Maybe he won't pick it up. I feel like I'm going to throw up."

Tuesday, August 13, 2011 – 12:45pm Mountain Daylight Time (18:45 hours Zulu Time)

Michael Bishop and Samantha Sloan held a regular update meeting throughout the months and years of their planning. There was no specific time or place, but they always managed to make it happen. On this day, Samantha met him for lunch at a golf course restaurant just outside of Denver, Colorado. Bishop was taking a few days in between a meeting he had just had with Nikoli in San Francisco, and heading back to Massachusetts. He booked an event room so they would not be disturbed, as the meeting would go far beyond a regular lunch. He played an early round of eighteen, and then following the meeting, he was hoping to get in at least another nine.

As they were getting settled, Sam looked out the window reflecting and said, "Do you think we picked the wrong place to make our stand? Colorado is supposed to be the Promised Land, you know. All of the innovation was here, the valley, the future."

Knowing that she was referring to their favorite book, Atlas Shrugged, "You are the one with the superstitions around that book. I love the book, but I am more attached to the message, not the place." Bishop said, shaking his head in dismissive reproach. "I think too many people are making too many connections with that book and we have to put a stop to it. We didn't set out to carry out the ideals in that book. It is simply a great book with a fantastic message, one that I still think is relevant today, but we have to be careful, Sam. We need to be taken really seriously and if anyone thinks we are bunch of cult loons following some mandate of that book, we are going to lose, and lose fast."

Samantha felt stupid. It wasn't as though she wanted to follow the book word for word, but the way Colorado was described, and as much as she'd gotten to know it, she felt connected to it. She really felt a sense of untouched promise. The air was crisp and fresh as if saying that anything could be done here. She wished she had come here sooner to live permanently, and live like someone who knew nothing about any of this.

"Yeah, I get it," she said and starting the update. "Today the announcement should come out that Cooper is seeking the Republican nomination, do you think he'll get it?"

"I don't see why not, and can you imagine how it would go if he does? He wouldn't be able to come with us but he could make the move a lot less dangerous to everyone," replied Bishop.

"So you saw Niki yesterday, where is he with his group, and are they ready for the conference? Are we ready to schedule who will be in attendance, and when?"

"No, I think that is still premature, but we are getting close."

"Are you waiting to see whether Jack gets the nod?" asked Sloan.

"No, logically that wouldn't be something to wait for, although from a strategic standpoint it could be. The San Francisco bunch has a lot going on right now, not that everyone doesn't. But it would be bad timing, I think. I am guessing mid-June to start. I have a million things to tell you about what is happening with them, so first fill me in on Holden, and Sharma. Also, I haven't heard from Pearson or Corrigan. Should I be concerned?"

"Actually no, Mr. Pearson has virtually been a machine, organizing everything on that end, and Harris has really picked up the pace as well. He and Holden have really become confidants and great friends. I think Harris needed that. I haven't seen him so happy, ever... let alone organized and efficient. It is nice to see. As for technical specs of the finished buildings and schematics of the drones under construction, those are on your tablet. It's also time to send another note, you know?"

"I don't think we should right now," Bishop answered changing the subject to technical details of buildings that had been recently completed.

Accepting Bishop's answer, Sam moved onto other topics, "Also, we finally have processes for Texas industries to stay and how to deal with them if they do, as well as those who want to leave. We are not taking hostages and this procedure addresses that. People, companies, industries will all be informed, and then they will be able to make their own decisions."

After three hours of updating and planning next steps, Samantha couldn't wait any longer, so she had to ask. "Are we going to talk about the leak? You can't just ignore it Mike."

"I'm doing no such thing." Bishop responded.

"How many rounds of golf have you played since hearing about the news?" Sloan asked inquisitively.

"A lot." Bishop answered with the most serene look on his face, not mad at being questioned, and completely in control. "But I think I played the most rounds I've ever played the week I released my part of the algorithm to the team at MIT working on the quantum computer, and that turned out pretty well."

Smiling, she could see his look of 'I've got it under control' and just shook her head. He was certainly a force, but she also new he was avoiding this.

"We knew Wallace could be unstable and now it is what it is," said Bishop. "I'm more worried about this Assange guy. He makes liquid Ebola look appetizing and it's not because of his self proclaimed technological brilliance. He is a loose cannon and he has the ridiculous idea that it is his role to expose material out of a sense of morality, yet he runs around in disguises looking over his shoulder all the time. If he were truly righteous, he would stand up in front of those he is exposing and ask for a real back and forth. No, I've thought a lot about this. This isn't going to hurt us like we thought at first, and your conversation with him convinced me of that. He is an egomaniac hiding under the airs of a crusader without doing the work."

"But now, our identities might get exposed and that could jeopardize what we are trying to do," replied Sloan, trying not to sound panicked.

"And if we are, then we will do just what I said, stand up for what we believe and try for some back and forth with the administration. The administration doesn't want everyone to know about AmendX anymore than AmendX wants to be known publicly. 44 did exactly what I thought he would. He would have so many questions to answer on so many levels that they don't want to know who we are. This gives them deniability. Besides, they can't possibly find out about enough of us to make the plan fail. They might find me or they might find you and that affects me and you not the group, so don't forget that."

"I don't know how you can be so calm. When I talked to him it was like he was on a mission to find out who we were. He was like a zombie," she said looking down at her completely ripped up fingernails.

"It is what it is. You have been planning this for the better part of your adult life. There is nothing you can do to change what has happened so keep doing what you're good at and let's move through this. Plus, I think he has enough to deal with, Gram-ma spiked his site and he has been reeling ever since, plus his personal problems and if he really does think everything is about him like you said, then we are fine."

***

It was only about six weeks later that Bishop was ready to have the conferences begin. The leak got everyone looking and listening but not much else came of it. But that was the perfect evidence Bishop needed to move forward and finalize everything via the conferences. Sitting with Nikoli and Samantha at the Sensedatum offices, on a secure telepresence, he sat down and got ready for the address. Jackson Cooper was to be in the room with him, but he had just undergone an experimental surgery for his back and was recovering quite nicely in Texas with his family. He would be listening in, with about one hundred other leaders within the group, including Michael Pearson and Randall Quinn, both of whom were listening in from Quinn's home across town. Pearson wanted to say something to the group before Bishop began speaking.

"This is a situation I never thought I would find myself in," he started. "I have given this country the better part of my life out of a sense of pride and duty. No one loves the foundations of this country more than I do. Having said that though, you all know where we think the country is going. I have watched Bishop grow up from a boy to a man and he has been special since his first day in this world. I had occasion during some continuing education to hear a lecture from professor Dr. Daniel Robinson from Oxford University. He spoke about the history and the ancient foundations of the human condition and how wisdom is gained. I would like to quote what he said. *'If there is a nation of fools, finding out what fifty-one percent of them want isn't very helpful. You can't count on majorities; you can't count on the enumeration of opinions as these show up. What you are looking for is the one who actually gets it right, the one that does understand what the nature of the human condition is and what's right for it. What you need is a philosopher king. You need someone who is, by nature, and as a result of philosophical guidance, has attained a degree of wisdom otherwise unavailable to the masses.'* "I believe we have our philosopher king in Michael Bishop. He has had an undeniably focused compass on the fundamental concerns of the human existence most of his life and it is because of this that I chose to join this group. Thank you Michael for letting me have this time."

Bishop blinked nervously. He hadn't expected that introduction. "I'm not even sure how to respond to that praise and the confidence Admiral Pearson has in me, except to say I am the king of no one and I don't profess to be, but I will work to the death to make this group successful. It is each one of you and your individual talents and hard work that have gotten us here today. You know, we didn't even know what we were doing when this started. I can't speak for Niki and Sam, but I know I certainly didn't. We just thought there had to be a better way to get things done, or to even get things done at all, and over the years we found people that agreed with us. Then more did, and then more. Also, as we all know and agree, it isn't just about doing things in a different manner. This country is so polarized on almost every issue, it's a wonder anything gets done, and that has caused conspiracy theorists to go wild. The common man has no idea what is really supposed to be going on because the machine is too massive. I am the last person to say we need to denounce the comforts of what technology, medicine, and the like has brought us, and go back to the dark ages, but we do need to simplify many, many things in the name of streamlining, transparency, and understanding. Again, do not misunderstand me. I do not think 'we the people' need to know everything that is going on in every bedroom, boardroom or war room. There are things that, for the sake of our own security, we do not need to know about, but on the flip side of that particular argument, there needs to be a level of trust that those with that secret knowledge are not corrupt and out for some other gain. As far as the polarization though, I think once the people are so deadlocked, it is time to separate and move on. Every society must compromise to live peacefully with each other, but the chasm has grown so huge, I believe it is time to detach from those that do not believe in the life we want. I do not judge those other people, but I should not have to pay for a lifestyle I am utterly against.

I would like to briefly talk about some of the major items that will be discussed in detail at the upcoming conferences. The media. Where do I start? The media is such a vital part to our freedoms and our knowledge base, but the wheels, truly, have come off the wagon. We are literally in our neighbor's bedrooms, and why? Who cares what the famous actor does in his off time? Are our lives so empty that knowing these things fills the chasm? Go learn something new, go outside and breath the air, pet a dog, watch a baby experience everything new...do those things a couple of times, and you'll soon realize how ridiculous the rest of the gossip is. The first amendment of the United States has been so misused and abused it is shameful. I'm thinking that not infringing on the press was written because there was so much oppression in the days those words were written. Those who penned them wanted to give the people the true, unbiased, untarnished news. Not the right to invade people's privacy, or print secrets that our enemies can read and use against us, or spin a message in any direction. That brings up another point that I feel is important to bring up; the founding fathers wrote the constitution trying to address future concerns but in no way could foresee everything. I would bet my life that they never intended those words to help or be relevant to everything from the freedom of Internet porn to frivolous and innumerable law suits tying up our legal system into knots...the likes of which will never be untied. The media is out of control and needs to be reined in.

Speaking of spinning a message a certain way...Partisanship and polarized views is what got the media into that game in the first place. In the beginning of this country, many men and women left a place where their voice was not heard. Even though many of their voices were in conflict with each other, they knew that working together to create something new was of the utmost importance. Now, the sheer size and number of conflicts cause me to believe it is time for another break. Once there seems to be an argument or discord about anything and everything, it is assumed to be time to align with the faction you agree with most and move on with no thought to compromise or working through the issue. We can't agree with everything or everyone, but we can find those big-ticket items that matter the most to us and annex based on those, cutting out those who don't and that is where AmendX is taking us. We have found those hills to die on, and we will create the newest frontier with those like us. Like us only in ideas, but with great diversity among people giving us the best chance of open, new perspectives in which to help govern and pilot us into a new emancipation and new way of living.

The word government means different things to different people - big government, small government, too much government, not enough. Who knows? All I can tell you is William of Occam had it right; keep it simple. When we have big government, we get more bureaucracy, departments within departments… convolution. When we have too little government we get dictators and rulers with no regard for affecting the larger population. The economy goes with that. I go again to Occam's razor…when we continue to add to already complex things, we get contradictions. One example comes to mind is the tax code. Exactly how many times does it contradict itself? Keeping our house clean and free of waste will ensure those contradictions do not destroy us.

Let's talk for a minute about resources. Do you believe there really is a water shortage or an oil shortage? If there is, we are the dumbest group of people ever! I live in an area that someone comes and checks the water meter twice a month and then I get a bill every three months for past usage. If there is a leak or I'm using more water than recommended, it is not discovered until up to three months after the fact when your bill is five times what you expected it to be. How much water could be wasted in that time? Do you still think there is a shortage with that kind of waste being allowed? And by allowed, I don't just mean by regulation. I mean also by acceptability. If we truly wanted to save a resource like water a detection grid could be set up for communities quite easily. Actually one has already been set up and has been working in a neighborhood by one of our members, and the user and the provider can access it with real-time usage numbers. Once something happens out of the ordinary, a leak in your sprinkler system for example, the detection system immediately notifies both parties so it can be fixed straight away… saving both the resource and money. Now think for a minute, are we really trying to save our water? We currently have several types of energies that can replace fossil fuels and other scarce resources, but because of politics and secret deals with other countries we don't use them…solar comes to mind. We have multiple ways to harness the power of the sun to replace other resources and we just don't. Trade agreements and back room deals that are made to benefit those outside of this country negate those other options from ever being used. If we closed ranks until our own house was taken care of, that might be a good start. Then we would also be stronger to help other peoples in need.

"Education." Bishop paused for a long moment. "The top priority of the government of any people should be that of educating them.

With education, we can give the gift of self-sufficiency...the idea that you are able to do anything is quite powerful. You know, that old idea of the American dream? Well, through education, it can come true. Not the American dream of those professional athletes that got passed through university because they could catch a football, go to the pros, make a ton of money, and be permanently injured by the time they are thirty. Then retire with possible brain trauma and broken bodies, blow through the money while they are playing because no one taught them how to take care of themselves, and finely end up with nothing. Does that sound good to you? How about the ones that passed their classes on their own because they wanted their education? They played the same dangerous game, but invested in the future that they knew would not include sports, and had their degree field to fall back on. The architects, lawyers, the guys returning to school for their masters' degrees because they understand a sport cannot last forever. The ones involved in their community, starting families and making lives for themselves. We are doing such a huge disservice to those exceptional athletes by not insisting on passing their classes on their own and getting the education they deserve while they are in school. But education shouldn't be for just the athletes that stand out, or the rich. It should be there for the rich, the poor and everyone in between and if we truly want to see our people educated, we will find ways to get that done.

The Criminal Justice System and jurisprudence is, like all of the other topics I've discussed already, a complex one. There has to be a goal in mind when framing the axioms. Are we making rules and laws to control, discourage, or protect? Is it a little bit of each of those? Then, when someone breaks our rules, do we look at intent? Should willfully, recklessly, and knowingly be a part of a heftier sentence or how should responsibility and accountability be governed? The ramifications that make up the definition of right and wrong and the analogous treatments, sentences and practices that go with them are massive. But once again, I believe they can be stripped down to their basics while still being compelling. Common sense just has to remain a big part of the process and I believe that is the most of what is missing.

Like everything else I've talked about, our medical industry and healthcare system are bogged down by red tape, and costs have gotten so out of control that it needs to essentially be scrapped and started again. Would it be great to give healthcare to all of our citizens? Of course, but in the interest of our economy, we can't continue to spend more than we make, or take from a population that has more and give to a population that has less. It does those people a disservice and keeps them on the dole, needy and dependent. In our great-grandparents' and grandparents' day, there was no health insurance, and they were expected to pay from their own pockets under fee-for-service. This meant that if you went to the doctor, you paid your bill right then and there. Billing wasn't even a practice until well into the 20th century. The doctor offered his services for a fair price and the patient paid it. This also meant they didn't go to the doctor for every little ache or pain they experienced, and frivolous lawsuits were unheard of. Sometimes even mistakes by doctors went undiscovered or uncompensated because, like any other time, human error does occur and a big payout is not going to change anything about that. The first types of insurance covered lost wages for on-the-job accidents, but medical bills still had to be paid by the individual. Later, catastrophic coverage started, like the word implies, for horrendous accidents or illnesses that incurred large expenses that could wipe out a family. Common, everyday healthcare was priced fairly and paid for immediately. As time went on, more and more bureaucracy caused the prices to go up and up and up. We started being billed for our appointments, which meant the office needed someone to send out the bills, and that person needed to be paid for their work, so the office visit fee had to go up. I won't go down the list of every way the fees increased and I really won't even go into how absurd malpractice insurance caused fees to skyrocket, but it is fair to say, we are in a place now that maybe ten percent of the costs we experience are due to our actual consultation and treatment with a doctor for our illness. Everyone does not need health insurance. What we need is to get rid of most of the insurances we have and start again; we need to pay for the everyday things out of pocket, and if it is too expensive, like anything else, we will stop using that doctor and find one who offers a fairer fee for the consultation. For those who cannot afford a basic appointment, free clinics can be offered by doctors and other volunteers who want to give something back to their community… Not be forced to pay higher insurance premiums for those who cannot or will not. Without the enormous lawsuits we might also see a more rapid acceptance of new drugs and procedures to the market. Now I'm not one to support irresponsible green lighting of drugs, but again, without the myriad steps of bureaucratic processes, we could get more speedy access to clinical trials and research that is being done. Let the individual take control of, and responsibility for, their health. If someone wants to get into a trial and they have done their homework and have been told of the risks, who are we to say they can't. Please don't misunderstand me, like I said, controls do have to be put in place. We can never allow something like the Tuskegee experiment to ever happen again, but right now we are over-controlled, making this country not so free after all.

I've said essentially the same thing for many of the different areas I've addressed. Responsibility, accountability and independence are becoming extinct characteristics and this group formed to bring them back to life. Gluttony, laziness, apathy, selfishness, rudeness, meanness, hypocrisy…all have become epidemic in this country. This isn't about hating this country, quite the contrary; this is still the best thing going. There are, however, many issues that, if they aren't taken seriously, it won't be the best thing going. Going to Texas is about a certain perspective being demonstrated, ours, and scaling the problems down to see if they will work. Personally, I think they will. But now it is time to put them to the test."

Bishop paused again for a very long minute, as if he was trying to decide to go on…and finally said, "Proverbs says, 'whoever walks with the wise becomes wise, but the companion of fools will suffer harm.' Isn't it time to want to walk with the wise again? To get in the game, do great things, reach for the highest goals? We are all capable; we just have to want it again! I am the person this group chose to be our speaker. We do not have one leader because the US doesn't have one leader; they have a figurehead that does, in fact, make some final decisions. However, groups of very intelligent people, elected by more intelligent people, debate and vote on how our lives will move forward, how our laws will be governed, and how our values will change over time will be the standard operating procedure.

We are a think tank of individuals with very specific ideas in mind. We are just a microcosm of how the US should run but has become so bogged down in entitlements both for themselves and for the citizens that think it is their right to know what is going on exactly when it is going on in spite of the fact that it also tells our enemies the very information that can and will change the lives of the citizens we are trying to protect.

Power is a crazy thing. Some abuse it others fight against it. What we have tried to put together is a balance, so no one person or group can get carried away and go to the extreme in any one way. We are coming from a place of genuine desire to make a country strong, and wealthy in every sense of the word, with morals and values that the US once had. Companies will endeavor to make a profit, but also create a environment workers will want to come to. Pharmaceutical scientists and companies will research and make new drugs that will help our citizens, for a price they can afford, and still make a handsome and well-deserved profit. If through research, the drug turns out to be too much of a risk, it will be scrapped... the end goal is not to make money while killing our citizens, it is to balance discovering new technologies, drugs, ways of living, and profiting from them, but not at the expense of the common man. Honestly, I do not have the understanding of how an individual can act with malice, hatred, or apathy just for a buck, and I have made plenty of money. You do not need to hurt anyone to be successful, so I've never understood that kind of person, and we will certainly weed that out of the new society.

Being a part of something like creating and passing an amendment, being a part of the administration that puts someone on the Supreme Court, is extraordinary! It is my belief this country was made on the majority vote, the vote of the people. 'I'm so-and-so, and I approve this message' has gone so far beyond what is good and true. How did we get to this point? The Supreme Court of the United States has a tradition that before a new term they shake hands. It is symbolic of a righteous philosophy, commonly shared. The problem is, however, the rest of the US, the masses are not included in the philosophy, and now not even the etiquette. How did the masses forget who we are, what we stand for and how we make people's lives better?

It is so easy to become complacent; we wake up every morning, get ready for work, come home, eat some fast food, maybe do some Internet shopping, veg out in front of the television and just watch commercial after commercial between shows that have no common sense or substance, then get up the next day and do it all over again. How can that be called living?

The idea of the original thought, the original person, is gone. Albert Einstein failed out of school, yet we are still unraveling his theories. An education is obviously a great thing, but conventional schooling does not fit everyone. Why can't we look beyond the degree and see what is in the person? Those stupid jokes about 'oh, you have an MBA, ok, let me show you how to do this,' started for a reason; we are cattle.

Texas is going to scale down the problem and make these issues manageable. If we are successful, we will be the first to dedicate our time, efforts and money to help the US incorporate what works. The powers not delegated to the United States by the Constitution, nor prohibited by it to the States, are reserved to the States respectively, or to the people. I cannot stand by and watch the country I cherish fall to mediocrity and debilitation. I will find a way to see this country's ideals come to fruition."

Taking a deep breath and letting out an audible sigh, "I know it seems as though this journey has taken forever and now everything will seem rather abrupt, but it is indeed finally time. We've matured over the years, as have our ideas. But unfortunately the country and world stayed on the same path. Now, I talked with my two best friends in the world, I trust my life to them and their judgment and they agree; we think we can do better and now it's time to prove it. Over the next two days, get the word out to your areas and go to your predetermined locations. Your representatives will meet for the conferences and then the next steps will be taken. Finally, thank you to everyone who has sacrificed and worked toward this cause. Thank you for believing in me and for wanting something better for yourself. Thank you."

Samantha watched Bishop in a sort of awe. She knew his faults and flaws. She knew what he was good at and how he shined when he was involved with something he was passionate about. She also knew that she was in love with him.

Michael Pearson and Randall Quinn hung up the call and got ready to leave. The house was all boxed up and ready for the move. His wife and kids had gone ahead to Austin to get settled in their new home. Quinn didn't love the idea of leaving California; he loved it, but he knew sacrifices had to be made. Quinn disassembled the video unit and placed it in the last remaining box.

"How are we on time?" he asked Pearson.

"We're good. We need to meet Norman at his plane at SFO at 5pm. He wants wheels up right after that." Replied Pearson.

The two men were hitching a ride with a friend and fellow Xer, Norman Buchanan, who was also making the final move to Austin. He had originally planned to bring seven others with him on his G200 aircraft, but most of the seven headed to Colorado to get ready for the conferences. Buchanan wasn't going to be in Colorado for a couple of weeks so he thought he could get settled in Austin in the interim. Quinn wanted to make sure his family was getting settled and then he would head to Colorado. As for Pearson, the Admiral was on vacation, according to his command, to be followed by his official retirement. It coincided nicely with the group's plans and he would be able to participate fully in the conferences without any deception, which he really preferred.

"The car is out front," Pearson said to Quinn.

Quinn grabbed his bag and walked to the front door. Opening it, he let Admiral Pearson go out first then he stopped, turned around and looked at the interior of his home one last time. Now that 13-C was private again and most of the inner workings were already in Texas, moving the executive offices wouldn't be hard at all, but he would certainly miss northern California. He shut and locked the door. Pearson was already in the black town car waiting for Quinn. He turned and walked toward the car.

AUTHOR'S NOTE

Wake up every day and set your intention. Do your best throughout the day, smile inside yourself and love yourself. Then, smile and look at those around you, look at them and really see them, for they are endeavoring to do the same thing you are. If we all live with a little more awareness, that is half the battle. Thank you for reading this book. Thank you for allowing me into your heads and hearts. I am blessed to have been able to do this.

Because this book is self-published, editing is taken on by a few friends and myself. We tried to find errors, but I welcome any readers to contact me if you come across some as well. I can be contacted through the Taking Texas website, Facebook, or Twitter.

http://www.takingtexas.com
https://www.facebook.com/takingtexas
https://twitter.com/takingtexas

Niki Chesy

Printed in the United States
By Bookmasters